Praise for bestselling author Michele Hauf

"Hauf delivers excitement, danger and romance in a way only she can!"

—*New York Times* bestselling author Sherrilyn Kenyon on *Her Vampire Husband*

"With action-packed excitement from start to finish, Hauf offers an original storyline full of quirky, fun characters and wonderful descriptions. And the sexual tension between CJ and Vika sparkles. Readers won't want to put this one down."

—*RT Book Reviews* on *This Wicked Magic*, Top Pick!

"This quirky story has a fair amount of humor and a lot of heart as well."

—*Harlequin Junkie* on *The Vampire Hunter*

"Nothing at all tame about this book. Lots of messy, dangerous sex, complete with teeth, the way vampire sex should be."

—*Brazen Reads* on *Beautiful Danger*

"I love the world building this author creates in her books."

—*Romancing the Dark Side*

"*Kiss Me Deadly* is an addictive read, one that won't be put down until the final page is completed."

—*Examiner.com*

Michele Hauf has been writing romance, action-adventure and fantasy stories for more than twenty years. France, musketeers, vampires and faeries usually populate her stories. And if Michele followed the adage "write what you know," all her stories would have snow in them. Fortunately, she steps beyond her comfort zone and writes about countries and creatures she has never seen. Find her on Facebook, Twitter and at michelehauf.com.

Books by Michele Hauf

Harlequin Nocturne

The Saint-Pierre Series

The Dark's Mistress
Ghost Wolf
Moonlight and Diamonds
The Vampire's Fall
Enchanted by the Wolf

In the Company of Vampires

Beautiful Danger
The Vampire Hunter
Beyond the Moon

HQN Books

Her Vampire Husband
Seducing the Vampire
A Vampire for Christmas
"Monsters Don't Do Christmas"

Visit the Author Profile page
at Harlequin.com for more titles.

MICHELE HAUF

Enchanted by the Wolf

and

Captivating the Witch

ISBN-13: 978-0-373-60197-4

Enchanted by the Wolf and Captivating the Witch

This edition published by arrangement with Harlequin Books S.A.

For questions and comments about the quality of this book, please contact us at CustomerService@Harlequin.com.

Printed in U.S.A.

CONTENTS

ENCHANTED BY THE WOLF 7
CAPTIVATING THE WITCH 311

ENCHANTED BY THE WOLF

This story is for everyone who believes in faeries.
They believe in you.

Chapter 1

"What's going on behind closed doors?" Kir asked Jacques Montfort, the pack's scion, and his best friend. The men stood outside the pack principal's office door, and Kir had caught Jacques with an ear tilted to listen through the door.

The dark-haired wolf, who was built like an MMA fighter, shrugged back his shoulders and lifted his chin. "An emissary from Faery is in there with my dad."

Kir whistled and leaned against the concrete-block wall. Etienne Montfort was principal of pack Valoir, an old and revered group of werewolves that had been a cohesive group for centuries. Kir had been born and raised within the pack.

Both men tilted their heads toward the door. With their heightened werewolf senses, they could hear much through thick walls, but something about the conversation was muted. Faery glamour? The idea of a being from

Faery visiting their pack was too interesting for either one to stop eavesdropping. And neither could deny they had a tendency to get into trouble together. They'd been raised side by side, more brothers than most siblings could claim.

"You ever meet a faery?" Jacques asked. His blue eyes twinkled with curiosity.

Kir shrugged. "I've seen them in the nightclubs. They're…colorful."

"That's for sure. And their wings are freaky. So, you ever…you know."

Kir knew Jacques's unspoken implication was that he wanted to know if he'd had sex with a faery. "Haven't had the pleasure. If you can call dodging wings pleasurable."

"I hear they're delicate."

Smirking, Kir let that one go. Jacques was the one with the fiancée. And a raging curiosity for all things female that had gotten him in more trouble with the little woman than a man should have to deal with. But his bride-to-be was a werewolf, so Jacques won the King of the Perfect Score award in the men's minds. It wasn't often werewolves mated with their own kind, because of the rarity of the female. Even those wolves in packs often had to look elsewhere for a mate because most of the female pack members were spoken for upon birth.

Jacques was a lucky wolf.

Kir, on the other hand, had gone without a date for months. The idea of a delicate faery didn't appeal to him. A match with a fellow wolf would feed his sexual desires perfectly. Beyond his species, the only other option was mortal women. Some proved open to his aggressive needs. He could also withstand the occasional witch, but they tended to be unpredictable and sometimes just plain creepy.

Ah, hell, wasn't as if he was looking for love anyway. He didn't believe in love.

Hookups were fine for now. Besides, there was a certain danger involved when pursuing a wolf from another pack. Packs tended to protect their females fiercely.

On the other hand, life wasn't worth the ride without risk.

"Twenty bucks says he's trying to negotiate the hunting grounds again," Jacques said.

Etienne's goal was to appeal to Faery so the pack could be allowed to hunt in their realm. The more the mortal realm evolved and the cities pushed out into the country, the less safe it became for a werewolf to hunt without risking discovery by humans. Their breed required vast acreage unhampered by hunters with guns and curious human eyes. Faery offered that. And, if a portal to Faery were opened right here in Paris, the trip to the hunt could be quick and easy.

"Let's hope, for the sake of the pack, you won that bet," Kir said, "and that he's successful."

A harpie in human guise sat across the office desk from Etienne. Arriving without notice, she'd waited ten minutes in the office while he'd been summoned on this bright weekday morning that had seen him lingering in bed beside his wife's warm body.

The visitor was tall, slender, wore her hair in a short black bob, with eyes equally as dark. Her skin was dark brown, smooth and utterly flawless, and yet Etienne avoided staring at her overlong. Look at one of the sidhe the wrong way or too long? A man could sprout horns.

"I'll get right to the point," the harpie said. She spoke French with ease. Etienne knew that the sidhe had the ability to pick up languages foreign to them almost as if by magic.

"First, if I might have your name?" Etienne asked carefully. Faeries did not give their full names freely, but he could hardly refer to her as Mademoiselle Harpie.

"You may call me Brit. And you are Etienne Montfort, principal of pack Valoir, *oui*?"

He nodded. He'd been principal since the 1940s and had witnessed remarkable changes in the mortal realm. But he'd rarely had experience with faeries until lately. Apparently, someone had taken note of his campaign to gain access to hunting grounds.

"To what do I owe the pleasure of your visit?"

"I have been sent as an emissary representing the Unseelie king, Malrick."

Etienne sat up straighter. This sounded promising.

The harpie splayed her long, graceful fingers before her over the wood desktop. "You are aware there are portals to Faery here in your mortal realm?"

Etienne nodded. He was aware but had no clue as to their location. Not that he hadn't, on occasion, considered searching. He did know that unless a portal was marked with faery glamour, it wasn't visible to any but the sidhe. Yet he would never attempt to breach Faery without permission. He prided himself on maintaining strong alliances with the various species.

"A portal has recently been unlocked by sorcery and it opens directly onto Unseelie territory," Brit stated in a businesslike tone. "This is a source of much misfortune and annoyance to my kind."

"I can imagine. Are mortals entering the Faery realm?"

"All sorts. It is, in a word, disgusting. My king, Malrick, requires a guard posted on this side of the portal until specific magics can be conjured to close the portal. It is a difficult task summoning such powerful magic to seal a portal that we did not open, so it will take some time."

"A guard?" Etienne suddenly sensed the gist to this visit. Perhaps not as fortuitous as he'd hoped.

"On behalf of the Unseelie king, we would request pack Valoir take on the task of guarding the portal. It would not require more than one man posted outside the portal. You could assign shifts. Fighting back curious humans should cause you no more trouble than growling at them."

"Indeed, it would be a simple post." And pack Valoir was large enough to provide the wolves for the job. "Have you an estimate on duration?"

"Your mortal time moves much differently than ours." She shrugged, obviously at a loss.

"We'll leave it as an open standing agreement." But Etienne wasn't about to shake hands just yet. "And what would my pack receive as recompense for taking on such a task?"

The harpie spread her hands on the desk and smiled warmly. Her eyes glowed violet now. Etienne was ever charmed by sidhe eyes. Or was it that their charm was so powerful he could not resist? He had to remind himself not to stare.

"The Unseelie would grant pack Valoir the right to hunt on our land," she offered.

"In Faery?" Etienne said on a gasp.

"Indeed."

That was immense. To be allowed such freedom in a realm that offered what was rumored myriad hunting opportunities? Why, it was unprecedented. "Pack Valoir will be allowed free rein. Only, we request you do not hunt as a pack. Only one wolf in timed intervals. A measured means to hunting."

"That can be done."

"Do you accept the assignment, Principal Montfort?"

Etienne sat back in his chair, not bothering to hide the

grin that curled his mouth. His pack would shout and howl at such fortune. And, truly, the task of guarding the portal would be minimal. It would not disrupt their lives, and he shouldn't think those who worked enforcement would have to be tasked for the job.

He nodded decisively. "Yes, I agree. On behalf of pack Valoir, I accept the bargain issued by your king, Malrick."

"Excellent. And know, because of the unique nature of this agreement, my king requests a specific requirement to sealing said contract and to make it binding."

"Uh… Oh, oh, yes." Twining his fingers together, Etienne leaned forward. "What exactly is required?"

"It won't tax your pack, I promise. In fact, it will only require the compliance of one pack member of your choosing."

Damned faeries were all about ceremony and pomp. And Etienne suspected that one pack member would not like what the harpie next requested. But if it would allow the entire pack to hunt freely? Sacrifices must be made for the good of the pack.

When the door had opened to let out the visitor, Jacques and Kir shuffled down the hallway. They watched her walk by, and just when they thought the coast was clear to slip around the corner and out of the back door, Etienne called out to Kir.

Damned werewolf senses. No wolf could hide from another's sense of smell. Jacques nodded to him that he'd see him later.

With the office door closed behind him, Kir waited with hands stuffed in his back pockets.

Etienne paced over to a window that overlooked the Seine in the 16th arrondissement. "You drew the short stick," he said to Kir.

"I wasn't aware there was a drawing, Principal Montfort," Kir said lightly. "What nasty task have I been assigned today?"

"This weekend, actually." The leader steepled his fingers before his lips. Pale brown eyes assessed. "Sunday. In the forest edging Versailles, where the pack often celebrates midsummer's eve. Malrick, king of the Unseelie court—"

"A faery?"

"Yes. I've just finished speaking with a liaison he sent with a most exciting offer that will benefit the entire pack."

"You're bargaining with the sidhe now? Do you think that wise?"

"Of course, if it will grant us access to Faery for hunting."

Kir's jaw dropped open. So his guess had been right. Etienne had actually managed to snag hunting rights in Faery!

"That's a generous offer," Kir said. "What did you have to offer in return?"

"Kirnan, this deal affects the whole pack." The sudden serious tone in Etienne's voice alerted Kir. His principal saved that dour bass tone for announcing bad news or chastising those in need of an attitude adjustment. "Seems Malrick is concerned about a portal from this realm into Faery," Etienne explained. "It's been cracked by common humans, and the Unseelie are experiencing an influx of the idiots landing in Faery. He wants our pack to guard the portal until the proper magical spell can be conjured to close it."

"How long will that take?"

"Not sure. Could be weeks, months. Hell, the way the time is screwy in Faery, it could be years. It is a minimal task, according to the liaison with whom I spoke. And we've the manpower. I expect you and Jacques will not be required to hold post, since you both have the enforcing that keeps you busy."

"The enforcement team is solid. If you should need

one or the other of us, I'm sure we could manage a day now and then."

"Good to know. So in exchange for us guarding the portal—a simple task that will require one-man shifts round the clock—our pack gets to hunt in Faery. In an orderly and scheduled fashion, of course. Malrick doesn't want the entire pack running loose in his realm, but a few wolves during the days preceding and of the full moon will be tolerated."

"Of course, you accepted this offer?"

"I would have been foolish not to!" The principal's enthusiasm spilled out in a gleeful clap of hands.

And Kir was right there with him with the enthusiasm. Until he recalled what Etienne had said to him when he'd entered the office. "So where do I come in holding this short stick?"

The principal's demeanor drew to a solemn yet regal stance. An uneasy feeling trickled up the back of Kir's neck. Etienne was a kind, elder wolf who rarely used aggression or faced down his pack members to keep them in line. He left that to his scion, Jacques, who took to such tasks with relish. Yet he sensed in the man now a certain dire reluctance.

"The sidhe have ceremonious ways to seal bargains. Something we merely consider good fortune may be considered a grand boon to them. And the liaison pointed out that this is a unique bargain that must be honored. So to seal this pact, Malrick proposes to offer one of his daughters to marry one from our pack. The couple will bond, thus providing the final seal to the deal."

"A marriage? That's…extreme."

"Not for the sidhe. Their bonding rituals, which are elaborate and varied, are the stamp of approval, so to speak, for such an extraordinary bargain. Either that, or they request a life sacrificed or one of our firstborn. You know how the sidhe can be."

No, he did not. As he'd indicated to Jacques earlier, Kir hadn't much contact with the winged ones. Marriage seemed a bit much to ask. On the other hand, a sacrifice or handing over one's firstborn seemed more extreme.

The poor wolf who had to step forward to marry some faery he'd never seen before would certainly not like it.

Kir met his principal's hopeful gaze. His leader was pleased to have scored such a propitious arrangement for the pack. Indeed, it was a valued prize—but a marriage?

"Sunday," Etienne said. "You will be ready for a day of ceremony and pomp."

"Of course." Likely the entire pack would have to don suits and pin on tiny flowers or whatever it was wedding parties were required to wear. He could deal with that.

"You're taking this rather well. Good man, Kirnan. Good man."

"Whatever details you need me to arrange, I'll see to them. I assume that's what you intended when you said I drew that short stick?" He smiled, but his leader only matched it with a shake of his head. And an imploring lift of brow. "Wait."

The more he thought about it… If *he* had drawn the short stick…

Kir's heart stopped beating for a full three seconds. He swallowed, flexed his fingers at his sides and then croaked out, "You mean *me*?"

Etienne nodded. "We went down the chain of command. I, of course, am happily married to my beloved Estella. Eighty years and counting. And my son and the pack scion, Jacques, as you know, is engaged to sweet Marielle. So the task falls to the third in command."

Kir spoke before thinking. "Oh, hell no." Now that he

understood he was the unlucky sap, he smacked a fist into a palm and paced before Etienne's desk.

"It must be done, Kir. You are young. You have no current romantic entanglements."

Not for lack of want. A guy didn't need to be in love to have a good time.

"You are an excellent offering."

"An offering?" Kir winced at the word. It sounded so... sacrificial. A burn of bile stirred in his throat.

"I shouldn't have put it that way," Etienne added.

"I can't marry a woman I don't know. Principal Montfort, when I do marry I want to marry for love."

"Are there any females in the pack whom you desire?"

"No, I—" Kir shoved his fingers roughly through his hair. "As you've said, I'm young yet. Twenty-eight years is but a pup in a werewolf's lifetime. I have never given thought to marriage. Well, hell, yes, I have. I do want family and a happily-ever-after. But I want to date freely until I've met the one."

"The one." Etienne smirked. "Estella and I were an arranged marriage. Do not rule out the possibility of an interesting match, Kirnan."

"Interesting?" The word felt vile on his tongue. *Interesting* was not *love*. "You and your wife are an amazing couple, Principal Montfort. But I'm not like you. Not patient or, apparently, so accepting."

And, hell, his dad had screwed up his marriage; what made Kir think he could manage a loving family without an eventual nasty divorce? And abandoning the children to scar them forever?

"I've my work with the enforcement team that keeps me busy," Kir tried. "I don't have time to dote on a wife and...do the things a husband needs to do."

Like what, exactly? He didn't know. And he didn't want to know! Not…this way.

"Isn't there another wolf in the pack with equal standing?"

Etienne shook his head. "It would shame Valoir were we to offer a male who had not an esteemed rank. You are the highest ranked wolf who is available. Please, Kir, I'm asking you to do this as a favor. I'm not commanding you."

Pacing before the window, Kir's brain zoomed from standing at a dais and getting a first look at a woman he must vow to shelter and love forever to running away from the pack, becoming a lone wolf, free—yet forever ostracized and alone. Like his father.

He didn't want to repeat the sins of his father.

"She will be one of the Unseelie king's daughters," Etienne added with a hopeful lilt.

One of them? How many daughters had he that the man could deal one out as a seal to the many bargains he may make?

"Our breed gets along well with the sidhe," Etienne tried. "Er, regarding when it comes to mating. And faeries are very often quite lovely. I don't think you should worry about how she looks. And I have heard that wings can be quite—"

Kir put up a hand to silence his principal. He needed to think about this. Sunday was two days away. He was captain of the enforcement team, alongside Jacques, who was the lieutenant. His job required he police the wolf packs in Paris, and it kept him busy much as a nine-to-five job would.

He didn't need a wife. He wouldn't know what to *do* with a wife. If his own family's history was any example—well, that was it; his family was no example of how to live and love in a happy, healthy relationship.

Kir wasn't prepared to welcome a woman into his home. Nor did he want to stop looking at other women. He didn't want to stop having sex with other women. What must that be like to sleep with only one woman? For the rest of his life? And to be castigated by a wife for looking at another woman?

Heart pounding, he caught his palm against his chest.

"So it's agreed, then," Etienne finally said. "The ceremony is scheduled to begin at twilight. I'll have my wife arrange all the necessary suits and whatever else is needed. All that wedding frippery, you know. You're a good man, Kirnan. Thanks for doing this for pack Valoir. I've got to rush out now."

Etienne walked Kir to the door and down the hall to the front door of the nondescript concrete building the pack used as a headquarters. The principal flagged down his driver, who waited at the curb, and, with a wave, was off, leaving Kir standing on the sidewalk, hands hanging at his sides and jaw dropped open.

Married in two days? To a woman he'd never met.

Kir felt like the last one standing on the gym floor after all the rest had been chosen for sides. And he was the odd man out, not needed for either team, both of which stood on the sidelines laughing and pointing at him.

And, to make matters worse, he had no one to confide in, no one to ask for guidance. His father he had not seen for a decade. His younger sister, Blyss—it had been years since she had been estranged from the pack. They spoke on the phone because she summered in the United States with her new husband. But she wouldn't be interested in his dilemma. She had just given birth to a new baby and was busy with life and marriage.

That left his mother, Madeline, whom he tolerated and begrudgingly respected at best.

"Married?" he muttered.

The clenching in his chest seized up his breath and he gripped his throat.

Chapter 2

The forest shivered with a warm midsummer breeze that seemed to sing in a language Kir recognized but could not interpret. It was a joyous sound, which helped to settle his crazy nerves. Overhead, thousands of tiny lights darted within the tree canopy. Faeries. Kir was surrounded by his pack and all sorts of sidhe. Jacques stood at his right side, shrugging his shoulders within the tight fit of the rental suit. The scion's attention also wandered high to follow the flickering lights.

The woods had glowed from afar as pack Valoir had arrived en masse. A stage set for a performance, waiting for him, one of the main players. Faeries had clasped Kir's hand and bowed to him, greeting, acknowledging, surmising. He'd not been introduced to the Unseelie king and wasn't sure the man was even here. Etienne had briefly introduced Kir to Brit, the harpie who had brought the deal to the table. She'd been stunning in a silver sheath that had revealed more than it hid.

But it had all been a whirlwind since he'd arrived. Dozens of strange and interesting faces, elaborate and glamorous clothing and costume, delicious peach wine and tiny cakes that tasted either sweet or savory but was always too small to satisfy his fierce appetite. And the greetings and silent perusals. He hadn't had time to think in the few hours that had passed since his arrival.

Or to escape.

And now he stood, knees locked and fingers flexing nervously at his sides. The suit was tight across his shoulders and it was hot. He wanted to scratch at the starched shirt collar but wasn't sure his fingers could perform the move because they felt so far away and detached from his body.

Kir couldn't concentrate on the words the officiant spoke because beside him stood *her.* The woman soon to be named his wife. And after that they would dance and drink, and, well, he'd heard there was a honeymoon cabin erected not far from here.

Something sweet, like flowers or fruit, or maybe even sugared fruit topped with flowers, tickled his nostrils. The petite woman who stood beside him, the crown of her head below his shoulders, smelled like dessert.

He did like dessert.

He didn't want to like her. Because that would mean he was cool with this stupid agreement. One that stuck him with a woman he didn't know or want.

For the rest of his life.

Werewolves could live three centuries or more. That was a hell of a long time to spend with one woman. Especially a woman he had not chosen.

He wanted to look down—the top of her head was capped with flowers and fluttery butterflies that seemed to hold the veil in place—but he dared not make the blatant once-over with the audience behind him. He'd remain stoic and say all the right things. His pack was watching. He was doing this for them. They had better appreciate his sacrifice.

The ceremony officiant rambled on about loving the other until death did part them and enduring magic most vile and exquisite through eternity.

Vile magic? What the…?

Kir closed his eyes. His heart did a weird dive and then free-fell within his rib cage. It didn't land with a splat, though, because something distracted his imaginary death-dive. She smelled *really* good. His mouth actually watered, and he cursed inwardly for not having eaten all day. Too nervous.

There would be food later. And drink.

There was not enough whiskey in this realm to get him to the point where he could accept this situation.

Behind him, he felt the gentle sweep of wings as the woman beside him shifted on her feet. As she'd walked down the aisle, she had worn a long sheer pink veil over her head that fell over her body and to her bare feet. Her feet were decorated with bright arabesque violet designs, like some kind of *mehndi* artwork. Her wings were unfurled to display gorgeous violet and red gossamer with darker shading in the veins. Her hair was dark. He could see that much beneath the veil. But he could not determine if she was pretty.

They'd wrapped her up as if she were a gift, and he didn't like it.

Suddenly feeling as though he was forgetting something important, Kir lifted his chin and focused as the officiant announced the twosome had been joined in matrimony by the authority of the Unseelie court. And later they must seal that promise by bonding.

What a way to start a marriage.

When he had, at the last minute, thought he'd need to buy a ring for his new bride, the liaison harpie, who had arrived early to ensure the details had been handled properly, stated rings were an offense. Mortal metals must never be worn by the sidhe. All that was required was that the two bond as Faery decreed.

A ring would have been so much easier.

"Join hands," the officiant announced. "And bind yourselves to one another."

What? Right here? The bonding? Kir looked over his shoulder and caught Etienne's eye. The elder wolf nodded. And beside him stood his mother, Madeline, with a tear in her eye.

Oh, this was not cool. He couldn't—

His new wife lifted her hand beneath the pink veil and Kir took it, deciding it was fragile and felt too light. He might break her bones if he squeezed. Awful thought to have. He would never harm a woman. But he felt as if she were something that must be protected and watched over.

He didn't have time for watching over a tiny faery. She had better be able to care for herself.

Her head did not tilt up to look at him. He breathed in through his nose and exhaled in preparation. If they had to bond before an audience—and his mother.

Pushing aside the veil, the officiant wrapped a red silk band about their joined hands, draping the ends over their wrists. As he recited some words that Kir assumed were in the sidhe language, he traced an elaborate symbol in the air above their hands.

Behind them, the audience of sidhe began to…hum. It was a beautiful, wordless melody that twinkled in the air and stirred the leaves. Animals scampered nearby in the forest and Kir felt the hairs on his body prickle with vital awareness. Connection to nature. Elation expanding his lungs, he noticed a design began to show on the top of his and his new wife's hands. A gorgeous, delicate tracing that wound in and out and curled and arabesqued like something etched upon a Moorish ruin. Or perhaps it was similar to the designs on her feet and ankles. It didn't hurt and, in fact, felt as if a piece of ice was being traced under his skin. The tracing crept over the side of her hand and Kir felt the design spread across his skin.

"Bonded," the officiant announced.

With applause from the sidhe court, the design on their hands suddenly glowed brightly, then faded to the pale etching. But seriously? *That* was the bonding? Whew! Kir could not be more thankful that Faery's means to bonding was different than his breed, which meant having sex.

His new wife dropped her hand and then her attendant pulled the veil away from her head. Slowly, the pink fabric glittered under the glow from the faeries overhead, and her dark hair, woven through with tiny blue flowers, was revealed. She looked up at him with a small smile. It was forced.

Not so pleased about this marriage, either, he guessed. Poor woman.

Poor, gorgeous woman. As a consolation he had gotten a pretty one. And yet, what color were her eyes? Pink?

When the officiant said they should kiss, the audience clapped and cheered. Kir felt a blush ride his neck, and that disturbed him. Performing for an audience? Yikes. And, yet, the kiss was a standard wedding tradition.

With a smirk, his wife reached up and bracketed his head with her hands, boldly bringing him down to her level. And then…

She kissed him. It was soft and tentative at first but quickly warmed and grew bold. Her lips were soft and pliant. Sweet to taste, as sweet as her scent. And quietly stunning. She knew how to kiss, and parts of him stood up and took notice. He could kiss her all day. If he hadn't an audience.

So there was a bright moment to this horrible day.

And when she opened her eyes, he saw that, indeed, they were not the usual sidhe violet but instead pink. Which indicated she was a half-breed.

Kir's heart suddenly did drop to his gut. What the hell had he married?

Following the vows, and that unexpectedly delicious kiss, Bea had danced the expected dance with her husband. It was an ancient sidhe dance that required barely holding hands and walking down an aisle of fellow revelers. It involved bows and hops and all that ceremonial nonsense that her elders so adored.

Her new husband's name, which she had only learned during the ceremony, was Kirnan Sauveterre. And his hand, when it had finally touched hers, had felt warm but shaky. Nervous? Surprising, coming from a big, bold wolf such as he. The man had filled the air beside her with a reluctant confidence. Yet she sensed he was a force when not out of his element, such as they both were now.

After their kiss, he'd barely spared her more than a few glances. And during the dance his eyes strayed everywhere but onto her. Was she so hideous to look upon?

After the dance, Bea excused herself to find something to drink. Her husband had let her go without a word, turning away to quickly find and chat with one of his pack mates.

Perhaps he was as freaked by the whole event as she was. She guessed that, because he'd stood stick straight amid a swarm of congratulating friends, his eyes unfocused as he nodded mechanically. And she suspected that tiny smile was more a what-the-hell-have-I-done? smile than of genuine nuptial bliss.

Pity. The wolf was sexy. Tall, too. She liked them big, tall and strong. And now that he'd relaxed a bit, he radiated a stoic command. The dark brown beard wasn't her favorite, but he kept it neatly trimmed, and the mustache, as well. She'd have sex with him if she had to.

And she did have to.

"For the rest of my freakin' life," she muttered, and grabbed a wooden goblet of mead from a passing waiter's tray.

Downing the sweet amber liquor in one shot, Bea winced at the honey bite. The bees that had made that batch must have gotten into a patch of thistleberry. Always gave the drink a tang. Then she grabbed another to have something to hold in her hand while she wandered among the well-wishers and those who had imbibed far more mead than she had.

"Let the drunken debauchery begin," she declared to no one but herself. "Might as well celebrate the end of my life with a good ol' rainbow yawn in the morning. Not like I expected something better in life, eh?"

Princess though she was, growing up in Malrick's household had been a lesson in endurance. Bea had never strived for more than survival among her dozens of sidhe siblings; the majority of them were full-blooded faery. She, being a half-breed of dubious heritage, had received the brunt of Malrick's disdain.

So to stand now amid the revelers and receive their congratulatory handclasps only increased the nervous roil in her belly. It was a show they put on, a product of much mead and the desire to please their king. They cared little about her.

As did her father, who was, not surprisingly, absent this evening.

The hum of voices and laughter receded from her thoughts. Bea understood the French language with ease. The sidhe could assimilate any mortal realm language merely by listening to it. Fortunately, France had always interested her. If she were to visit any place in this realm, she was glad she'd landed in this country.

Wandering to the edge of the merriment, she found and followed the flower-petal-laden path that twisted through the dark forest depths until the laughter and conversations grew to but a murmur. A trio of sprites danced in the air before her, sprinkling the path with their violet dust. Beyond an arch of fern fronds, she followed the sprites to the nuptial cottage, which had been erected for their wedding-night bonding. The walls were formed from plane trees growing high, and their branches curved and spread out thick leaves to fashion the roof. It was private, save for the narrow alcove nestled near the doorway, where she knew the witness would be positioned while she and her husband did the deed.

Yes, someone had to witness their wedding-night bonding. Bea shivered at the thought of performing the sexual act with a witness. Faeries were big on ceremony and the observance of royal deeds. And since her father was the Unseelie king, that made her wedding a Big Deal.

Not that she'd ever felt remotely princess-like. Shouldn't a girl's father, at the very least, show up for her wedding?

She ran her fingertips over her embroidered and bepearled pink gown. Beneath the gossamer layers she felt the blade she always wore strapped to her thigh. Growing up in Faery as a half-breed should have been a wonderful thing. The sidhe embraced half-breeds; they even sought to procreate with most other breeds to create such progeny. With all but the darkest, which included demons and vampires.

Bea's non-sidhe half—of which she wasn't clear what it was, though certainly she'd assumed it vampire—had made her a pariah among her own. Through his inattention, her father had made it very clear she disgusted him. Which explained why he'd been so eager to offer her as a seal to this bargain with the Valoir pack.

"Unwanted and unloved," she whispered. "And now I've been thrust into a realm that frightens me and will be forced to live with a wolf I don't know."

A shiver traced her skin and she wrapped her arms across her chest in a hug that felt more pitiful than comforting.

There was a bright side to look at. She'd always dreamed about escaping her father's household.

"Perhaps I'll like the mortal realm," she decided. "And maybe my husband will even grow to like me."

Turning to gaze back toward the celebration, her wings fluttered and she had the thought to fold them away. Wings and sex, well…she wasn't ready for such soul-deep intimacy with the new husband. Stones, she just hoped to get through the evening without saying something stupid or landing in an awkward sprawl on the bed.

She spied her husband near the feast table, speaking confidently to another wolf she guessed was a good friend, for he had stood beside Kirnan during the ceremony. Kirnan Sauveterre. She wondered about his surname. What did it mean? It felt honorable and bold as she whispered it.

Kirnan stood the tallest amid the crowd save for a few sidhe. He held his head proudly, shoulders back. Soft brown hair curled about his head, and a slightly darker beard and mustache framed his long face. A regal nose. And ears tight to his head. No points, though, Bea noted as she stroked the gently pointed tip of her ear. So she'd learn to like him despite that physical fault.

A hand-tooled black leather vest stretched across a broad, muscled chest, and his leather pants wrapped muscular thighs that she imagined often ran through the forest, both in man form and as a wolf. The sprig of dandelion in the boutonniere he wore at his breast pocket portended faithfulness.

If only she could get so lucky. She touched the blue anemone in her hair. Chosen for luck.

Bea sighed. Her husband looked like every woman's dream of the rescuing knight. All he needed was the white stallion and a suit of silver armor.

And perhaps he should look into that set of armor. Because she was armed and would not allow anyone to harm her. If he turned out to be an aggressive, demanding wolf, she would have to put him in his place. No one from this realm was going to mess with her. She'd had enough practice sticking up for herself that she never took a step without first casting a look over her shoulder.

After wandering into the wedding cottage, Bea sighed and plopped onto the end of the massive bed. She stroked the bond mark on the back of her hand. The first seal. Sex would close their bond.

She inched her gown up along her leg, and, from the thigh strap, she tugged out a gleaming violet blade and stabbed it into the tree branch that formed the canopy bed frame.

"Please let him be kind," she whispered.

Chapter 3

Kir stumbled into the wedding tent. He'd put back a few drinks but hadn't thought he was drunk. Must have been that tree root at the threshold. Although, the honey mead had been some powerful stuff. Whew! He and Jacques had done a couple mead shots before Etienne had suggested he go seek out his bride.

His bride. The words felt foreign tinkering about in his brain.

Tilting back his shoulders and taking things in, he could only marvel. How this makeshift tent slash honeymoon debauchery cottage had been erected was beyond him. The walls grew up from the ground—mature trees that had long ago rooted—and the branches bent over to form a roof as if they'd grown that way decades earlier.

And it smelled great in here. Like flowers, honey and sweet things, and…her. Yeah, she'd smelled like candy. And her scent had found a place in his nose. And that was a bit of all right.

The new wife stood on the opposite side of the cottage, fingers nervously tracing the bed linens. Clad in sheer pink silk that imitated flower petals, she looked like a lost girl, veiled in black hair with bright eyes. Her wings weren't out, or maybe they were folded behind her back.

What was with those eyes? Pink? Kir had thought all sidhe eyes were violet. And if she was a half-breed, then he wanted to know what her other half was before they got too cozy. He didn't do creatures like vampires and demons. There was a vast range of "other" she could be if she were not full-blood faery.

Either way, you have to do this. Right. What a way to ruin a good drunk. Sex with a stranger, who would then follow him home. And stay there. He'd thought getting the mark on his hand was the whole bonding ritual. Not so, Brit had explained to him, when he'd asked after his bride after losing sight of her at the revelry.

"Hey." She waved at him. She remained by the bed, perhaps as nervous as he about this? Surely the idea of having sex with a man she'd known all of a few minutes could not appeal to her.

At least, Kir hoped that kind of sex didn't appeal to her. A fast-and-loose faery wasn't his idea of perfect wife material.

Ah, heck, why was he being so judgmental? They were in this together. And if his guess about her nervousness was right, then he'd do what he could to alleviate some of that worry. Starting with a firm attempt at clinging to the last vestiges of his sobriety.

"So, let's get this over and done with, eh?" He stretched an arm toward a little nook at the entrance, where she could catch a glimpse of their witness. "We do have a spy to entertain. But, so you know, I really don't want to do this with you."

"Way to make your wife feel loved, big boy."

"Love? Are you—" He eyed the carafe on the bedside table and aimed for it, but when he drank, he found it was only fresh, clear water. Kir spit out the not-alcohol over the moss floor. "Are you on board with all this?"

"I haven't much choice," the woman said. "Nor do you, apparently. Sacrificed for the good of your pack, eh?"

What was her name? Oh, yeah. Beatrice.

"Listen, Beatrice, if sex is what is required by your kind to seal the bargain, then sex it is."

"Yes, we sidhe are a weird bunch. And daddy Malrick is a twisted bit of dark sidhe."

"Says the half faery."

She lifted her chin at that statement. Defiant? Defensive?

"Your eyes," Kir said, pointing at her face. "Am I right?"

She nodded.

"So what is your other half?"

She shrugged. "It's not important. Is it?"

Not with a swimming head and the strong urge to dive onto the bed, close his eyes and wish the nightmare would end.

"Nope. Guess not."

Kir tugged off his vest and shirt and tossed it to the floor, his back to her. Bea could see that the wolf was raring to go. And would you look at those muscles? They bulged and rippled and formed a vast, solid surface. She felt sure she'd not seen the like, ever, in Faery. And she had dated more than her share of sidhe in all shapes, sizes and even colors. This wolf? He was, by the blessed Norns, beautiful.

She dashed her tongue along her lower lip. If she had to do this, she may as well try to enjoy it. Take one for the team, right? Let the big, handsome wolf put his hands all over her naked body? She'd force herself if she had to.

As his fingers drew down the zipper of his leather pants, he turned. "So how do you want to do this?"

"Down and dirty." Bea shed a thin strap from her shoulder. "Get 'er done." Because if not now, she'd lose her bravery and fly for safety.

"I agree. Quicker is easier."

Flicking off a strap from her shoulder, her wedding dress dropped to a puddle at her feet. And the wolf's eyes dropped to her breasts. They were small but high and perky. She was well made for aerodynamic flight.

Kir exhaled and averted his gaze to the side. Was he getting all shy on her? Or perhaps a gentleman hid behind the steely muscles and bite-worthy abs? Aw. Sweet.

But Bea couldn't get behind forced niceties after that wince she had seen him make during the ceremony. It was her eyes. They freaked him. The dude did not like her. And if the werewolf knew what her other half was? He'd go running with his tail between his legs.

Now all she had to do tonight was keep her dark half subdued. Fingers crossed.

"Pants off," she said, turning toward the bed and patting the mattress. "We'll get into the swing of things, then you can shift, and we'll seal the deal."

Kir chuckled. "Is your definition of *foreplay* the swing of things?"

"Yep. You got a problem with that, big boy?"

He narrowed his gaze on her. "Are you always so cold?"

"Nope. But how many times have you been required to have sex with someone you've known only minutes? And with a witness not a leap away whose heavy breathing I can hear!" she said loudly.

The heavy breaths were instantly muffled. Bea rolled her eyes.

Kir smirked at the obvious disaster that had become their lives. "Right. Sorry. This is tough for us both. I just want you to know..."

He hooked his hands at the waistband of his leather pants and stared off toward the ceiling. Above, tiny sprites hovered, but Bea didn't mind. They were always around in Faery. She was quite sure she'd never had sex with a man completely alone. But sprites didn't tell tales. Unless you pissed them off.

"What I want you to know," he started, "is that despite the surprise of only learning about this two days ago, I'm going to give this my all. This marriage. I never do anything half-cocked."

Bea laughed and averted her eyes to the opened fly on his leather pants. "Half-cocked?"

"It's an expression. And even though I don't know you, any woman deserves my best."

"Honorable words. Have you been practicing that speech all day?"

"No, it's— Hey, take me or leave me. I drew the short stick. Now I intend to do the best with the situation."

"The short stick?" Bea crossed her arms over her breasts, feeling not at all embarrassed by her nudity, but oh, so curious at the wolf's comment. "What in mossy misery does that mean?"

"The short stick? You know. When there's a less-than-desirable task to be done, someone breaks a bunch of sticks and holds them in his hand, with their length concealed in his fist. Whoever draws the shortest stick is the loser."

"I see. So I'm your short stick?"

He shrugged and offered a wincing nod.

"Peachy." She swallowed back the scream that vied for

release. She'd only hoped he would be nice. Not cruel like her father. Foolish of her to wish for so much.

"Sorry, I shouldn't have explained that to you," he said, rubbing a palm against the side of his head. "Do you want a drink? I brought in a bottle of wine."

"No, I'm cool. And I think you have imbibed far too much already."

"Mead," he said with a drunken grin.

"Yeah, from the little I've seen at the reception, you mortal realmers can't handle your mead. Let's get this done with so the witness can go to bed, and I'm really tired, so..."

"Yeah, me, too. So it's just business between us? Doing this for the home teams?"

Bea smirked. Some home team she was on. "I'm not even *on* the team. When teams pick sides, I'm always the one left standing."

He cast her a curious raise of brow. "I've had that same thought. Huh."

"Right. For the team," she agreed with as much enthusiasm as she could muster, which was zero.

The werewolf strode closer, and Bea climbed up onto the bed but didn't take her eyes from his, which swept over her body appreciatively. Was the wolf actually hungry for her? Good. That would make this go quicker. She could do this. She didn't have to feel anything for him; she just had to go through the motions. Seal the deal. Worry about the whole happily-ever-after crap in the morning.

He slid a hand below her breast and leaned down to lick her nipple. Bea sucked in a breath as that contact flamed over her skin and tickled her into an appreciative wiggle. Wow. Most men would have started with a kiss and worked lower, but she had no arguments about this mode of attack.

Business, and all that. The wolf was already at the *getting* in the getting-'er-done part.

Stones, but he really knew how to stir her system to alert, all nerves fired and ready to receive. He moved to her other breast and laved her tight nipple, then he chuckled.

Chuckled?

"What the heck?" Bea asked. "Why am I so funny to you?"

"You're not." He shook his head, then nipped her skin quickly before giving her another deep chuckle. "I'm just… nervous. This is—"

"Weird?" She raked her fingers through his soft hair but enjoyed the sensation so much she abruptly pulled back. "Uncomfortable? So wrong it's almost right?"

"Yeah. Don't misunderstand me. I'm hot for your body, Beatrice. It's just, we're doing this backward. Normally a couple gets to know one another before *really* getting to know one another like this."

"Like we have a choice?"

He followed her gaze to the alcove by the door. The feet were now crossed at the ankle. "I guess not."

"I'm nervous, too." She stroked his cheek. His beard was soft, and she tickled her fingers along it. He nuzzled his face into her palm like a cat seeking strokes. Except he wasn't a cat. And she was as cool with this moment as she could get. She'd love to take the time to run her fingers over his skin and map out his muscles, but… "The longer we put on a show for you-know-who, the freakier it gets."

"I agree. I'm hard as a rock. Ready to go. But I want you to be ready."

"That's thoughtful. But don't worry about me. You are some kind of sexy. Just looking at you gets me hot. I've been ready for a while now. So come inside me, husband. Let's seal this deal."

She lay back against the pillows, sitting half-upright,

and beckoned him closer. Kir slipped off the leather pants and his erection slapped up against his stomach. Bea sucked in her lower lip. Great Goddess of Goodness, that was a nice one. She could imagine taking her time with that thick column later. When they were alone.

The wolf got on the bed and knelt between her legs, lowering his body over her. Avoiding eye contact. Oh, stones, did she appreciate not having to stare into his gorgeous brown sparklers at this particularly sensitive moment. *Just get it done. You can do this.*

She grasped his hot length and guided him inside her. He stretched her sweetly. She bit her lip, thinking she'd gotten the long stick for sure.

Heh. This nervous anxiety was making her silly. But better to go with humor than to turn into a crazy, jittery nerve-bucket.

Slowly, he slid in and out of her, the thickness of him tugging at her pinnacle and teasing her insides to a quivering anticipation. This was already better than ninety percent of her dates back in Faery. Because…well, just because. She didn't want to go there.

Because surrendering to the moment worked right now. It made her forget. About everything. This was actually… pretty freakin' awesome.

She moaned, and Kir stopped his thrusts. "Am I hurting you?"

"Oh, no, wolf. What you're doing feels great. Faster."

"If I go any faster, I'll come, and that can't happen until I shift if we're going to do the bonding correctly."

"Right, you werewolves bond in shifted shape. I sense this is going to get interesting."

"Real fast. You ready for my werewolf, little faery?"

No. And maybe. And, stones, yes, she was ready.

This day had been insane, what with being forced to

leave her home with nothing more than her bridal gown and the blade strapped to her thigh. No mementos, but she hadn't needed any. She'd even stood in the forest and watched as sidhe magic built her wedding dais and this bonding cottage, all the while her heart thudding faster and faster, wondering if this world could be worse than her own.

And then to stand beside the wolf, her heart thundering, and promise to love and honor him without knowing what kind of man he was. Kind, domineering, cruel or, perhaps, weak?

But it was going to end on a high note if she had any say about it. And that note would come from her as she cried out in pleasure.

"Let's do this," she said, shuffling back on the bed. She wanted to come right now. She wanted…foreplay and emotion and his hands all over her, both inside and out.

But tonight wasn't for any of that. "Let's get 'er done."

The faery's bright pink eyes widened as Kir's body began the shift. It took only a matter of seconds for his bones to change and his skin to stretch over lengthening muscles and shifting interior organs. Fur sprouted from his pores and his jaw grew longer and teeth made for tearing meat filled his maw.

When in his half man/half wolf werewolf form, he had thoughts as a man and as a wolf. He could understand some spoken language, but for the most part, he acted on instinct. And instinct told him a ripe female waited for him.

She scrambled off the bed, seemingly fearful of his towering form, but when she stopped at the headboard, she turned. A tiny smile curled her pink lips and she crooked a beckoning finger at him.

The werewolf recognized that as an invitation.

* * *

Gasping, Bea caught her hands on the headboard fashioned from woven branches while the werewolf howled behind her. He had reached orgasm, as had she. And, man, that had been a cosmic thing. She could now entirely get behind the meaning of bonding in werewolf terms. Big furry wolf man, meet the quivering, sexually satisfied faery chick? Fur and claws? She could deal. And she had. In werewolf form Kir was mostly man-shaped anyway, and his cock was all man.

Yet she was suddenly ravenous. And not for food. She'd been born with an inexplicable hunger, which had been sustained by drinking ichor from her fellow sidhe ever since puberty. Here, in the mortal realm, she had prepared herself for her first taste of mortal blood. Because, if not ichor, the only other option was blood. It sustained. And satisfied. It was tied in to sex and the orgasm and the desire to pleasure herself as deeply as possible.

And she would not ignore that hunger.

Much as Bea assumed the wolf was not going to like what she did next—she twisted about and hugged the big furry lug about his wide, panting chest. Sinking in her fangs at the werewolf's throat caused him to whip back his head in protest. A talon cut down her thigh as he attempted to pull her off him.

Bea clung. The blood spilling into her mouth was hot and thick and tasted better than mead or even ichor.

Now, this was her kind of bonding.

Chapter 4

Suddenly the fur Bea had clenched in her grasp receded and her fingers slipped over male skin slickened with his own blood. Kir's exaggerated form, which had been mostly human in werewolf shape, save the wolfish head, returned to his regular structure. He pulled his neck away from her mouth. Her fangs dripped blood onto her thighs.

Her new husband pushed her into the pile of pillows jammed against the headboard. Kir slammed the mattress with a fist. "What the—" He slapped a palm over his neck, though she had landed the bite much closer to his shoulder than she'd intended. "You bit me!"

"Yeah? What did you expect? You shagged me in the literal sense, buddy. Shaggy fur and all."

"We needed to bond. You knew that had to happen. You agreed to it!"

"That I did."

"But what's the bite about?" He gestured to her fangs. "You...you..."

His panicked expression was comical, but only until Bea realized he had been blindsided, and she should have waited to answer her hunger until after he was more familiar with her *needs*.

"I was in the moment." She retracted her fangs and pushed a long tangle of hair over her shoulder. Dragging a finger through the blood droplet on her thigh, she then licked it clean. Mercy, that tasted incredible. "I needed to feed."

"Feed?" Kir exhaled. "What the hell are you? Oh." He fisted the air. "Hell no! You can't be. No, no, no. Please tell me you are not half vampire."

She sat up pertly and wiggled her hips, more from fresh nerves than defiance. And, really, sarcasm and snark were her best means of defense. "Did the fangs give me away? You are one perceptive werewolf."

"Bea? Tell me what the hell I married."

She definitely did not like his angry voice. But, seriously, what had he expected? It wasn't as though Malrick was going to hand over a valued full-blooded sidhe daughter for marriage.

"I may be half vampire," she conceded, unable to meet his accusatory glare. "But I don't know. I've lived on ichor all my life. Ichor is equal to blood in the mortal realm. And my eyes are pink. I know, right? Most sidhe eyes are violet."

Kir crushed his palms across his forehead and over his skull. "I can't believe this! Malrick is your— What is your mother?"

Bea shrugged. "Never met her."

"Didn't your father tell you who or what your mother was?"

"Daddy dearest? Pfft. He likes to keep secrets. Only, he never lets me forget what a disappointment I am to him.

Which is, I suspect, why you got stuck with me. Sent the rotten egg of the bunch off to the mortal realm. Like you said—" she pointed a thumb at herself "—short stick."

Kir wiped at the bite marks on his neck. "I assumed Malrick would not send a favorite. But a vampire is…"

"Not your first pick for a wife, eh?"

"There's nothing wrong with vampires, I just… You know werewolves develop a nasty blood hunger from a vampire bite? That is not something I want to happen to me. I pray your vampire taint did not have a chance to enter my bloodstream."

"Sorry." Way to make her feel special. Not. "If it makes you feel any better, it's never been confirmed that my non-sidhe half is vampire. But I have been drinking ichor since I was a teen."

"Never been confirmed?"

"My father won't talk about my mother. I guess she was vamp, though, because I have these fun things," she said as she tapped her fang, and she caught her husband's wince. "Right. I'm used to that look. Now I'm kind of glad I bit you."

He gripped her by the upper arm. "You will not do it again. A blood hunger is the worst for a werewolf like me."

"Then you'd be like me. A disappointment." Bea tugged from his grip and scooted away from him on the bed.

Yeah, so she'd known this wasn't going to be a romance-and-roses wedding night. She probably should have asked to bite first. Her bad. She had barely gotten a taste, but the drops she'd licked from her lips were hot and thick and so, so tasty. She'd bite him again in an instant. But she had probably spoiled the chance of that ever happening again.

"Yeah, whatever," she offered, using dismissal as defense. "No more biting. I'm excited to taste mortal blood anyway, because yours was—"

Bea caught Kir's openmouthed gape. It was too familiar. And she did know how to protect herself by pulling on the cloak of indifference. "Quit looking at me like that. I'm not the enemy. Or evil. You're just like everyone else. Hating me because I'm different. A dark one. Something Malrick despises. I—I hate you!"

"I hate you, too," the wolf muttered.

He sat there, fingering the bite wounds at his neck, wincing and growling. She had barely broken the skin! And Bea couldn't feel at all ashamed for taking what she'd wanted. He'd taken from her. He'd slammed her up against the headboard and filled her with that hot werewolf hard-on. And she had taken it all because—oh, mercy, it had felt great.

Wasn't that what a marriage was all about? Give and take?

Very well, so she could feel the tiniest bit of regret at having possibly ignited a blood hunger in her werewolf husband. But really? Did the guy even realize his erection was full mast again? He was so ready for round three, or four, or whatever round came next.

And so was Bea. Because the slight blood scent on him had aroused her to some kind of wanting, needy bit of lust and faery dust.

A glance to the doorway and she did not spy the feet dangling from behind the wall. Their witness had fled, evidence secured. Would he report their wedding-night fight? Did it matter? Malrick hadn't come to the ceremony. He'd gotten rid of the dark one. The daughter he'd wished had never existed. What did he care what happened to her in this realm?

With this wolf. Who was sending out waves of anger that gushed from his skin and surrounded her like a foul mist. Skin that sparkled with glints of faery dust. Faeries had a tendency to release dust during orgasm. Couldn't be avoided.

Bea looked over her shoulder at her new husband. Stones, he was gorgeous. The perspiration pearling his glinting skin looked lickable. She didn't need blood anymore. She just wanted more wolf cock. Inside her. Slower this time. And sans audience.

A teasing desire lowered her voice to a hush. She traced a fingertip along his knee and up his thigh. "Want to have sex again? Promise I won't bite."

Kir swiped a hand over his neck and studied the blood. He gritted his jaws and growled. She kissed his shoulder and slid a finger down his hard length. "I'll let you be on top again. I'm wet for you, wolf."

With a shake of his head, he answered resoundingly, "Yes."

A bird chirped outside the wedding cottage. Either it was too early, or Kir had drunk too much last night. Either way, he'd never felt like growling at a bird until now.

It was the mead. Had to be.

He strode about the cottage, picking up his clothes from the cushy moss floor. The leather pants were still clean. Good enough for work, so he pulled them on. Outside the tree-trunk-walled room, the only living beings were the birds and squirrels. The wedding guests had left throughout the night, finally giving them peace. He'd seen the redcapped brownie who had been in the alcove by the door scamper out, as well.

The humiliation at having been watched while having sex was a new one. But it wasn't as though hundreds of sidhe and wolves from his pack hadn't been outside and within hearing distance. The music and revelry had been loud. But when he'd howled during orgasm?

Don't think about it, man.

Well, hell, he'd not thought about it while in the moment. So maybe he wasn't feeling as humiliated as he could.

He retrieved his shirt from the moss, and when he stood and accidentally elbowed one of the braided tree branch bedposts, the faery on the bed turned over and stretched out an arm. Her breasts were pert and hard, and sunlight sheened across her pale belly. On the top of her feet the skin was decorated with fancy violet swirls, similar to the bond mark on the back of his hand yet much more elaborate. Everywhere she…glinted.

"Faery dust," he muttered, and swiped a palm over his forearm, which also glinted faintly. The stuff was fine and not easy to wipe off his skin.

He didn't want to wake her. He didn't know how to do the morning thing. Were they supposed to do a morning thing? Generally on dates, if he ended up in the woman's bed, he slipped out early or else offered to take her out for breakfast, which she usually refused because the getting-ready part always took so long. He knew the drill.

He rubbed his neck, feeling the faintest abrasion from the bite mark. After what she'd done to him last night, he was ready to toss her out and let her sleep in the backyard shed.

But really? The sex had been great. And he'd had more sex with her *after* the bite. What kind of crazy was that?

He just wished he'd had some warning before the fangs had come out. So he could have defended himself. He'd married a half vampire? Or so she thought she was half vampire. How insane was it not to know for sure? Well, it was obvious. Fangs and a hunger for blood? Sure, there were other species that boasted fangs—even werewolves had thick, fanged canines—but how many sought blood for pleasure?

And what now? Would he develop a nasty hunger for blood? This was not cool. First thing he would do when he returned to Paris would be to look up a wolf doctor and have himself checked out.

Beatrice blocked the sunlight with her hands. "Ugh! The sun!"

"Does it burn you?" He looked about for a curtain beside the windows, but there wasn't one. The sunlight beamed through the twisted tree canopy. No way to block out nature. "Are you okay?" He grabbed the tangled sheet but wasn't able to pull it up to cover her.

"Dude, what's your deal? The sun is not going to burn me. Just…who wakes up so early? Do humans actually tread the earth this time of day?" She pulled the gossamer sheet up over her face and spread out her arms to each side. Putting up one finger, she noted, "I'm only half vamp. Sunlight doesn't bother me. I much prefer the moonlight, though."

He did, too. But thanks again for reminding him that he was now married to someone who could give him a nasty taste for blood. Doctor's appointment? Coming right up.

"It's eight o'clock," he said. "And, yes, the mortal realm is up and at 'em."

"Eight? Oh!" She buried deeper into the sheets and pulled the pillow over her head. "Wake me after high sun."

"I take it that's the faery way of saying noon? I have to head into work and stop by the, er…" She didn't need to know how freaked he was about developing a blood hunger. "I'll give you a ride home."

"Home? I don't have a home anymore," she muttered from under the sheet.

"To my house. Er, *our* house. Can't stay out here in the middle of the forest forever."

"In theory, I could," she said, her voice muffled. "You could leave me in this little cottage and come visit me every once in a while. When you want sex." She sighed, the sheet billowing above her mouth. "Just so you know, the sex was fantastic."

"No argument on that one. Next time I hope it's just the two of us."

"I can so get behind that one."

He chuckled at her levity. And, yes, private sex—without the fangs—was something he could look forward to, as well.

"Seriously, Bea, I have to get going. I work six days a week. Today's no holiday because I got married last night."

"Yeah, yeah. And as soon as we both step foot outside this place, it'll cease to exist. So there goes my plans to hole up here all by myself."

"Really? It'll disappear?"

"Faery glamour, don't you know. Is there a change of clothing laid out for me somewhere?"

"There is." Grabbing a pale green dress laid across the table by the bed, he tossed the garment onto the bed. "Ten minutes. I'm going out to…"

Relieve himself and hope upon hope that his vehicle was still parked nearby and not decorated with shaving cream or crepe streamers.

An hour later, Kir parked the Lexus—undecorated—in front of his house and led Bea inside. She leaped from the car, not wanting to touch any part of the steel frame, even after he'd suggested that nowadays human-manufactured vehicles were produced with less iron, and none of that was cold iron. Still, she'd been cautious and fearful.

He was already late for work, so he didn't do the grand tour. He wanted to grab a clean shirt and head out. He needed to get away from Bea and orient himself to what had happened last night. So many things going on in his brain. He had a wife. He'd had sex with a witness watching last night. The sex had been awesome. Until the bite. A bite that he could no longer feel. His skin was healed. Would Jacques notice? Could he get in to see the doc this afternoon?

"You're on your own today," he said, striding down the hallway toward the laundry room. "Take a look around the place. I guess it's your home now, too."

"Peachy." She stood in the hallway with arms crossed over the sheer dress that barely hung past her derriere. Barefoot, the markings on her feet drew his eye. "Get a new wife. Toss her in a little box and head back out to your normal life. I get it."

He was not doing that. Okay, he was, in a manner. He'd have a talk with her later. Didn't she understand that people needed to work to live and survive in this realm? If she was a faery princess, the concept may be foreign to her.

"I'll leave my cell number on the kitchen counter if you have any questions. You know what cell phones are?"

"Yes," she snapped. "It's those stupid little boxes humans talk into when they don't want to talk face-to-face. Duh."

"Or when they can't be face-to-face but just want to check in on each other."

"Is there iron in them?"

"I— No. Very little iron, if any, in the house, too."

"Fine, but rubbing against it burns like a mother."

Touching iron wouldn't kill a faery, but it would give them a nasty burn—he knew that much. And frequent contact with iron? Eventually it would bring their death.

Kind of like what happened if he came in contact with silver. A nasty burn. And if it entered his bloodstream? Bye-bye, wolf.

"I'll try to swing by on my afternoon break to see if you need anything," he said, tugging on a clean shirt and buttoning it up.

"More sleep for me, less wolf. Peaches and cream, buddy. Peaches and cream."

"Right." Slapping a hand to his neck, Kir wasn't so fond of the faery right now, either. Despite the satisfying sex. He headed down the hallway toward the front door. "I'll see you later."

"I hate you!" she called out from the kitchen.

"I hate you, too, Short Stick," he answered.

A smirk lessened any vitriol he felt with that statement. He'd never hated a person in his life. Hate was not good for the soul. But extreme dislike felt damn good when it involved a bloodsucking faery who had no compunctions about taking a bite without asking first.

Chapter 5

The wolf owned a lot of hair products in bottles that listed so many strange ingredients it made Bea's eyes cross.

"Makes sense," she said as her eyes wandered over the array of scented shampoos, conditioners, creams, potions and lotions lined up on a glass shelf in the huge walk-in shower. "The guy is a wolf. I wonder if his werewolf ever showers in here?"

She'd initially been shocked after Kir had shifted to werewolf form. Oh, she'd seen werewolves before and had known what they looked like fully shifted, but she'd never stood so close to one before. Or gazed upon his magnificent hard-on. Or, for that matter, touched said hard-on.

Giggling, she flipped on the shower stream, which blasted her from the walls and overhead.

"Yes!" She skipped about within the water, dancing, arms flung out and head back. "It's like a rain shower. I could so get used to this."

She unfurled her wings and let the water spill over them, which sent scintillating shivers along the wings and at the muscles and bones where they connected to her spine. She'd worn them out all the time in Faery yet had been warned that in the mortal realm it was not wise, even if she wore glamour.

She'd never been one to follow the rules. Like what was so wrong with biting your new husband if you hungered for a little sip?

Kir had really been angry with her. Justified, coming from a werewolf.

"Too bad," she sang, opening her mouth to the water stream and spinning. "You're stuck with me now, wolf. Deal with it!"

Because look at what she had to deal with: hair, hair and more hair. And a tail. And talons that had cut down her thigh when he'd tried to pry her fangs from his neck. She couldn't blame him for hurting her. It had been a defensive reaction. And the cut had been shallow; it was already healed.

So now she had a shifter husband who— Okay, so he wasn't ugly in werewolf form, just big and growly and noisy. He was also a bit of a stick-in-the-mud, from what she could divine. Not pleased to be her husband, that was for sure. Something about drawing the short stick.

Yet they had both given their all for the wedding-night sex. Again and again. And while the sex had been great, Bea wondered how long before the luster wore away and she'd be jonesing for a return to Faery. At least there she'd always been able to find a willing bite. And along with that bite had usually been some reasonably satisfying sex.

"Never going to happen." She switched off the water and shook her wings vigorously. "I'm not going back!"

Because nothing could make her return to Faery, and

the tyranny of her father's reign over her. She was free. As free as she could be considering the mark on the back of her hand that bonded her to a wolf.

And now that she was here, she could begin her mission. To find the mother she had never known.

Jumping out of the shower, she performed a shiver of wings to flick away the wet, sending droplets across the walls and mirror. She twirled and leaned onto the vanity before the mirror. Eyeing the wet faery, she winked at her.

"Aren't you a sexy chick? You know the wolf wants to eat you up. But he won't because you've got fangs."

She ran her tongue along one fang that descended to a pointy weapon. In Faery she'd been a pariah. Half-breeds were favored for strengthening and adding genetic powers and attributes to the sidhe lines. But vampires were shunned. Filthy longtooths. They were nothing but scum who liked to feed on faery ichor as their favorite drug. They were disliked almost as much as demons. A half-breed sidhe demon was labeled The Wicked and was the lowest of the low. So she did have that going for her.

"Not quite the dregs of the barrel, are you, Bea?"

She decided her father had had the affair with her mother for the reason she must have been forbidden fruit. Something lesser than Malrick. Dark and forbidden. He'd wanted to try her out. And he'd never let Bea forget that.

But in the mortal realm vampires must hold a certain status. Bea hoped so. Because she was done with the shame and ostracism. She wanted to shine, to grow and finally become the fierce woman with wings and fangs that had been stifled in Faery.

"So long as the hubby doesn't get in my way, I'll be golden."

Winking at her reflection, she rummaged through the vanity drawer and found Kir's comb. She hadn't been allowed to bring any of her things to this realm. The comb was not like the crystal prize she'd once owned, but it smelled like him. Woodsy and wild. It would serve until she could go shopping. But to do that she needed mortal money. Of which, she hoped the hubby had a lot.

Her übersexy hubby who really knew how to get right to the point concerning orgasms.

"I hate him so much I can't wait until he gets home."

Tossing the comb onto the vanity and skipping down the stairs, she decided to explore, as Kir had suggested. It felt great to walk around skyclad, wings unfurled. She didn't mind the narrow hallway that bent back her wings as she strode into the kitchen.

The note on the counter detailed a phone number and was signed "Kir."

"Like he thinks I won't guess who the note was from? Silly wolf." Though she traced a finger over the name and lifted the paper to give it a quick kiss. "My hubby."

Tiptoeing about the vast stone-tiled kitchen, she ran her fingers over the granite countertop, not sensing the energy that she normally felt from stones. But the fieldstones paving the kitchen floor were alive, which lightened her steps as she spun and traced her fingers across the glossy stovetop and the sink. No iron here!

At the icebox, she flung open the door and peered inside. Lots of clear plastic bottles holding energy drinks in various pale colors. Fruits and vegetables. "Go, wolf." And meat. Sliced, chopped, chunked, shredded and cut. "Blech. My hubby likes to eat things that once had a heartbeat. Bad wolf." She'd married a carnivore. That would be a new one to deal with.

On the other hand, she couldn't claim complete vegetarianism. Now that she was in the mortal realm, she'd get the opportunity to feast on mortal blood. And that had a heartbeat. Getting a sip of wolf last night had been like popping her red-blood cherry. Blessed be, he'd tasted good.

And she wanted more.

Plucking out a vine of green grapes, Bea danced through the kitchen and into the next room, which was a cozy living area walled on two sides with books and carpeted in what looked like ancient tapestry. Deeply varnished wood and curvaceous carvings gave the room a medieval appeal. It felt solid and earthy.

"Just like my wolf."

Sitting on the back of the big leather couch, she tilted back her head and nibbled the grapes from the vine. Toppling, she laughed as her feet went over her head and she tumbled off the sofa and onto the floor. She upset the books stacked on the coffee table, and one landed on a wing.

"Ouch." She pulled up the heavy book and read the title, *Exotic Fantasy Figures*.

Inside were gorgeous colored plates featuring fantastical creatures that she felt sure did not exist in the mortal realm or Faery. Though a few depictions were close to some of the sidhe she'd known. The text said they'd been created using a computer. She wasn't familiar with mortal technology but had learned about computers during her mortal realm lessons. The devices were carriers of information.

She needed to get her fingers all over one of those computers if she was going to track down her mother.

Flinging aside the book to land splayed open, she sprang up and skipped to the floor-to-ceiling window and pressed her nose to the glass. Outside lay a small yard with browning grass and some pitiful flowers.

Bea's smile wilted. "Poor grass. I'll have to give you some tender loving care."

A shed stood at what she guessed was the back of Kir's property.

"Doesn't own much land. Hmm…let's hope that means he put all his money in gold, because this girl needs to do some shopping."

Popping another grape into her mouth, she twirled and flung out her arms, delighting in the warm sun that shone through the window. She only stopped her dance when she felt the odd sensation that she was not alone.

Standing in the archway between living room and kitchen was her new husband, his mouth hanging open and hands to his hips.

"What?" Bea pulled a wingtip forward and preened it over her shoulder. "Close your mouth, big boy. You act like you've never seen a naked faery before."

Kir's astonishment dropped and his eyes crinkled. The man's gentle laughter scurried over her naked skin like warm summer rain. And she did love to dance in the rain.

"I have some work in the area, so I stopped in to see if you're doing okay. I guess you are."

"Peachy! Your shower rocks!"

"It does." He walked in and picked up the book she'd tossed on the floor, carefully placing it back on the table. "Let me guess. You need clothes."

"Why?" She propped her hands akimbo. "You got a problem with naked faeries?"

"Uh. No. I don't think I do."

His eyes took her in from feet to knees to loins, and up where he lingered at her breasts. Bea felt his desire follow that warm rain like delicious sun. Mmm, come here, hungry wolf.

"But all creatures wear clothing in the mortal realm," he said. "So. You need clothes."

"And combs and jewelry, shoes and purses. Makeup. Perfumes. All that girl stuff. And to get that I'm going to need some mortal cash. Please tell me you have bajillions of the stuff."

"Bajillions?" Another soft chuckle. "Sorry to disappoint."

Bea's shoulders sank, as did her wings.

"But I am comfortable, as they say. You won't starve or be forced to live in a cardboard box anytime soon. I promise."

A cardboard box? Did mortals do that? Bea shivered. She'd once had an aunt who would curl up to live in a crustacean shell. Ugh.

"What's your job?" she asked. "Brit said something about you being an enforcer. Is that like a wolf cop?"

"In essence. Our pack polices the werewolf packs in Paris. Keeps an eye on them. Investigates the blood games and tries to ensure that no wolf makes the front page of *Le Monde*. That's the local world newspaper."

"Cool. So when do you have to guard the portal to Faery?"

"Not sure. Etienne, my pack principal, suggested I probably would not, since I've already gotten—"

"The short stick. I remember. You've sacrificed so much for your pack. Taking on a wife who is actually interested in having sex with you whenever you desire? Whew! That is so tough. I shed tears of pity for you, wolf."

"Whenever I desire?" The wolf's eyes twinkled. Actually twinkled.

"Pretty much." She fluttered her wings.

"I thought you hated me."

"Oh, I do." She crossed her arms and tucked her wings down tightly, a forced show of dislike. Her new hubby's chuckle made it difficult to keep her nose up and her back straight. So she put her wings away. "Wings are too much for you to handle."

"I bet they are. I can take you shopping later," he said. "Uh, you might need to wear something of mine, though."

"I do have my wedding dress."

"Which was so sheer every wolf in my pack blushed."

"Not cool for shopping?"

He shook his head. "Paris may be avant-garde when it comes to fashion, but I don't think it's quite ready for a half-naked faery. Look through my closet and see what you can find."

"You are twice as big as me. You're troll size. Dwarf troll, at least. And I'm not keen on working the leather. You know an animal used to wear those pants before you decided to tug them on? But I'll see what I can do. So, you got time for a quickie before you go back to work?"

He quirked a brow. "I thought you hated me."

"Oh, I do. But I like this." She danced up to him and drew her fingers down his chest and tapped his cock through the leather pants. "You saying you don't like this?" Flinging her hair with a tilt of her head, she thrust back her shoulders, proudly displaying her breasts.

The wolf lunged and encircled her in his arms, his mouth landing on her nipple. Bea squealed in delight as he lifted her and laid her on the couch. "I have time," he said.

Jacques always rode shotgun and, yet, mastered the radio when they were out on a job. He'd flicked the radio to a rap station, so Kir had turned the volume down. They compromised like a married couple.

Is that what marriage was about? Compromise? Seemed to Kir he and Bea got along just fine. When naked together. An afternoon quickie had put him in a great mood. Even if work was intense.

He'd heard about a pack in a northern *banlieue*, a city suburb, that was into something weird, and vampires were dying in stranger ways than the usual starvation, death by blood loss, or fighting to the death that some packs had a tendency to inflict upon them. They'd received a frantic phone call from a vampiress who was not in a tribe. Her boyfriend had escaped imprisonment from a pack and now lay on her floor, puking up black blood.

They arrived at the address in record time. Kir shifted the vehicle into Park and looked to Jacques, who smirked and stared at his hair. "What?"

"My man, you sparkle."

"I— What?"

Jacques couldn't hide his goofy grin. "So I guess it's true what they say about faeries when they come, eh?"

What the hell did they say about faeries coming? And who were *they*?

Bea had come quickly this afternoon on the couch—ah. Kir glanced in the rearview mirror. Sunlight glinted in his hair. He slapped at the faery dust. "It's all over me."

"It has been since you came in this morning, but it looks like more since that quick stop at home." Jacques's laugh thundered inside the car.

The stuff was hard to get off, and he had some smeared above his temple. Still, he didn't regret the quickie. Though he wasn't going to allow Jacques one more moment of mirth.

He slammed his hand up under his friend's jaw and silenced his laughter. "One more chuckle and you'll be chewing spine."

Jacques put up his hands in defeat and Kir dropped him immediately. It was an empty threat. They both knew the other would never hold good on a promise to violence, teasing or otherwise.

"Is it that noticeable? Maybe I shouldn't go inside."

"You got most of it off. Call it a night at the club. Let's go in and check this out. Vamp shields up?"

"Activated," Kir replied. Since childhood the two of them had shared an aversion to vampires and had playfully pulled an invisible shield of protection over themselves when they'd play vampires and werewolves.

If only he could do as much with his wife.

A wolf should be more upset about being married to a vampire—even if she was only half. But did a wolf who hated vampires have sex with one three times within a twenty-four-hour period? Something wrong with that.

And, yet, something so not wrong with sliding inside Bea and losing himself against her soft, petite body, drawing in her sweet perfume, drowsing him into some kind of all right.

"You coming?"

Jacques had started up the front walk while Kir was still contemplating running home for another round with his half-breed, pretty-smelling wife. But he couldn't afford to let his thoughts stray in a vampire's house, he thought, and followed Jacques inside. Vamp shields up, indeed. It wasn't possible for a werewolf to do that—put up some kind of magical protection shield—but just thinking that he could bolstered his confidence. He knew to avoid the fangs, and the cross on the stake he'd stuck in his back pocket gave him reassurance.

A male vampire, probably late twenties, lay on the kitchen floor in a pool of black liquid. It looked like blood, but Kir couldn't be sure what it was. Vampires bled red blood. Demons, and a handful of other species, bled black. And the victim's girlfriend, who was sprawled beside his body, insisted he was all vamp, formerly a mortal who had been attacked and turned only a year ago by a tribe of vampires that had then abandoned him.

"Is he going to live?" the blonde with a skimpy top that emphasized her narrow waistline asked. Her red-painted fingernails were stained with the black substance that seeped from her boyfriend's mouth.

Kir looked to Jacques. His friend's brow lifted. Both knew the answer. And was the vampiress blind? Her boyfriend was literally skin and bones, starved to the marrow. They could see his veins, and those veins were not plump with blood. And what was he coughing up in thick black globs?

"You got a stake?" Jacques muttered.

"Of course."

"What?" the girlfriend shrieked. "I trusted you guys!"

Kir grabbed the woman by the arms, trying to settle her. "Your boyfriend is not going to survive. He's in great pain. The stake will be a kindness. Can you understand?"

Eyes frantic and filled with tears, her lips tightened and she winced. She collapsed against his chest, her breaths heaving out. Her fingernails dug into his arms, but she wasn't trying to hurt him. She was trying to accept.

Kir couldn't relate to such a painful loss. And then he could. His father had left him and his sister when they were little. He could never fill that hole left behind in his soul.

Just when he reached to put a comforting hand on the woman's shoulder, she stood up and whispered, "I'll get something." When she returned to the room, she handed a stake to Kir. It had a pair of initials carved on it. "It was a backup in case either of us wanted to jump ship. He didn't ask for vampirism. He wanted the stake months ago, but I begged him to stay alive for me."

The vampire on the floor whispered, "I love you," to the vampiress. And then he said, "Get them. The…the…"

Kir and Jacques both bent close, hoping the vampire

would give them a clue that would lead to the pack that had kidnapped him.

"The what? Who?" Jacques urged. "Can you tell me what pack did this to you?"

"The...denizen..." The vampire's body stiffened, his muscles tightening and his jaw snapping shut.

"The denizen?" Jacques looked to Kir.

Denizen was a term for a group or gathering of demons. The very idea of demons being involved caused Kir's jaw to tense. The last breed he wanted to deal with was demons.

The girlfriend grabbed the stake from Kir's hand. Before he could take it from her to perform the offensive task, she lunged over her boyfriend and staked him in the heart. Jacques grabbed for her, but it was too late. They'd get nothing more from the pile of ash.

While the girlfriend wept over the ash, Jacques and Kir stepped outside the house. "Demons?" Kir asked. "So, this isn't werewolves?"

"I don't know."

"Well, if it's not, it's not our problem."

"Right." Kir clenched and unclenched his fists. "Let's give her a minute, then see if she'll let us search his things for clues."

The wolves waited out on the front step until the sobbing settled. A half hour later, quietly and respectfully, they went through the house but found nothing of use for the investigation.

"You have a safe place to go for a while?" Kir asked the vampiress.

"You think they'll come after me? The pack?"

"Not sure. Why do you think he was taken by a pack? He said something about a denizen. That's demons."

She shrugged. "He'd mentioned something about a wolf

following him a few days before he disappeared. I assumed."

"Usually the packs grab a vamp off the street. I don't know what the hell your boyfriend was coughing up. Or what a wolf could have done to him to make that happen."

She nodded. "I have a friend who will let me stay with her. Thank you."

"You shouldn't thank us for what happened here."

Her eyes wandered to the stake sitting on the pile of ash. "I couldn't have done it alone. I wish he could have been more help to you."

"We'll find the pack or denizen responsible for his death. I promise you that."

Leaving her at the door, Kir joined Jacques in the car.

"Let's hope it is demons," Jacques said. "We have enough on our plate already."

"I promised her we'd help her. No matter what."

"Ah, man."

"She's a woman. Alone. Who lost her boyfriend."

"She's also a vamp, and it's not clear wolves were responsible for that vamp's death."

"I'm won't let her down."

Jacques sighed and shifted into gear. "You and your damned sense of honor."

Damned or not, if it wasn't a pack, and they weren't required to bother with this crime, Kir wanted to stand true to his word. Because he couldn't stand back and allow anyone, even a vamp, to die for reasons unknown.

Chapter 6

The faery had never been shopping before. Bea had told Kir that in Faery she could pull on a glamour to change her clothing and look, but since arriving in the mortal realm her glamour was weak and it was a no-go for clothing changes. So when she strode into the high-end clothing shop on the rue Royale, her squeal might have been heard by dogs.

As well as by wolves.

And Kir liked the sound of her joy. It went a long way in erasing the lump that sat in the pit of his stomach after the call to the vampiress's house this afternoon. He never liked to destroy another living being or witness it. Since he wasn't able to get in to see the doctor he'd contacted until tomorrow morning, he decided putting some clothes on his wife would relax him after a long workday.

A salesgirl with brilliant red lips to match her nails led Kir and Bea into the back area of the shop that was more private than the sales floor. He sat on the designated "boyfriend couch," which was shaped like a huge pair of red lips, sipping champagne and refusing the chocolates offered by the cooing salesgirls while he waited for his wife to slip into the first outfit the staff deemed fitting for her.

The dressing room door opened and out wobbled a faery in a white sheath that hugged her petite figure yet went all the way up to her neck. Pink high heels, higher than the Eiffel Tower, hampered her walk as she clung to the wall and tried to stand upright and maintain a modicum of dignity.

"High heels are new to me," she said. "Who'd have thought, eh? So is lace. There's so…much of it. I don't think white is my color."

"Nope," Kir said.

Bea's lips dropped into a sad moue.

"I won't lie," he offered. "It's too much," he said to the saleswoman. "She's brighter and more fun. And sexy."

"And maybe not so tall?" Bea said as she wobbled behind the saleswoman back into the fitting room.

The next outfit was introduced with a jump as Bea landed expertly on heels half as high as the previous ones. She wore black suede thigh-high boots that were laced with white ribbons from thigh to ankle. The skimpy black dress was cut out at the torso to reveal both hips, and the neckline exposed her breasts nearly to the nipples.

"Now, this is me," she said, sashaying before Kir. She bent over and flashed him a view up under her skirt. Hot-pink panties. "You like?"

Kir croaked, then he checked himself and sat up straighter, catching the saleswoman's knowing smirk. "Uh-huh, that one's good. Shows off your…fun. Right, your fun stuff." He cleared his throat. "But you need more than one outfit. You can't wear that all the time."

"I'll mostly be wearing nothing around the house, but if you insist..." Bea twirled into the dressing room and called for more, more and more.

Wearing nothing at all around the house? Kir could handle that. He'd probably have to put up curtains, though, since the neighbors' yards hugged his closely. He didn't want to risk anyone catching a glimpse of his naked and winged wife. He worked hard to maintain his secrecy among the humans. If they were to learn his true nature, it could affect not only him but the whole pack.

But he suspected Bea was going to be one hot little number to keep under control. Yet, if he could appease her with clothing and jewelry, he didn't mind doing so. The joy and the utter delight she displayed at receiving such things went a long way toward securing his comfort with her.

Maybe this marriage thing wouldn't be so awful. His new wife appealed to his lust. He wouldn't mind having sex with her daily, if she was on board with that. The fangs were an issue, but he'd keep her in line. And he didn't feel a hunger for blood, so he was crossing his fingers the doctor said he was in the clear. And she was self-sufficient, taking care of herself while he worked. So far, this marriage was a win-win situation.

Next up: a pink dress. It was made out of high-gloss latex that hugged her body and pushed up her small breasts nicely. Black thigh-high stockings that sported matching pink bows at the tops ended in pink heels as glossy as the dress. Kir gave the look two thumbs-up.

A punky black number with a big white cross slashed across the shirt that stopped just below her breasts was paired with tight red jeans that sported black zippers down the sides. Black sandals that exposed her delicately marked feet? Yes, please.

Bea danced out of the dressing room wearing a long

sheer black dress that had patches of flowers embroidered here and there. The embroidery covered nipples and her crotch—and nothing else. She wore a black fedora pulled down over her eyes. Her hips shimmied seductively, having mastered control of the high, black heels. He could see almost everything beneath the dress, and what he couldn't see he could imagine running his tongue over and tasting until she came in shouts of pleasure.

And faery dust. He absently brushed his fingers over a temple.

"My favorite," he offered, setting the champagne goblet aside and focusing on the sashaying faery.

"You want me, werewolf?" she teased, dashing out her tongue and tipping up the brim of the hat with one finger. A nod of her head toward the dressing room spoke louder than any audible invite. "I sent the sales chick away for a bit."

Kir lifted a brow. Here in the store? He had no argument with that; nor did his erection, which had sat up to take notice.

Standing, he tossed Bea over his shoulder and strode into the dressing room, closing the door behind them. The floor was scattered with dresses and various pieces of colorful clothing. Shoes toppled here and there. He stepped on a long heel and wobbled but landed an arm against the wall, pinning Bea's back against the floor-to-ceiling mirror.

Pink eyes danced with his. He could feel her smile moving over his skin and teasing at his desires. He shimmied the long skirt up around her thighs as he dived against her neck to kiss up under her chin. She smelled like the perfume she'd been doused with upon entering the store. Chemical but a little spicy. He preferred her natural candy scent.

Grinding his hips against her mons, he milked a wanting moan from her. Her fingernails dug in at his shoulders. Yeah, he liked it rough. Kir growled and bit at the fabric over her breast. No time for complete undressing. He wanted inside Bea now.

Fortunately, the pink panties were history. With a flick of her fingers, she unbuttoned his leather pants and drew down the zip. He shuffled them down to his knees. Bea wrapped her legs about his hips and coaxed him closer.

As he glided inside of her, his wife said, "Oh, yeah, that's the sweet spot, big boy. You're so thick. You really want this, don't you? Yes!"

He pumped inside her twice before he came in a shuddering, thundering orgasm. But he never forgot about the woman. Thumbing her clit as he came gave her a rousing cry of release only moments after his.

"I love shopping," Bea said as she wilted against his chest, panting.

"Hell of a lot more interesting than I'd expected it to be." Who the hell cared that Bea had been loud and the whole store might have heard?

"Whew! We're going to have to buy this dress now that it's gotten a workout."

"I have no problem with that at all. You think you got enough for a while?"

"Enough? Hardly…" She glided her hand down to her breasts and fluttered her lashes at him. "Oh! You mean clothes, not sex. I'm good. But let's hit the jewelry store next. I need some sparkly things."

Kir laughed against her hair as he felt his erection soften while still sheathed within her. She was already at the next store, and he was just getting his breath back. The woman liked sex. But maybe it was like candy to her. She wanted more and more and could eat it or not, but never refused a treat if offered.

Pulling out and zipping up, he stepped back as she tugged down the dress skirt and sorted through the shoes on the floor. He ran his fingers through her hair lightly; she didn't notice the touch.

"You know what you want?" he asked.

She popped upright, her pink eyes flashing on him like some kind of Christmas lights inviting him closer for a present.

"I mean with the clothes," he said. Stroking a hand down his chest, he took some pride in the fact that she wanted him. But upon inspecting his hand, he noted the faery dust.

"Everything," she said, nodding, hands on her hips. "Absolutely everything."

Bea sat on the king-size bed surrounded by clothing, jewels and shoes. She'd never thought personal items could mean so much, but these frilled, glossy and sparkling bits of pretty were all hers. No one could take them away.

She pulled the T-shirt with the rhinestone skull emblazoned on the front over her head. Who would have thought mortal fabrics could feel so sensual against the skin? The pink panties with the bright purple bows at each hip were more decorative than to actually cover anything. Didn't matter. She wore them because they were pretty. And the blue high heels with the red soles were her favorite.

Or maybe the chrome heels with the spikes on the toes.

No. She grabbed the green sandals with the gossamer laces that wrapped up her ankle and put on one of those. Kicking out her feet, one still wearing the blue shoe, the other in the lace-up sandal, she squealed.

"I take it you are pleased," Kir said as he landed on the top of the stairs that opened into the attic bedroom. He strode over. "I ordered in some food. I'm starving."

"Me, too. And, yes, I am pleased with all my goodies. You like?"

"The whole look?" His eyes danced over her attire: skull shirt, pink panties and mismatched shoes. "I don't think you should be caught on the streets in that getup, but it works for me."

"I bet I know which part of this outfit you like the best." Bea rolled onto her palms and knees and wiggled her derriere at him.

The wolf lost his footing against the mirror and had to catch himself in an awkward save.

"I don't understand why mortals like to wear a string between their butt cheeks, though. It's uncomfortable." She tugged off the panties and flung them toward Kir.

He caught them and crushed the pink fabric in a fist. "So, that's what it takes to make you happy? Pretty shoes and sparkling jewels?"

She dangled a fine silver chain before her, deciding she could weave that into her hair later. "Mostly. Though I have to be careful with mortal metals like this. Can't wear it for too long without getting a rash."

"You're easy." He crossed his arms and brought the panties to his nose. "Mmm…"

"I know what it takes to make my wolfie husband happy, too."

He looked at the panties, as if realizing what he'd been doing, then shoved them in his pants pocket. "There is that. But isn't there anything else?"

"What do you mean?"

"Like something you want to do. To aspire to? What would make you happy beyond the material things?"

"Wow. Heavy conversation much?"

He shrugged and sat on the corner of the bed and toyed with a tuft of purple fringe on one of the dresses. "I have my work, and that, to me, is satisfying. You're new to the mortal realm and have much to learn and discover, but I have to wonder if there wasn't something you used to do in Faery, or dream about, that you still aspire to?"

"Huh." Leaning forward to toy with the glossy leather toe of the blue shoe, Bea mulled over how keen the wolf was to learn about her. And here she'd thought him only capable of sex and howling. Not that either were offensive...

Could she tell him? She didn't trust him yet. They'd known each other only a few days. But he was her one friend here in this strange and wondrous realm. And he was much nicer than she'd initially thought him to be—though, in principle, she still hated him. "I do aspire to something."

"Great. Tell me?"

"You first. Tell me about this job of yours."

"What do you want to know?"

"What do you do? I mean, I always thought wolves ran in packs and that was their family, and...well, what else is there to do?"

"In the mortal realm we need to hold jobs to make money so we can survive."

"Sounds tedious."

"I suppose being royalty you're not familiar with the concept of work."

"Nope. Should I be?"

He chuckled and that sexy crinkle at the corner of his eyes drew Bea's attention like an arrow to a target. She'd kiss him there if he were a little closer.

"You don't have to work, Bea. I'll take care of you. That was an implied promise I made with our marriage vows." He studied his hand, the one with the bonding mark that faintly showed against his lightly tanned skin. "Pack Valoir was chosen by the Council to be enforcers a couple years ago. The Council is a sort of governing body made up from all paranormal breeds. So my job description is an enforcer."

"So that's what, like, wolf cops?"

"Sort of. Like I said before, we police the packs in Paris and the surrounding area. Mainly we focus on controlling the blood games, trying to keep them minimal. I'd love to stop them completely, but that'll never happen."

"Is that where the wolves pit vampires against one another to the death?" she asked eagerly.

"Yes." He narrowed a brow on her. "I'm sensing far too much curiosity in your tone. Don't tell me you'd actually watch such a match."

"Uh..." Apparently, a bloody good match did not appeal to her new husband. It had been a great way to pass the time in Faery, watching the trolls beat the rock-shifters to a dusty pulp. "No. 'Course not."

She'd best not tell him about the kelpie matches that had entertained the court on many occasions. She had made a pretty mint betting on those fights. She did have her talents.

"Bloody fights? Ugh." She screwed her mouth into a distasteful moue. "That's nasty stuff."

"It is. As well, we keep an eye on all irregular activity among the local packs. I've a new case that landed on my desk. It's a strange one. Vamps who have escaped from the packs' clutches are dying. In strange ways. Lots of investigating in the coming days, I'm sure."

"Sounds boring. Except the part where you might have to break up a fight."

"Admit it. You love a good fight."

"For the right reasons."

"When is fighting ever for a good reason?"

"When it's to protect yourself from the stupidity of others," she said without thinking. "Just because a person is different doesn't mean it's okay to beat on them."

Kir tilted such a concerned gaze on her that Bea had to

think about what she'd just said. Oops. That had revealed a little more than she'd intended. She didn't trust him that much. Time to redirect this conversation.

"So let me guess, you must have some kind of record book on all the wolves, eh? A means to find out information about them?"

"We do, but it's not a book. Our files are digital. The database is vast and covers other species, as well. We recently managed to tap into the Order of the Stake's computer database and downloaded their files before they could put up a firewall."

"Everything you said sounded like gobbledygook to me. And I tend to like gobbledygook. So long as it's warm."

Kir stood and paced to the triangular window sized as large as the wall that looked out over the front yard and the street below.

"Let's just say we can look up info on pretty much any paranormal species within Europe and the outlying countries. Comes in handy when we need to crack a case."

"So, do you list faeries in that database?"

"No." He returned to the bed and sat beside her. Brushing the hair from her face, he lingered with the tip of his finger on her ear-point. "Your realm is like another planet to us who live in the mortal realm."

"Yeah, well, this realm is more than kooky. I mean, mortals walk around with dogs on leashes. How cruel is that? And cars." She shuddered. "So much iron."

"Why all the questions about the database?"

"I, uh…" She toyed with the green sandal strap.

Dare she tell him? If she didn't, she had no clue where to begin her search in this big, vast city. A city that may not even be the correct starting place for her search. How to know where to begin?

Going up on her knees before him, Bea trailed her fingers down the front of his leather vest, landing at his hip, where a tuft of her pink panty stuck out from the pants pocket. "There is something I want, beyond all these pretty material things you've given me."

"Tell me. I'd like to know what would make you happy."

She believed that he did, too. The wolf was kind. He had valiantly accepted the challenge his pack had asked of him because to refuse would go against some kind of honorable code he obeyed. At least, that's how she dreamed he was. This knight's armor was fashioned from leather and truth.

"Bea?"

"It's something I've wanted since I was a child and I used to sit in the shadows watching my half sisters and brothers play. They'd always exclude me because Malrick made it known how unfavorable I was. The dark one."

He stroked her hair, and she flinched at the soft touch. She hadn't expected such tenderness from a growly wolf. And when her teardrop landed on his wrist, she quickly swiped it away and turned her shoulder to him, coiling forward as she sniffed back more tears.

What was this? She didn't cry. She was too tough for that. Her skin had hardened to armor over the years of neglect and abuse. Where had she put her blade? Stones, but she had lost track of it!

Kir embraced her, and he tugged her against his chest even as she tried to pull away to escape the unwanted kindness. She wasn't deserving. She was the dark one. The one no one wanted to touch.

And then something inside her cracked open and reached out for the touch. For a moment of understanding. She sank into Kir's arms and he cradled her to his warm chest, his heartbeats lulling her, urging her to curl up against him and tuck her head beneath his chin.

"All I want," she whispered, "is to find my mother."

Chapter 7

Dinner arrived via delivery and Kir set out the plates and poured red wine while Bea pulled herself together upstairs. He'd held her weeping and shivering in his arms. Never had a woman opened herself up to him like that. It had felt fragile to him, a moment he'd best handle carefully and with a reverence, given the faery's tears. He felt honored she'd shared that with him.

But how to help her find her mother? Bea had no clue who the woman was. Malrick had never given her a species, so she literally had nothing to go on. She wasn't positive her other half was vampire. And the database the enforcement team kept wasn't so precise a guy could type in a random faery name such as Bea's and get anything beyond a blinking cursor.

And really? If any in the pack knew he was allocating precious work time to help his wife track a suspected vampire, they'd have harsh words for him, for sure.

Yet he was compelled to do what he could. He preferred Bea giggling and fluttering about—even naked, if she chose—so he'd see what he could do.

Thinking about fluttering… A lithe faery skipped down the stairs and landed on the parquet floor with a barefoot bounce. Sashaying into the kitchen, her wings fluttered behind her bare shoulders. And bare body.

Kir's eyes took in skin and softness and nipples and, oh…that sweet vee between her legs. "Uh…usually dinner is eaten clothed."

Why had he said that? He had to get his head around the notion that the woman preferred skyclad. And, as a man, he was all for the blatant tease. But he did need a few safe respites from the kick in his libido. Like eating. Mealtime should be clothed. Maybe?

"Slip on something now," he said, setting the filet mignon delivered from a three-star restaurant on the table, "and after we're finished, I promise to slip it off you. If… that's what you'd prefer."

The faery squealed and clapped and spun out of the room, wings dusting the walls as she scampered upstairs.

And Kir chuckled and shook his head. He'd just asked a woman to put *on* clothes. What on earth was wrong with him?

The wolf did like his meat. Bea did the polite thing and tasted a bit of the pink beef. The sauce was savory, but she had to gag down the meat. Ugh. Good thing plenty of vegetables also sat on her plate. But the thing that distracted her from the distasteful meal? Mortals had food delivered to their front door in boxes. How cool was that?

"I'll do what I can to help you," Kir offered after a sip of wine.

She lifted a brow and stabbed a carrot slice with her fork. "Help?"

"Find your mother."

"Oh, yes! Thank you."

"It's the least I can offer you. Family is important."

"Knowing that packs thrive on tight bonds, I'm not sure my definition of *family* is the same as yours."

"They are all different, but I think love is a common bond in all families."

"Then my definition is really far from yours." Because love? Yeah, that wasn't a word she'd ever heard muttered in her father's demesne. Love tended to be tricksy for the sidhe.

"So your pack is your family?" she asked as she sipped the cool red wine and made a dessert out of watching her husband devour his food. "How many brothers and sisters do you have?"

"One sister," he offered, pushing his now-clean plate away from him and sitting back to savor the wine. "Her name is Blyss. She married recently and now lives part of the year in Minnesota with her redneck werewolf husband."

"What's a Minnesota?" Bea asked around a crunch on a string bean.

He chuckled. "It's a place."

"Oh. I didn't do very well in mortal realm geography classes."

"It's in the United States, which is on a different continent from this one. About a nine-hour flight west."

Bea's eyes widened. "You fly?"

"Not with wings. Though, can your kind fly across an entire ocean?"

"Probably not. We'd have to stop and rest on a mermaid's head or chill out on a whale's back. So, a sister? And just the one? Now I can understand how you manage to embrace family."

"A family that is too distant lately. I miss her, but Blyss and her husband return to Paris for the winter and spring.

I still haven't seen her new baby, but she sends me emails and texts pictures all the time."

"Emails and texts? Is that computer stuff?"

"Yes." He pulled out a cell phone from his vest pocket and aimed it at her. "Smile for me."

Wiggling her shoulders, Bea assumed a pose with a bright grin. Something flashed on the back of the phone and she gaped. "Did you just steal my soul?"

Kir chuckled. "Not even. I just made an image of you. Or the camera in my phone did. Now I have it with me all the time so I can look at it whenever I like. See."

She inspected the image on his phone and it was her! "That's amazing. But I'm still a little worried about my soul."

"I promise you I've no such magic. So now if I wanted to I could send your picture to my sister with the click of a button. I did tell her about our marriage. She's excited for me. I still haven't told Blyss about Edamite, though. Want to ease her into that one slowly."

"What's an Edamite?"

"Edamite Thrash is the man's name."

"Sounds villainous."

"It is a perfect villain name, right? He's my, er…half brother. My mother kicked my father out years ago after she discovered his marital indiscretions. I didn't know about Ed until recently. Apparently, my father has a taste for darker things."

"Like vampires?" she said with a perk up of her shoulders. Heck, if the man's father had a child with a vampiress, then Bea should expect as much understanding from the son, right? And they had something in common: dads who did dark things. Yay! Not.

"Not vampires. Demons. Vampires, I tolerate. Demons, I despise," Kir said. "And leave it at that."

"Ah. So that means you don't like this Edamite guy?"

"He's…okay. We're learning to accept one another. Hell, my family is messed up, there's no way around that one. Until recently Blyss denied being a werewolf. She took pills to suppress her wolf."

"Really? How'd that work for her?"

"Well, for a while. But then she met Stryke Saint-Pierre and he brought out the wolf in her. Much to my relief. A wolf who denies her heritage? That's just wrong."

"You're proud of what you are."

"I am." He offered his goblet across the table and Bea met it with a *ting*. "To werewolves!"

"And their half-breed wives," Bea offered before she sipped.

Kir paused before sipping. His eyes met hers. He smiled behind the glass rim, then drank. "To my half-breed wife, who isn't quite sure what her other half is, and who promises to keep those fangs out of my neck. Yes?"

She set down the goblet and curled up her legs to sit kneeling on the chair, catching her chin in hand as she considered his proposal. It wasn't much to ask. And she really did not want to give him a blood hunger if it was unnatural to his species. She should be thankful this arranged marriage seemed to be working out so far. The man was kind, sexy and all sorts of virile.

"Yes," she said with a smile. "I can promise that. But I'm going to have to satisfy the hunger I have, just so you know."

"With a human?"

"Yes. And soon. This is a new venture to me, being in this realm, not having any friends who will offer their necks for a snack when I need one. I'm not sure how to go about it."

"Is it a sex thing?"

She sensed the worry in his tone and shook her head. "No. And yes. Most times when I've taken ichor it's been while having sex. But I don't *have* to have sex just to have a bite. And now I'm a married woman. I do take our vows seriously. Weird as it is to marry a stranger."

"It is weird, but we're adjusting."

"We are." She raised her glass for another toast. "Now, you had mentioned something about getting me out of these clothes?"

They started up the stairs, but by the time Bea's foot made it to the fourth runner her dress was off and Kir nipped at her ankle. She giggled and turned to pull him up by a hank of his curly hair. The wolf liked it when she was rough with him, she had noticed, so she dug in her fingernails at his shoulders.

"Right here?"

"Good a place as any," he said as he bowed to her mons and lashed his tongue over her pulsing clit. He pushed up one of her legs and she gripped the stair rail so she wouldn't slide down, but it seemed he had a good hold on her. Bea realized she wasn't sitting on the stairs, because he supported her completely in his big, muscular embrace.

Tilting back her head, she squealed with delight as he dived in deeper and fed on her. The man knew how to get directly to the point, and it wasn't long before she was gasping, gripping his hair and fighting the urge to release. And then she did not fight it. She bucked her hips as her wolf shoved down his pants and pushed himself to the hilt inside her.

He gripped the stair rail to the left and slammed a palm on the stair riser to her right. Bea's head bumped into a stair above her. "Ouch!"

"Sorry. Let's take this upstairs." Without sliding out of

her, he managed to crush her against his chest and take the remaining stairs up to the bedroom.

They landed on the bed amid her giggles and his huffing pants. "You think this is funny?"

"Yes, you crazy wolf." How did she get so lucky to have been married off to such a fun and amazing man? It felt wrong, but she didn't want to go there, so Bea, instead, tilted his head up to look at her. "You're good to me, wolf. Why?"

He shook his head and kissed her stomach. "Because I'm honoring our marriage vows." He kissed her mons. "And you're worth being good to." He slid lower to kiss along her leg. "And you make it a lot easier to do this marriage thing than I had expected."

She could get behind all that. He made it easy, too.

"Tell me about these," he said, tapping his fingers on the violet designs covering her feet. "Sidhe markings?"

"Yes, they are significant to the Unseelie. They are what connect me to the earth and make my nature glamour work. I won't come into any magical sigils for years. The older we get, the more powerful we grow. Of course, being a half-breed, I'm not sure what's in store for me, magicwise. I'm just thankful I can bring out my wings. You know, I can't rely on glamour here in the mortal realm?"

"Is that like becoming invisible?"

"Yes, making it impossible for the human eye to see me among them. I wonder what that's about?"

"Not sure." He kissed the Unseelie marks and then clasped her hand.

"I like holding your hand."

"More than this?" He glided up and kissed her breast.

"Yes and no. I think I need more time to consider the question. Maybe you should do that a little more."

"Your wish is my command."

Chapter 8

Kir woke in the morning and stretched his arms over his head. Bea's spot on the bed beside him was empty. Had she gone down to make him breakfast? He suspected she had no clue how to cook. Likely a princess was used to being served and waited on. Yet he'd been surprised by her confession about not being loved by her family.

He'd always felt loved by both family and pack. That is, until his father had left. But that had been twenty years ago. He'd not forgiven Colin Sauveterre for his rash decision to leave his family because of a demon lover; nor had he forgotten the pain of such a betrayal. Yet he refused to allow that harsh memory to weigh him down.

He'd lived a good life, had great friends and a good job. So it was difficult to understand how Bea's father could be so cruel to her as to make her feel as if she were unloved. A pariah. Had she no friends in Faery?

Well, he'd do his best to show her how good family

could be. Soon the pack would welcome her, too. He'd gotten lucky that she wasn't some kind of horned creature that wore a scaly skin. Though the vampire side bothered him more than he'd ever tell her. He rubbed his neck. She may have tasted his blood, but she couldn't have gotten a good drink. Surely, if a blood hunger was going to develop, he'd have noticed by now. Maybe?

He had an appointment this afternoon with a non-pack doctor in the 7th arrondissement. He couldn't risk seeing the pack's doctor because if he did harbor a blood hunger, that would surely get him banished from the pack. No matter what happened, he needed to deal with this quietly.

Slipping on a pair of jeans, he padded downstairs. Out from the kitchen sprang a naked faery wielding a samurai sword. The blade flashed before him and landed at his neck.

"Fuck," he whispered.

"Oops."

Bea retracted the weapon, performing the sweep to clear off the blood—thankfully, none had been shed—then putting it in the imaginary holster at her hip she should have worn had she been a real samurai.

"Oops?" Kir grabbed the sword and marched into the living room, where he displayed a wall full of ancient weapons. He put the weapon up on the wooden holders from where she'd stolen it. "What the hell?"

The faery pouted and stomped her foot. "I thought you were an intruder."

"In my own house? Why are you playing with these weapons?"

"I'm not *playing* with them. I know how to handle a blade. I never went anywhere in Faery without one. Never knew when an assassin would spring out of the shadows."

"Seriously?" Kir shook his head. It was too early. He wasn't in the mood for this. And she was...naked. It was hard to be angry with a naked faery. "I'm going to work. I'll be home around five. The clock is on the wall there. So, when you hear the door open and shut around that time, you'll know it's me. Your husband. Okay?"

She gave him an impudent tilt of her nose.

"Damned naked faery," he muttered as he strode toward the entryway.

"Jumpy ol' grump of a werewolf," she spit in his wake.

"Short Stick!" he called back.

No reply.

Bea slumped onto the couch and pulled up her legs, tucking her chin between her knees. He'd called her that awful thing about being a short stick. She didn't want to be the thing the loser was forced to live with. She just wanted him to like her. She had begun to believe he actually did like her. If she judged from the sex they'd been having, he was over the moon about her.

Maybe the sword had been too much. She had been playing with him! She'd keep her hands off his weapons and stick with her own blade. But she wasn't going to drop her innate cautionary instincts. She knew nothing about this realm. A girl had to protect herself. And if her husband was always away at work?

"I can take care of myself. Always have. Always will."

She wandered through the kitchen and tapped the granite countertop. "This is so boring! I need to get out. Explore the city. Learn the landscape. Scope out the enemies and determine who are my friends. Yeah. Good idea, Bea. Time to explore. And—" she tapped a fang "—time to feed this ache for satisfaction."

* * *

"Demons bleed black," Jacques said. He set a cup of coffee on Kir's desk and hiked up a leg to sit on the corner of the desk.

Kir looked up from the computer screen he'd had his eyes glued to for over an hour. When had he last blinked? He rubbed his eyes, then tilted the paper cup in a toast before sipping the lukewarm brew. The coffee machine in the office was ancient and if it ever spewed out anything close to hot he'd probably have to hug it.

"You think the vamp the other night was coughing up demon blood? That doesn't make sense. The packs pit vampires against one another."

"I know. But the vamp did mention a denizen."

"You're right. We can't rule out demons. But I didn't think vamps actually bit demons by choice."

"The vamp had been tortured. He could have been forced to drink demon blood, or even attacked a demon in defense. Maybe the packs are changing things up. Pitting vamps against demons. I don't know. I'll keep muddling the idea over. So, uh…is it okay if I tell you that you're sparkling again today—because you seriously need to get that glitter off your cheek, man—or should I just let it go?"

Kir swiped his cheek. Sure enough, a fine dusting of sparkle imbued his skin. Every time Bea came…

"You two must be getting along pretty well, eh?"

Kir chuckled and crossed his arms as he leaned back in the office chair. "If you call my wife coming at me with a samurai sword getting along, then yes, we're swell."

"What's up with that? Did she ever tell you what her other half is? And are her eyes really pink? That's crazy, man."

"They're pink. She doesn't know what her other half is. And we have work to do," he said, dismissing the conversation before it got too personal. Jacques would go there if he didn't nip it in the bud while he was ahead. And he had no idea how to tell his best friend his wife was possibly half vampire. "There are only two packs in the suburb where we found the tortured vamp. Royaume and Conquerer."

"I know a guy in pack Conquerer."

"Then we start there," Kir said. "Let's head out for a few hours, then break for supper."

"I'll have results from the blood test in a day or two," the doctor said as he placed a narrow glass vial of Kir's blood in a plastic holder on his desk. "But I suspect, if you haven't noticed symptoms yet, you're in the clear. You said the vampire didn't get a good, deep bite?"

Kir had avoided telling the doctor it had actually been his new wife who had done the biting. If he had taken on the vampire taint, it would show whether or not the doc knew exactly what kind of vamp it had come from.

"No, I reacted quickly. Shoved the vamp off me."

"You haven't craved red meat lately?"

"More than usual? No. I eat red meat every day, though."

"Right. What about hearing pulse beats from those around you?"

"Not that I've noticed. Do vampires hear the pulses of their victims?"

"They are more attuned to such a thing, though we wolves can hear it if we concentrate."

Kir nodded and pulled his shirt back on. The exam had required only the blood draw and the usual checking of eyes, nose and throat. Shouldn't there be a test for vampirism? Wait. There was: stakes and holy water.

"I'll call you as soon as the results come in," the doctor said, shaking his hand. "And be careful around the long-tooths, Monsieur Sauveterre."

"I do my best."

Striding out and getting into the car, Kir headed for home, disappointed that he hadn't learned definitively whether or not he was in the clear. The uncertainty was making him paranoid. He felt his pack members were giving him the eye because they knew something was different about him. Beyond the fact he'd just been forced to marry a faery.

Yeah, that was probably it. Maybe his pack members were jealous. Bea was gorgeous, but he doubted any wolf would be jealous of him pairing up with a half-breed faery.

Passing through a neighborhood that blended small businesses with residential homes, he noticed an iridescent flicker out of the corner of his eye and slowed the Lexus to a stop. Down the alley he saw the unnatural sight that any mortal would have freaked out to see. Even he, a paranormal breed, was stunned to see it. And the worst part? It was his wife.

"Wings out in the middle of a Parisian neighborhood? Bea, you're smarter than that. Maybe." He pulled the car to a stop.

Didn't she know how to pull on a glamour? He hated to think that he'd have to sit her down and have a talk with her, like a child, on how to act in this realm. Apparently, recalling his encounter with the samurai sword this morning, it was necessary.

"At least she's not naked."

He got out of the car and strode quickly in her wake. Ahead, he smelled a familiar scent. Animal. Angry. And he felt, more than scented, the fear from another being. One unfamiliar with this realm.

"Bea." It was his wife's fear.

He rushed forward into the shadowed alleyway and jumped over a toppled garbage can, landing behind a growling dog. The breed was a Rottweiler mix with something he couldn't guess at and the dog's ears were torn, a sure sign it had been used for fighting. No collar. No tags. It was not tame. How could such a beast be out on the streets? It must have escaped captivity.

Like Bea? The thought was so sudden it served to knock Kir aside the head. No, she wasn't a captive. What was he thinking?

The dog barked at the faery who clung to the brick wall. Bea's wings were still out. And…was that blood on her chin? Had the dog bitten her? No, she would bleed ichor. Kir could feel her fear, and as his heart went out to her, he couldn't begin to sort out why she was here.

"Don't move, Bea," he instructed as he approached the dog cautiously. "But put your wings away, or someone will see."

"I can't. I'm too scared! They pop out when I'm afraid."

Growling a warning, Kir defied the dog with a commanding tone. The insolent beast did not turn to him but instead stepped closer to Bea. Spittle dripped from its maw. It was ready for a fight.

"Kir!"

The dog lunged for Bea. Kir leaped, landing his hands on the hind legs of the beast, which snarled and twisted around to snap at his face. In an attempt to avoid its jaws, he flung the beast against the wall. It landed with a yelp and a whimper.

"I don't want to hurt you," he said in a commanding tone, lowering to a crouch to put himself on level with the dog. His hackles bristling and canine teeth lowering, he smelled the dog's aggression and he had to focus to keep his werewolf from coming out. "I don't know who has hurt you, but she won't. Nor will I. Friends," he said, and hoped the dog was not too damaged to feel his gentle but firm intent. "Cease."

The dog's head dropped, perhaps recognizing that command. It whimpered and stepped toward Kir. Willing his canines back up, Kir put out his hand, palm up, offering peace. The dog sniffed at him. They were two different breeds, but they did carry a common gene; however, that didn't mean they were instant friends or allies, by any means.

He felt Bea's hands curl over his shoulders and she hugged up against his back. Her body shook and her wings shuddered. The dog had scared her. As well, her wings could have alerted the dog. She was not a creature it had ever dealt with before so that may be why it was aggressive.

He cooed a reassuring noise and the dog licked his fingertips. "Good boy."

He wasn't sure what to do. If he left the dog here, it could go on to torment another person, perhaps cause harm. But he couldn't take it home with him. He wasn't a pet kind of guy. And while werewolves tolerated dogs, keeping them as pets was macabre. If he took the dog to the pound, it would likely be euthanized.

"Can you take me home?" Bea asked nervously.

"I have to take care of the dog first."

He tugged out his phone while the dog continued to sniff and lick at his fingers. Dialing the office, he asked Violet to look up a no-kill pound. After a few minutes, the secretary returned with a giddy reply. There was a rehabilitation pound less than a mile away.

"I guess we're going for a walk," Kir said. He scanned the alley and noted a coil of nylon rope lying near a rusted ladder. "Get that for me, will you, Bea?"

"We're not taking that beast home?"

"No, but I can't leave him to run loose and possibly hurt someone who doesn't have a manner of communicating in a nonthreatening way with it."

"Great." Bea picked up the rope and handed it to him. "I go out for an exploratory walk and I end up with two dogs on my ass."

Securing the rope about the dog's neck, Kir stood and looked down on his wife. "I am not a dog."

She hooked her hands akimbo. "You both growled and snarled at me."

"Not a dog," he reiterated firmly. The animal at his feet growled. Kir tugged the rope gently, and it settled. "And will you put your wings away?"

Bea stepped back from the warning. With a shiver of her shoulders, her wings folded down but did not recede. "That dog isn't wearing any clothes."

"What?"

"You said all creatures in the mortal realm had to wear clothes."

"He's not a— Bea, can we talk about this later?"

"Yes."

"You weren't hurt?"

"No." She blew out a shivering breath. "Just shaken."

"Because you have blood on your chin."

She swiped her chin. "Oh."

He understood now. She'd gone out to satisfy her hunger.

"Maybe I should walk home and meet you there," she said.

"You know your way? Can you possibly get there without flashing your wings at everyone you pass?"

"What's wrong with wings?"

"Not in the mortal realm, Bea. Can't you pull on a glamour?"

"I told you I've tried. No luck. The air is different here. Sort of like I have a big fuzzy sweater on me at times. I need to come down from the fear."

"Wrap them around you like a shawl or something."

She did so, clutching the gossamer red-purple wings across her chest. "I can retrace my steps. I think I've had enough of big bad Paris for now."

"I suspect big bad Paris is tired of you, as well." Kir inwardly chastised his defensive annoyance, but he didn't like to be called a dog. And Bea must learn to follow the rules mortal society pressed upon their kind. Blood hungry or not. "Go straight home. I'll be there in an hour."

"Fine." She tromped down the alley like an admonished child yet called over her shoulder, "I hate you!"

"I hate you, too," he said, but he didn't raise his voice. *Hate* was such a strong word. It belonged to people such as those who would train the dog at the end of this rope to be cruel and vicious.

"Come on, boy."

Chapter 9

Kir arrived home two hours later. The rescue shelter had been pleased to take in the stray and promised they would place the dog in a good foster home designated and trained for rehabilitation. It was the best situation he could have provided the animal.

Now he wandered into the living room, collapsed onto the big leather easy chair, and put his feet up on the hassock and toed off his boots. Jacques was stopping by later with the file on the job. Kir wanted to look through it at home, away from the office, where urgency demanded his high attention. Sometimes he did his best work while relaxing and allowing his mind to wander. And he didn't want to muddle over the blood test report. He wasn't a worrier; he liked to be an optimist.

He grabbed the remote and clicked on the music. Led Zeppelin's "Kashmir" was cued up and he cranked the volume and closed his eyes. Best way to unwind after a long, trying day.

Robert Plant's crooning, snaking lyrics slithered off the walls and thudded in his heart. To create such a sound that had made itself so evocative of a certain period in time was an amazing accomplishment. He often wondered what he had done, or would do, that could change the world. Enforcing took a few packs out of the blood games and saved dozens of vamps, but did it really matter?

Perhaps bringing a dog to a shelter had made a small but indelible mark. Yes, he could be satisfied for that accomplishment today.

Opening his eyes, his vision caught the movement of red-and-violet wings near the window. Dark hair swirled in a veil across her face. Her hands swayed and danced, her fingers an intricate interpretation of the music. And her hips shimmied toward Plant's call to surrender.

Once again, the naked faery strikes. Smiling at such fortune, he kept his eyelids half-mast. He wanted to watch awhile without her being the wiser. How had he forgotten that he had a wife? He'd come home and slipped into the usual routine without remembering he'd left Bea in the alley after rescuing her from the Rottweiler. She'd been so afraid she hadn't been able to put away her wings.

Apparently, she'd recovered from her fear. Oh, had she recovered. The woman was petite and lithe, but she knew how to work the curves that shaped her body. Small breasts perked up in rosy jewels and those hips could shake a house. And now her wings didn't shiver in fear but instead glowed and rippled to the music's beat.

Kir licked his lips. The bonus in this arranged marriage was sex whenever he wanted it. Although, to think about it, he hadn't yet made love to her. They'd only had sex. Lusty, frenzied, give-it-to-me-because-I-need-it sex. There had been no emotion involved.

He shouldn't complain about getting his physical needs

met by the more-than-willing faery. But they had bonded. Both in Faery terms and by the ways of his kind. They were in this for real. So the idea of seeking a more intense intimacy that would ultimately lead to lovemaking appealed.

As well, he wanted to get to know his wife. Emotionally. Personally. She sought her mother. Her father had been cruel to her. Dogs frightened her and made it impossible to hide her wings. What else made the faery tick?

Bea sashayed toward him, having spied his sneaky observation. "Do you mind if I dance?" she called over the loud music.

He adjusted the volume down so they could hear each other. "Not at all. I love the way you interpret Led Zeppelin."

"Is that what you call this music? I like it!" She spun and then jumped onto the coffee table and snaked her hips up and down in a sexy stripper move. "It's so…exotic. It gets inside me and makes me move. You want to dance with me, Kir?"

"Nope. I like sitting in the audience."

The faery closed her eyes and ran her palms over her skin, from breasts to stomach and down her thighs. The air sweetened with her candy scent and he inhaled deeply. He could drown in her and not bother to swim for shore because to die inside Bea felt too delicious. The woman inspired his marvel. And that was a precious thing.

The song ended and segued into "Stairway to Heaven." Bea plopped onto the chair arm and leaned in to ruffle his hair with her fingers. "How'd it go with the vicious dog?"

"Found a shelter that was happy to have him. They'll rehabilitate and find him a new home."

"Well, good for the beast. It almost tore my leg off."

"I think you flew out of its reach in the nick of time. Much as you should not be seen walking about Paris with your wings out, I think they saved you from serious injury. But promise me you won't do that again."

"Get attacked by a dog? I'm not sure that's in my control."

"I mean bringing your wings out in public."

Bea shrugged and leaned forward, resting her elbows on her knees. Her wings were folded down her back. "What is so wrong with wings?"

"How many winged creatures have you seen walking this realm?"

"There are birds everywhere!"

"Bea."

"Fine," she conceded with a grumpy pout. Twisting, she stroked his cheek, then fluttered her fingers over his beard. "I want you to know I'm sorry for calling you a dog. My bad."

"Apology accepted. *Dog* is a slang term used against us. My species is not like the domesticated dog breeds the humans employ as pets."

"I get that. And wouldn't the mortals freak if Fluffy suddenly transformed into were-Fluffy?"

"What were you doing in that alley anyway?"

"I was bored. I needed to get out and breathe in nature. It's difficult to find nature in this city, you know that?"

"There are parks everywhere. I'll take you to the Bois de Boulogne this weekend. It's a huge park. I think you'll like it."

"Yes! Points for the werewolf hubby."

"So you were bored? Nothing else?" He tapped her lip where earlier in the alley he'd seen blood.

"I have to feed," she said softly. "Please don't be angry with me."

"I'm not. It's something you need to do to survive. I want the two of us to be honest with one another, okay?"

She nodded. "And if I take blood from humans, then

I won't be so tempted to bite you. But, stones, you taste so good."

"I think that's a compliment, but it also kind of makes my skin crawl."

"Sorry. Just giving you the honesty you asked for."

Now she slipped off the chair arm and onto his lap. Her bare limbs snuggled against his lap and chest. With a shimmy of her shoulders her wings receded and disappeared with some kind of faery magic Kir didn't understand.

She put her palms to his chest and met his gaze. "I've been thinking about us," she said. "I want to piss off all the naysayers that were shaking their heads at our wedding ceremony. And, like you said to me that night, I want to make this marriage the best it can be. We need to get to know one another."

"I was thinking the same."

"Wow, so we are on the same wavelength. What do the mortals say? Cool! We do have some things in common. We both like to eat and have sex."

"That's a start. We also both have an interest in weapons."

"You see? And we like to shop."

"I'm not so sure about that one."

"You like to watch me shop."

"I'll give you that one. Interesting, though, that you've no desire to wear the pretty things I've bought for you."

She tilted her head and now he noticed the silver chain strung through her hair from one ear, over the crown of her head, to the other ear.

"Subtle, and very fitting a princess." He kissed her forehead. "If you're a princess, does that render me a cool title by virtue of being your husband?"

"Only if you are sidhe. But I'm sure an honorary title can be managed. How about the Princess's Main Dude?"

He chuckled. "I'll wear it with pride." He stroked her arm; the skin was warm and only a little sparkly. He'd have to start looking in the mirror before leaving for work. "I've been thinking, too. *Hate* is such a strong word."

"Huh. Well..." She bracketed his face with her hands, peering into his eyes. "I still hate you. I mean, that's what it is. Faeries and species who inhabit the mortal realm? We don't have reasons to want to embrace."

"Other than sex?"

"There is that."

"If you have to hate me, then do what you must."

The doorbell rang and Kir sniffed the air, catching a subtle but familiar oaky scent. "That'll be Jacques. He's brought some files that I need to review tonight."

He got up and Bea followed him down the hallway to the front door. "Goodie! I get to meet one of your pack members. Was he the guy who stood beside you at the wedding?"

"Yes, my best man. He's also my best friend. We grew up in the pack together. I consider him my brother." He grabbed the doorknob and turned to catch his bobbing, giddy wife with hands clasped in gleeful expectation. "You forgetting something?"

She gave him a confused purse of her lips.

"Clothes?"

"Right!" She dashed off and up the stairs.

Kir invited Jacques inside, but he couldn't stay. Looking over his shoulder, most likely to catch a glance of his sparkly wife, his friend handed him the files. "Your brain works well when you're kicking back. I get that. Let's hope you can figure something new in this case."

"I'll give it my best. See you tomorrow, Jacques."

* * *

Bea heard the door close before she got her top on. Arms tangled in the pink shirt, she looked out the window and followed the werewolf's retreat. He was as big as Kir, yet had short dark hair and a bounce to his step.

Had Kir made him leave so he wouldn't have to introduce the winged wife to his pack mate? Not like she was a big secret. Though, as she'd mentioned to him, there had been snickers and derisive glances at the wedding ceremony. While the sidhe and werewolves held good relations, no doubt Kir's pack was aware she was a half-breed.

And that other half was nothing good. Nothing that a werewolf wanted to deal with, anyway.

Plopping onto the bed and tossing the shirt to the floor, she pulled up her legs and jammed her chin on top of her knees. "Stupid half-blood faery. You don't even know what your other half is."

She doubted Kir could locate her mother; nor should she expect so much from him. He was a kind man. But who was she to ask anything of a man who had already sacrificed his freedom to marry her as a means to seal a bargain?

"Jacques couldn't stay," Kir said as he took the stairs up. "Otherwise, I would have introduced you two." He wielded a manila folder stuffed with papers.

Bea finished pulling on the T-shirt, suddenly feeling exposed as the big, hulking wolf crossed the room and stood before her. "That's okay. I know I'm not the pack's favorite person."

"Why would you say something like that?"

She shrugged. "Half of me is not something wolves generally like to chum around with."

"The other half of you is."

"Well, then, which half do you want? Please pick the top half because I don't know what I'd do without a head."

"I'll take the full package." He knelt before her on the floor and set the folder on the bed. Bea sat up straighter. What did he have in mind? The pose seemed entirely too princely. "I'm one hundred percent behind the plan for us to make this marriage the best it can be."

He stroked his hands up her calves, setting a warm fire slowly up her limbs.

"Be damned what everyone else thinks?" she asked with hope.

He nodded. "They probably don't hate you as much as you think they do."

"Oh, they do. But I'm used to it."

"It bothers me that you are used to it." He kissed her knee, then the other. The brush of his beard quickened the fire into a blaze that rocketed up to her loins. "No one should be treated as if they don't belong or aren't right."

"Aren't you the positive Pete. Don't worry about me, wolf. I'm a survivor. I just, well, I really do want to find my mother."

"I said I would help you."

"But you also said you probably shouldn't."

"I'll figure out a way to do it on the sly. But if you don't have any information..."

"I have her name."

"That will help."

"It's Sirque."

"Cirque. Like in the circus?"

"No, it's spelled with an *S*. It's the only thing my father ever gave me about my mother. I used to write her name in the sand gardens, then quickly erase it if one of my brothers or sisters came sneaking up."

"I'll check the database tomorrow when I'm at work."

"Thank you, Kir."

He moved between her knees, and she cupped his face and kissed him on the mouth. He caught her hands, surprise dancing in his eyes.

"What?" Bea asked, a little freaked by his reaction.

"That's the first time we've kissed."

"No, we've— Really?" She thought about it. Huh. "What about our kiss at the ceremony?"

"Doesn't count as a real kiss."

"You're right. So many people were watching. And I was nervous. So, just now, that was our first official private kiss." She touched her lips. "You…okay with that? I mean, if I'd known, I would have gone for something a little longer, more…romantic."

He pulled her to him and pressed his mouth over hers in a connection that scurried through Bea's system faster than her wings could flutter. And the fluttering combined with the warm stirring at her loins and alchemized a heady, needy desire.

The wolf's arms moved down her back, bracing her tightly to his chest as he dived deep into the kiss. Tasting her. Feeding upon her. Claiming her. She had never felt more wanted, more appealing and desirable than in this moment. And his touch went beyond the frenzied slide of skin against skin they'd been sharing the past week. With the werewolf's kiss, he entered her in the most intimate way possible.

And she never wanted him to leave.

Pressing a palm to his chest, she wished he wore no shirt or vest. Still, she could feel his life thundering against her fingers, racing closer, as if a wolf were on her heels. And Bea sighed into the kiss, releasing all the negative feelings and emotions she'd brought out of Faery with her. In Kir's arms, everything was better.

"Need this," she muttered, and he twisted his mouth to the side and dashed his tongue against hers.

His hand slid up to her breast and squeezed the nipple none too gently. Bea moaned into the kiss and moved her breasts against his chest, wanting to put herself so close to him he couldn't force her out. She wanted to find a safe place. A place where she could be a half sidhe, half whatever and be accepted.

Not yet, though. She knew he couldn't accept what even she didn't know. But she would enjoy this moment while she could.

"On our wedding night," he said, pulling from the kiss yet keeping his mouth close to hers. "Your wings were out. But my werewolf didn't care. It just wanted..."

"To do the nasty."

He nodded. "That's usually the way it goes on the night of the full moon, and when I'm in werewolf form."

"I knew what to expect. And I did put my wings away before we did the nasty."

"We've been pretty much doing it the same fast and frenzied way ever since. But why do you always put your wings away beforehand?"

"Wings out is the ultimate intimacy, Kir."

"I understand that. Do you think it's too soon for us to try it?"

She shrugged.

"Being in my werewolf shape is the ultimate for us wolves. But I don't want to push you. I know it will take time for you to trust me. I'm curious, is all."

He wanted to do the wing, eh? Well, Bea would not argue some wing sex. Because...? Because she did trust him. And curiosity was never a bad thing.

"Maybe if we slowed it down," he said, and nudged

his nose along her earlobe. "And… I know that when you touch a faery's wings…"

"Mmm… Yes, I want that intimacy with you. Let's do it."

"I don't want to pressure you."

"Oh, please, no one tells this faery what to do. If I want to have winged sex, I will. And I think you'll like it, too."

"Okay." He kissed her mouth lightly, his mustache tickling her skin. "How do we start?"

"Diving right in always works for me."

She unfurled her wings and they brushed the air with her summer scent. Dipping one forward, she dashed it across Kir's hair. "Touch all you like, big boy. But know—" she touched his lips with a fingertip and met his wanting gaze "—such a touch drives me completely mad."

"A good mad?"

"A very good, orgasmic, giddy, sex mad."

Kissing along her jaw and down her neck, his other hand played over the uppermost radius bone and the soft gossamer fabric that stretched between it and the ulna bone. The touch felt like a finger to her clitoris. It was that intense and intimately attuned to her pleasure.

"Ooh, by the blessed Norns." Bea rolled to her side, going on her hands and knees, and giving him easy access to her wings. "Yes, right there. Oh, baby, you've got the touch."

Kir explored every portion of her four-quartered wings, dancing delirious sensations throughout her system and gathering them all into her core, which hummed and moaned and ached for release. His hot breaths shimmered over her wings. Barely there touches ignited a coil of flame that sizzled in her being.

And with a surprising ease, he fitted himself against her back, kneeling over her from behind. He slipped one hand across her stomach and down, finding her moistness that ached for contact. First touch released a gasp from Bea's lips. And it was the kiss to the base of her wings, where the wing bones segued into her spine, that pushed her into a giddy, soaring, moaning orgasm.

As Bea came she wrapped her wings backward and about Kir's shoulders and back. He shivered at the gossamer caress. It was warm and alive, shuddering through his system and overtaking him in orgasm.

He breathed in faery dust, and it tasted sweet, turning liquid and like honey mead to quench his thirst. Burying his face in her hair, he held her there, the two of them giving everything in the frenzied shivers their bodies shared. For the touch had gone beyond anything they had previously shared. He hadn't even slipped off his pants. Connection, pure energy shared between them, had brought them both to climax.

He fell to his back, taking her with him. She sprawled, exhausted and elated, across his chest. Her heartbeats thundered against his.

"That was freakin' amazing," she gasped against his throat, then licked his skin. "I dusted you."

"You always dust me when you come."

"Sorry. It's what happens with sidhe."

"It tastes…like mead."

"Really? You like to taste my dust?"

He shrugged, pushed her hair from her eyes and pulled it through his fingers. "I didn't do it purposely, but, yes, it was delicious."

"Kind of how drinking your blood would be to me." She eyed his neck where the carotid, no doubt, pulsed madly.

"Don't think about it, Bea."

"I know. But would it be so awful if my bite gave you a hunger for blood?"

"It would. My pack would banish me."

"Oh. Really? That seems extreme."

"Wolves would never harm a human, nor do we ever wish to rely on them—including drinking their blood—for survival. Such a hunger would result in my banishment from the pack."

"I hadn't considered that. You'd lose your whole family."

"Exactly. But I'll know soon enough—"

"Know what?"

"Uh…"

"What aren't you saying, Kir?" She smoothed her hands over his hair and studied him intently with her sex-softened gaze.

"I, uh, went to a doctor to make sure your bite hadn't tainted me."

"Oh."

Her reaction wasn't the angry rebuttal he'd expected. But her disappointment stabbed at him perhaps even harder. "I have to know, Bea. As I explained—"

"That's fine. You should get yourself checked out. I'm sorry. It was a stupid mistake." She rolled off him and onto her back, her wings tucked under her. "I'll never bite you again, but I seriously do need a bite. Like tomorrow. I'm starved for the vitality I get when I take from another person."

"Promise you won't take from any in the neighborhood. You have to keep a low profile. Just like the vamps do. And no wings."

The offending wings fluttered, sifting dust over their embrace. "Promise," she said, then reached over the side of the bed. "Your papers fell."

"I need to read through them before going to bed. Will you mind if I lie in bed with the light on?"

"Not at all. But what's this?" She studied the file folder.

One of the papers had slipped out and was crinkled from her rolling on top of it. "You're looking for a demon?"

Kir rolled over beside her. She tapped the word Jacques had written. "Denizen? That's what you call a group of demons. I thought you didn't like demons."

"Hate them. We're not sure who or what tortured the vampire we found. Could be werewolves, could be demons. I promised the vamp's girlfriend I wouldn't stop until I found out."

"That's very noble of you, but I thought you policed your species? So you're helping a dreaded vampire?"

"Bea, I don't dread vamps. Just their bite."

"Right. Okay, I get it. You don't have anything to fear from me."

"I don't fear you." He tugged her to him and kissed her quickly. "I like you."

"Really?"

He nodded.

"But you can't like someone and hate them."

"Exactly. But don't let me stop you from hating me."

"I don't want to hate you," she said on a whisper. Now her lashes fluttered and she avoided eye contact with him. "I'm just not sure I know how to do anything but."

He directed her to look at him, and before he could speak, the tear that spilled down her cheek caught him and he swallowed hard. "Don't be sad, Bea. This realm is new to you. Marriage is new to you. You can go as slow as you need to in finding your place here. And here." He took her hand and placed it over his heart.

And Bea spread her other arm across his chest and laid her head down beside the hand over his heart. "Thank you."

Chapter 10

Bea sensed the moment Kir walked in the front door. She didn't hear the door open and close. It was a visceral pull in her muscles that sat up and stood at alert. He was home, this man who knew how to touch her wings with such expertise he had made her cry out in utter joy.

She stood up from the dried flowers she'd been studying in the garden bed out back and almost ran toward the house. Almost.

Relaxing her shoulders and dropping her expectant posture, she reasoned, "Girl can't up and run every time her man walks in. He'll start thinking I like him. I do not." Just because he'd admitted to liking her didn't mean she had to jump on board as quickly. "I hate him. Right?"

Stepping lightly across the newly greened lawn, she took her time, fighting the urge to run all the way.

Kir strode through the patio doors, blocking his vision with a hand. The sun was high and bright. He was home early. "Hey, I found a faery in my garden!"

"Oh, make a funny about the faery, will you?" She tried to act affronted, but the wolf's surprising humor made her want to leap into his arms and wrap her legs about his hips.

"You making my flowers grow?"

"You think all faeries can touch a flower and bring it back to life? Okay, I'll give you that. But I don't think there's much hope for this science experiment gone wrong. Those decrepit shafts of brown matter died a noble death, I'm sure. Though I did bring some life back to the grass."

He looked over the green grass. "So you did. This is great! The old lady a couple houses down used to come and tend the flowers once a week. I haven't had the desire to test my brown thumb since her death last year."

"Oh, sweet. You and the little old ladies have a garden party."

He tilted a wonky look on her. "You're particularly snarky today."

Bea flexed her bicep. "Gotta keep the snark muscle exercised. So, why are you home early? Looking for some more wing action?" She almost unfurled her wings but then remembered his warning about keeping them concealed in places where she might be seen by humans.

"I searched your mother's name in the database."

She dropped the teasing tone and stepped up to the wolf. "You did?" Her heart fluttered in anticipation and she bounced on the balls of her feet.

"No vampires named Sirque."

"Oh." Her shoulders deflated. "Did you search other species?"

"I, uh, didn't. Sorry. Didn't think beyond vampire. You think I— Yes, of course. You said you weren't sure what your other half is. It was a quick search. Didn't want anyone at work to see me doing it. I'll look again."

"Thank you. I thought for sure she was vamp."

"She could be. Our database isn't complete, and if she's out of Europe, then…" He tilted up her head with a finger to her chin. "You okay, Bea?"

"Peaches and cream. I've been a half-breed whatsit for so long, I can handle it for another day. Or three. Or even forever."

He pulled her into a hug. "Something will turn up. And you're not a whatsit. You're a pretty faery."

"Thank you for looking for my mother's name. I appreciate it more than you will ever know."

And his hug was all she needed. Bea couldn't remember a time when she'd received such a genuine, unconditional hug. Sidhe didn't do the touchy-feely stuff. Or maybe that was what she'd grown up to believe. Her family, especially, had been into the royal entitlement thing. Bowing to one another had been de rigueur.

She could get used to hugs. Especially the ones that surrounded her with wolf.

Kir took her hand and they strolled into the living room. "So, my mother asked about you today."

"She did? The mother-in-law, eh? I don't think I met her at the wedding. Is her interest in me good, bad or ugly?"

"It's good. She wants to take you out with a couple of the pack females for a lunch and shopping date tomorrow."

"Shopping? I can dig it!"

"I thought you would. I think this is a great chance for you to get to know the pack ladies. I'll let her know when to pick you up. Oh, and, Bea?"

"Yes?" She stood on tiptoes, pushing her palms up his chest, to peer into his eyes.

"Please wear clothes when you go out with my mother."

"Gotcha."

"And, uh…you might not want to mention the whole

half-breed vampire thing. Not until we know for sure what you really are."

She gave him a thumbs-up. His mother would be a challenge, she sensed that from his worried remarks. She could handle her. Maybe.

Bea was nervous about her clothing choice. She had no idea how a pack wife was supposed to dress. But the television shows she'd been watching about housewives and divas had given her a few ideas. Bling seemed very important. Of which, she had some, thanks to Kir's generosity. But she wasn't sure if she'd balanced bling with style well enough.

Skyclad would have been much easier.

As she stepped out of the limo that Kir's mother, Madeline, had sent to pick her up, she tugged at the short pink skirt, trying to pull it to her knees. Normally short stuff felt great because it was as close to naked as she could get. And the green high heels that laced around the ankle had added to the sex appeal she'd felt looking in the mirror as she'd dressed.

But as Madeline stepped forward to greet her, the werewolf matriarch's smile fell and her eyes dropped to Bea's breasts, which were nicely pushed up by the tight, hugging fabric the salesgirls had raved over. Latex, the thing to wear. And Kir's eyes had almost dropped out of his skull at the sight of this dress when she'd modeled it for him.

Seeing Madeline's horrified expression, she compared her ultra-sexy housewives-meets-divas look to her mother-in-law's tidy plaid skirt and top set that was tailored to emphasize her narrow waist yet revealed no bosom whatsoever. And her black red-soled shoes were understated and classy.

"You must have brought clothing from Faery," Madeline

commented as she leaned in to buss Bea on both cheeks. A curl of subtle spice perfume lingered after her retreat.

"Actually, your son bought this dress for me. Is it wrong? Kir said it was lunch and the day is bright, so I wanted to wear something summery."

"Dear, you should be cautious whom you expose your assets to. I don't want my son's wife to look like a hoyden."

Bea wasn't sure what a hoyden was, but she didn't think it was good. Resigned to nod and play along, she followed Madeline into the back of a quiet, cozy restaurant that boasted high ceilings with massive ferns hanging along the walls and framing the stained glass windows. It was bright but proper, too.

Madeline introduced Bea to three women from pack Valoir. Marielle was a pretty, dark-haired wolf who wore her collars high and her skirt hem low. Too thin, as well. Bea thought her hand might snap in her grip when they shook hands. She was engaged to the pack scion, Jacques Montfort, who was also the pack principal's son, Madeline explained. Marielle tried not to look at Bea's breasts as they shook hands but was incapable of disguising her dismay at the sight of them.

Bea suddenly wished she had a purse so she could hold it over her chest, which did expose a good bit of her breasts. So the dress had been a wrong choice. But surely they must be impressed by her bling? The shiny rhinestones on her wrists clanked and glinted and made her so happy.

The other two women were hastily introduced. Valery and Paisley. Apparently, they didn't warrant face time because they had not a high-ranking male underarm. Valery was married, but Paisley, with gorgeous corkscrew blond curls, seemed young, perhaps still in her teens.

Bea sat before the round table that was decorated with a silver tea service and a pristine white cloth. At least she didn't have to worry about her bare legs bothering stern ol' Madeline. It was hard to believe the woman was Kir's mother. Where Kir was open, Madeline's lips were drawn so tight thin lines radiated up from her top lip toward her nose. And Bea wagered if she wanted a kind word from her she'd have to commit hara-kiri and hand the woman the sword when she was finished.

After tea was served and a few terribly insufficient sandwiches were downed, the questions started in. Bea was happy to entertain the younger women's curiosity because it was easier than trying to make conversation with the mother-in-law.

"Are you finding married life exciting?" Marielle asked eagerly. Bea assumed the woman would be most comfortable if she were wearing an apron and with a kid propped at her hip.

"Yes, Kir is very kind." She glanced to Madeline. The woman tapped her teacup with long, pink fingernails. What else to say? She couldn't drop the sex bomb, how she and Kir did that more than anything else. "I'm looking forward to having a family of my own."

Where had that confession come from?

It was true. Bea had always wondered what real family could be like, and so the idea of creating her own and doing it with someone who loved her appealed. Though certainly she was nervous about whether or not she could pull off the whole domestic thing. And motherhood? She had no example to follow.

Bea sighed. Perhaps it was best if she stuck to sex and keeping her man happy.

Madeline scoffed and set her teacup down with a click. "Faeries don't know the meaning of family. Of close bonds and devotion to one's blood. Do you even know what love is?"

"Well—"

"Yes, my son is kind," Madeline continued. "He takes after me. It's a pity that he was saddled with a species not our own."

Bea fluttered her gaze to the other women, who all occupied themselves with the stupid sandwiches. Apparently, they were as cowed by the woman as she was.

"I'm doing my best," Bea offered, finding she had to shove her shaking hands under the table to keep from spilling tea. "I know it wasn't an ideal situation. For either of us. But I want to make your son happy."

Again, Madeline scoffed, then busied herself with straightening the silver spoons to the right of her plate.

Bea felt tears wobble in her eyes and a pulling strain that threatened to turn into a torrent. Why couldn't the woman like her as her son did? In spite of her heritage, was she so awful? Truly, she was the dark one. The half-breed that did not deserve kindness. She quickly sipped her tea, hoping no one would notice the teardrop that landed in the lukewarm brew.

The remainder of lunch was spent in near silence, with a few comments about the elite shops along the rue Royale. The women had planned to spend time shopping, but after the bill was paid Madeline announced she had another appointment she'd forgotten about and apologized for not taking Bea along.

Of course, Kir's mother left with her three protégés. None of them offered Bea a parting glance.

Alone in the cab Madeline had summoned for her, Bea kicked off her shoes and tilted her head against the leather seat. It was apparent if Madeline didn't accept her, then no one else in the pack would. And she suddenly hoped that her husband's marriage to the half-breed faery would not result in his losing face with the pack. She didn't want that for him.

How to win the pack's approval? And did she want to? This marriage was a sham. It had been a political move on the pack's part, an opportunity to dispose of the dark one on her father's part. She'd be surprised if Malrick allowed Valoir to continue to hunt in Faery for much longer. Couldn't have rabble streaming in.

Such as his daughter?

Crossing her arms, Bea sank deep into the soft leather seat. She closed her eyes, but that didn't stop the tears from streaming down her cheeks.

Demons and werewolves. And vampires.

Kir couldn't connect them, but he was determined to do so. More and more, he believed the vampire they'd watched get staked by his girlfriend had tried to communicate something about demons to him and Jacques.

Jacques knew a guy who knew a guy who could hook them up with a demon informant, so until he heard from his partner, the rest of the day was a bust. He'd considered contacting Edamite but would use that contact as his last recourse.

"I'll try the informant first," he muttered, to assuage his guilt over not trusting the half brother he had no reason to hate but, deep down, knew that he did.

But really? Hate? After he'd told Bea such a vile reaction wasn't for him?

"Yeah," he muttered. "Demons deserve my hatred." Because his eight-year-old self was never going to forget what his father had done to the family.

Leaving the office, he hopped in the Lexus. With rain splattering the sidewalk, the sky had darkened early. It was nearing supper time, so he stopped at a Greek restaurant and purchased a big order of chicken gyros and pomme frites with extra tzatziki sauce.

His phone rang as he was pulling up in front of his home. The doctor's office.

"You're in the clear, Monsieur Sauveterre. I can find no vampire taint in your blood sample."

"Thank you, Doctor. That's what I wanted to hear."

He hung up and, with his spirits soaring, skipped up the steps and into the house.

Bea greeted him with a ho-hum kiss and took the take-out bag from him to dish the food out on plates.

"What, no 'Hi, honey, I missed you'?" he asked. Way to bring a man down from his elation.

"I didn't have time to miss you today," she said, sorting the food onto the plates. "And really? Honey? I hate you."

"Ah. Right. Forgot about that."

She was in a fine steam today. What had happened between last night—when they'd had great sex—and now to make her so irritable? And then he remembered. "So you must have had an interesting outing with my mother."

Bea sorted through the utensils for forks and knives. She didn't meet his gaze, and yet he thought he saw her roll her eyes.

"Bea? What's wrong?"

"Nothing at all." She gestured with a flutter. She set the forks by the plates. "I had a lovely tea with your mother and three others from your pack. Paisley, Valery and… I forget the other one."

"Marielle?"

"Yes, right. The apron wearer."

"The what?"

"They were all so…domestic." Bea's entire body performed a disgusted shiver.

"What's wrong with that?" He sat at the table as she poured a goblet of wine for each of them.

She slid across the table from him with only shredded

lettuce and pomme frites on her plate. Her sigh told him so much.

"There's nothing wrong with being domestic, Bea," he said. "It simply implies those women like making a home for their husband and families."

"Family," she said softly. She prodded at the wilted fries. "Do you think *I* need to be domesticated?"

"There's a big difference between domestic and domesticated, Bea. You will never be tamed. And should not. But as for caring for the home..." He bit into the gyro stuffed with savory shaved chicken.

"You want me to be the little housewife who cleans and cooks? I watched some of your television. I prefer bling and high heels. I don't think I can work the apron."

"What if that was all you wore? Just the apron?"

Her eyebrow quirked. He'd earned a little smile from her.

Kir clinked his goblet against hers. "To naked faeries in aprons."

Her reluctant smile grew larger. "Just make sure the apron is pretty and has lots of ruffles."

"What if I can find you one with rhinestones?"

"Then I will so do the domestic for you. But seriously? Am I to be stuck in this house always? Your backyard is greatly lacking in size and the garden is a desert. And in case you didn't notice, I'm a faery. I thrive on nature. I need to breathe, Kir. To let out my wings. What about that park you said you'd take me to?"

A park was still no place for wings. But...

"I've got something even better." He couldn't believe he hadn't thought of it until now. It would be a gift to her that would put her over the moon. "If you can wait until the weekend."

"What is it?" Her eyes twinkled. "Will I need my pink

shoes with the red soles or the green sandals with the lace-up straps?"

"Neither. You can go as naked as you desire. I own a cabin about two hours out of the city. Nothing but forest for leagues in every direction."

"Oh, blessed Herne! I think I don't hate you at this very moment."

He winked. "I'll take that non-hate and raise you a genuine like."

Bea perked and leaned across the table to kiss him. "I'll count the minutes until the weekend starts. And so long as I don't have to go anywhere with your mother ever again, I'll be the good little wife you desire."

"That's not what I desire, Bea. What I desire is your happiness. Happiness for myself, as well. Together, we can probably figure that out, eh?"

"Your mother thinks I'm wrong for you."

"Madeline believes wolves should marry other wolves. She wasn't pleased to learn about me drawing the—"

Bea looked up from her food and defied him with her gaze.

"She'll get over it," he offered. "Give her time. Once she gets to know you, I can't imagine her not liking you. You're a very likable faery."

She wiggled on the chair at that compliment. "I am, aren't I?"

"Except for when you attack me with a samurai sword."

"You should be thankful I know how to protect myself when you are not around."

"I am, and I'm not. I don't want you to ever worry about being unsafe. I promise to protect you should you ever need it."

"My knight in shining armor."

He shrugged. "It's not so shiny."

"So long as it's not fashioned from iron, you're good."

"How about leather?" He rapped the leather vest he wore.

"Perfect. You'll have to tell me about the designs worked into the vest you wear. It's so intricate. Is it a family crest?"

"No, but that's an idea I might have to try next time. I did this myself."

"What? You made that?"

"It's a hobby. A guy in the pack tans the hides and makes the leather workable, then I put the design on it."

"Wow. Make me something."

"I thought you weren't cool with leather."

"I can be cool if it's made by you. For me." She clasped her hands near her cheek and fluttered her lashes. "Maybe a sexy little corset or bustier?"

"As you wish."

"So simple as that? You've given me everything I ask for, Kir. What can I give you?"

He didn't want anything more than her bright smile and effervescent presence. But if she was asking… "Your like. And no more hate."

Bea's pink eyes beamed. "Done."

Chapter 11

They'd had sex the first night they arrived at the cabin. And the next morning up against the kitchen counter while Kir had been making eggs and bacon. In the afternoon when he'd taken her on a walk to show her the family of partridge who nested near the stream, they'd torn away their clothes and satisfied their insistent hunger for each other, and that night they'd fallen asleep entwined in one another's arms after delicious orgasms.

Usually Kir headed out to the cabin every full moon. It was only the half-moon and yet he'd let his werewolf out on the second night because—well, because he could. He'd run most of the night while Bea had been tucked in the cozy bed, knowing what he was doing and happy that he could escape to the wild.

On the third day, after Kir had spent the afternoon chopping wood for the fireplace, he'd helped Bea to make a stew. (His mother actually prepared the stew and froze it in Ziploc bags, so all he had to do was heat it up. Bea had felt so accomplished.)

They clinked their wine goblets and Kir leaned in to kiss Bea's nose. "Tonight," he said, "we're going to make love."

"That's what we've been doing, big boy. Or did you somehow lose all memory of our antics when you wolfed out and pushed me up against the tree yesterday afternoon?"

"Bea, you know what I mean by making love."

"Right, the slow, touching stuff." She wiggled on the chair and blushed. "Not that there's anything wrong with sex. I like sex. Stones, I *love* sex. And I happen to know you do, too."

He chuckled. "I do, but tonight, I'm going to make love to you. Slowly."

He kissed her eyelid, softly, gently. Bea felt the kiss tickle down her cheek, over her lips, and scurry to her breasts, where an inhale lifted her nipples against the silk robe she wore. Her body ignited.

"Sounds good," she whispered. "But why the sudden need to make love?"

"Because I care about you."

"You do?"

"Yes. Why does that surprise you?"

She stopped herself from saying *because that's never happened to me—ever* and instead shrugged.

He kissed her lips, lightly brushing them as if to savor, always linger. "And I want to show you that I care about you."

"I'm yours, lover boy. But, just so you know, I think you're too good to be real. I've been walking in a dream ever since coming to the mortal realm. I hope the dream never ends."

Leaving the supper dishes for later, he lifted her in his

arms and carried her up the stairs to the dark bedroom. Flicking on the light switch with an elbow softened the unbleached timber walls to a warm glow. But he didn't lay her on the bed; instead, Kir sat on the bed, with her on his lap, and moved aside the hair from her neck. He kissed her at the base of her hairline, tendering the skin as if to learn every pore.

"Wings out?" she asked on a tone that belied her desires with a hushing gasp.

"Not yet. We're taking this slowly."

Damn, he was determined to prolong the foreplay. How many guys that she had known in her lifetime had wanted to do that? She could dig it. But really? Could she last that long before getting to the big bang? The wolf always managed to instantly find her hot zones and zap them like a muscleman hitting the bell with the big hammer. This slow, methodical exploration—his tongue now traced the top of her spine—would try her patience.

Kir tickled his tongue in circles, seeming to move one vertebra at a time. The silk robe slipped to a puddle at Bea's hips, and she crossed her arms over her breasts and bowed her head as an agonizingly delicious trace of hot tongue over her skin stirred up a moan.

Right there, where normally her wings would unfurl, was the sweet spot. No man had ever discovered it before. And Kir took his time, circling, tracing, tasting her skin…

"Merciful stones," she muttered, and clutched the bedsheets.

"You want me to stop?"

"No!" She felt his smile against her skin. "Yes, right there. Oh, lover, that…is…so…"

"You smell good here."

"Different than elsewhere?"

"No, more intense. Summer and flowers and candy. It's

your unique scent, Bea. Like your dust. It's faery. You taste better than summer."

"Nothing is better than summer." She leaned forward, burying her face against a pillow, and stretched out her legs to take in Kir's amazing touch.

When he moved lower on her spine, she felt so dizzied from the touch up near her wings that she was thankful for a respite. The good didn't stop, but it was sustained now and she could breathe more freely, not expecting orgasm to jump right out at her. Yeah. Slow and lingering.

Making love. Who would have thought?

His thumbs smoothed over her Venus dimples and he pressed his tongue into each dent. She wiggled her derriere. The skim of his tiny jewel nipples slipped over her thighs and away as he tongued her delicately, deeply, hungrily.

And then his tongue found the join of her derriere to her thigh and lashed her roughly, licking her summer scent, making her spread her legs. She wished he'd turn her over, but he passed by her aching core and mastered a trail down the back of one leg—oh, she was so sensitive behind her knee—to her ankle. He nipped her playfully there, and on the arches of her feet. His actions made her curl her toes and grip the sheets in glee.

A tongue tickling between her toes? By the blessed Norns, she was so over sex. From now on it must be lovemaking. Always. She would insist upon nothing less.

Grasping her foot, which was well and thoroughly sexed, Kir moved to the other to give a repeat performance. "Turn over," he said, and she gladly complied.

While her toes curled and her arches were worshipped, Bea cupped her breasts and squeezed, heightening every touch he granted her. Her moans had become a song, and he punctuated the melody with a sexy, wolfish growl.

When he reached the apex of her thighs, her husband nuzzled his face against her, lashing her deeply, tickling her tender skin with his soft beard and cupping her derriere in his wide, strong hands.

She tilted her hips, seeking, demanding as much as he would give her. Too much, she asked for. Everything, he gave her.

One of his hands joined hers at her breast, and he squeezed her fingers around her nipple. Bea moaned loudly, pressing her mons against his face. He lapped at her, tending her swollen, aching clit as if it were a treat of which he could not get enough. He took his time, suckling, licking and breathing hot hushes over her skin. And when he slid a finger into her to curl upward, she nearly lost it.

"Not yet," she gasped.

"Why not?"

"I want you inside me. I need you hard and thick in me. Don't you want to feel me shake your world?"

The wolf didn't argue. Pants off in seconds, he then mounted her, pushing her legs open with his knees. His heavy erection landed on her clit, the wet head of him slicking across her as he directed it over and up and along her.

"Bea, you make it hard to go slow. I tried, but—"

"But you did it. I mean, as slow as we could manage. It was amazing."

"We'll practice the slow stuff more often," he said through a tight jaw.

"Sounds good. But practice is over, wolf. Now I need it fast. And deep. Please."

He entered her quickly, filling her with his solid length. Burned by him, Bea cried out as her humming core cheered the intrusion. He pumped inside her, each movement dragging his length out and along her clit. The friction was insane. She clawed her nails down his back. Her fangs tingled, wanting the rich, sweet blood that usually came with skin contact.

She would not bite him. But she needed to touch the tip of her fang to his skin. To tease at the want, the incredible need…

The wolf growled and grabbed her by the back of the neck, pulling her up to kiss roughly, deeply. And he never stopped his pace. Hungry and focused, he claimed her as he had never claimed her that first night of their marriage. For he had honored her this night with patience and love.

And thinking about that sent Bea over the edge and into the night where the wolf howled and her faery shouted in joy and dusted them both in a glittery cloud.

During the ride back to Paris, Kir lifted his hand to shift the truck into second gear when he realized he was holding Bea's hand. They'd been holding hands since he'd driven onto the autoroute half an hour earlier.

Huh. He was holding his wife's hand. Smiling at Bea, he received a beaming smile in return. She squeezed his hand and nodded her head to the rock and roll blasting through the radio.

And he wondered why he'd never considered handholding a boon before. It was definitely something he wanted to do more of.

Out the corner of his eye he noticed the patterns that had been sealed into his flesh upon the marriage bonding. They glowed. Bea's hand glowed, too.

"You see that?" he asked.

She nodded, then closed her eyes. The smile never left her mouth. And the glowing slowly ceased, but he thought about it all the way home.

Chapter 12

The groceries Kir had brought home proved no end of delight to Bea's curious nature. He'd specifically selected items that needed only to be unwrapped and placed in the oven, or that were fresh fruits and vegetables. But the powder to make water taste like cherries fascinated her.

Filling a glass with water, she marveled over the silvery flash the sunlight caused in the liquid as it sat on the granite countertop.

"I used to swim in a stream that glinted like that," she said, and sighed. Some things she did miss about Faery. Never her fickle family, but always the nature. "I sure hope he takes me back to the cabin. Soon."

Tearing open the packet of flavoring, she tilted the bright red powder into the water and watched the particles disperse and transform the silver water into a bright pink. With a quick stir of a spoon, she then tasted it—and spit it out.

"Oh, that's awful. What the heck?"

She looked at the packet but couldn't read the French words that she could innately understand when spoken out loud. "Kir said you put it in water. Ugh."

She dumped the pink brew down the sink. "I'll stick with the clear stuff. Some human foods baffle me. Guess it's time to head out to the yard and see if I can rescue the dead things out there."

Kir and Jacques sat in the Lexus out in front of the warehouse where they'd been tipped off that they'd find the demon that pack Royaume was working with. After reviewing the files, Kir had determined that between the two packs Royaume and Conquerer, Royaume was most likely involved in dirty dealings.

The little he knew about Royaume was that the pack was small and not well-known. They didn't have intel on who the pack leader was. Which was odd because it wasn't so easy for a wolf pack to go unnoticed by others of their breed in the city limits. Out in the country? Stealth and privacy was easier to maintain. But the fact they could be of few numbers was probably the reason they were unknown. They had never raised a blip on the enforcement team's radar.

Good enough reason to check them out.

Sunrise teased the horizon. Kir had left a warm faery at home in bed to sit here with Jacques while sucking down stale coffee. Something wrong with that scenario.

"How are your wedding plans coming?" Kir asked.

"Wedding planning is a lesson in torture, my man. We had to pick colors and doilies the other day. Seriously. Doilies? I didn't know what a doily was until then. And I can't believe I know what it is now."

Kir chuckled.

"And tomorrow we have a date to taste petits fours. What the hell is a petit four? Sure doesn't sound like meat."

Kir laughed. "I think I dodged a bullet by not having to do all the wedding stuff."

"Be thankful for that small mercy. Marielle wants to control everything. Even the groomsmen's boxer shorts! Don't laugh, man, you are going to be a groomsman."

"I'd be honored."

"Yeah, you say that now. Wait until you have to wear pink boxers."

"Will she ask Bea to be a bridesmaid?"

Jacques's laughter ended abruptly. He swiped a hand across his jaw and glanced out the window. "I don't know, man. Yes?"

That was the least believable lie the man had ever tried on him.

"She went shopping with my mother and your fiancée the other day," Kir said. "I assumed Bea had been welcomed into the pack."

"Right. The shopping trip. Marielle said it didn't go so well. Your little faery probably didn't want to say anything about your mom—"

"What about my mother?"

Jacques shrugged. "That's girl stuff. You ask your wife to tell you about it. Hey, look! We got action in the window."

Much as he wanted the lowdown on Bea's lunch with his mother, Kir couldn't ignore what was more important. "Let's go."

They got out and crept up to the house, a nondescript two-story painted white with flaking brown shutters. Jacques, who carried a pistol loaded with salt cartridges, signaled that he would go in first. Kir would follow with a stake and a salt blade. He also knew a few demon wards in Latin, if necessary.

Once inside the house, they didn't have to threaten violence. A scrawny demon in human form wandered down the dark-paneled hallway, a glass of milk in hand. At the sight of Kir and Jacques, he dropped the glass and lifted his hands. "I didn't do it!"

Jacques wrangled the compliant demon into the living room and shoved him onto the stained plaid couch. Kir stepped carefully over the broken glass, his heavy rubber heels crunching a few pieces. He took in the room and cast his gaze down the hallway. He listened…sniffed. Faint scent of sulfur and sweet milk. Stale furniture and dust. No others in the house whom he could sense.

"We've got questions about a pack," Jacques said, leaning over the demon and playing the bad cop, as was his mien. "You're going to answer them."

"If I know anything, I will." The nervous demon clasped his hands between his knees. "I don't mess with wolves, man. You guys have sharp claws and I tend to bruise easily."

A battery of questions was quickly answered. The demon knew nothing about the packs because, as he'd shown them, he liked to keep his distance from werewolves. He wasn't a member of a local denizen.

And yet, he did let something interesting slip. "That vamp you two found was probably used for V."

"Vee?" Jacques looked to Kir, but Kir could only shrug.

"It's V like the capital letter," the demon clarified, and put up two fingers in the shape of the letter. "It's the hot new drug for us demons. We suck it straight from the vamp's veins or get it infused directly into our carotid. The vamp is restrained, so it's all good. But sometimes our blood flows back into them and that's a mother for the vamp."

And would such a harrowing return flow of demon blood lead to the vamp vomiting up black blood?

"Demons are drinking vampire blood now?" Kir asked. "Why?"

"Don't you know, man? Vamp blood is the ultimate. It's laced with so many different kinds of human blood. All that live, fresh vita racing through their systems. The first taste is like a superhit. If your vamp was choking up demon blood, he must have fought for his life to escape. Probably sucked some demon blood in the process."

"And how are werewolves involved in this V?" Jacques asked.

"I don't know. Maybe it's the wolves who collect the vampires? All I know is V is a hard substance to get. Not like a couple of us can keep a vamp hostage and feed off him. The vamps are too smart for that. And it's controlled. Only a few V-hubs in the city. Expensive shit."

"V-hubs." Kir shoved his fingers through his hair. This was new and interesting. And it gave him a very bad feeling. He'd heard of the vampires who went to FaeryTown to get high on ichor, but demons getting high on vamp blood? "You're going to take us to one of those hubs."

The demon shrugged. "Not possible. They move, like, every day, man. The only way to find one is to know someone who knows someone."

Jacques's cell phone rang and he gestured to Kir that he had to take the call as he wandered out toward the front door. Probably his fiancée with more ridiculous wedding planning details.

The demon on the couch crossed his arms over his chest and stared at the broken glass out in the hallway. He'd been forthright and helpful. He didn't want any trouble. So maybe Kir could learn one more thing.

He leaned in so Jacques couldn't hear. "You ever hear about someone named Sirque?"

The demon's smile was greasy and black. "What a delicious memory of a demon well spent."

"You know her? She's demon?"

"'Course she's demon. Didn't you just ask about her? You think she's involved in selling V? What's your game, wolf?"

"What she is or isn't involved in is none of your business. I'm trying to locate her."

"For what price?"

Kir twisted the demon's hand backward, snapping the tendons at his wrist.

"All right! Let go!"

He gripped the wounded wrist, pressing his thumb against the narrow bone. Demons who occupied human bodies suffered the weakness of the flesh. They felt all the pain, breaks and bruises, and couldn't heal as quickly.

"Jeez, it takes me a hell of a lot longer to heal than you crazy dogs."

"Dog?" Kir growled, showing his teeth. "Talk fast, sulfur head, or I'll tear out your throat."

"All right! According to the rumors, Sirque ventured deep into Daemonia to find the dark treats she was looking for. That demoness was never satisfied."

"Satisfied?"

"You know." The demon pumped his hips lewdly. "Sexually."

Not a topic he wanted to learn too much about if the demon he spoke of was really Bea's mother.

"How does one get to Daemonia?"

"That's a good one." The demon chuckled nervously.

"Idiot wolf. It's the info about V or Daemonia. Take your pick, 'cause I'm only giving up one."

"You don't get to tell me how to run the show—"

"We good to go?" Jacques asked as he returned, tucking the pistol into the holster under his arm. Gliding a hand over the salt blade at his hip, he asked, "He remember where to find one of those hubs?"

"I'm waiting to see what your partner really wants," the demon provided.

"Cocky bastard, eh?" Jacques lunged for the demon, gripping him by the throat and laying the salt blade against his cheek. The salt seared the demon's flesh and it growled.

"You want freedom?" Jacques looked to Kir.

Kir couldn't stop him and didn't want to. He'd gotten what info he could about Sirque. She was a demon? Daemonia? It was a good lead.

He nodded once, and Jacques jammed the blade up through the demon's jaw. The demon spasmed. Jacques stepped back. And Kir turned to the side and put up a hand to block the explosion of demon dust that dispersed into the room.

"Bea!"

Kir strode into the kitchen, opened the fridge and realized he'd not stocked up on wine in a while. The wire racks were bare. And Bea, well, why not? She could manage a trip to the grocery store. So long as no unleashed dogs barked at her. He'd give her a credit card and put a limited amount on it so she didn't go overboard.

A faery fluttered into the kitchen, carrying a bouquet of yellow-faced white-petaled daisies in hand. Her wings were furled and receded into her spine. And she was not naked.

Disappointed by her lacking display of skin, Kir reached

into the high cabinet and pulled out a glass flower vase for her. "You couldn't have found those in our desolate wasteland out back."

"The neighbor behind us brought them over when I was muddling on how to bring life to the dead shrubs. She expressed her sadness over the pitiful dead stuff and gave me these. I think she has a crush on you."

"And why would my ninety-year-old neighbor have a crush on me?"

"Who wouldn't? Just because you're old doesn't mean you stop noticing the fine. How old are you, anyway?"

"Twenty-eight."

"See? You're close enough in age for the cougar out back. How long is twenty-eight?"

Kir laughed. "Faery time and mortal time have always been very different. Do you know what a Faery year equals in mortal years?"

"We don't have years. But we seem close in age, yes?"

"I think so." He kissed the top of her head as she stuck the flowers into the vase. "I'm yet a pup in werewolf years."

"Really? And I was beginning to wonder why you hadn't married until now."

"Pup. And… I hadn't found the right woman, I guess."

"So you thought you'd wait around until someone forced you to it?"

"You got that right, Short Stick."

"I hate that stupid name."

"Come on, I like it. I got stuck with something I was expecting to be terrible and it's turned out to be pretty amazing."

"Really?" Her pink eyes brightened. "Okay, then. I guess I could keep on being your short stick."

"You've no choice." He slid onto a bar stool before the kitchen counter and tapped the flower vase.

"I'm working on your flowers in the yard," she said. "Takes a lot of faery magic to bring up new from dead, though."

"So you can grow flowers?"

"With the right conditions. Though my glamour has been weakened by this realm. Normally a walk across the yard would do it. I don't know what you've done to kill your flora, but you killed it good."

"I do mark my territory out there once in a while," he said with a wink.

"That'll do it." She laughed. "Be thankful the grass is now green. I figure if I give it some time the green will wander closer to the brown stuff and then I can mingle them and create new life."

"It'll be fall soon enough. The winter will kill everything, so you might as well wait for spring."

"Yes, but it's a challenge I can't resist. So how was work? I watched a television show today and it was about a married couple. The wife asked the husband about his work and made him brownies. Do you want me to make you brownies?"

Kir perked, his shoulders straightening. "Do you know how to make brownies?"

"Only the annoying little ones who sneak into a person's house at night to clean. Well, I don't *make* them. Although I did make it with a brownie once…" Bea giggled and hugged Kir. "Mmm, you always smell so good."

And he was getting a hard-on. Par for the course, but only because he absolutely refused to imagine Bea getting it on with a brownie. But he'd better tell her about today's work before they got to the sex. Or would it be better if he got some *before* revealing details? No, he wouldn't do that to her. For good or for ill, he had to tell her what he'd learned.

"I think I got a lead on your mother today. She's not vampire."

"How can you be so sure? Did you find a way to verify that?" She pulled out of the hug and stumbled backward until her shoulders hit the fridge. "That doesn't make sense." She tapped her incisors. "Fangs. And the blood drinking."

"Lots of species in the paranormal realm have fangs, Bea."

"Yes, but what else could she have been?"

"Demon?"

"What? No, you're— Why would you suggest that?"

He sensed her nervous anxiety in the way she bounced on her toes and clasped and unclasped her arms across her chest. Maybe demons were as nasty to faeries as they were to him.

"We apprehended a demon today, in conjunction with a case I'm working, and I had a moment to ask if he had heard about Sirque."

"Why would you ask some random demon about my mother?"

"Bea. I didn't think this would upset you—"

"I don't understand you, Kir. You don't even like demons," she accused. "They are nasty to you. And if I had a demon mother—"

"Bea!"

She pressed her back to the fridge, casting him a fearful look. Kir checked his tone. He had not raised his voice to her, ever. But she was being irrational and he hadn't even spilled details.

"The demon had heard of her and confirmed she was demon."

"Because there's only one Sirque in the world? Come on, Kir—"

He grasped her upper arms gently and held her tearing gaze. "Bea," he said as gently as he could. "This is what he told me. He said Sirque was rumored to be in Daemonia, because she had to go deep for what she was looking for."

"What does that mean?"

"I have no clue. He intimated it was sexual."

"Yuck, don't tell me."

"I won't. That's all he told me. But it gives us a place to look for your mother. Daemonia. Aren't you at the least pleased to have a lead?"

She bowed her head. Her delicate shoulders shook in his grasp. Maybe learning that she was one step closer was too much to handle. She must have thought about her mother every day, and now to be closer—shouldn't she be happier?

Bea shoved out of his grasp. "You're telling me that I'm part demon?"

He could only offer a shrug.

"I need to think about this." She ran up the stairs.

And Kir put his palm over his heart. She was upset. Because of him. It hurt to know he'd been the cause of her pain. But he'd give her some space.

Maybe.

Hell, he couldn't follow her. He wanted to. He needed to circle her in his arms and tell her he would protect her. Because he wanted to protect her, to give her everything she desired, even if that meant going to Daemonia to do so. But how to get to the Place of All Demons?

And did he really believe he could go there? The one place in the world occupied by the breed he hated most?

If Bea's mother was demon, that meant Bea was half demon. Kir's heart thudded.

"Hell."

Chapter 13

Bea rushed into the bathroom and closed the door. Her head spun with what Kir had revealed about her mother. It couldn't be right. Sirque was not a common name, but surely more than one in this vast mortal realm possessed it?

He'd found the wrong Sirque. She was sure of it.

Because to suddenly be told she could be half demon had reached in and clenched her heart in a painful twist.

Half vampire, she could deal with. She'd been dealing all her life thinking as much. Her stepsiblings had shunned her and she had learned to live in the shadows. And drinking ichor, and now blood, was not at all terrible. It was simply a part of who she was.

And always her father had made her feel less than worthy. Which was why she found it hard to know what to do with the unconditional acceptance Kir gave her.

But demons had created those shadows she had clung to for comfort. Demons existed in Faery. They were reviled.

Their blood was black and their eyes red. They exuded a foul scent and had been birthed from Beneath. Beneath was a realm away from Faery and the mortal realm. It was not spoken of but always induced a shudder when the dark and twisting evil that writhed within its confines were thought about. Never were they mentioned by name.

Those demons who managed to mate with the sidhe produced half-breed offspring who were never accepted by the faeries and could never be accepted by their own. If a faery saw one of the half-breeds, they whispered of The Wicked. Such half-breeds were filthy and not to be dealt with.

Demons were the sidhe's one bane.

Bea remembered once seeing a demon lurking in the shadows. Its red eyes had glowed brightly and she had screamed.

"Red." She wandered to the vanity and looked in the mirror. "And silver?"

Her father's eyes were silver. Elder faeries' eyes always changed from the common sidhe violet to silver or sometimes turned white. If her mother's eyes had been red…

She recalled mixing the red drink powder into the water that had shimmered silver in the sunlight and marveling over how it had turned the water pink.

Tears spilled from Bea's eyes as she stared at the pink irises her mother and father had created. Was she one of The Wicked?

Breaths caught at the back of her throat, making it impossible to swallow. She clutched her neck, wincing. She should have never sought her mother.

A knock on the door startled her. She sniffed back a tear. "You okay, Bea?"

"No." She would never again be okay. Not if she truly were half demon. On many occasions her husband had plainly stated he did not like demons. In fact, he hated them. Oh!

The doorknob turned and Kir walked up and stood behind her, meeting her gaze in the mirror. He didn't touch her. She might shove him away if he did. She might not. She didn't know what to do right now. How could he bear to stand so close, knowing she could be half demon?

"I can't be demon," she whispered. "That's the worst."

"You are what you are. You're good, Bea. You will not become what you expect from such a creature."

"Creature," she muttered. "Oh, Kir, do you know we sidhe call them The Wicked? They are vile."

His arms bracketed her at the moment she felt her knees weaken, and she sank against his strong, solid body. He felt like sanctuary, a world apart from the horrific world she'd been thrust into. Here stood a man who would protect her.

But could he protect her from herself?

"It's going to be okay," he said in a quiet tone. "I'll be here for you, no matter what."

"You will? But…but you don't like demons."

He stepped beside her and slid his hand into hers. The bonding marks on the backs of their hands flickered, then glowed briefly. She gasped at the sight of it. "It did that in the car, too. I think it means…"

He lifted her hand to kiss it, and again the mark glowed briefly. "Our connection makes it brighter."

She nodded and caught a gasp in her throat. Could that mean that he was falling in love with her? That she was falling in love with him? What cruelty had saddled Kir into a marriage and then to learn that he had bonded with something he most hated?

Bea looked up to her husband's face and he bent to kiss her.

"We'll get through this," he said. "If you want me to

continue to track your mother, I'll do what I can. If you want to drop it, we can do that, too."

She nodded. "I need to give it some thought. Kir, why are you taking this so well?"

"It's easy enough when you are involved."

"But you hate demons."

"I do have a demon half brother."

"That you never speak to!" She exhaled a breath. "I think… I need to be alone. I'm not sure. Maybe I need you here. I'm just so…hungry. Stones, I need blood. I should go out."

He tugged her hand as she started to leave the bathroom. "I don't want you going out in the condition you're in."

"But I'm hungry. I… Blood. I know that will take the edge off. Maybe it'll help me to relax and sleep after everything I've learned."

"Then take from me."

"No. Kir, you said I couldn't bite you again. I don't want to give you the blood hunger."

"If you're not a vamp—"

Bea put up her hand. "Don't say that. We don't know what I am."

"The blood test came back from the doctor. I don't have vampire taint in me. And it's probably for this very reason."

Bea moaned miserably. The word *taint* sounded like something associated with The Wicked. She didn't want to taint anything. Most especially, her husband.

He led her out of the bathroom and into the bedroom, where he directed her to sit on the bed. Disappearing into the closet, Kir returned holding her blade. The setting sun flashed in the iridescent violet that sheened the black blade. "If you cut me, it's not a bite. Yes?"

"Maybe. Oh, it's the same thing. I'll still be consuming your blood."

"Yes, but your fangs won't enter me. If you are vampire, the vampiric taint won't enter my system."

That did make sense.

"I'm willing to let you try. I want to be what you need."

He strolled into the bathroom and returned with the glass he kept on the vanity. He didn't even wait for her to stop him. He put the glass in her hand. Then he slashed the blade across his wrist. He held it over the glass, filling it with half an inch of his blood before pulling away and pressing his thumb to his wrist to stanch the bleeding.

Seeing the warm red liquid catch a glint from the overhead light, Bea traced her fingernail along the rim of the glass. When she had thought she was half vampire, the idea of consuming blood hadn't bothered her. It was what she needed to survive.

But if she was half demon, what did that mean? What demons consumed blood? Had an innate need for the substance? Thinking about it made her shiver.

Kir tilted the goblet and she drank, allowing him to feed her. The first taste was warm and thick. Lush. It burst on her tongue and she swallowed it all, closing her eyes to the heady flavor of pure werewolf. Bea hummed deep in her throat and smiled.

Kir kissed her forehead. "Good?"

"Beyond description," she murmured. And yet, something was missing. She couldn't name the something, though. She needed… Oh, it didn't matter. "Thank you. I…don't know how to say it enough."

He kissed her mouth and tapped her nose with a finger. "Why don't you run yourself a hot bath and relax. I'm going to order in something to eat. I'll bring up the food when it gets here."

"I'm good. Just get something for yourself. A bath

sounds like the perfect thing to lull me to sleep. You don't mind if we don't...?"

"We can't have sex every night."

"We can't?"

He chuckled. "We can, but tonight I think we just need to snuggle and hold one another."

"That sounds like a treat better than your blood, husband. Come snuggle with me after you've eaten."

"I will."

He strode down the stairs, and Bea whispered, "I hate you, wolf." And she filled in for Kir's reply with, "I hate you, too."

Then she shook her head and smiled. "But not really."

The blood he had given her warmed her all over and she wrapped her arms about herself, reveling in his selfless sacrifice.

Kir wandered about the kitchen after he'd called for delivery. He rubbed his temples. Clasped his hands in fists, in and out. Paced the hallway from the front door to the kitchen. The possibility of Bea being part demon was not cool. He didn't love Edamite, that was for sure. Now to accept that his wife could be part demon?

What hell had he fallen into?

He rubbed his wrist where the cut had already healed. A blood-drinking wife. He'd never in a million years have thought that was what his destiny held. A destiny he'd been forced into. But if she was not vampire, then he had no fear of developing the blood hunger. That should make everything between them right.

He wanted to make this work because...because of Bea. He adored her. And really? He rubbed the mark on the back of his hand.

Was he falling in love with her? Or had it already happened?

He exhaled. “Part demon?”

And now the investigation was leading him toward demons, as well. The last thing he wanted to associate with was fast becoming the only way toward answers. Answers for questions he was sure he’d never in a million years purposely ask.

He had never wanted to follow in his father’s footsteps, and, yet, he was inexplicably tracing those very steps right now. He’d engaged in a relationship with a woman who was part demon. Possibly?

“Fuck,” he muttered.

Chapter 14

Standing out in the backyard, considering her options for the flower bed, Bea rubbed the back of her neck and turned her face up toward the sun. It wasn't as bright here in the mortal realm. Nothing wrong with that. The sun in Faery had been cruel at times. She'd preferred her cool yet bright rooms, and when she had spent time out in nature it had been in the shaded forest that hugged her father's demesne.

She should be able to make these flowers grow. For some reason, this morning she didn't feel as spunky and go get 'em as she normally did. And that was odd, because she'd drunk Kir's blood last night. Blood always got her going.

Did she need to take blood directly from the vein? Had drinking it from a glass somehow robbed it of vital nutrients she needed for survival? Could her other half be holding her back? Now that she was in the mortal realm, it was possible her vamp—or demon side—was stronger. A drain to her faery magic.

She dug her toes into the dirt and concentrated. No flowers. Not a bud or green leaf.

If she had a mother to talk to, she might get some answers to those questions. But if her mother was demon, she wasn't sure anymore that she wanted to hear the answers. No wonder her father had protected her from Sirque's true nature all these years. Allowing her to believe she was half vampire had been a mercy when the other option was demon.

"I'm not even a dark one," she whispered. "I'm one of The Wicked."

If she really was half demon, then why did she drink blood? Did The Wicked live off blood and ichor? Ugh. Just thinking the word *demon* gave her a stomachache. And knowing that The Wicked were ostracized and hidden away in a part of Faery the sidhe never traveled to made her shudder. That was where she belonged.

She sat on the grass and extended her legs. Leaning forward, she stretched out her arms over the soft green grass. She should plant her feet and draw up the vita from the ground to transfer it to the flowers.

Could it be her demonic half that was zapping her nature vita?

She wanted to unfurl her wings because that might help, but Kir's warning about nosy neighbors kept them safely concealed. And she always remembered now to put on clothes when going outside. She suspected the face that often appeared in the second-floor window in the house to the left was an old man. Probably hadn't seen a naked woman in ages.

Thinking about being naked segued her thoughts to skin and heat and Kir's impossibly muscled body. She could really use some of that right now. Anything to keep her mind from the dire thoughts of living secluded away from all others and labeled one of The Wicked.

She squinted up at the sun. Funny, she'd never been so sexually hungry while in Faery. She'd gotten some maybe once or twice a month. Here in the mortal realm? She would really be pleased to have it every day.

And what was that about?

Must be what having a sexy hubby did for a girl.

"Here's hoping he can adjust to having a demon for a wife. Ugh, Bea, don't even say that. Stop thinking about it!"

The flowers shivered near her legs and she beat the ground. "Stupid, dry, lifeless plants. I'm going to infuse you with some vita if it kills me."

The struggle to bring life to this garden, at the very least, would distract her thoughts from more dire issues.

Kir set the take-out bag on the kitchen table and decided he'd look up chefs in the directory later. He didn't expect Bea to learn to cook and felt it was sort of an ingrained thing. A girl grew up learning how to cook at her mother's side. Bea hadn't a mother or, apparently, anyone who had cared much to spend any time teaching her.

Fluttering into the kitchen, his wife, sans wings, infused the room with a burst of pink.

Bea rubbed her hands together in glee. "What is for dinner tonight? You know how much I love that you can pull a full meal out of a bag."

The pink dress number barely covered her breasts, and Kir wanted to peel back the candy-colored latex to get to the good stuff.

She snapped her fingers before his face. "Up here, husband. You can have dessert later."

"Right, uh...crepes. Let's eat quickly. I invited over the

Jones brothers tonight. They're dark witches who might be able to tell us how to gain access to Daemonia. Is... that okay?"

She settled onto the chair, open bag in hand, and peered inside, but he knew she was thinking too hard on what he'd just told her.

"Bea?"

A dramatic sigh melted her shoulders. "Yes, that's fine. If I'm half demon, I'd like to know once and for all. Daemonia, eh?"

"It's the Place of All Demons."

"I know what it is. When I was little, my cousins used to tell scary bedtime stories about faeries lost in Daemonia. But that was nothing compared to the tales about The Wicked."

Sensing her mood wasn't going to lift if they stayed on topic, Kir grabbed the bag and set out the meal containers. "Let's eat and save the demons for later."

"But what if we can never put them aside for later? What if I am one? Kir, your wife is a demon. One of The Wicked. Doesn't that make you angry?"

"Never angry."

"Appalled?"

"No, just..." Just yes! And no. And, hell, he didn't know how to feel about this. But he didn't want Bea to pick up on his lack of surety about their marriage right now. "Later, okay?"

"Fine. But I'm not so hungry anymore." She pushed her unopened tin forward on the table.

"Really? I bet you've never tasted banana-and-chocolate crepes."

She tugged back the tin with one finger and lifted the paperboard cover to peer inside. "Smells reasonably edible."

Kir dragged his finger through the chocolate that oozed out of his sweet meal and offered it to Bea. "Just a taste?"

Going up on her knees on the chair, she leaned across the table and licked his finger. Eyes closed, she moaned in appreciation. Had he noticed how bow-like her lips were? Or that pert tilt to her nose? She was pretty, no other word for it. Not glamorous or elegant, but simply pretty. And that set his heart racing. Because she was simple and sweet and good and she was his.

Yep, you claimed her, wolf. Did you hear that? You've claimed the woman you didn't want to marry. Who might possibly be half demon. So now you really are like your father. Sucker.

Bea opened her mouth and waggled her tongue at him. He swiped a finger through the chocolate again and this time she sucked his whole finger into her mouth. Her tongue tickled the sensitive underside and he leaned in to kiss the corner of her eye. He wanted to taste her. Now. Covered in chocolate.

May his heart be damned, if she was a demon.

He opened her tin and peeled back the top of the crepe to expose the gushy chocolate inside. Dragging his fingers through the warm ooze, he then held them up for her to lick, but as she got close, he tapped her nose with them and then caught her under the chin with his chocolaty fingers and kissed her deeply. She tasted sweet, but her giggles separated them from the kiss. He lashed his tongue across her nose, then dived to her jaw, where chocolate streaked her skin.

"You think so, wolf?"

Her fingers worked quickly down his shirt, unbuttoning it and peeling it back as he cleaned the chocolate from her throat. Then he felt Bea's fingers wiping the warm ooze over his chest. It was sticky and— Damn, he was going to enjoy this meal.

"Why haven't I tasted chocolate until now?"

"Not sure." He moaned as her tongue found his nipple. She licked and bit him gently, lashing him to a hard jewel.

"You like that?"

"Feels great. Probably the same way it does when I lick your nipples."

"Well, then, this must feel fabulous. They're so tiny, though. Poor men. Although you did get something even better."

Her hand slid down to unbutton his pants and the warm, gooey slide of chocolate coated the head of his erection. Bea slipped lower to kneel on the floor, and he obliged when she pulled down his jeans and gripped his cock. Reaching up to score some more chocolate, she then swathed it up and down him as if she was a talented painter.

"Remind me to bring home crepes more often," he said, and then growled with pleasure.

Kir toweled off while Bea dressed in the bedroom—the pink latex had taken on a lot of chocolate. His cell phone rang and he checked the screen. Edamite. He'd left him a text regarding the investigation.

He answered but spoke softly so Bea wouldn't hear.

"Hey, bro," Ed said. "It's been a while. You must need something."

Kir's heart dropped. Did he only ever contact Ed when he needed something? There was not a thing about the man he didn't like, beyond his breed. He should be able to embrace him as family and look beyond the fact that his very existence was proof of his father's infidelity.

"Have you heard of V-hubs?" Kir asked, trying to keep it as businesslike as possible.

"Since when are you in the market for vampire blood?"

"So you do know about them?"

"Not saying I do, but I'm not saying I don't."

Ed's status among the Parisian demon denizens was right up there with some kind of mafia leader. His brother was involved in things Kir would rather not know about. Yet there were times he sensed Ed was only involved in the evil stuff to ensure it didn't spread and catch innocents in its grasp.

"You're not involved with V, are you, Ed?"

A heavy sigh preceded his response. "You're investigating this? That enforcement team of yours?"

"We are. We found a tortured vamp and thought he'd come from a pack using him for the blood games, but the investigation has led to V. I suspect a pack may be involved somehow, but my source says a demon is in charge. If you're involved, Ed—"

"I can get a location of a hub for you, but beyond that, I don't have any info."

"Because you're protecting someone?"

"Nope. I don't dabble in that stuff. Got enough on my plate lately, as it is."

He should probably be the good brother and ask what the problem was, but Kir couldn't summon the concern. "I'd appreciate it, Ed. I owe you one."

"No, I think we're good. What we went through with our sister's boyfriend, Stryke? We're good."

They'd battled demons intent on summoning a demon prince from Beneath. Ed had been involved until he'd learned his involvement could harm family, so he'd withdrawn. Yeah, the demon had a conscience and that made him twenty times more favorable than any other demon Kir had met.

"I'll call you when I get a location," Ed said. "Give me twenty-four hours." The phone clicked off just as the front doorbell rang.

Bea answered the door and couldn't help but say, "Damn."

Both men standing on the stoop looked at one another, then back at her. They both had long black hair, dark eyes, narrow frames with muscles that didn't stop, and one sported many tattoos. Lanky and sexy, they wore their clothes as if someone had tossed the fabric at them and it clung to muscles for dear life.

"Sorry. It's not every day tall, dark and handsome shows up at my door," Bea offered. "Times two. You must be the Jones brothers. Kir didn't tell me you were twins."

"Is that a problem?" one of them offered.

"Oh, no. No, no, no." By the blessed Norns, these boys were hot. "I'm Bea. Kir's wife."

"I'm Certainly Jones," the one with an elaborately tattooed hand said, "and this is my brother Thoroughly."

"Mercy."

"Call us CJ and TJ," Thoroughly said. Bea decided he was slightly more built than the other and maybe a little taller? "Is Kir in?"

"Yep." Bea took in the dark gorgeousness of it all as the men awaited an invite to enter. But as soon as they stepped inside, then she'd no longer have them all to herself, so…

"Bea?" Kir's hand slid around her waist, reminding her of her attachment.

"Right," she said. "That's me. Bea. The chick married to the werewolf. So not interested in a dark witch sandwich—er, won't you two come inside?"

"What's up with you?" Kir whispered at her ear as they led the twins into the living room.

"You didn't tell me our guests were twins."

"Is that a problem?"

"Never. Nope. Double the sexy? I can deal. Here we are, gentleman witches. Have a seat."

Bea sat in the middle of the couch and gestured that the Jones brothers sit on either side of her. Until her husband grabbed her hand and pulled her to stand beside him.

"Sit down, guys," Kir said. "Whiskey?"

"Always," Certainly said. He and his brother sat on the couch. CJ pulled up a leg and propped an ankle across his knee. TJ scanned the room.

Bea tried to figure the logistics of squeezing herself between the two of them, but there wasn't much space... The brush of her husband's arm along hers straightened her and she saw him gesture toward the kitchen.

"Right! Drinks. Be right back."

She rushed off to play the domestic goddess that would please her husband. And impress two sexy witches.

An hour later, the men nursed the dregs of the whiskey bottle Kir had opened, and Bea sat on the arm of Kir's easy chair, having forgone the libations. Whiskey was too strong. She preferred wine but had been too curious to pour herself a goblet.

She'd taken in the brothers and had spent stolen moments looking at CJ's tattoos. One at his neck looked like some kind of language she wasn't familiar with. The entire left hand was covered, including his palm. At his opposite wrist it looked like a big *V* and she wondered what lay beneath the clothes. More tattoos, for sure. The witch's elaborate ink made the violet sidhe markings on her feet seem insignificant.

"So the only way to Daemonia is with a blood sacrifice." Kir repeated Thoroughly's suggestion. "How is that done? Have either of you tried it?"

Thoroughly, a man of no tattoos that Bea could determine, cast a dark glance toward his brother, who offered a sheepish shrug.

"I've been there," CJ offered. "And I will never do that again. I came back with passengers."

"Demons?" Bea's eyes widened.

CJ nodded. "It was not pretty. I wouldn't suggest a werewolf or a faery venture into Daemonia. The landscape is brutal."

"But if the werewolf wanted to go there," Kir insisted, "how would this blood sacrifice be made?"

CJ sighed. "You need vampires. Lots of them. Drink the blood from the heart of a vamp daily, for thirty consecutive days."

"Yuck." Bea clasped her throat, and she felt Kir's hand nudge her thigh. "What? That's awful. The last thing I would consider is to ask you to kill to get to my mother."

"Not like the city doesn't have vampires to spare," CJ said. "But if you so much as miss one day, you have to restart the thirty-day cycle. If all else fails, you need a mass killing and all the ash from those vamps. Thirty vamps in one day will do."

This was too terrible to listen to. And the men were discussing it as calmly and rationally as if they were planning a shopping trip. Bea saw nothing attractive about the twins now. Dark magic? Ew.

"If you'll excuse me." She wandered out of the room, aiming for the upstairs bedroom.

"You all right, Bea?" Kir called.

"Yep. Just had my fill of horror stories for the night. Nice meeting you, CJ and TJ!"

They called back to her, but she was already at the top of the stairs and aimed for the bed, where she landed face-down with a groan.

"Guess we won't be going after my mother after all."

Which, all things considered, was probably the better option. Bea had never dreamed there was a possibility her mother could be demon. She didn't know what to think about that beyond her obvious disgust.

And then she coiled in on herself and felt a teardrop splatter her cheek.

Kir said goodbye to the twins, but only after asking them what they knew about V. Neither knew much, but CJ suspected that it made sense that demons would involve themselves with werewolves. They needed the muscle to wrangle the vampires who would provide their product.

As the witches drove off, Kir's phone rang. Ed had a location. The V-hubs moved often, so he suggested Kir check it out immediately.

Casting a glance up the stairs, he listened for movement from Bea. Had she already gone to bed? It was only ten in the evening. "Bea? I'm going to head out with Jacques for a bit. Business."

"Uh-huh."

"You okay?"

"Are the witches gone?" she called down.

"Yes." He smirked. She'd been hot for the both of them until their true natures had been revealed. Served her right for mooning over them like a lovesick puppy. "I hate you?" he tried as he stood at the bottom of the stairs.

"I hate you, too," she called down, but softly. "I'll see you when you get home, big boy."

"Don't wait up. This could take a while."

Half an hour later, Kir checked the salt blade tucked

at his belt and secured the stake at his hip. He glanced at Jacques. His partner gave the ready nod. The hub was in the Bois de Boulogne, a huge city park that centuries ago had once served as a festive place to see and be seen, hold parties and entertain one's desires with whores. It hadn't changed much. Only the shadows beyond the archery range in the Jardin d'Acclimatation were what drew them both now.

"This section is a kids' park," Kir said as they strolled across the manicured grass and left the safety of the last streetlight. "I can't believe they'd operate so close."

"That shed." Jacques pointed to a brick building with paper coating the inside of the windows. The door hung open. "You go ahead and lead, buddy."

Smirking, because he sensed Jacques's unease, Kir walked ahead. Very few times had he been aware of Jacques wanting to turn tail and run. Must be the spooky atmosphere. Approaching carefully, salt blade drawn, Kir stepped up to the open door. He didn't scent anything beyond the stale, greasy odor of fried foods and animal droppings from the nearby zoo. Not a hint of sulfur. Or vampire blood, for that matter.

Stepping up to the door, he peered inside the empty shed and, with an inhale, made a sensory appraisal.

"What do you see?"

"Abandoned," Kir confirmed, and Jacques joined his side. "But maybe..."

Another sniff detected sulfur, faint and distant. "They were here."

He strode inside the shed, which was empty save for a few wood shelves on one wall and a couple of rusted chains hanging near a dirt-smeared window. He could see well enough without a light. Something glinted on the floor.

He bent and picked up the necklace chain and immediately hissed.

"What is it, man? Silver?"

"No." It had the faintest scent of— "I, uh, thought it was something else. It's evidence, though."

He tucked the chain in his pocket, not wanting to look it over too closely with Jacques watching. Because he didn't need to study it overlong. He recognized the iron circle pendant. Kir had seen his father wear this very chain and iron circlet when he was younger.

Chapter 15

Days later Kir couldn't ignore Bea's casual comments about wanting to help locate her mother. She wanted to find her. If she did find her mother, would that be like admitting she was one of The Wicked? He didn't understand that but could guess demons were as reviled in Faery as they were in his heart.

On the other hand, never having answers could drive her bonkers.

Bea would attempt witch magic to summon her mother in some manner. Kir suspected she would have no luck, what with her waning glamour, so he allowed her to play with the simple magical items Certainly had dropped by. The dark witch had promised she wouldn't hurt herself or open any voids to other realms with the stuff. He also suggested to Kir it required an actual witch to work witch magic, so…

It kept her busy while he was at work, and she'd not asked about his going to Daemonia since. The idea of sacrificing thirty vampires to gain access to the demon realm did not sit well with Kir. On the other hand, he lost no love for vampires. But he was not a murderer.

There had to be another means. And maybe Bea was on the right track. If the word could be put out that she was looking for her mother, maybe that word would somehow find its way to Sirque and she would come to her daughter.

On the other hand, Sirque had abandoned her daughter. Kir suspected she wouldn't come rushing in with hugs and kisses if she did hear about Bea's attempts.

How else could he make his wife happy? They'd been married three months, and they'd grown close. They had sex nearly every day, and it was now more making love than sex. They enjoyed both. The only thing that could make life any better was if Bea was truly accepted into his pack. But after Jacques had let it slip about Kir's mother and Bea, he wasn't so sure that was possible.

Kir had not asked his mother about how she felt about Bea. Hadn't seen Madeline in weeks. And, okay, so he had a certain level of respect for his mother that wouldn't allow him to disrespect her. So his avoiding her was probably his means to avoiding the greater issue about whether or not she could ever like his wife.

Jacques was actually pulling a shift watching the faery portal today because Jean-Louis had missed his shift. The guy wasn't exactly sick, but they did suspect he was more anxious about his wife, who was due to give birth any day now. Jacques hadn't minded; he was interested in the portal, and knowing that his turn at the hunt in Faery was the next full moon, he'd eagerly volunteered.

Kir hadn't gotten a chance for the hunt yet, but he'd been too busy to care. While the hunt would serve his werewolf the adrenaline rush it required and satisfy it on a feral level, he didn't need to bring down a small animal and tear it to shreds to satisfy any physical need his body had. It was just a bonus. A bonus he would accept when his turn came up.

He was actually glad Jacques wouldn't be accompanying him today, because the place he had to visit, he wanted to go to alone. And face the man alone. His father.

He eyed the necklace he'd found in the abandoned shed. Too familiar. And though it had been years since he'd spoken face-to-face with his father, the faintest tendril of his scent lingered about the chain.

Was Colin Sauveterre in pack Royaume? He didn't want to believe his father could be involved in the V trafficking, but if Colin was still involved with a demoness, anything was possible. The last time Kir had spoken to him—eight years ago?—he was still seeing Ed's mother, Sophie. Things could have changed since then.

Kir hoped they had and that Colin wasn't involved with demons or selling V.

Should he have asked Ed to come along with him today? When they'd initially found each other after Colin had told Kir about his half brother, they'd shared little about family life and more about casual stuff, best local bars, things they preferred in women, cars. But over the years Ed had dropped info about Colin and Sophie. That they were living in the 12th arrondissement. He visited them sometimes but not often.

Kir had listened with a sinking heart. Ed had a better relationship with his father than he did. Perhaps that was the real reason he couldn't embrace his half brother without judgment.

Now he pulled the Lexus up in front of the small house in the 12th that edged the 11th arrondissement and sat not too far from the Port de Plaisance de Paris-Arsenal that fed north from the Seine. Mere blocks from the Opéra

Bastille, the neighborhood was strictly humans. And the one werewolf.

His father had once said the best place to hide was in plain sight.

Kir agreed with that. To a point. He existed alongside humans and so had to walk among them, but he knew it was wiser to hide his truths than invite the retaliation the humans would reap should they begin to believe in such creatures.

Approaching the purple door that fronted the narrow two-story his father lived in, Kir picked up the scent of sulfur. And his heart dropped. This was going to be the toughest visit of his life.

Bea found the pack compound with ease because Kir had driven by it many a time and, once, he'd brought her in when he'd needed to talk to his principal. Etienne was a nice man, and when around him she'd sensed no hatred from him regarding her being a half-breed. But at the time she had only been inside the compound for minutes and hadn't been introduced to anyone else.

Kir had told her he'd be in and out because the investigation required he do a lot of footwork, but if she was hungry around noon she should stop in for lunch. She'd bagged a meal she'd made herself. Salami sandwiches and fresh-cut cantaloupe. She'd spread mustard on the bread, which she hoped Kir liked. A sprinkle of cinnamon over the mustard had added a sweetness that satisfied her taste buds.

She was admitted into the compound with a nod from the woman who sat in the lobby. Bea was pretty sure her name was Violet. The plain brick building could be mistaken as a business that mortals might visit. Though there were no signs indicating what it might be, Kir said a few humans did wander in on occasion. Thus, the receptionist was positioned out front to redirect them elsewhere.

"Is Kir in?" Bea asked as she strolled around Violet's desk toward the hallway that led to the inner sanctum.

"I'm not sure. I didn't see him leave, so you might get lucky and find him. I like the color of your dress."

Bea clutched the salmon swish of skirt that went all the way past her knees and didn't cling. "Thanks!" She'd specifically chosen something not low cut and had worn flat-soled sandals in anticipation of running into the monster-in-law—er, mother-in-law.

Bea couldn't help a giggle at her moniker for Madeline. She could entirely understand why Kir's father had felt the need to leave the marriage if she was such a stick-in-the-mud. But he'd left her for a demon?

Interesting. She wondered how Kir felt about that coincidence. His father had apparently loved a demon enough to end his marriage. And now the son was married to a possible half demon. That fact must kill him.

Bea shook her head. "Don't go there. I will never be to Kir what Madeline's rival was to his father." Whatever that was.

She spun into Kir's small office and found it empty. No handsome wolf sitting behind the desk, sleeves pushed to his elbows to expose muscled forearms. She'd entirely expected a scene out of one of those TV shows with all the letters—like *CSI* or *NCIS*, or whatever it was. Her shoulders sank. She set the paper bag on his desk and sat on his spinning chair. Maybe he'd show if she waited. That would give her time to snoop.

Kir knocked on his father's front door. In his pants pocket, he clutched the chain and pendant he'd found in the amusement park shed. He didn't want to do this. He'd avoided this confrontation for years. Since he'd been eight years old?

The door opened and the man he could never forgive for abandoning him smiled widely, his pale blue eyes crinkling in joy. "It's been so long, Kirnan. Come in, come in!"

The old man looked the same, as he probably would for another hundred years before time started to show with wrinkles and gray hair. There were days Kir envied the humans for their short life spans. They only had to endure family for so long.

And then he regretted having that thought. He didn't hate his father. Their relationship was simply distant and strained. It seemed they never had much to talk about. And it always felt like something new and awkward every time. So long as he didn't flaunt his demon girlfriend in Kir's presence, he could deal.

Hell, really? No, not really.

Colin Sauveterre led him into a bright living room with comfy leather sofa and chairs. A big-screen TV hung on one wall and artwork depicting odd geometrical designs mastered the two parallel walls. He'd never taken his father for an art lover. And the delicate glass vase on the coffee table? Hmm…a woman's touch.

Kir clenched his fingers into fists.

"It's always too long between visits, Kir," Colin said as he gestured Kir sit in one of the chairs.

Really? It had been nearly a decade since he'd last seen the man in person. "You do know where to find me, Dad," he offered, finding it difficult to release his fists.

"The compound? I'm never sure if your mother will be there."

"You also know where I live. Mom rarely comes by my house."

"Again, I can't risk that encounter. Besides, I don't want to intrude on your life. I know how you feel about me."

Hearing it spoken so matter-of-factly tightened the muscles at the back of Kir's neck even as it splayed his fingers into grasping claws. But he wasn't about to feel guilty for real feelings. Maybe.

"It's good to see you now. What brings you here?" Colin sat while Kir remained standing.

"I'm on an investigation for the enforcement team," he said.

"Another pack engaging in the blood games?" Colin wondered, then shook his head. "Vampires are certainly not my favorite breed, but that doesn't give me, or any other wolf, the right to harm them for fun and profit."

Yes, Colin had instilled in Kir that sense of honor, that all breeds were equal. And, yet, Kir had not followed that teaching after learning his father had left his mother for a demon. A child's heart is a fragile thing and not something that could be easily mended.

"It's something different this time," he said. Crossing his arms over his chest, he strode to the window to scan outside. There was no yard to speak of and the next building was an arm's reach away. "You know about V-hubs, Dad?"

Colin shook his head and stroked his Vandyke-style beard. "No. Should I? Why are you here if you say you are on an investigation? Am *I* under suspicion? Son, you know how I feel about the blood games."

"Dad, do you recognize this?"

Kir held the chain with the iron circle before him. His father gasped, then caught himself and stood.

"Looks like something I once owned," Colin said with a shrug. "Lost it, though. There must be any number of such things out there. Certainly I know it was not an original. Are you accusing me of something, Kir?"

"This necklace—" he set the chain on the coffee table "—was found at an abandoned V-hub. An ever-moving, mobile hotspot where V is sold."

"V?"

Was he really going to play it this way? Kir knew that was the very necklace his father used to wear all the time. Because it still bore his scent.

"V is vampire blood. Demons buy it, or so I'm learning. They drink directly from the vamp and get some kind of euphoric high from the infusion of human bloods mixed in the vamp's system. Jacques and I talked to one of those vampires who managed to escape. He told us it was demons, but we also have reason to believe a pack could be involved."

"And you are accusing my pack of such a crime? Pack Royaume is discreet and small. They follow me. I would never condone such a crime as harming another for profit. You know that!"

He did know his father possessed that kind of honor. Or so he once had. And Colin had just verified for him that he was in pack Royaume. How had a lone wolf managed to be accepted by another pack? Kir knew nothing about the man now.

At that moment the front door opened and in breezed a woman who pulled a blue silk scarf from her long brown hair. Her eyes brightened at the sight of Kir and he nodded to her, even as his spine stiffened in disgust.

"Sophie," he acknowledged his father's girlfriend. A demoness. Edamite's mother. The reason his father had abandoned him when he was eight.

"Kir, it's been so long. I'm so pleased you've stopped by. Isn't it wonderful, Colin?" She strode over to his father and kissed him on the cheek. "I won't bother you two. You must have so much to talk about. I'll bring in some lemonade, yes? Oh!" She bent to pick up the necklace from the coffee table. "You see, Colin? Here it is. I told you it would show up. He thought I'd lost it," she said to Kir as she strode out into the kitchen.

Kir swung a look to his father, whose jaw was tight.

"I think it's time you leave, boy," Colin said. The scent of his rising aggression grew obvious.

Fists tight again, Kir faced down his father. "Tell me what's going on, Dad."

"Trust me when I say I have no clue. But I will. Soon enough." They maintained a tense stare. Kir wasn't about to back down. So he was surprised when his father did. "Please. Will you leave me to talk to Sophie?"

He shouldn't. Sophie had just put herself at the scene of the crime by claiming the necklace. But Kir sensed his father was telling him the truth and that he didn't know what was going on.

"I'll have to keep an eye on the house," he said. "Standard procedure."

"You are your mother's child, Kir. Always playing by the rules. The pack is everything. Dare to take a chance on life, will you? I promise it will reward you richly."

Kir strode to the door and gripped the doorknob. "I have taken a chance. I was married recently. Part of an arranged agreement between the pack and the Unseelie king."

"You allowed yourself to be forced into marriage? How is that taking a chance on life, boy?"

"It's working out well." And he smiled, because Bea was one awesome thing in his life right now. That chance he'd taken? It had paid off. "I'll be in touch soon. Know that you and Sophie will be tracked wherever you go."

Colin heaved out a sigh. "I'll come to you if there's anything you need to know. I promise you that."

Kir nodded and left his father's house. If Sophie was running the V-hubs behind Colin's back, and utilizing his pack to do so, he certainly hoped Colin would do the right thing and walk away from her.

At the sound of a female rapping her long fingernails on the desktop, Bea sat up from snooping in the bottom drawer of Kir's desk.

"Uh, monst—er, Madeline." She kicked the drawer shut and clutched the paper bag with Kir's lunch in it.

The woman's blond hair curved over one eye, giving her a smoking temptress look that did not jibe with her high-collared, all-business navy blue pantsuit. "Are you rifling through my son's private things?"

"Uh, no." Well, yes, but. "Just blank paper and envelopes in there."

"You were looking for something, you filthy faery."

"I—" Bea snapped her mouth shut. The look in Madeline's eye was too familiar. Malrick had used it often. Condemning. Hateful. She wanted to cringe and hide in the shadows, but none were available in the bright office. "I brought Kir some lunch," she managed, though it took all her courage not to cry.

"Smells like mustard," Madeline said. "Kir hates mustard. You don't pay attention to your husband, do you? What are you good for? Who let you into the compound?"

"I…uh…" Could she run?

"Give me that." Madeline snatched the bag. "If Kir smells this, he'll retch. He's out on an enforcement call, so you should leave."

"I was going to wait—er, yes." Madeline stepped aside, a hand to her hip. With escape in view, Bea wasn't about to stay and participate in a losing battle. She slipped out the doorway and scampered down the hallway.

All she could think was Kir had the mustard in his icebox so he must like it. And then she wanted to unfurl her wings and fly swiftly down the hallway, but with a look over her shoulder she spied Madeline watching her retreat, the lunch bag crushed in her grip.

Violet called goodbye to her as she ran out the front door. Racing down the street, Bea's tears slid across her cheeks.

Kir found Bea curled up on the easy chair, gazing out the window at the rain streaming down the glass. She had clothes on. He had to admit that was a little disappointing.

When he sat on the chair arm, she sighed heavily.

"Bad day?" he asked.

"Terrible. I went to the compound to bring you lunch."

"You did?" He kissed the crown of her head. "I'm sorry—if I had known, I would have waited for you. I probably just missed you."

"Yeah, well, your mother didn't miss me. In fact, she wishes to miss me a lot. She's just…not nice."

"Give her time."

"You say that like it's the easiest thing in the world to do."

"I know it's not. Parents can be…difficult."

He slid onto the chair and managed to pull her onto his lap in the process. Bea hugged him and tilted her head against his chest. "Tell me about your day, my big strong wolf."

"It was probably as challenging as yours was."

"Oh, I doubt that. But, then, mustard wouldn't have killed you."

"Mustard?"

Bea sighed again. "Just tell me about your day?"

"Jacques and I have been investigating a case that involves a pack and demons selling vampire blood. It's complicated. But our investigation led me to Colin Sauveterre today."

She lifted her head and met his gaze. "That's the same surname as yours."

"My father. He's..." Kir shook his head. "I don't know if he's involved, but I think his girlfriend is. She's demon. I don't like her. Never have."

"Because she is the reason your father left you when you were little?"

He nodded. Swallowed. "If she is going behind my father's back..."

The stroke of Bea's fingers over his beard gentled his growing anxiety and Kir bowed his head against her hair. He didn't want to talk about work or his father. He didn't want to think about what would happen if he learned Colin was really involved.

"Can I get lost in you?" he murmured. "Forever?"

"I will certainly let you try. Kiss me, lover. Let me distract your thoughts from dire things."

He tilted his head and she met his mouth in a firm and lingering kiss. It tingled and warmed and it didn't move or try to open his mouth. It didn't have to. Their connection was solid. And Kir knew he had found something wonderful in his pretty faery wife.

Chapter 16

A week later Kir hadn't heard from his father. He'd told Bea that could be a good thing or a really bad thing. The watch they'd put on Colin's house hadn't turned up anything suspicious, which only made Kir nervous. Bea felt awful for him that his father may be the very criminal he sought. She hoped it wasn't so. But all she could do was hug him when he came home at night and make love to him before they fell asleep in each other's arms.

Now she sat on the end of the bed. The house was quiet. Kir was away at work. Afternoon sunlight filtered through the window in cool shadows. A weariness she'd never before felt gave her reason to draw her senses inward to do a sort of mental check on her body. And…she sensed something new.

So could that be the reason that drinking Kir's blood from a goblet hadn't seemed to perk her up? Why she wasn't able to fully access her faery magic to make the flowers grow? Because she was…

Bea spread a palm over her belly. It was flat, yet she felt a tickle within, in her very center. And while she'd never been in this condition before, she sensed a certain *knowing.* Something beyond herself had entered her life. And it stirred within her.

Was she?

She got up and padded into the bathroom to study her naked profile in the mirror. To imagine having Kir's child was— She'd never given it thought. But to consider it now made her smile.

His species thrived on family. And Kir would want more than anything to have a big brood. Could she give him that family?

Her smile fell and she turned away from the mirror, shaking her head. "It could be faery. Or could be wolf. It could be half and half. Or…it might be demon. He could never handle that."

Could she?

"Hey, Short Stick!"

Kir tromped up the stairs. Stopping in the doorway to the bathroom, he leaned there, hooking a thumb in a belt loop, and looked her over. "I will never get tired of coming home to find a naked faery waiting for me."

She stretched out her hand and he went to her, taking it. The bond mark glowed brightly, and it gave her the confidence she would need to tell him her suspicion.

Walking him backward until his heels met the tub, and Kir sat on the edge of the tub, Bea stood over him and drew her fingers down the side of his face, tracing the line of his beard and back up to his lips, which were warm and soft.

"You're such a fine man. So handsome. I've even grown to love your beard."

He stroked his chin. "You didn't like it?"

"Not initially. But now I couldn't imagine you without it. You're so good to me. We don't belong together, you know."

"Why not?"

"Would you have ever chosen a half-breed faery if you'd had the choice?"

"I wasn't given a choice. And I'm not at all displeased with the results."

"Really? You and your short stick?"

"Bea, what's wrong?" He took both her hands in his. "I thought you didn't mind me calling you that?"

"Well, it means you got something you didn't want."

"Right. But when I say it now, I say it because I'm glad I still have it."

"You are?"

He clasped her hand and turned it to display the glowing bond mark. "I don't think this would lie."

"No, it wouldn't. Oh, Kir." Her heart lightened. Her husband's regard felt like the sun on her soul. The one thing she'd never thought to possess was now hers. "I'm so happy. Are you happy?"

"Very. Can you be happy even if we never find your mother?"

"With you by my side, nothing else matters. Oh, but…" She sat on his lap and took his hand to place on her stomach. "There's something I have a feeling about."

He kissed her shoulder and nuzzled his nose along her skin. A delicious shiver traced her skin. "What is it?"

"This." She pressed her palm over his hand. "I'm pretty sure… I feel new life in there."

Kir sat up straighter. His arm and chest muscles flexed with excitement. He pressed a palm firmly to her stomach. "Really? Are you sure? How do you know?"

"I'm not positive. It's a knowing."

"Knowings are good. Right?"

She shrugged. "Would it be okay with you if I were pregnant?"

He kissed her so soundly she toppled backward and Kir had to catch her. Then he lost his balance and they both slid into the bathtub, giggling and laughing. With Kir's legs sticking up high and Bea pressed against him, they made out in the tub like teenagers.

And she knew from that moment forward, everything was going to be blessed.

Everything was not blessed. Morning sickness was a bitch that Bea wanted to beat with a club and toss into the river Seine. It had been two weeks since she'd told Kir, and her suspicions had been confirmed when she'd woken two mornings ago and rushed into the bathroom to toss her cookies.

She didn't like cookies and much preferred cake, but that's what Kir had called it when he'd heard her.

The room spun as she wandered back to bed and sort of rolled into a collapse onto the sheets. The roses Kir had brought her last night sat on the nightstand and their fragrance was so strong it made her woozy. They must be pregnant faery kryptonite.

"Must get rid of pretty things," she muttered as she swiped for the flowers. But she felt too weak to manage the move that would propel her across the bed toward the flowers.

Instead, she pulled the sheets over her head and groaned in misery.

Kir felt Bea relax as he worked his hands over her muscles and skin. He'd spent leisurely time on her back, thighs and ankles, and now she had turned over and he kissed her belly. It was still flat. She probably wouldn't show for months. Kir couldn't wait to be a father.

No matter what the child would become? his conscious tossed out there.

Their child could be werewolf. Their child could be faery. It could be half and half. Any of those he would adore. But as for the demon blood creeping into the mix, he wasn't sure how to accept that. His father's involvement with a demon had tainted his perception of the species. And now, though he'd put a tail on Sophie for weeks and had yet to turn up anything related to a V-hub, he still had his suspicions of her. She was not to be trusted. Because she was demon.

How to accept a demon child? What if it had red eyes?

Just because the person had a certain species' blood in their system didn't make them inevitably evil. He knew that because his wife was perfect, even though she still felt she was not because of her mother's black blood. Rationale always sounded wise and smart.

The key was to embrace that rationale.

"What are you thinking about, Long Stick?"

"What did you call me?" He rolled over on the bed to stretch out alongside her, smoothing a palm across her bare stomach.

"Well, if you get to call me Short Stick, then I can call you Long Stick." She snuggled her face up to his and kissed him. "And it's not your height I'm referring to." A squeeze of her hand about his cock hardened his erection instantly.

"Heh. I actually prefer when you call me big boy."

"Well, that's a given."

"You want to take the big boy out for some play?"

She slid her hand inside his pants and teased the head of his cock. "I thought you'd never ask. Your hands all over me for the past half hour has been great, but you know it's been a slow, simmering trip to must have, must need, right now, baby, right now."

"I like the sound of that."

She shoved down his pants and climbed on top of him.

"How long can we continue to have sex? It won't hurt the baby?" he asked.

"Please. I think he is the size of a pea right now."

"You think it's a boy?" His grin was irrepressible. To imagine raising a boy and showing him how to play sports and fix cars made him smile widely. "I'd like a boy. Or a girl. I'd like many of both."

"Many?" Bea smirked. "I suspected as much. But, yes, I do think it's a boy."

Straddling him, she slid his cock inside her and Kir groaned and pulsed his hips gently, easing himself in and out of her heat.

"Want to think of names?" she asked.

"Not while I'm having sex with my son's mother," he said, his jaw tight. "Later. Yes, faster. Ride me, Bea."

She rode him to a swift orgasm that saw them both crying out and then snuggling together in a sweaty yet blissful embrace.

Striding through the living room, his destination work, Kir bumped the book on CGI fantasy paintings from the coffee table and picked it up. He loved to browse fine art and was always surprised when an artist got the depiction of a paranormal being right. Were there humans in the know? Or was it that collective consciousness that, sooner or later, imbued the human imagination with a truth they would always believe a fantasy?

He hoped so.

Paging through, he found the one piece that disturbed him. The creature was a boy with wings perched on a fallen log in the forest. Small horns jutted from each temple and its eyes were red.

"Demon faery," Kir muttered, then slammed the book shut.

Outside a horn honked. Jacques waited. And Kir put the book on the highest shelf. He'd had enough of fantasy for now. His child would be wolf.

It had to be or the pack would reject it.

Later that afternoon Kir joined Jacques on a stakeout of a suspected V-hub in the murky streets of Chinatown in the 14th arrondissement. The windows were plastered inside with old newspapers. There was no visible doorknob but, instead, a security camera above the door.

They watched for hours, noting that only two demons entered and left, both looking not high but maybe… freaked? Was it the sunlight? Could be, Kir deduced, that drinking vamp blood would do that to a demon. Vamps could go out in the sunlight without instantly frying to a crisp, but they wouldn't last for long.

"Did I tell you my turn at the hunt didn't happen?" Jacques suddenly asked. He set his coffee cup in the cup holder and twisted his gaze toward Kir. "Something wrong with the portal. Couldn't get through."

"Really? That's strange. The pack have problems with it before?"

"No one has complained. Dad's trying to contact the Faery liaison to see what was up. Might have been a snag on the Faery side. Who knows? I was jonesing for the hunt, though. Man, I just want to tear something limb from limb."

His friend's macabre desires didn't startle Kir. It was innate to their species, that feeling of freedom, of living wild and free of mortal control.

Jacques suddenly sat up straight and pulled the keys from the ignition, cutting off the low radio. "Check it out."

The demon they tracked coming out of the V-hub was Sophie. She was even wearing the iron circlet around her neck as she scanned the street, and her eyes fell onto Kir.

"She's been in there the whole time. Didn't see her walk in earlier. Must be the big cheese. We taking her in?" Jacques asked. He already had the salt blade in hand.

Kir exhaled long and hard. He hadn't wanted it to be her. His dad did deserve some happiness. Damn her. Damn the demon.

Then he nodded. "Yes."

Chapter 17

Bea swung the katana sword through the living room, deftly avoiding the terra-cotta vase that she couldn't guess why Kir owned. The man wasn't much for decorations, though he did have some old lanterns and a chest that looked as though it had been tossed from the back of a carriage while the highwayman had made his escape.

She swung again, this time bringing the tip of the sword oh-so-close to the vase. Just a breath closer…

"No." Her imagination blurred away the expectant display of vase shards scattering at her powerful strike. "He must own it for a reason."

She quickly shifted her hips and jumped around to face an imaginary attacker, shouting out in warning as her sword connected with gut. The attacker fell. Bea raised her arms in triumph.

"Can't sneak up on me. No way."

She tapped the floor with the tip of the sword as she

decided what next to do today. She was beginning to understand that work, which kept Kir away and busy, was probably a good thing. There was only so much a faery could do in the house all day without craving a hobby or venturing out into the city. And with the pregnancy making her faery magic weak, gardening was out of the question.

Shopping, though…

"Too risky with dogs out there." She shivered. "Unless I had a driver who could take me from store to store? Hmm…"

She'd have to ask Kir about that one.

The television was interesting, but when she sat to watch a show she found she tended to remain sitting, and ended up watching things that didn't even interest her. It was a bad habit, so she strolled into the kitchen. She could try to make some food for her adoring husband. The stuff he brought home in bags or had delivered was excellent, but…

He had mentioned his mother's home-cooked meals. On more than one occasion.

"I'll give it a go!"

Scampering into the kitchen, she tugged out the recipe book that Kir kept tucked beside the stove and paged through it.

Supper was interesting.

Kir sat across from Bea at the dining table. He'd set the bag he'd brought home to surprise her in the hallway after smelling the food. One surprise at a time. And anything Bea did for him would always take precedence. Inordinately excited to watch him dig into the meal she had made for him, his wife wiggled on the chair opposite him. She'd made the food herself. It had taken her all afternoon. She'd followed the directions in the recipe book and was so proud.

He bit into the crunchy morsel that was supposed to be garlic bread, and— Mercy, that had a lot of garlic. He gagged but kept his expression stoic as he quickly grabbed the water to chase down the tear-inducing bite.

"You like?" she asked eagerly.

Kir's nod got stuck in a head shake. "That'll keep the vamps away."

"Right? Try the spaghetti. I didn't want to touch the meat, so the sauce is meatless. I chopped tomatoes all day! Well, okay, maybe like an hour. But it felt like all day using that little knife from the drawer. Should have used the katana."

"You didn't?"

"No, of course not."

He twirled his fork into the strands of spaghetti, noting they were not limp and didn't coil about his fork. Rather, they rolled on the plate because they were not even close to al dente.

Thinking conversation was a necessary distraction, he asked, "So what compelled you to cook?"

"I'm not sure. Maybe I'm nesting?"

"Makes sense."

Fearing the worst, but unwilling to let Bea down, he cut through the spaghetti with a knife, then forked in a bite. He chewed the hard noodles, nodding and forcing a smile. The sauce did give the crunchy noodles a bit of slickness.

"What do you think of the sauce?"

He swallowed a quick draft of water. "You do like to use garlic."

"I wasn't sure if a clove was the whole thing or just one of those sections that breaks off, so to be safe, I used the whole thing. Is it too much?"

He winced and slugged down another shot of icy water. "You'll know later."

"What does that mean?"

"It depends on whether or not you'll be able to kiss me."

He forked in another bite. It didn't taste awful, just… hard and garlicky. He'd eat it. Because he couldn't imagine pushing the plate away and seeing the disappointment on Bea's face.

"You're not eating?" he asked. She had only a piece of garlic bread on her plate and a puddle of tomato sauce to dip it in. "Still feeling sick?"

She nodded. "And not just in the mornings. It's hard to keep food down some days. I hope this passes soon."

"Maybe you should see a doctor. The pack has one, but…ah, I don't think he's trained to work with faeries. There must be someone in FaeryTown."

She shrugged. "I'll think about it. I know it's normal stuff for pregnant women."

Wincing, and downing the remaining glass of water, he pushed back from the table and went around to kiss his wife. "Thank you for the amazing meal." Then he gave her a big, sloppy kiss. He pulled her up into his arms; she wrapped her legs about his torso.

"Oh, you're right," she said. "Garlic!"

"Ha!" He kissed her again, and this time dipped his tongue across hers.

"Kir, no! That's really strong!"

He blew on her, teasing her with the smell, and then bent to nip at her breast, which, he had noticed, was feeling much firmer lately, maybe a little bigger.

"You can taste all you like, big boy, but no more kisses until you brush your teeth."

"You think your breath is so sweet?" He kissed her again, and even while she squirmed, she pulled him closer.

Enough of this unpalatable meal—he had something

more pleasing in mind. Lifting Bea into his arms, Kir dashed out of the kitchen and toward the stairs.

"The dishes!" Bea called.

"They can wait. Ah, but I almost forgot." He veered back into the hallway and snatched the bag from the floor. "I have a surprise for you, too."

"Yay!"

He bounded up the stairs and laid his wife on the bed, tugging off her pants and pushing up her shirt.

"What about my surprise?"

"This can't wait," he said. "I think your spaghetti made me horny."

He kissed her breasts and then nuzzled a path down to her hard, swollen belly. He loved to rub his beard against it, to revel in her giggles. He rested his ear below her belly button.

"Hear anything?" she asked, her fingers massaging his scalp.

"Yep, he's saying, 'No more garlic! I'm melting!'"

She slapped his head playfully. "It's not a vampire, you wicked wolf."

"Right. Vamps aren't repelled by garlic anyway. Though we'd be hard-pressed to find a vamp who would not run from the two of us right now. Oh, I told everyone in the pack today about your being pregnant. They're very happy for us."

"Really? Even your mother?"

"Of course. Why wouldn't she be?"

Bea propped up on her elbows. "Kir, you know Madeline doesn't like me."

"Eh, my mother comes off as cold. You two haven't spent enough time together to get to know one another."

"Some things a person just knows will never happen. Like your mom liking me."

"She'll love our child."

"And that's supposed to be my consolation prize?"

"Give her time, Bea. She's used to being the queen of the family, you know? Right now she's second in rank to the pack principal's wife. And with me being married, well…"

"Do I threaten her? Because seriously?" She splayed her arms to indicate her petite size.

"Maybe a little. What woman could be good enough for her son?"

"Especially if that woman is a filthy faery."

"A what? Bea?"

"I don't want to talk about this. What I really want to do…" She sat up and pulled up his head by a scruff of his hair. "Is march you into the bathroom and put a toothbrush in your hand."

"You think so, Miss Garlic Breath?"

He inundated her with tickles to her hips and thighs and there under her breasts where she was really ticklish. His tongue laved and suckled at her, luring her into a purring acceptance, and then his mood shifted to playful again and Bea shrieked with laughter.

"My precious short stick, I adore you so much."

"Then let me look at the surprise!" she said between giggles.

"All right." He grabbed the bag and handed it to her. He'd picked it up this morning, before the stakeout. The last thing he wanted to talk about was taking Sophie in for questioning, something he wanted to put off as long as possible. "I was thinking about our son this morning. I couldn't stop myself when I walked near a baby store."

She pulled out a tiny blue T-shirt that had a wolf screen-printed on the front. It read I'm a Little Howler in French.

"Oh, blessed Norns, Kir, this is adorable!" She crushed

the T-shirt to her chest and sniffed back tears. “I have never been happier. Thank you,” she said. “For marrying me. And for not running when you probably could have.”

“If I had run, I might have never known such happiness as lying in your arms. You’re going to make a great mother, Bea.”

“You think so? I don’t have an example to know if I’ll be doing things right.”

“I’m guessing it’s an instinctual thing.”

“Kir, my mother’s instincts were to abandon me.”

He kissed her quickly to stop the train of thought that could threaten to bring them both to tears. “I adore you. The baby will adore you. That’s all that matters.”

Chapter 18

Madeline Sauveterre was gorgeous—and she knew it—and the epitome of class. Bea guessed she wore fitted black dresses and hats with brims that she could look up at you from underneath. She probably wore gloves for fancy occasions. Bea had seen an old movie on television and couldn't remember the actress's name, but Madeline had that same cosmopolitan style. And despite being nearly a century in human years, she looked as young as Bea and Kir did. The woman had aged well.

She'd stopped in for a visit this afternoon, and Bea, surprised as stones about that, led her into the kitchen and opened the fridge, because she couldn't think what else to do.

"I'm sure we have some of that fancy bottled water in here somewhere."

"Don't bother, dear. I've brought you some flowers."

The woman tugged out a bouquet of red roses from her

expansive Chanel bag and smiled that straight, false smile that Bea associated with serial killers—so she watched a lot of television; what else was there to do?

"Oh, they're so…red." And the scent poked sharply at her ultrasensitive nose.

"I'll put them in a vase for you, dear."

"Oh, you don't have to—"

Madeline found a vase in the cupboard and started playing with the bushy bouquet. Every time she swished a flower, it filled the kitchen with an overpowering heady scent. A scent that would normally invoke most to lean forward to draw in a deep breath.

Lost in the intrusively cloying perfume, Bea felt her stomach curdle. "I need to sit down."

"Not feeling well, dear?" Madeline adjusted the roses. She wouldn't stop playing with them.

"I'm sensitive to smells lately. Roses, in particular."

"Oh? That's too bad. Perhaps Kir did mention something about that to me." Heels clicking dully on the fieldstone floor, Madeline set the vase on the table right next to Bea. "But they are too pretty to toss, don't you think?"

Kir had told her roses made her ill? Nice monster-in-law. Not.

Bea hadn't the heart to tell her they gave her a woozy head. She'd toss them as soon as she left. Besides, it had been a kind gesture. Had Madeline changed her colors toward her? Maybe having Kir's baby would bring them closer together.

"So, Beatrice, how far along are you?"

"Not sure. Two or three months?"

"You've not been to a doctor?"

"I'm not sure there are faery doctors in the mortal realm."

"Nonsense. I'm sure we can find one in FaeryTown. I

can't believe you'd ignore the baby's health like that. But what should I expect? You are so…different."

And a filthy faery. Bea was surprised she hadn't dropped that one on her yet. No, she hadn't changed colors. How silly of her to even dream.

Oh, those roses. Her head was spinning so wildly she had to clutch the chair arm to not spill over the side.

"I wonder what the child will be," Madeline tossed out. "Kir never has told me what you are, exactly. You are a half-breed, of course. It's evident to look at your odd pink eyes. We've all assumed vampire." She said the word with enough vitriol to drown an entire tribe of vampires.

Bea shrugged. "If I were half vampire, would that be a problem?"

She was in no condition to have a conversation, let alone correct her mother-in-law that she could be something worse. Because if Kir held demons as foul because of his father's affair, then surely Madeline marked them as the most vile, unforgivable creatures to walk this realm.

"You are aware that if my son's child were born vampire he'd be banished from the pack?"

Bea dropped her mouth open. She hadn't been aware of that. What would they do to him if it were half demon?

"I didn't know that."

"Yes, it's true. We take our bloodlines very seriously. Keeping them pure is a must."

"Then why did Kir's principal allow him to marry a faery in the first place?"

"Etienne is a peculiar one. He never thinks things through. Consequences are never fore in that old wolf's mind. He saw a means to gain access to hunting grounds and…well." She dusted the air with a dismissive gesture. "Unfortunately, I was not consulted on the matter."

"I love your son, Madeline. He loves me. And we will

love our child unconditionally, no matter if he's werewolf, vampire, faery or a crazy mix of all three."

Madeline looked as if she smelled a dead fish. "So my son says. He's another who never looks to the consequences. A half-breed grandchild?" Madeline sniffed. "Unthinkable."

"Look, I know you don't like me— Oh." Bea reached out to grasp something in an attempt to steady her spinning head. "I really don't feel well. It's the morning sickness, which is more like all-day sickness. I need to get into bed. Prone is my favorite position lately."

"My son's bedroom is up the stairs, yes?"

Bea nodded. Normally, she'd unfurl her wings and flutter up to land in a sobbing heap on the bed, but she had to keep it together. The last thing her judgmental monster-in-law needed to see was the filthy faery in wings.

"Let me help you up, dear. Wouldn't want you to take a nasty fall."

Bea felt the woman support her across the back and she walked blindly down the hallway, trusting Madeline would help her up the stairs. Nausea crept up her throat and dizziness spun her head.

"I don't want to do anything to jeopardize Kir's position in the pack," Bea managed as the stairs moved slowly beneath her bare feet. "Really."

"Yes, well, it's too late for that, isn't it? You should have used birth control."

"But Kir wants children."

And how dare she suggest such a thing? They were married. It wasn't as though they had done something unforgivable by making a child together. On the other hand, giving Kir a demon child would not keep the bloodline pure. Stones.

Landing on the top stair, Bea sensed the bed—and a

much-needed collapse—loomed close. A renewed wave of rose perfume made her wobble—and Bea didn't feel Madeline's arm supporting her.

"Watch it, dear."

"Help me," Bea managed, before her equilibrium gave out and suddenly she was free-falling.

Her shoulder hit the stairs hard. She screamed. Her body rolled, taking each step painfully, as if her bones were being knocked out of their sockets. And then she lay sprawled on the floor at the base of the stairs. Warm ichor seeped from her nose.

The click of Madeline's heels sounded near her head. "Funny. I always thought faeries could fly."

And she walked away, arm swinging the single red rose she held. Her heels echoed in loud clicks until the front door closed, and… Bea blacked out.

Kir's phone rang as he walked on the sidewalk up to his house. It was Colin. He hadn't told him yet that he had taken Sophie into custody.

"Dad," he answered, and paused before the front door without opening it.

"Kir, she's gone. I haven't seen her in days. I don't know what's happened. I know I told you I'd call you with anything if I suspected she was dealing the V and… Oh, Kir."

"Is she, Dad?"

He sensed more than heard his father's reply. It sent a shiver up his spine. But, really, he'd caught Sophie at the scene of the crime. While no vampires had been found inside the hub at the time of arrest, the paraphernalia linking her to drawing blood from vampires had been there.

"We've taken her into custody," he provided because hearing his father weeping unnerved him.

"What?"

"We picked her up at a V-hub, Dad. I'm sorry, I forgot to call you. We're going to question her soon."

"Soon? What does that mean? You've had her for days? What are you waiting for? I have to talk to her."

"I will call you after we've questioned her. I promise."

"But, Kir—"

He couldn't do this. He didn't know how to show empathy toward his father. So Kir hung up and shoved the phone into his pocket. It hurt his heart a lot more than he expected it would.

"Bea!"

Bea came to and realized she was sitting up, supported by Kir's arms. She looked around. Had she been lying at the bottom of the staircase?

"Did you fall? What happened?" She could feel his fear and anxiety as his hand moved down her arm, giving her a few testing squeezes, and to her stomach, where his palm pressed as if to divine the heartbeat within. "You need to lie down."

He carried her up the stairs and laid her on the bed. Every bone ached, and she cried out as he set her down.

"What happened?" He touched her forehead, then rubbed the darkened ichor between his fingers. "You're bleeding from a cut above your eye. And your ichor is dark, not clear. You need a doctor."

"Not a wolf doctor," she said softly. "I'll be fine. Just… took a tumble."

"Down the stairs!"

Yes, thanks to Madeline. Had her monster-in-law pushed her? Bea had been too woozy to know for sure. The woman had been helping her to climb the stairs, her palm at the small of Bea's back, and then…it was not. And she remembered wobbling, reaching for something, anything to stop from falling. Madeline hadn't been there to catch her. And she had left her there at the bottom of the steps. Bea could not get the sound of the woman's high heels clicking away from her out of her brain.

"It was..."

She couldn't tell Kir his mother had been here. He loved his mom and respected her. And without full knowledge of what had really happened, Bea didn't dare make accusations.

"Morning sickness. You know how it makes me dizzy. I'm sorry."

"Don't apologize. I just... Hell. Is the baby okay?"

"Not sure. I'm sore everywhere. My elbow really hurts."

"I need to find a doctor for you."

"FaeryTown?"

"You think? I'll go there right now. No. I can't leave you." He clasped her hand and pressed his forehead to her stomach. The brush of his beard always made her smile, but this time her smile ended in a wince. "I shouldn't have left you alone. Not when you've been feeling so awful. Bea, please forgive me?"

"It's not your fault, lover. You have work to do, and I should be more careful. Go to FaeryTown. I'll be fine as long as I'm on the bed, and it's not moving. Just bring me some water before you leave?"

He dashed down the stairs and returned to her side in record time. Sipping the water, she settled into the comforting touches as he stroked the hair from her face. He pulled back his fingers and studied the ichor that glittered there. *Did* her ichor look a bit foggy? Darker? Hmm...

"Just bumps and bruises," she reassured. "With rest, I'll be peaches and cream."

"I'll find a doctor just the same. Give me an hour or two. I'm not familiar with FaeryTown."

"You're going to need some glamour."

"What?"

"Kir, you can see me because I let you. I don't wear a glamour. Though I'm not sure I could if I tried. Been feeling so drained lately. I suspect it's the pregnancy. I also suspect FaeryTown is completely glamorized. You'll need to *see* the faeries if you want to talk to them."

"How do I do that?"

"I have some magic for that. Maybe. I'll give it a shot."

She touched the bridge of his nose between his eyes and closed hers. Summoning from her core, she imbued him with the sight. Maybe. Who knew if she could do the simple trick with the way she'd felt so drained lately?

"I felt something," he said. "A zing that coursed through me."

"Then it worked. The glamour should allow you to see all sidhe, whether or not they wear a glamour. Should stay with you a few hours. Or...minutes, depending on my fading mojo. Hurry back."

He pressed his face to her stomach again and she could hear him sniff tearfully. "I won't be long."

Two hours later, Kir smelled the ichor when he entered the front door to his home. He'd found a faery doctor who had agreed to come within the hour, but she had been on her way to tend a sprite mother who was delivering at that moment. It was the best he could do. So he'd rushed home to be with Bea until the doctor arrived.

The scent of his wife's ichor pierced his nostrils sharply. It was too much ichor. Sweet and grassy, overlaid with something darker, like smoke. Not right.

He dashed down the hallway, punching the wall as he reached the stairs. Letting out a howl, he charged up the stairs. She wasn't on the bed, tucked within the blankets.

He followed the glittering spots of ichor on the floor that led into the bathroom.

Bea looked up from her position sitting before the bathtub. Her face was covered in ichor. Her hands, as well. On the floor puddled more of the sparkling, clear substance.

Not so clear, he thought. Darker than usual. But he couldn't worry over the color right now.

In that terrible moment Kir knew. He fell to his knees before her.

"I'm so sorry," she said.

Pain tore up from his lungs and crushed the sweetness living in his heart that could have been his child. Kir howled as he had never howled before.

Chapter 19

Kir had failed Bea. And pack Valoir.

He stuffed the tiny T-shirt he'd purchased weeks ago into a trash bag, tied up the plastic and wandered out to the backyard. The sun was too bright. The birds were too loud. Traffic fumes caught in his lungs. Even the grass, which had turned green under Bea's attentions, had returned to its usual brown, crunchy state.

Jacques had called repeatedly. When was he going to question Sophie? Did Kir want him to do it for him? No, just wait, he'd said. He needed…time. Hell, he didn't know what he needed. But he hadn't been able to tell Jacques about Bea's miscarriage.

Everything was wrong. Too much wrongness. Unbearable to his heart.

He slammed the garbage bag into the tin can and put the cover on, then kicked the base of it. The can crashed against the wall of the stucco shed and almost toppled over.

Driving his fingers through his hair, he walked in a tight circle behind the shed, not wanting to risk Bea seeing him in this state. It had been a week since she'd miscarried. They hadn't talked about it other than him asking how she felt and her nodding and curling up in bed, or lying on the couch to watch television. He hated leaving her alone all day—alone with her morose thoughts—and tried to skip out from work an hour or two early. Sophie needed to be questioned, and he didn't care. He didn't care about anything.

And he cared about everything.

He didn't know what else to do. He felt helpless. He wanted to make it better for Bea so she could smile. All he wanted was for his faery wife to smile. She hadn't danced about the living room naked, wings unfurled, for weeks. And the brightness in her eyes had clouded.

He figured it would probably take a while for her to grieve and move beyond what had happened, but…

What about him? He…needed. Something.

He needed to wrap his arms about Bea and let loose the tears, to get them all out and scream and whimper and know that he still had her. That's all he wanted—her. They could try again at having a baby. Had he cursed the unborn child with his thoughts? He regretted thinking how difficult it would be to raise a demon within the pack.

He peeked around the shed wall. The living room curtains were drawn. She'd been watching TV when he'd come home tonight and had only picked at the salad and croissants he'd brought with him. She would take a bath in a few hours and move into bed without saying goodnight to him.

She was slipping away from him.

Kir fisted his hands at his sides.

"I won't let that happen."

* * *

Bea sat up on the couch as Kir knelt on the floor before her. He took her hands and kissed them, then pressed them over his chest. A heavy inhale lifted his powerful pecs beneath her fingers. The shiver in his breaths as he exhaled startled her. She didn't understand.

And then she did. He was struggling. She didn't know how to help him. She didn't even know how to help herself. She'd never felt such an immense loss.

"I'm not going in to work until we figure this out," he said. "I won't leave you alone all day to sit and think about what's happened. It's not right. I want to be here for you, Bea. For whenever you're ready to talk about it. Because… I need to talk about it. *We* need to talk about it."

He rested his head on her lap and she stroked her fingers through his soft hair. The man gave her everything she asked for, did not deny her a thing. He'd given her blind trust. He'd given her his very life by agreeing to marry her.

The pack will banish Kir if the child is a half-breed.

He'd sacrificed his home and the love of family for the child.

Bowing her head to his, she closed her eyes and tears spilled down her cheeks and dripped into his hair. "I wanted to give you a child."

"We can try again." He looked up and held her head between his palms, their foreheads touching. "This one wasn't meant to be. Maybe. I don't know. Bea, I hurt, too."

"I know you do. I've been so thoughtless. Sitting about, moping. I can see how hard it's been on you. You don't walk with your shoulders thrust back proudly. You shiver in the middle of the night when you're sleeping."

"I didn't know I did that. I admit, I've been having some white nights."

"I know, because I've lain beside you watching." She stroked his hair. "How...how can I make it better?"

"Just hold me?"

She beckoned him onto the couch and they entwined in an embrace that, at first, hurt her heart desperately. She wanted to push him away and hide her face and cry to herself, scream that it was so wrong. And then all she could do was cling, pull him closer and let the pain seep from her pores to mingle with his.

Tucking his head against her shoulder, her strong, proud werewolf husband sobbed in her arms. His body shook against hers and soon she found her tears had stopped and she cooed reassurance to him. Touching him softly on his cheek, kissing him there. Stroking the line of his nose and admiring its straightness. Tears wet his cheeks and she kissed the salty pain. She kissed his mouth and their pain sealed something neither of them could name, but both knew would forge their bond stronger.

And when they clasped hands, the bond mark glowed so brightly that the room, which had darkened with twilight, was brighter for it.

"We will have a child," she whispered. "When it's supposed to happen."

He nodded and pulled her in. "I love you."

"I love you."

"No matter what happens," he said, "I will never stop loving you. You've gotten into my heart, Bea." She wiped the tears from his eyes. "You made a nice little nest in my heart and I'm too much of a softy to kick you out."

"I like it here in my nest. Cozy. But do you really love me?" Bea's heart thundered with anticipation. "You've... never said it to me."

"I haven't? By the gods, Bea, I love you. So much."

This was the first time anyone had ever said that to her.

And it felt so real. Perfect. And it could have only been said by her loving husband. "I love you, too. I loved our baby."

He bowed his forehead to hers. "I did, too. Philipe," he whispered.

"Huh?"

"Our child. I wanted to name him Philipe. Is that okay?"

She nodded. "Yes. Philipe. He's ours, Kir. In our hearts."

Bea leaned over her husband's shoulder, intently watching as he worked the small metal tool across the surface of the leather vest. Each tap of his hammer impressed in the soft leather, forming a design with the curved tool. The rhythmic taps of the wood hammer against the tool composed a song.

She reached down and traced a finger along the curve embedded within the soft, oiled leather and, without even considering whether or not to ask, imbued it with faery dust. "Is that okay?"

"Yes," he said softly, his attention divided between the work and talking. "I like that. A part of you infused into my clothing. Will you trace it all?"

"Of course." She moved around and he pulled her onto his lap. With Kir's direction, she traced the design.

He'd stayed home with her for two days, saying the work would get done without him. He'd mentioned something about having to question a demon in custody, but that she would keep.

"Do you want to head out to the cabin tomorrow?"

"Oh, yes! I've desperately wanted to go back there."

"Me, too. We need the break from the city. You could let your wings out and fly to your heart's content."

"Oh, my great goddess, I can't wait!"

"Thought you'd like that."

"Let's finish this before we go," she said. "I want to

see you wearing it." She drew his hand up and, taking one of his fingers, used it to trace the design and seal the dust she'd placed on his handiwork. "This is my knight's shining armor."

Bea woke to her husband's kiss. The warm, musky scent of him coaxed her to tug up her knees to her chest and coo a satisfied chirp amid the tangle of sheets and pillows.

"I got a call from Jacques," he whispered, setting the cell phone aside on the nightstand. "My dad just walked into the compound and confessed involvement in the sale of V. I have to go in."

"Of course you do," she murmured, still half-asleep. "Will it be hard for you?"

"Yes."

She clasped his hand and kissed the bond mark. "I love you."

He kissed her mouth. "You give me strength, lover. Thanks for that. I haven't forgotten our plans to head out to the cabin. Pack some things. I'll be home as soon as I can. Love you."

Another kiss to her forehead and she felt him slide his hand down her bare stomach. His fingers glanced over her thatch of soft hairs and tickled the tops of her thighs. A moan clued her he was having a time of it getting out of bed. But she wouldn't keep him from family.

"You had doubts your father was involved," she said. "You'd better go. He may need you."

"Right. Later, Short Stick."

"I'll be ready."

She nuzzled under the warmth of the sheet and listened as her husband dressed and, in the bathroom, brushed his teeth. Down in the kitchen he made some toast, and it sounded as if he took it with him, because the front door closed soon after the toaster had popped.

"I love that wolf," she whispered, and drifted back to sleep.

Kir was determined not to repeat his father's betrayal. And the only way to do so was to be there for his father now. To show him that he held family in regard. That it meant something.

That he could not, and never would, be like him.

When Colin should have gone directly to Kir, he'd instead turned himself in to the pack. Fortunately, Jacques had taken him in hand at the compound and had placed him in a semi-secure office before Etienne had gotten word of the surrender. Not in the dungeon behind bars where the principal would have put him.

Kir spoke to Jacques and learned that Colin hadn't said anything to him other than that he was entirely responsible for the V-hubs and the kidnapping of vampires by pack Royaume. Sophie was blameless.

"You believe him?" Kir asked Jacques.

"He confessed. You don't believe him? Kir, I know he's your father, but—"

"But the demoness is wicked and could have him bespelled," Kir said.

"Bespelled? Can demons do that?"

He had no idea. But it was easier to believe that than to succumb to the truth—that his father had acted of his own accord. "Give me some time to talk to him."

"That I can do. But Etienne is itching about the collar to place the man in shackles."

"My father has never wronged Etienne. Tell him to cool his heels."

Jacques whistled and stepped aside to allow Kir through

the doorway to the containment room. Inside was an empty desk and chair and a pullout futon. A gallon jug of water sat on the desk. The only window, placed near the ceiling, was no more than a foot high, but a determined wolf could certainly break the glass and make an escape.

Colin stood when Kir entered. His father looked drawn and tired. And Kir noticed now the brown hair that he always wore clipped close to his head was strewn with gray strands. Had those been there when he'd visited at his father's home the other day? He looked worn.

"Son."

Kir sat on the corner of the desk, arms crossed high over his chest. "Jacques says you confessed."

Colin nodded. "I am the mastermind behind this vicious act you've been investigating. Lock me up and release Sophie."

Kir nodded. Now he knew the reason for Colin's surrender. He wanted to save his girlfriend. Was the demon worth sacrificing his own freedom?

"I don't believe you," Kir said. "You're lying."

"What the hell is wrong with you, son? You get a confession and you refuse it?"

"Tell me how the V is administered," Kir said.

"The demons drink it from a restrained vampire's veins. Or, for a more direct infusion, the recipient is hooked up to the vamp with a tube. Instant high."

"You've done your homework. But I still don't believe you knew anything about this. You knew nothing that day I was at your home. We caught Sophie at a V-hub. What's happened since then?"

"What's happened is that you have kept someone I love locked up for over a week. What for? Why detain her without allowing her to contact me, a friend, anyone?"

"I've been busy."

"Busy? So busy that you would leave a helpless woman to rot in a cell—"

Kir growled at his father and fisted a hand, but did not approach him.

"It is unthinkably cruel," Colin insisted. "Either question her, or release her."

"I've been…" Kir winced.

The past week and a half had been horrible, but last night he and Bea had reconnected. Not completely, but they were beginning to join hands and start down the path to understanding and acceptance. He couldn't believe he'd not told her he loved her until last night. Thankfully, that had been remedied.

Softly, he said, "Bea miscarried. I've been taking care of her."

Colin bowed his head. "Oh. I'm…so sorry, son. I didn't know. Is she…doing well?"

"She is grieving. As am I. But that doesn't excuse my ignoring Sophie. I apologize for that. I'll make sure matters are taken care of today."

"But please." Colin crossed the floor to stand before Kir. He entreated his son with a gesture of hands. "I love Sophie, Kir. I cannot bear to know she will be deported to Daemonia. What will I do without her? Surely you must understand how it is to love someone so much?"

He did. And yet, the eight-year-old in him shook his head and stomped the floor with a foot. It wasn't going to be so easy to appease his broken heart. "The questioning is merely to affirm what we've learned about the V-hubs. We caught Sophie red-handed. Jacques has scheduled her deportation for this evening."

"No." Colin gripped Kir's shoulders and held him firmly. "Please, son. I know she's guilty. But…send me instead. Please. Allow me to stand in her place."

"That won't remove the offending party from this realm. She sacrificed her freedom when she chose to commit a heinous crime, Dad."

"I'll talk to her. Make her stop. I'll take her away. Far from here. I'll keep an eye on her. I won't allow this to happen again. She's addicted, son. I had no idea. And the addiction forced her to sell so she could afford more V. It's horrible. I know!"

Kir growled in warning, showing his teeth.

Colin shuffled away and his back hit the wall, his head bowing. The old werewolf, whom Kir had once looked up to, admired even, had been reduced to begging. For a demon.

"Demons can never be trusted," Kir hissed. "That woman took you away from your family. Now I will take her family away from her."

Colin's growl preceded his lunge for Kir. He gripped him by the throat but did not press hard, only warningly. "You are out of line, boy."

Kir hadn't had to struggle to step out of the old man's grasp. Yet, though he was stunned beyond belief his father had lunged for him, he couldn't bring himself to retaliate. The man had never raised a hand to him. Ever.

"You see what she has made you do?" he asked. "Always you chose her over your family."

"Kir, no. How dare you."

Drawing back his shoulders and looking down on his father, who now leaned over the desk, Kir said sharply, "You left me and Blyss and Mom. You just...left. For a *demon*."

Colin looked up abruptly, his eyes teared. "It wasn't that way," he said. "Kir, no. I loved you. I have always loved you. I would do anything... Your mother twisted the truth. You only know her version of the story."

Now what lies would his father concoct to save the

demon? Hadn't the years of their lacking connection and communication proved how little Kir cared for his lies?

Yet, try as he might, he could not walk away from Colin, not so quickly. He splayed his hands before him. "So what's your version?"

Colin nodded and sighed. A sigh so heavy Kir felt it enter him and settle in his gut. "I fell out of love with your mother long before I ever left pack Valoir, Kir."

Kir crossed his arms tightly, drawing up his chin. He didn't want to hear this. And he did.

"Madeline is a cold, hard woman," Colin continued. "Difficult to love. But I tried and was successful for a while. I was once passionately in love with her. When you children were little, we made some lovely memories."

Kir paced behind his father. The clear memories he had of family were the few times they had all gone to the country cabin and spent weeks there romping in wolf shape, chasing rabbits and sleeping in the wilds.

For a moment he thought of Bea, sitting at home, waiting for him. What tormented childhood memories did she have because her father could never love her?

Because of a demon.

He would never betray her love as his father had betrayed his mother.

"I left pack Valoir because I was empty," Colin said. "And living with Madeline only carved that emptiness deeper. I wasn't banished, but Etienne made it clear I could never return if I left. I suspect Madeline had a word with him. They had an affair, you know."

Kir gasped. Etienne and Madeline? He couldn't believe it. Etienne doted on his wife, Estella. They were in love. Had been for eighty years.

"I lost my love for her after that," Colin stated plainly. "I had to go."

"If that is so…if you really had fallen out of love with Mom…" He struggled not to raise his voice. Clasping his fingers into an ineffectual fist, he asked, "What about me and Blyss? Was it so easy to walk away from us? Why didn't you stay for us?"

"I wanted to. But when I brought it up to your mother, she gave me an ultimatum. Either I remain married to her and stay with my family, or I had to leave and never see the two of you again. Etienne backed her up. It was a cruel threat. I couldn't bear one moment longer in her presence. Nor could I live under the control of a principal who would cuckold me. So I left.

"And do you know? The moment I set foot outside the compound my soul lifted?"

Kir shook his head. How easy was it for him to make up such lies?

"She had brought me so low, Kir. I don't ask you to understand or to forgive me. Just know, leaving was the only option for my sanity."

No, he didn't understand. And he would never forgive his father for walking away from him when he was so young. Sure, Kir understood that some marriages failed, were never meant to be and could be loveless. He didn't want to believe that had been his parents' case. And yet, he himself knew Madeline was a cold woman.

Bea feared her? He exhaled.

Accept his father's choice? No. But perhaps he could sympathize.

"I always thought it was Sophie who led you away from the pack."

"I met her months after I'd left. It was quick, I know. And it's probably why you remember it that way. You do recall I did find ways to see you and Blyss those first few years?"

Kir nodded. Madeline had often taken them to the Jardin de Luxembourg, where he'd rent a toy boat and sail it on the pond before the former royal palace. While Blyss and his mother had been off strolling through the flower gardens and getting lemon ices, he'd sat on the shore beside his father, who had always kept one eye over his shoulder.

"None of this matters anymore," Kir said. "I hate demons. Sophie will be deported tonight."

Colin grabbed his wrist and Kir tightened his jaw. "You can hate Sophie," his father said, "but you can't hate the entire demon race because I fell in love with one of them after your mother annihilated my heart."

A truer statement had never been spoken. But Kir's eight-year-old self's memory wanted him to cling to the hatred for them all. To punish the one responsible for his shattered childhood.

"Please, son," Colin pleaded. "If Sophie is sent to Daemonia, she will never find her way out again. She will perish there. She's accustomed to living in the mortal realm. Daemonia is harsh. And her absence would kill me."

Kir tugged from his father's grip. "Walking away from your family killed an eight-year-old boy's sense of safety and trust." He left the room, slamming the door, and marched down the hallway.

Jacques met him as he turned the corner and matched his strides along the quiet, dark hall that led lower, toward the dungeon, where Sophie was being held.

"You going to question her?"

"I'm going to prepare her for deportation."

"Tonight?" Jacques confirmed. "I've contacted the Reckoner. He can send her to Daemonia."

Kir heaved out a sigh. "Just give me a minute." He stopped before the iron-barred gate that closed before the door to the dungeon. "Is she guarded?"

"No. She's a weepy mess. I always thought demons were tougher. More wild."

"I'll be right back."

"I'll go with you."

"No, I'm not in any danger from Sophie."

Jacques put up both palms in placating acceptance. He knew Kir was stubborn and he would not interfere.

Kir opened the gate and the steel hinges creaked closed behind him. Down two stories of twisting stone stairs he spiraled until he landed in the cool darkness. No lights? There was electricity down here. The cell doors operated on a code system. He could see well in the dark, though, and wandered forward, past two empty cells.

The pack rarely used the dungeon, but there were occasions when a pack member needed a little cooling-off time, or perhaps a blood-crazed vampire they'd rescued from the blood games needed to chill before being released.

They'd kept the demoness down here too long. His fault. He should have questioned her immediately and then deported her. But now with this new information his father had given him. Really? Colin had met Sophie *after* leaving his family?

Kir stopped before the third cell, his shoulder facing the bars. He didn't look inside, but he could scent the demoness. Faint trace of sulfur and, above that, a sweet, cloying perfume tainted with the salty mist of tears. She was a woman who prided herself on her appearance, much like Madeline. Yet she hadn't been allowed personal comforts, only two meals a day and some books. He could hear her shiver and knew she was aware of his presence.

His father hadn't met Sophie until after leaving the pack and his family. Remarkable. Had his mother been so impossible to live with? Kir knew Madeline was a difficult woman and was very controlling. Hell, Bea was afraid of her. Yet he had only ever respected her.

She'd had an affair with Etienne? Did Estella know? Dare he ask Etienne? It could be the only way to get the truth.

But would the truth change things? Bandage his broken eight-year-old self's heart?

He turned to face the bars and located the dark figure huddled in the corner on the bare mattress placed on the cold concrete floor. The darkness didn't allow him to make out more than a froth of hair and shapeless clothing. And yet, the faintest glint glowed briefly on her face. Two red irises.

Bea's eyes were pink. Faery eyes were normally purple. So when a faery mixed with a demon… That didn't make sense to him. Purple and red making pink? Probably it didn't work that way. His mother's eyes were blue and yet he'd gotten his father's brown eyes.

He loved Bea. Half demon or not. He could love the demon within her. He must learn to. And it wasn't fair to blame an entire race for the sins of one woman. Who may not have been responsible for his father leaving him in the first place.

By the gods, everything he believed was now being tipped on its head.

"Will you tell Colin I love him?" The tiny voice came from the darkness. "And I'm sorry. The addiction is so… so powerful."

Kir swallowed and gripped the cell bars. "Could you overcome the addiction?"

"I…" A sweep of fabric across the floor as she stretched out a leg. "Perhaps. Not in Paris. Too easy to access V here. It calls to me, Kirnan. Even sitting here for so many days… I can still taste it. It is a wicked mistress."

"What if Colin took you away?"

Sophie's head lifted. Red glowed in the darkness. "You would not banish me to Daemonia?"

Such hope in her voice. Had he a right to play judge and jury? She had tortured and likely killed many vampires to obtain the V she not only used but also sold. She was guilty of a crime. But perhaps not guilty of stealing Colin from his family—only loving him. Maybe she had been the one to put back together the pieces of his father's broken heart.

"Kir?"

He stepped back. Waited for her to speak.

"My son…" Sophie crawled forward on hands and knees. "He mustn't know what I've done."

Edamite's relationship with his mother was good.

His heart thudded. Why was this so difficult?

"Be ready for transport soon," he stated.

Kir walked away, without another word. At the top of the stairs, he gave Jacques orders for this evening.

"Jacques is taking my place on the hunt tonight," Kir said as he drove the Lexus out of the city limits. "That is, if the portal works."

"It doesn't work?" Bea adjusted the radio but did not stay on a station for a complete song. He suspected she liked playing with the dials more than the actual music.

"It didn't last time Jacques attempted to pass through it. I'm not sure a fix has been made yet."

"Interesting." But her tone was more accusing that wondering. "When will you hunt? Isn't it an instinctual thing for you?"

"It is, but it is a pleasure instinct, not a survival thing. There is plenty of food here in the mortal realm to keep me alive. And, besides, you are a much more pleasant evening."

She stroked the vest he wore. "This is your armor, wolf."

"I like how if feels. A different fit than other vests I've made. I think it's your faery dust."

"You are my knight in leather and fur," she said. "And I am pleased to be your damsel."

"Something tells me this damsel can protect herself."

"I probably can, but I'll always swoon for you. How did it go with your dad?"

Kir sighed. Yet, for some reason, his heart felt lighter even if he didn't want to accept that lightness. "He's not involved."

"He confessed that?"

"Yes, among other things I'm still trying to wrap my brain around."

"Want to talk about it?"

He checked the dashboard clock. Sophie had been transported half an hour earlier. "Much as Colin wanted us to take him in hand and release Sophie, I wouldn't allow it."

"So is his girlfriend going to be sent back to Daemonia?"

Kir signaled a turn and followed the queue of red taillights exiting the city limits before him. Jacques had left the compound with Sophie in hand. And as far as Etienne had been informed, the act had already been completed. The demoness had been transported to a Reckoning service across town.

But if the transport vehicle got a flat tire and Colin Sauveterre just happened to be in the vicinity at the time…

"Everything will go as it was meant to be," he said.

Chapter 20

Standing on the porch, bare toes wiggling over the edge of the unpainted pine floorboards, Bea closed her eyes and spread out her arms. Splaying her fingers, she took in her surroundings through smell, taste and sensation. Oncoming autumn smelled light and only a little foreboding. She looked forward to experiencing her first cold season in the mortal realm. In Faery, winter was vile and wicked, and she had rarely ventured outside her little palace room for fear of the freeze that turned the Unseelie lands to virtual glass.

So she had led a pampered life, albeit as the black sheep. Just because the walls had been crystal and the foods fine didn't mean she hadn't felt a vast and pining desperation for compassion and a loving hug. Connection. Family. Simple love.

Kir loved her unconditionally. And because of his love for her she was rising from the intense grief that had wrapped her soul for the past weeks. Kir grieved their lost child as much as she. She adored her husband. And the feeling was so huge and overwhelming she caught an arm about the porch column and hugged it as she thought of her fine husband, off loping about the forest.

All alone.

"I should have gone with him."

Why hadn't she thought to do such a thing? Since she'd been in the mortal realm, she'd not flown or shifted shape to small. Surely she could. Her glamour may be weakened, but if she could bring out her wings, then shifting shouldn't be a problem. Unfortunately, she'd never had a reason or a place private enough to afford such luxury. It hadn't even occurred to her to try the first time they'd visited this cabin.

Giddy with anticipation, Bea spun once, then shed her yellow cotton sundress and scampered off the end of the porch that opened onto the forest floor. But her feet did not touch the leaf-strewn earth. Instead, she shifted, transforming to a small shape, her wings unfurling and carrying her high through the trees. She passed an emerald-capped hummingbird that could not keep up with her zipping pace, and she laughed, the sound of her glee falling to the forest floor in glints of faery dust. Arrowing through close-spaced branches, she lifted a hand to slap one as she passed, sending a scatter of desiccated leaves fluttering to the ground.

Soon enough she spotted the brown-furred wolf tracking the forest floor below. The beast loped casually, pausing to sniff the base of an oak tree, then dashed ahead, playfully, and darted this way and that. He headed toward the stream that curled among stacked boulders and majestic pine trees.

Bea arrowed toward her husband and flew alongside

the wolf for a while before the beast noticed her presence. The wolf stopped abruptly, sniffing the air that glittered about her, and sprang up on his hind legs to bat the faery dust with a forepaw.

She landed on his head, her toes sinking into his fur, warmed from his run. He didn't try to shake her off. Even in wolf form he knew her. Bea spread her fingers through his fur and snuggled to give him a hug.

The wolf wandered to the stream with her sitting between its ears. He dipped his head to drink in the cool water, and Bea turned onto her stomach, digging her fingers and toes into his fur to hang on.

"Never had a wolf's-eye view of the world. I could so rock this. We can race through the forest with me calling 'Mush!'"

She laughed and turned onto her back, but her giggles upset her hold and she slid down the wolf's nose as if on an amusement park attraction. She landed with a splash in the water.

"Oh, this water is cold!"

Shivering, she soared upward, her wings flapping double time to shake the water from them and her bare skin.

The wolf howled.

"Was that a wolf laugh? Seriously?"

Within two blinks, the wolf's body shifted and lengthened as it transformed into Kir's human *were* form. He came to man shape, laughing, his hands in the water as he knelt on all fours.

Bea flew to his shoulder and landed, gripping a hank of his hair to secure hold. "I don't think that was funny."

"Did you say something?" he said. "I can't hear anything but little bells. You're so tiny. And naked!" He sat back on his haunches and held out his hand. "Come here. I've never seen you in this form. The forest called to you, too, eh? It's paradise out here. There are days I think I could stay in wolf form forever."

Bea lit on his palm and sat, cross-legged, leaning back on her palms to look up at him. He seemed to be a giant. His big brown eyes were sheened with gold and tenderness. Funny to remember now how frightened she'd been to walk down the aisle, and, still, on her wedding night, she had inexplicably trusted her new husband. He was true to the core, a valiant man.

He touched one of her wingtips and she curled the long filament of it about his finger in response. He couldn't hear her voice when she was in this small shape, but it was nice, this meeting of their worlds in different forms.

She crawled forward and lay on her stomach, leaning over the edge of his palm, and looked down. At his lap, his erection jutted like some kind of Greek column she'd fly into at her father's home if she hadn't been looking. She wouldn't be able to wrap her arms around it in her current form, but the thought to try…

Fluttering her wings, she lifted from his palm, and he leaned back, catching his palms against the shore stones. She landed her feet on the head of his cock and stood with arms akimbo, looking up at him.

"You think so, eh?" he asked.

His cock suddenly bobbed, and Bea put out her arms for balance. Well, she *was* in a certain mood. The day was too perfect not to be. So…why not?

Fluttering down aside the huge column, she stood next to it and gave it a hug. It was as tall as she. The vein that ran the length of him pulsed against her cheek. Bea licked his skin. It tasted saltier than usual but also like the fresh, cool forest. She hooked a leg along the curve of his erection and stretched out her arms, performing a pole-dance shimmy. Oh, the things she had learned watching television.

Spinning and pressing her back against his warm, steely length, she sashayed her hips down along him. Kir groaned and…laughed.

"Come to your normal size," he said in that deep, husky voice that always cued her it was time for sex. "I'm struggling between horniness and a good belly laugh."

With a shudder of her wings and a focus inward, she stirred her glamour and her body transformed, her bones growing and skin stretching. It didn't hurt. She came to full size with a spill of faery dust sprinkling over them.

She kissed him, spreading her fingers through his hair as she had done with his fur. "It felt good to shift and soar through the sky. I should do it more often, but someone has forbidden me to do so in the city."

"We could come out here more often."

"Nothing would make me happier."

A shift of his hips placed the head of him at her folds, and she directed him inside her. He glided in slowly, sweetly burning a path to her core. She groaned and leaned forward, hugging his chest and nuzzling her head at the base of his throat as he lazily pumped inside her.

"Tell me this will never end, Kir. Us."

"It will never end. I promise. I love you, Bea."

They clasped hands and the bond mark glowed brilliantly as they made love until the night snuck in a chill that chased them home. Once in the cabin, Kir started a fire, and they made love on the woven rug before the amber flames.

They hadn't planned to head back to Paris for another day, but Kir got a phone call around seven in the morning from his principal asking him to meet him in an hour. Etienne had insisted it couldn't wait. And Kir recognized his leader's serious tone because it was rarely used.

Had Etienne discovered his sleight of hand with the demon Sophie? Jacques had promised his silence, and he knew that it had been a lot to ask of a friend. Not wanting to discuss it over the phone, Kir said he'd head into Paris immediately.

Bea was disappointed they wouldn't have another night out in the quiet of the country, but she helped him batten down the hatches so they could quickly get on the road. She lay across the front seat, her head on his lap all the way home.

She'd told him that shifting to small size yesterday had tired her. She wondered out loud if it was her demon half growing stronger now she was in the mortal realm. Kir didn't say anything. It had been amazing to see her in that shape. That she had trusted him enough to show that side of herself.

Etienne was an easygoing man who was young for a pack leader. Probably only a hundred and thirty years old, he assumed the command and presence of a much older wolf, one who had seen much and had learned from experience.

And Kir would never forgive him for forcing him to marry Bea, because to forgive would mean he regretted the marriage. And that was something he could not do. He should thank Etienne for the gift he'd given him. Kir did respect the man.

And then he did not.

Had his principal had an affair with his mother? Could Etienne and Madeline's relationship have been the catalyst to Colin leaving? He wasn't sure how to bring it up. And depending on what Etienne had called him in for, it could be the wrong time to do so.

He'd play it by ear.

"Kirnan, have a seat. Sorry to call you back in early from the cabin. I didn't make it to retreat this full moon. How pitiful is that?"

Kir remained standing. "You're busy, principal. If you need me to do more…?"

"You and Jacques are doing an incredible job enforcing. You got the Royaume situation tied up?"

Apparently, Etienne had not heard of the demoness's escape. Whew.

"Settled. The, er, demoness has been deported. And the V-hub that was in current operation has been burned."

"I always hate to mete punishment. Especially when this case was so close to home. How is your father?"

"I suspect I won't be speaking with him for some time, Principal Montfort."

"I'm sorry, Kir."

"Royaume is a small pack. Sometimes a pack follows their principal, even knowing what they are doing is wrong. The pack members look up to their principal."

"I trust the two of you will handle it accordingly. As for guarding the portal, that's been going smoothly. Only had a few encounters with humans thinking they were wizards trying to pass through. The things humans get to these days. The idiots have seen too much TV and played far too many video games. Although, Jacques said he again wasn't able to access Faery to hunt again last night."

"Really? What's that about?"

"You should sit," Etienne said.

Kir sensed discomfort in the man's tone. Too curt.

"I'd rather stand. I've been driving. Need to stretch out my muscles."

Etienne leaned forward across his desk, placing his palms flat. "Sit. Please."

Kir sat on the wood chair and drew up an ankle to prop

across his knee. He'd done nothing wrong. Unless Etienne really did know about the situation with his father and Sophie. No, Jacques was discreet. Although, he had asked his best friend to make a move against his father.

Was it something about him and Bea? Couldn't be. He hadn't told Etienne about Bea's miscarriage, but surely word had carried to him.

Though Etienne rarely involved himself in the enforcing schedule, Kir had to ask. "Is there a new case?"

"No. I'll get straight to the point. The passage is not working, and we've learned why just this morning. Malrick refuses to honor the accord made between Valoir and the Unseelies."

Kir's mouth dropped open. He didn't know what to say or how, exactly, to process that information. They'd only gotten to use the passage for a few months. He hadn't even hunted in Faery.

"We offered one of our best wolves—you—in exchange for a promise that both sides would honor the alliance," Etienne stated. "But for the past month we haven't been able to access the passage at all. And my contact, who has been keeping tabs on Malrick, says he is indifferent to what the pack wants. Sounds like he made the agreement merely to pass off an unwanted by-blow on us."

"How dare you." Kir sat up halfway but stopped himself from reaching across the desk to grip his principal by the throat.

"Settle, Kir. I'm sorry. I shouldn't have used that term. It's what Malrick calls her, you know."

Sitting down, Kir nodded. He could believe as much. But that didn't mean Etienne had a right to repeat it. "Bea has been made to believe she is less than worthy. She grew up knowing her father had no love for her."

"That's a sad thing. And I'm sure you have found a common bond, the two of you, with such histories."

Kir's muscles tightened. The man was putting up a front. He sensed it. He had had an affair with his mother. Kir knew it.

"Principal, I have to ask you something."

"Kir, wait. You must hear this first."

He nodded, but his fingers curled into fists. Suddenly his father seemed a much kinder man. But where did Etienne stand on the scale of honor to one's own?

"I have to act swiftly to show Malrick we will not allow him to treat us with disrespect," Etienne said.

"I agree. The pack must stand its ground. What are your plans?"

Etienne sighed and leaned back on his chair. He rapped the desk with a fist, then said, "We have to send her back."

"Her?" Kir heard the word, but he processed it as if it traveled through his brain ten times slower than Etienne had spoken it. *Her.* Her?

Her.

That meant… Bea.

"No! She's my wife."

"I'm sorry, Kir. It's politics."

"Absolutely not!" He stood, tilting the chair back in the process, which landed in a clatter on the hardwood floor, echoing his anger. "I won't give her back. Etienne, we're in love." He held up his hand to display the pale mark that now glowed every time he and Bea clasped hands. "We've bonded."

"Kirnan."

"You understand about bonding, Principal Montfort. We wolves take it very seriously. It is a lifetime commitment!"

"And so I had assumed the sidhe did, as well."

Kir stepped back, fisting the air. Insanity! That his principal could even suggest such a thing. And yet, Etienne did not obviously hold the bonding in such high esteem if he had… "You and my mother," he blurted out. "You are the reason my father left."

"Kir—"

"Colin told me. You've hidden it from me all these years."

"Boy, you watch your tone."

"You have no idea what real love is, do you?"

Etienne moved swiftly, gripping Kir by the throat and slamming him against the wall near the door. "Your mother seduced me," he growled.

Kir managed to fling his principal away. "My father left me because of you!"

"Because of your mother, son. Because of Madeline. I thank the gods every day that Estella took me back, and yet still I must live with that woman so close."

"Damn it!" Kir slammed his fists against the wall behind him.

"Knowing all this now doesn't change the present situation, Kir. We have to send the faery back."

"No! I have to think about this."

"I won't change my mind."

"You will. You must. How can you conceive— You owe me!"

"Kir."

Now he was acting like the eight-year-old who had just been told his father had left. Stricken. Angry. Vengeful.

Kir shook his head and ran his fingers through his hair, pulling tightly against the pulsing in his temples. "Just… give me a day. I can come up with a better solution."

Etienne breathed out a heavy sigh through his nose. He nodded once.

Kir turned and marched out of the room, leaving the

door open. They would not send Bea back to Faery. He would not allow it! That…man. His principal had destroyed his family years ago. He would not allow him to destroy the new family he held dear.

At the sound of the front door slamming, Bea looked up from the pan of brownies cooling on the counter—easy to make from a box!—and rushed out to greet her husband in the hallway. He growled at her and punched the wall.

"Kir? What in mossy misery?"

He raked his fingers through his hair and turned away from her, pacing back and forth.

"What happened?"

He punched the wall again and again. The plaster cracked and sifted to the fieldstone floor.

"Kir!"

He turned to her, and when his eyes blazed and she had the fleeting thought he might hurt her, he suddenly pulled her to him and clasped her so tightly she choked on her breath.

"Don't ever want to let you go," he muttered, his arms banding across her back.

She wrapped her legs about his hips and clung, though really, she needn't try to hang on. He was holding her as if to loosen a single muscle would conjure up a storm that would whisk her away from him.

"You don't have to let me go," she squeaked. "But you do have to take down the steel grip a bit. You're squeezing me."

His muscles flexed as he relented. Enough that she could breathe easily. But she didn't want to. Something was wrong. She could feel it in the subtle shiver that tracked his bones and vibrated against her own.

"I need to hold you," he said.

"You can hold me all day and night. But can you smell the chocolaty goodness?"

"What?"

"I made brownies."

He pulled back from the tight clasp to study her eyes. "You baked?"

She nodded eagerly. "It came out of a box, but I had to mix in eggs and water. I promise it's much better than the Garlic Spaghetti From Hades. You want me to serve you up a nice warm chunk and then you can tell me about it?"

He squeezed her again, and Bea had the feeling even a whole pan of brownies was not going to prepare her for what was troubling her husband.

He carried her into the kitchen and looked over the pan. So the edges were black.

"I can cut out of the center," she offered. "And we have vanilla ice cream."

He snickered, but it wasn't his usual joyful sound. "I'll eat the whole middle. Later."

He set her on the counter and pressed his forehead to hers. Standing there, he slid his hands along her face and into her hair, stroking it, feeling her, taking her in. Bea didn't reciprocate the touch. He was fighting some inner demons right now. The man had to do what he had to do.

And then she remembered. "What did your principal have to say? Is it something bad? It must be. Oh, Kir. Talk to me."

"Malrick has reneged on the alliance."

Breaths gasped from her mouth. Her heartbeat sped up as she felt her lungs deflate and she wasn't sure she could ever draw in breath again. It wasn't a surprise to hear her father had reneged on an agreement. That was his MO. But that Kir was so upset about it warned she wasn't going to like what came next.

He started to speak, but she pressed her fingers to his mouth. She shook her head, not wanting to hear it. She wanted to stop the world. Freeze time.

He clasped her fingers and kissed them. "I love your skin, Bea. Your sweet candy scent. Your pretty pink eyes and your long fluttery lashes."

Oh, hell, this was going to be bad.

"I dream about kissing you, about pushing my cock inside you, even when I'm lying beside you with my arms wrapped about your warmth. Is that crazy?"

She shook her head, not daring to speak because she sensed to open her mouth would allow a cry to spill out.

"You are the most interesting woman I have ever known," he continued, still clasping her fingers against his lips. "You're goofy. You're flighty. Literally. You do naked like a pro. And you're the first woman who has ever given me a pole dance."

She managed a small smile.

"I love you, Bea, with all my heart and every bit of my soul. You make my life feel vast. Wondrous." He reached for her hand. The bond marks glowed, signifying their love. "We belong to one another."

"What is it?" she insisted. "Please, Kir, tell me."

"Do you love me?"

"More than anything. More than I love shifting small. More than I love flying. More than I love sex."

"Really?"

She nodded.

Again he pressed his forehead to hers. Bea felt sure he could hear her heartbeats, so loudly did they thunder against her rib cage. She gripped his shirt and clung.

"My principal wants to act swiftly to show Malrick the pack's disdain for his actions. He wants to send you back to Faery."

Chapter 21

Bea's tiny, keening moan pierced Kir's heart as if it were a silver arrow. He clutched her head and held her to him, forehead to forehead. He'd not felt more helpless than when he'd found her sitting before the tub in a puddle of ichor after she had miscarried their child.

And yet, he would not be helpless about this. He would not allow it. No one would rip his wife from his arms. Even if that meant he had to steal her away and leave the country.

He suddenly knew exactly how his father felt when he'd been forced to choose between family and happiness. And Kir could only be glad he'd made the rash decision to help Sophie escape.

"It will not happen," he insisted. "No one is sending you back to Faery."

"I love you," she said on a gasp that segued into tears.

"I told Etienne the idea was ridiculous. You are my wife. We've bonded. We are in love."

"Malrick wanted to get rid of me."

"And, in doing so, he gave you to me. I have never received a finer gift."

"But your pack can't step back and allow Malrick to spit upon them. Your leader is right—"

"Bea, don't say that. Would you willingly return to Faery?"

"No! Never. I mean that I understand about your principal's decision. Oh, Kir, my heart hurts."

She fell into his arms and he carried her down the hallway. "I told my principal I needed to think about this. I have to figure out a better plan. There's got to be something pack Valoir can do instead of sending you back. Something that will show the Faery king we will not tolerate broken bargains."

"Promise you won't let them send me back?"

He kissed her. "I cannot conceive of parting with you."

They stood in the shower, Bea's legs twined about Kir's torso as he lifted her up and down, thrusting his cock within her and pulling almost all the way out, until she would dig her fingernails into his shoulders and beg him to go faster, not stop, to bury himself and get lost inside her.

After the shower, they made it as far as the middle of the bedroom floor. Towels lay strewn across the floorboards in their wake. On the bed, Bea knelt on all fours as Kir took her from behind. His hand clasped her breast, his other clung to her hip. She loved it when he took her this way. It was the position that he enjoyed most, wolf that he was, and she felt as though he touched her high inside. Perhaps, even, he touched her soul.

He slapped a hand on the bed, and she slid her hand over to clasp with his so the bond marks glowed. Nothing could break their bond.

And later, laughing, they spilled off the bed, getting tangled in a tumble of sheets and the soft patchwork quilt. Yet when Kir pulled aside the sheet and Bea quickly sniffed away the damning tear, he paused and sat up abruptly with her on his lap.

"What's wrong, Short Stick?"

She kissed him and stroked his beard and sniffed back another tear. "What if this is the last time we make love?"

"No, Bea, I will never let you go."

"Promise?"

"Yes, I promise. They'll have to send me with you if anyone thinks to remove you from this realm."

She chuckled through her tears. "You might like it in Faery. Lots of good hunting."

And then neither of them wanted to talk about that, because it only reminded them why she was crying in the first place.

Kir lifted her into his arms and she dragged up the sheets and quilt as he did the same. Not making the bed, but letting the blankets fall into a nest, the twosome curled up together and kissed and snuggled until they fell asleep.

Sunlight woke Kir. He sat up in a puddle of sheets and quilts and smiled at his and Bea's antics last night. And then he frowned and shoved his fingers through his hair. Before they'd had sex she had been in tears. Nothing in this world should have hurt his wife so that she had cried. He needed to stop it.

Bea's fingers tickled up his spine, tapping, tapping, a ticklish morning greeting. While he wanted nothing more than to lose himself in all the goodness she offered him, he knew if he didn't act quickly he may lose that bright splash of faery dust forever.

"I'm going to talk to Etienne. I'll not be gone long." He

stood and tugged some pants out of the dresser drawer and found a T-shirt to pull on.

"Hurry back before the nightmare comes."

"The nightmare?"

"The one where I'm standing alone, without you."

Burying his face in her hair, he squeezed her against his body, not wanting to leave but knowing he had to talk Etienne out of his plans before it was too late.

Principal Montfort paced the floor as Kir, this time, sat calmly in the chair. "Kirnan." Etienne eyed him cautiously. Yesterday he'd accused him of tearing apart his family. And the man had not denied it, only tried to focus the blame on Kir's mother.

It required two to ruin a relationship. Kir knew that.

"Principal Montfort."

"So what did you come up with regarding a plan?" Etienne asked.

Did he sense a smirk in his tone? Why did Kir suddenly know his principal had abandoned him long ago? That perhaps Etienne could not have gotten Colin out of the pack fast enough? Did Etienne and Madeline still have something going on behind Estella's back?

He didn't want to divide his focus, and he really didn't want to consider his mother's illicit liaisons, so he pushed that aside. Bea was more important to him than stupid childhood abandonment issues that he could get over if he simply chose to do so.

"We're making assumptions that Malrick doesn't want to keep the agreement," Kir said. "Has anyone from the pack spoken with him? Maybe there is simply a problem with the portal. They've obviously been trying to close it to humans. Something could have gone wrong. We need to discuss this with all involved parties."

"I don't think it's possible to talk directly to the Unseelie king. He sent a liaison to deliver the news about reneging on the bargain. The harpie, Brit. Kir, I know this is difficult for you—"

"You can't begin to fathom how much this hurts my heart to know you would consider giving my wife away. To know…how you have betrayed me since I was a boy. I thought family meant everything to you? The pack is family. I am your family, Etienne. Does that not count for anything?"

"We should not regard past mistakes in present problems, Kir. The two are not related. How can you claim such steadfast love for the faery? You were reluctant about the marriage."

"My heart changed quickly. I love Bea."

"I understand, and I do believe you genuinely love the faery. But she is a half-breed, Kir. What? A vampire?"

"Demon," he announced proudly. "Most likely."

The principal lifted his chin and gave him a knowing look. Yes, so the son had followed in the father's footsteps. But Kir now knew that Colin had fallen in love and had followed his heart *after* he left the family and the pack.

"Demon," Etienne muttered. "You know she would not be allowed to bring a demon child into the pack, Kir. It may have been a blessing she lost your child—"

Kir pounded the desktop with his fist. "How dare you."

"I speak on behalf of the pack, Kir. We have expanded our arms far enough to welcome a faery."

"At your command! And now you change your mind, so you think you can reverse it all? If you insist on sending Bea back to Faery, then you'll have to send me along, as well."

"You are young and rash, Kirnan." Etienne sighed. He

rapped a fist on the windowsill. "Doesn't matter," he said, staring out the window. "It's already done."

"Done?"

Kir's hands grew instantly clammy. His heart dropped to his gut and thudded roughly. He knew exactly what that word meant.

"No," he said on an aching gasp.

"It had to be done, Kir. And I'm sorry for doing it this way."

"No!" He shoved the chair out of the way and headed for the door. "If she's not at my home, I will tear you apart!"

The pack wolves were directed by Madeline. Jacques was absent, though. As a precaution, he hadn't been invited along. Bea succumbed to the strange-smelling chemical that the wolves pressed over her nose with a cloth. She hadn't had time to scream. Her eyelids fell shut.

Her last thought was that she would never see Kir again.

Kir kicked open his front door and rushed inside. He didn't call out for Bea. He couldn't scent her. Instead, a mournful cry keened from his mouth as he tracked through the kitchen, slashing an arm across the bowl of apples on the counter. They landed on the stone floor behind him with a crash. In the living room he walked around the furniture, pushed open the French doors and stomped out into the yard. The bright sun angered him and he growled, fisting his fingers.

Back in the house, he ran up the stairs. The bedsheets had been torn from the bed and pulled across the floor. They'd left the bed in a mess after making love last night, but the sheets had been pulled up on the bed this morning. He remembered that exactly. Had a struggle occurred?

If anyone from his pack had hurt her…

He howled, loud and long. A warning cry that birthed from his soul.

Rushing outside, he drove like a madman back to the pack compound. Once there, he didn't take a moment to breathe or calm his anger. He needed the fury and rage. They would see how they had hurt him. His pack had betrayed one of their own.

Shoving aside Jean-Louis, who was but a lackey and who could have had nothing to do with the taking of his wife, Kir strode down the hall. Jacques stepped out and stopped him. The wolf shook his head and held up his hands placatingly. But the hairs on his head stood up.

"Tell me you were not the one who took my wife from our home."

"I did not, Kir. I wasn't invited to go along. If it had been anyone else, we would have had to do the same. Think about this."

"I love her!" He lunged for Jacques, shifting to werewolf as he did.

Jacques began to shift, and that rallied half a dozen pack members, who shifted to answer the call to protect and secure one of their own. Kir raged at them, slashing his arm and catching a shoulder or thigh with his deadly claws. Someone jumped on his back and pulled him down.

He heard the principal shout in his *were* voice. The tones were to stop it, to settle, but he ignored them. He wanted blood. He would not stop until he held his wife in his arms again.

Kir's mouth was dry. His muscles ached. He was no longer in werewolf shape. He wore jeans and no shirt. Blood scent alerted him, but then he unclenched his muscles. It was his blood. He'd taken a beating. And he'd delivered a beating.

He didn't regret his actions. If he had harmed one of the pack, it was because he had been hurt. Betrayed by the very wolves he called family.

Betrayed for so long.

"Had to do it," his principal said.

Looking up, Kir noticed Etienne stood in the corner of the dark cell. He'd not scented him. The fight had decimated his strength and his remaining strength felt inaccessible, out of reach. Now he realized the pull in his shoulder muscles was because his arms had been yanked back and up. His wrists were manacled with silver lined with leather. It wouldn't burn, but the silver so close to his skin would subdue him. Bastards.

This was the very cell in which they had held Sophie.

"You did not have to do it," he muttered.

"Give it a few days and your anger will lessen. It's tough. I understand that."

"I love her!"

"Yes." Etienne kicked his heel against the wall behind him. "Love sometimes hurts."

"No. That's what people say when they want to cover up their mistakes."

"Your father left you for love."

"No, he didn't! He left because his heart was cold from living with my mother. Because you took her away from him. My father escaped the pack and then found love."

Etienne shrugged. "Colin has always been weak. Madeline fell out of love with him long before I stepped in to soothe her aching, empty heart."

Kir winced. He didn't want to know. It was too late for truths.

"So many lies. And now you take away the one thing that meant everything to me. You betrayed me!"

"Betrayal is a strong accusation, Kir."

"It stands. Pack Valoir means nothing to me now. I won't apologize for loving my wife. Bring her back to me. Or I will leave the pack."

"Think those words through carefully, Kir. Leaving the pack is a serious deal."

He knew that. He'd be banished, forever branded an omega wolf. No pack would ever take him in. He would no longer have family.

The door closed, leaving him alone. Family? Had he ever had family? Or had it merely been a twisted fantasy?

Kir strained against the chains, pressing his body forward, knowing he could not escape the silver manacles. He howled for hours, endlessly, until his throat was so raw he could only whimper.

He'd promised Bea they would never be separated. He'd not kept his word.

Chapter 22

Bea woke sprawled on a cold stone floor. Shadows fell upon moss-covered rocks scattered haphazardly around a murky, moss-frosted pool of stagnant water. Weremice scampered nearby, their spiked tails scratching through the dust. Insects that could get caught in a faery's hair and steal away strands for their nests skittered along the stones. A blue-winged crow sat in the high cross-barred oriel that was open to the violet midnight sky.

She recognized this place. And such recognition curled dread about her spine. When younger, she and her cousins had snuck in here through an underground tunnel and played spook. It was the place her father sent those awaiting trial or punishment. The tower. Which wasn't much more than a tall column of fieldstone mortared together with silted clay from the bog witch's pond. It was the spell upon the stones that kept inside whatever needed to be restrained.

She smelled the stench now; it never lessened. Rotting

flora and dead things. The only way in was through an underground chamber, which must be close to the mossy grating.

Bea clasped her knees to her chest and shivered.

She was back in Faery.

Kir had not returned home to protect her.

Kir moaned in his sleep. "Bea."

Or was he caught in a waking reverie? Surely he'd sat in this cold, dark basement for days. And when not sitting he paced in an attempt to keep his muscles limber. Push-ups focused his thoughts. His mind was growing dark with worry over things he could not control. And revenge.

A pack female had brought him food and bottles of water. He'd eaten little—no appetite—but had consumed all the water. He needed to maintain his strength. It was difficult to force food down his gullet when worry about Bea occupied every moment, every breath.

Was she in Faery right now? Had to be. Etienne had acted swiftly. Had the principal's act of taking Kir's wife away from him been further retaliation against Colin, for whom he had held such hatred over the years? It was hard to fathom. Etienne had treated Kir well, as if he were his own son.

Was that it? They'd gotten rid of Colin and had acted as though he'd never existed. Kir and Blyss had grown to consider Etienne their father. He wondered how Estella felt about it all, with Madeline still in the pack. What weird sort of relationship did the threesome have?

He couldn't think about it. Didn't want to go there. All that mattered was his wife. Were they treating Bea kindly? Surely her father would not be pleased to see her returned.

Kir prayed Malrick allowed Bea back into his home.

What was he thinking? He didn't want Bea to be welcomed back into the family that had treated her so poorly. He wanted her here, in the mortal realm, at his side where she belonged. Because he accepted her, no matter what. Half demon? It didn't matter to him. He was over hating an entire race. And Sophie could no longer be blamed.

The door swung open to reveal two pack members. Kir blinked through the dullness to make out their faces. Etienne directed Jacques to unlock the chains.

"It's been three days," Jacques muttered as he twisted a key in the manacle lock that secured Kir's wrist. He slapped Kir's shoulder. "You over it yet, man?"

Kir eyed his friend and swallowed back a vicious retort. Hadn't the man the compassion to understand how he was feeling? How would Jacques feel if the situation were reversed with his Marielle?

But he couldn't blame Jacques for not understanding. He'd never had someone he loved literally torn away from him. Hell, the man's wedding was in a few weeks. He'd understand soon enough.

"Three days," Kir muttered.

He was three days separated from Bea. Three days distant, surmounted by the greater distance of a different realm. She must believe he had abandoned her. What else could she think?

"Can we trust you won't explode again?" Etienne asked.

Kir nodded. Now was not the time for anger and fighting. Now he must think and conserve his energy. He would need it if he was going to find Bea.

"Go home and sleep it off," Etienne said. "Return to work enforcing next week."

"Nothing has changed," Kir said. He dropped the manacle that had wrapped his wrist for days. The skin was abraded, but he'd heal before he stepped foot off the compound. Weakness from the silver would continue to challenge him. "By keeping me here, giving me time to think, you've cemented my decision, Principal Montfort."

Etienne stepped up to him, his shoulders squared and chin lifted. The elder wolf had always held Kir's respect. Until now. "And what decision is that?"

Jacques muttered, "Ah, hell."

"I'm leaving the pack."

"Don't do it, man," Jacques said.

"Will you bring her back?" Kir asked his principal.

"I cannot and will not undo what has been done." Etienne did not back away from his stance before Kir, but his face softened, his gaze less stern. "Kir, please. You must view this from my position. Even if Malrick did offer another alliance, I wouldn't trust him the second time to accept it. I'm sorry, but this was a spoils of war situation. We've already ceased guarding the portal. Faery will have to deal with their mistakes on their own."

"You did what you had to," Kir said, though he didn't agree with those actions. "So now I will do what I have to."

"What does that mean?" Jacques asked.

"I'm taking the war to Faery." Kir straightened, looking down on his principal. "I will bring her back."

"Are you insane?"

"Wouldn't you do the same for your wife?"

Etienne thrust back his shoulders. "That's different."

"Why? Because she's a wolf? Not a half-breed faery who the pack has sneered at since the day we took her in. The day I agreed to the marriage vows, the day the entire pack seemingly accepted Bea into our family. You made that decision when you accepted the bargain from Malrick and assigned me to marry her. Now look how you show her our respect."

"She has not earned our respect!"

Kir fisted his fingers but, wisely, held back the urge to

lay his principal flat. "Admit that no matter what she did she could have never done anything to earn your respect."

Etienne noted Kir's fist with a lift of his jaw and a snarl to show his fangs. "I don't want to discuss this anymore. It's been done."

"It has. Let each man take responsibility for his own actions." Kir looked to Jacques. "You're my brother, but I'd never ask you to stand beside me. I have to do this alone. I hope you can forgive me."

Jacques opened his mouth to reply but instead nodded, holding a tight jaw.

"Banish me tonight," Kir said to Etienne. "I need to have that ritual over with so I can go after Bea."

Kir strode out of the basement room, his intention to take a shower in the pack barracks and put on some clean clothes. He wouldn't go home. There was only one way out of a pack. And that required a test of strength and fortitude.

Chapter 23

The summons was a surprise. Bea had wallowed in the tower for what she guessed had been three days with little more than a few wilted mushrooms she'd dug out from the moss and stale water to drink. Just when she felt sure she would be left to die, a hob popped its knobby head from below, pushing up the moss-coated grating. "He wishes to see you."

So Bea followed the wobbling bit of gruff and smell down the dirt tunnel that was wrapped in tree roots and dripped with dank liquid. Topside opened into a small chamber off the main receiving room in Malrick's castle. Bea recognized it by the smell of humble-bees carrying pollen from the plethora of dewblooms that spilled down the chamber walls.

After crossing the quartz-floored chamber and to the far wall, the hob pulled back the iron-banded rowan door and nodded she make haste and follow. Bea scampered after her jailor, entering the receiving room that ever dazzled. Black-and-pink quartz-fashioned floors and walls.

Her father, tall, slender and aged, stood with his back to her, his fingers rattling impatiently near the leather strap that holstered a fine crystal scythe at his thigh. On those fingers glinted the tribal markings that were also magical sigils he could control with but a touch. It would take years, perhaps even mortal centuries, for Bea to master such magic with her burgeoning sigils. His thick black hair spilled over narrow shoulders and contrasted with the royal blue tunic he wore to his thighs. A decidedly medieval look for him.

Now that Bea had been out in the mortal realm, she could compare Faery fashion to some of the older mortal centuries. The Unseelies were quite behind the humans in some things. But not weaponry. The crystal scythe was just for show; the glamour-infused tattoos were the man's real weapon.

"I am displeased," Malrick hissed without turning to acknowledge her.

Shivering and weak, she rubbed her palms up her arms and fought to remain strong. She would not let this man reduce her to the cowering servant she had once been. Yes, a servant in her own home.

"I have done nothing to earn your displeasure," she said. "It is you who did not honor the bargain between pack—"

"Silence!"

Malrick swung about gracefully. Bea stepped back. While his face was beautiful, his eyes were silver. She'd never known them to be violet. Aging faeries' eyes faded and grew silver, but when that happened they were older than some worlds. Bea thought the color ugly, always had.

"You don't want me here," she said carefully yet firmly.

She lifted her chin, maintaining her courage. "And I don't want to be here."

Malrick gestured toward the door. "Then leave."

So simple as that?

She knew that if she were to venture beyond her father's demesne she would never find her way back to the mortal realm and would likely get lost or, worse, attacked by something she'd only imagined in her nightmares. She may have wielded bravery in the safety of her husband's presence, but here?

"Would you direct me to a portal?" she asked with hope and a staunch determination to maintain that bravery she had tried on and found she liked. "Send a guide? Ensure my safe leave?"

Malrick scoffed and lifted his chin. "You'd never survive. You've been pampered all your life."

"Pampered?" Bea could only gasp and search the ground, unwilling to meet his cruel gaze. All her life she'd been treated as less than, and now to discover such treatment had been Malrick's idea of pampering?

"At the very least," she started cautiously, "you could have told me about my mother."

"I told you as much as I could stomach."

That her father held such disgust for her mother ripped at Bea's insides. Truly, the woman must be evil incarnate. "She is demon?"

Malrick looked down his nose at her, a haughty glare that ever made her want to cringe into her skin and become small, disappear even.

But she remained strong. "I can understand why you hate me. Of all the mixed blood sidhe who roam Faery that are your progeny you surely cannot embrace one who has demon blood racing through her veins. That makes me one of The Wicked. But seriously? You're the one who had sex with a demon in the first place."

"I will not discuss— You try me, Beatrice!"

"As I must! For I've never had the fortitude to stand up to you until now."

"And why is that? Do you see what a little time in the mortal realm has done to you? It has made you—"

"Stronger." She stepped forward, confidence straightening her spine. "And smarter. And...kinder. And curious. Always curious." And it was all because of Kir's patience and loving manner. Within the safety of his love he'd allowed her to blossom. "I know you do not love the hundreds of women who stream through your life, and I can only guess a demoness was some kind of forbidden fruit to you."

Her father gestured dismissively. "I have my fetishes."

She didn't want to hear about that. She'd lived it. "Will you at least tell me what my mother meant to you? Did you love her at all?"

Malrick sighed heavily and closed his eyes. The heel of his hand caught against the jet hilt of the crystal scythe. "Bea—"

"Please, father. It is the last thing I will ever ask of you."

"I shall hold you to that." And his eyes met hers in a discerning once-over. Bea held his gaze, defiantly. Proudly. "Her name was Sirque," he finally said. "But I have told you that."

"It is all you have ever told me. You left me to concoct a make-believe image of a mother from the few clues of my own nature. The fangs and the cravings for ichor? I thought I was half vampire."

He smirked. "And you behaved as such. Abominable."

She clasped her arms across her chest, but the hug was far from the reassurance she sought from the only man she trusted. "But then to learn my mother was demon? I've only known to despise demons, more so than vampires."

"Demons are not an eloquent breed. Too attached to Beneath and their Master of Darkness, who ever insists he is greater than all of Faery."

Himself, the Master of Darkness, the Prince of Demons, did rule over Beneath. Mortals called it Hell. Himself insisted he ruled over the sidhe for they were halfway between angel and demon, and he, the devil Himself, had once been angel. Bea had been told the legends and myths of most breeds as she'd grown up. Faery tales, all of it. And those were the truest tales of all.

"Sirque..." Malrick lifted his head and offered quietly, "Pursued me. She...well, I won't say. The less you know about your mother, the better."

"You must tell me! I have a right to know."

"And I have a right to protect that which I love!"

Bea dropped her fist at her side. His words did not ring true. "What? Don't you dare use that word. You don't know the meaning of love."

"And you do? The Wicked cannot know love."

Yes, she had heard that in the faery tales, as well. But she now knew that to be false. Because she did love. Fiercely.

"Love is this!" She thrust out her hand to show him the bonding mark, which did not glow now that she had been separated from her husband. "Love is the ache in my heart that will never go away because I have been separated from the only man who has ever shown me kindness."

"I grant you a kindness by allowing you back into my home," Malrick said in a low, measured tone.

Bea knew it was a tone she must fear, but this time—no. She thrust back her shoulders and defied the Unseelie king by meeting his cold silver gaze. "You welcomed me back and into your dungeon. Some kindness."

"I did not order your death."

Indeed, he would see that as a form of compassion. Repulsed that this man's ichor ran through her veins, Bea could almost bring herself to embrace her demon mother if given a choice between the two. Any creature must possess more heart than this cruel Faery king.

"Allow me to leave your home. I promise to never return, to not ever darken your days with the evil that I am."

"You are not evil, Beatrice."

"At the very least I am wicked. And I remind you of her."

He nodded and turned away. "Her eyes were red. Yours are bright and wondrous. You will never be like her." He cast a glance over his shoulder at her. "And for that you should be thankful."

Such a cruel man. "What can you tell me about her habits, her desires, her needs? She gave me a blood hunger. Is that normal?"

He nodded, without facing her. "Could be. I never question my fetishes."

"Your dark sexual desires made a child, Faery king. And you treated me like dirt all my life. Just let me go. I want to leave Faery and return to the mortal realm, where I am loved."

"Leave, then. But I'll not direct you to a portal. Take only the clothes on your back and abscond from my sight." Malrick gestured to his lackey, whispered in his ear and sent him off. "I would ask you to stay. You will, at the very least, be alive in my home."

"Alive but never happy. I'll take my chances out in the Wilds. It can't be that treacherous."

"It's not, for one who has grown up in the Wilds."

Yeah, so the man wasn't on Team Beatrice. What was new?

"Could you at least, uh…direct me in a way that's not so harrowing as all the rest?"

Malrick smirked and as his lackey returned carrying a box, he approached Bea. "I care for you more than I will ever be able to admit. And, in proof, I will do this small favor for you."

Bea thrust up her chin, unwilling to show the slightest glee at his sudden step toward compassion. It wasn't kindness. It was simply what he thought she wanted to hear.

"When you leave, travel straight until the underforest ends. Then turn to your right, fly over the end of the forest and journey on from there. You must not pass through the end. The landscape is brutal. But if you make it over, you'll have a good chance of survival. With luck, you may locate a portal that leads away from this realm."

Sounded so not like a party Bea wanted to attend. But she'd been practicing with weapons all her life. She knew defense. And defense would be key when traveling the Wilds, for even she wasn't familiar with half the creatures that inhabited Faery. Though she innately knew that lacking knowledge had kept her obliviously safe all her life.

She nodded, maintaining a stoic resignation. She would not show her father how desperately she needed him to touch her. Perhaps hug her and send her off with his good wishes. Impossible. Malrick was forged from something so cold and adamant it had no name. He thought demons were the cruel, despicable ones?

The lackey opened the wood box and Malrick drew out a crystal blade, hilted with finely worked metal that glinted in all colors with a red sheen. He held it between them. Waning daylight danced in the clear crystal, flashing out brilliant red beams. *Like demon eyes.* Yet there in the center traced a black vine as if the spine of the weapon.

"This is yours," he said, and handed it to her.

Bea took the knife. The hilt was warm, and it seemed to conform to her grip, but that was impossible. Metal didn't do such things. The curved crystal blade was so clear she could see her hand through it.

"It was your mother's," he offered. "Sirque left it behind when she was— Well, it is yours to own now."

"This was once my..."

She couldn't afford a blink when the blade flashed brightly across her vision. Beguiled by the beauty of it and the knowledge that her mother had once owned this, she could only revere the gorgeous object. And then she feared it. Was the crystal threaded through with the blackness that was her mother's blood? The same blood that ran through her veins and had darkened her ichor?

"You've been trained to use weapons properly. I know," Malrick added. "I made sure my best trainers were available to you as you were growing up. None but the finest education."

That startled Bea. She'd always thought to sneak a lesson here and there from some in the household troops and had sworn them to never breathe a word of it to her father. Malrick had instigated those lessons?

No, don't step over to his side. It is not your side.

"I can hold my own," she said. "I've had to protect myself from my siblings and others in the household all my life. But much as you claim to be the instigator in my training, you'd never admit to knowing I had to fight for survival."

"Beatrice, I..." Malrick exhaled heavily and swept a hand before her, gesturing to the blade. "Use it with care. I send you off with blessings, and the sincere wish that you will not encounter such opposition that you will need to use it. Goodbye, my daughter of Sirque."

Bea lifted her head and found in her father's silver eyes a strange glow. Similar to the one she had first seen in Kir's eyes that summer evening when they had been forced to bond in marriage. Was it compassion?

Impossible.

"Thanks, Malrick." She chucked him aside the arm with a fist, and he flinched.

Mossy misery, he was still the same cold Malrick. No kindness in his heart.

With the insurmountable task of breaching the Wilds before her, Bea sought levity to encourage her first steps into the dangerous unknown. "So, I'm off."

"Indeed you are." Malrick turned, and his lackey followed him out of the receiving room, leaving her standing there alone and—she could admit it to herself—afraid. Her father had left her as if she were nothing more than a nuisance merchant attempting to ply her useless wares upon him. Never to see her again. Never.

And she was good with that.

She turned to the massive doors that opened out into the courtyard. And beyond that, the forest. And beyond that, the Wilds.

Tears spilled from her eyes. "Shouldn't be so difficult to march away from an asshole like him. I'll pretend he's just my bitchy werewolf monster-in-law."

Yet she stood there for a long time, the crystal blade clutched tightly against her breastbone. At one moment, she almost looked back. Might Malrick have twisted a glance over his shoulder after her? She would not look. She must not…

Bea turned around, her eyes tracing the long hallway strung with direwebs and dripping humble-bee mead. The glow from the bright Faery sun made her blink. Malrick was gone.

She let out her held breath.

"Alone," she said. "Get used to it, Bea."

* * *

Kir clenched the steel bar suspended a foot above his head and gritted his jaws. A claw cut across his back, tearing open his skin and nicking bone. He'd chosen not to have his wrists bound to the bar; instead, he would receive the ritual banishment due an unbound, free wolf.

Shifted to werewolf shape, the pack males had reluctantly queued up for the ritual that a wolf must endure as a means to ceremoniously oust them from their home—their very family. Half the pack had already cut claws across his skin. He had only ten more lashes to go.

Another cut into his flesh. And another.

He'd not yet cried out, though he clenched his jaw mightily. The claws were delivered swiftly, yet deeply. And they'd been dipped in wolfsbane, the wicked punishment to this trial. He felt every cut as a betrayal. His pack should have stood by him and protected Bea. Instead, following Etienne, they had chosen to make a grandstand act of defiance to show Malrick their disdain.

It could have been handled differently. But he would no longer question or argue. He wanted this done so he could get to her.

Five more wolves cut into his skin. Two more left. Etienne stepped up and paused. He could hear his principal's rapid heartbeat. The werewolf was both excited by the release of endorphins, the blood and the pain, and also reviled.

Blood poured from Kir's back, and he knew the muscles would take days, perhaps weeks, to heal properly, for the wolfsbane fucked with the healing process. He hung now, his fingers barely clinging to the bar. It was all he could do not to let out a long moaning cry.

"Do it!" Kir yelled.

And Etienne's claws cut into his rib bones. Kir's knees

bent. He clung. *Mustn't let go. Show them strength and face this trial with honor. Walk away from Etienne, who betrayed me and my sister, a proud man.*

Mercy, but only one wolf remained to mark him. Jacques.

Kir and Jacques had grown up together. They'd been close—brothers—their families a blend, and many times Kir had gone to Jacques's mother for the things he needed and vice versa. Jacques knew Kir's dreams and hopes, his desires. He knew that Jacques could not have found a better woman to love than Marielle. He hated that walking away from the pack also meant severing the bond he had with his wolf brother.

But some things were more important. Like the trust he had given Bea.

His best friend stepped up behind him. The werewolf had not a human voice in fully shifted form, yet Kir could sense his friend's distress in the acrid scent that oozed from him.

One more. Just do it, he prayed. *Make it end.*

Jacque's claw dragged down the back of Kir's neck, cutting into his vertebra. Kir howled and dropped the bar. He fell to his knees in the puddle of his blood.

Jacques shifted instantly. His hand landed on Kir's bloodied shoulder. "Come on, man. I'm taking you to the infirmary."

"No," Kir gasped, heaving for a breath. "Home."

And he blacked out.

Kir woke in the infirmary facedown on a cot, a flat pillow crushed against his cheek. The white-tiled walls were spattered with his blood. The odor of dried blood repulsed him. He cried out at the pain on his back and realized he'd been bandaged, for wide strips of gauze wrapped around his chest.

Reaching back was a lesson in patience. Every muscle ached and felt as if it had been shredded to ribbons. He tugged at the gauze below his rib cage, and the thin medical fabric pulled at the wounds. Howling in pain, he didn't stop until the bloody gauze had been torn away.

As his eyelids fluttered and he tumbled off the bed, he noticed someone standing across the room. A sniff scented her chemical perfume. Madeline.

"I can't believe you have done such a thing, Kir," she said. "For what? That filthy faery?"

For the first time in his life Kir saw his mother's vile soul, and he did not like it. Had he the strength, he would have lashed out at her. If only he had known she had been his ultimate betrayer.

"You are just like your father."

Perhaps he was. His mother may have grown to believe her lies over the years, but he would not stomach them one moment longer.

"You..." he muttered. It hurt to move, to open his eyes, but he did and managed to focus on the woman standing with arms crossed over her chest. "And Etienne."

Madeline gasped. An admission. The only one he would ever get.

"Leave me," he said.

"Kir, no, I—"

"Go!" He growled at her, and his mother fled, the click of her heels racing down the hallway the last thing he ever wanted to hear from her.

Hours later, Kir agreed to let Jacques help him into the shower to clean up, but he wouldn't let the nurse put on more bandages. He would heal. Eventually. He didn't have time for this. He needed to find Bea!

"I'll drive you home," Jacques said as Kir pulled up a

clean pair of leather pants and shoved his feet into a borrowed pair of boots. "But you're not bleeding in my car. Put a shirt on, man."

He caught the long-sleeved shirt Jacques tossed him and pulled it on but didn't button it up. The wounds had scabbed and would be healed in a day or two. It would take a lot longer for his pack's betrayal to resolve in his soul.

Without saying a word, he strode by his friend and down the hallway toward the car park.

Jacques didn't say much on the drive home. There wasn't anything to say. He was pack scion; he'd had to follow his principal's orders or risk his own banishment. Hell, he would never step so far beyond his father's rule. And Kir understood that. The good of the pack always came first. It was a rule he had abided always.

Until now. Rules must be bent to accommodate real life. And real life was messy and unexpected, and—when love was involved—demanded a man follow the rules of his heart.

Pulling up before Kir's house, Jacques shifted into Park and grabbed Kir by the wrist before he could turn and get out. "I know what it's like to love someone as much as you, man. What you feel for the faery has gotta be strong if it allowed you to do this."

Kir nodded, accepting Jacques's form of an apology. An apology that wasn't necessary. Both knew what was required to leave the pack. And he couldn't in good faith have remained with a family that would not accept the woman he loved.

"We had good times," Jacques offered. "You will always be my brother. Hell, I wish you could have been my best man. I'll feel you standing there beside me, Kir. Know that."

Kir nodded. "Keep up the good work with the enforcement team. Don't let the packs indulge in the blood games and keep an eye out for V-hubs."

"Got it under control. But it won't be the same without you by my side. Go and find her, man. Hold her tight and never let her go."

He clasped Jacques's hand and gave it a squeeze. "Bea and I will be fine. Thanks for the ride. And…thanks for all of it, brother."

Jacques nodded and turned his head away quickly.

Kicking open the door, Kir slid out and waved as his friend drove off. He might see him again someday. He hoped that he would. And they would be civil to each other, but Kir's banishment would not allow Jacques to show him any sort of friendship or companionship. Never could he return to the compound without facing swift and wicked retaliation.

Never again could he speak to Madeline. So be it.

The sun slashed a wicked heat across Kir's neck. The shirt stuck to his back where the scabs had cracked. He pulled it off, sure none of his neighbors would see the ravaged mess on his skin on his short walk up the sidewalk to his front stoop.

But as he arrived at the steps, he saw a woman standing there. Tall, dark, slender and beautiful. She wore what looked like black abraded leather on her legs and body. A sheer black veil covered her face down to her top lip so he could not determine her eye color. And spiraling out from each temple were long ebony horns.

No need to see her eyes. Kir immediately sensed what stood before him.

The demoness stepped down toward him. "I understand one of my daughters has been searching for me."

Chapter 24

The day was going much better than anticipated. Bea marched toward the underforest. And she did so with a sigh of relief. No dangerous intruders had leaped out at her; nor had she been attacked by anything swooping down from the azure sky. She wasn't starving, though she certainly wouldn't refuse something to eat and drink.

If the Wilds were all they'd been made to be, she should be bleeding and shivering in fear for her very life right now. Begging for rescue from a valiant knight armed to the teeth with weapons of all sorts to combat any creature he should encounter.

So far all she suffered were sore feet and an annoying itch at the back of her neck.

She swatted at a nuisance sprite who had been dive-bombing her hair all afternoon. "If sprites are all I've to worry about, then this adventure shouldn't be so taxing. I'll be home before I know it."

Then she smiled because now when she said *home* she meant the mortal realm. Never had a place welcomed her more.

And then she frowned. If she did get back to the mortal realm and to the place she called home with Kir, *would* he welcome her back? She only assumed he was upset about her kidnapping and subsequent return to Faery. What if he was not? Perhaps he may have been initially upset to lose her, but what if, after a few days without her, he'd determined that it was best she remain in her land and he in his?

Clasping her arms across her chest, she shook her head fervently. "He loves me. He has to. I need him to."

Because if he did not, then she truly had no home.

The glint from a pool of water distracted her dire thoughts. It was a good size, probably a lake. Bea eagerly rushed toward it. Colorful stones and boulders scalloped the shore. Hoping to quench her thirst, she carefully navigated a path to the vivid blue water.

The water was so cold it gave her brain freeze, but she lapped it up, knowing her journey could turn perilous and there was no guarantee if or when she'd next come upon fresh water.

She was hungry, though. "Should have asked the old man for a last supper before he sent me off."

On the other hand, her hunger was more for blood, not food. She'd not known that demons required blood, or ichor, for survival. Was it all demons, or just the particular breed that was her mother? What sort of demon had Sirque been anyway?

That Malrick had been able to dismiss her a second time with the same disinterest as he had the day of her wedding no longer bothered Bea. What did was that he'd thought he was protecting her by not providing details about her mother. So Sirque was demon. And Malrick hated demons, and through the years, he had ingrained that hatred in Bea.

Kir held a similar hatred.

But seriously? If she thought about it, what was it about demons she and her husband need fear and hate so much? There were all sorts in Faery. Demons had easy access for the very reason Himself, the Dark Prince, considered himself one who could rule Faery. Some breeds of faery were once of the angelic realm, as were the major demons, from which all demonic races had birthed. At least, that's how Bea understood it from the stories she'd read as a child. School had not covered demons in detail for the very reason they were looked upon as a lesser, vile race.

"The Wicked," she muttered.

Somewhere in Faery there was a cold dark place where the half-breed demons were exiled, forced to live away from all others. A place where she apparently belonged. Why had Malrick not sent her away? Perhaps the man did have an inkling of compassion behind those hard silver eyes.

Bea sighed.

Would it have been better to be half vampire and suffer the mere disgust the sidhe had for the blood drinkers? She didn't know anymore. She didn't know anything. She was wrong. Different. Disgusting.

Even her husband couldn't completely accept her. If she had been half vampire, it would have been easier for Kir to accept his fate to remain her husband till death did part them. Perhaps that was why he'd not come after her?

A ripple in the water flashed silver, then wavered to a turquoise ribbon that dispersed away from shore. A spatter of water droplets sprayed Bea's face. She sneezed and blinked as something rose above the surface. Her attention riveted as another something, and another, also surfaced.

Bea shuffled back against a slick, mossy boulder, her bare feet two steps from the water's edge.

Bobbling in the clear waters, three sirens stared silently at the faery hugging the boulder. Long, silken green hair swished about their shoulders, frosting the water surface in slick spills. Their skin matched the mossy stones and their eyes were as silver as Malrick's eyes. Gills at their necks and the tops of their breasts breathed in and out.

"N-nice day, ladies," Bea tried carefully.

She needn't fear an attack from creatures who existed in the water. As long as she didn't go in for a swim, she should be safe. *Should be* being the key words in that thought.

"Been walking all day without rest. I was thirsty. Just getting a drink."

The thin one in the center blinked and a milky sheen slowly peeled back from her eyes. "Take freely from our home."

Bea wrinkled her lips as realization stabbed at her. She'd been drinking from their home. Where they swam and did all sorts of bodily function kind of stuff.

She wasn't thirsty anymore.

"We offer you respite," the middle siren said. She was apparently the leader, for she floated in the fore. "You look as if you have been on an arduous journey."

"I have," she said, pleased that they could communicate in a language she understood. "That obvious, eh?"

Though she wouldn't mention the most trying challenge of the day had been untangling herself from a meadow of bramble vines after she'd lain down to rest a bit.

"I've...been sent away from my father's home. He doesn't want me there. I'm trying to find my way back to the mortal realm. Do you know the way to a portal?"

All three shook their heads no. "Why does your father not wish you in his home, dark one?"

Bea leaned forward, cocking an elbow on her knee. "He hasn't been a big fan of me since the day I was born. To get rid of me the first time, he married me off to a werewolf in the mortal realm."

The sirens gasped in harmony.

"Oh, that was a good thing. The new husband is fine and faithful and he really likes sex."

The mermaids blushed, if she could consider them growing greener in the cheeks and neck a blush.

"Everything was going swell until my husband's pack decided to send me back to Faery because Malrick didn't honor the wedding deal."

"Oh, Malrick," the center one said. "He's so dashing."

Bea didn't want to consider her father dating a mermaid, but it wasn't strange when in Faery. And he did like to mix it up with the breeds. A lot. Would she have been happier born with fins and gills instead of a thirst for ichor and blood? Swimming wasn't her strong suit, so nix that.

"You know my father—er, Malrick?"

Two of them bobbed their heads eagerly. The third growled at her sisters, revealing short, pointed teeth. Okay, some tension there. Wasn't as if Malrick was the most compassionate lover, surely.

"I'll put in a good word for you with my father if you can direct me to a portal," she tried.

"Oh!"

The two sisters who had not exclaimed slapped their hands over the other's mouth. "We surely don't know," one said quickly. The other agreed.

Bea could smell a liar when they all tried to hide that lie in unison.

"Darn. And here Malrick has been looking for a new

consort. Or so I hear. King of the Unseelie, you know. Big-time boyfriend material there."

The one who wanted to speak, but whom the other two were determined to keep quiet, wriggled against her sisters' grasps but to no avail.

"Why do you want to return to the mortal realm?" the middle one asked while she held a firm hand locked across her sister's mouth. "It is distasteful and odd. There are entire areas covered in dust without a drop of water to be had."

"I love my husband. I miss him. And, well, I am trying to find my mother. She's a demon."

All three blanched and the one whispered, "The Wicked."

"I know, right?" Bea couldn't completely get behind that statement, though.

Why did a demon have to be a bad thing? Her mother's DNA ran through her. Did that make her a bad person? "What are you doing in this part of Faery, wicked one?" the other sister observed. "You've gotten out of exile."

"I was never exiled."

Although, when she thought about it, maybe the mortal realm had been Malrick's means to exiling her in a manner he felt was less threatening than the unknown horrors she guessed The Wicked experienced.

"I'm not wicked," she insisted. "I'm just Bea." She tapped her lips with a finger. "So I wonder if my mother—Sirque is her name—"

One of the sirens shrieked so loudly Bea's ears popped. Another dived under the surface, her tail flapping the air. And the third growled like a dog and, fangs bared, lunged for Bea's throat, fixing her bony, clawed fingers about her neck.

Chapter 25

Far from fully recovered following the banishment, Kir's back ached with every step he took. The cooling autumn air should have soothed his lacerated skin, but instead it felt as if it were cutting through his flesh again with dull claws. He strode through the front doorway and turned to invite Sirque inside. She dipped her head and entered, her horns inches from slashing the wood door frame.

A chill traced his forearms, and Kir knew it was a visceral reaction to having allowed a demon to cross his threshold. Yet he would be wise not to judge. His hatred for demons had been instilled by observing his father's affairs. But his heart had turned. Not all such creatures were worthy of his scorn.

And if he showed any hate toward this woman, that would bleed through to his wife. And he loved Bea, no matter what.

"You've been through a trial," Sirque said as she noted the cuts down his back.

"I was banished from my pack. There is a ritual…"

"I am aware of it. Your species claims such familial love among their packs, and yet they can be unforgivingly brutal to their own. Why were you banished?"

"I chose to leave of my own accord because my pack betrayed me. Why don't you wait in the living room. Right through there. I'm going to run up and put on a shirt."

"You will heal more quickly if you leave it off." Sirque walked by him into the kitchen. "Take all the time you require, wolf."

He would love nothing more than to relax and rest and allow his body to restore, but he hadn't time. The longer he was away from Bea, the less she might believe he would come after her. He couldn't allow her to think that.

Striding up the stairs, at the top where he avoided the crushed railing splinters, he paused in a sunbeam and looked over his hand. The bond markings were pale. He squeezed his fingers into a fist. "Wherever you are right now, Bea, know that I am not far behind. I will trek worlds to find you."

He took a quick shower and slipped on jeans, but no shirt.

Thanks to the wolfsbane, the wounds would scar, unlike a usual wound that healed to fresh, unmarred skin. It was a ritual that had been passed down through the centuries. Now the scars were the flag of disrespect he must wear so that others would know he'd been banished.

"Whatever," he muttered, and padded barefoot down the stairs. It didn't matter what other wolves thought of him. The only opinion that carried any weight with him now was that of his wife.

Bea's mother had come to visit? All the way from Daemonia? For what reason? And why now? The mystery intrigued but only because the answers could help his wife.

He would spare her some time before rushing blindly off into Faery.

In the kitchen, he grabbed an energy drink and tilted the whole thing back. "Can I offer you wine?" he called.

"Yes, please. Something dark."

"Something dark." Like the demon sitting in his living room? He selected a dusty bottle of Malbec from the rack on the counter, bit out the cork and poured two goblets.

Sirque sat on the easy chair where he usually sat, a regal queen upon her throne, crowned with twisted black horns. She still wore the half veil down to her nose, but he could see her eyes, for it was sheer. Red irises glowed at him. Sulfur touched his nose. Any other creature might not detect it, but werewolves lived and died by their sense of smell.

"How did you hear that Bea was looking for you?" he asked as he handed her the goblet.

He did not sit, only because he wanted the air to circulate across his back. So he stood before the bookshelves. His gaze wandered to the sword on the wall. He'd give anything to have Bea sneaking about the house right now, naked, sword in hand, jumping out at him as if he were an intruder.

"Word from all realms reaches Daemonia quickly," the demoness offered. "I've a lackey who reports to me all items of interest."

"Why have you never come forward to visit Bea until now? How could you abandon her? Don't you realize what a tough life she's had living with Malrick, who has only given her disdain all her life?"

Sirque bowed her head. The great horns glinted, as if with mica flecked upon hematite. "Malrick has not treated her well? Bastard."

Did he detect true concern in her tone? "Had you expected differently?"

She shrugged. An odd gesture coming from a horned being. Too…human.

"Bea has been treated like a pariah for being a half-breed. Growing up, she has always believed she was half vampire."

"Vampire?" Sirque shuddered. "Why so?"

"Malrick would never give her the truth. She has a hunger for ichor. She drank ichor when in Faery, and here in the mortal realm, she drinks my blood and blood from humans."

"Such a taste cannot be for survival. And if so, it was not something I could have passed along to her. Although, I do favor the taste of blood." Sirque tapped a long black fingernail against her pale lip. "It is a delicacy I tend to indulge."

"Bea seems to think she needs it to survive. When she drinks it, she says she feels renewed."

"I assume she takes blood during a sexual encounter?"

Kir lifted his chin. In a sense, he was talking to his mother-in-law. The long-missing mother of his wife. But still. This topic of conversation made his skin shiver.

"It is the skin and sex that is required for my survival," Sirque explained. "Bea gets such contact while taking blood, yes?"

"Yes," he said. "Perhaps that's how it was in Faery. I don't understand, though. I know she doesn't do it like that with humans. And the last time she took blood from me, I let it spill into a cup before she drank it. There was no skin contact."

"Is she growing weaker?"

Kir shrugged. "She can't utilize her glamour since coming to the mortal realm. And there was the miscarriage. That took a lot out of both of us."

"I am sorry to hear that. Children are..." The demon bowed her head quickly.

"Why does Bea need blood?"

Sirque rose, setting the goblet on the glass table. Her long, pointed black fingernails tinged the delicate glass as she let it go. She strode toward the French doors overlooking the backyard, a grand thing of darkness, though oddly desiccated.

"I am an afferous demon," she explained. "Skin contact, the warmth of the vita flowing through the blood, is what I thrive on. And sex? Well. What better way to be served the life-giving vita than through the intertwining of bodies, skin against skin?"

She turned to gauge his reaction. Kir didn't swim for the hook. Her eyes moved slowly down his body, lingering at his abdomen, where some of the lashes had cut around from his back, and then lower. She was checking him out, and it made his skin crawl.

"Is she insatiable?" the demon asked.

"Uh..."

Sirque nodded, seeming to know the answer already. "Now that she's away from the confines of Faery, her demon side is rising up within her. And her sidhe half grows weaker. The demon in Beatrice seeks vita. She, like me, thrives on skin contact."

Bea was insatiable. Had been since their wedding night. So the blood hunger wasn't a necessity but rather an acquired taste? Perhaps that was why he hadn't developed a blood hunger from that initial surprise bite. He could hope so. Well, she wasn't vampire. And he'd never known a demon bite to give a werewolf a blood hunger.

"Apparently, I passed on my innate need for vita to Beatrice," Sirque said. "Though I would make a wager it is not as strong as mine, since she has Malrick's ichor running within her, too. Faery ichor and demon blood. When she bleeds, what does it look like?"

"I..." He almost said he hadn't seen her bleed, then the horrible night he'd found her beside the bathtub returned to his thoughts. "It looks like ichor," he managed softly. "Maybe a little darker. I thought it looked foggy."

"Hmm. Interesting. I'd expect it to be black by now. Well, as I've said, she is new to this realm yet. It'll take some time for the demon within her to place its stake."

"It matters little to me what color she bleeds. I am only concerned for Bea's welfare. For her heart. I love her, Sirque. And it tears me apart that she had to fight her way to me. What happened between you and Malrick? Why did you abandon your daughter?"

The room fell silent. Sirque's shoulders tightened, lifting as she tilted her head back. Kir was pushing, but he had every right to an answer, as did Bea.

"The afferous demon tends to drain her lovers rather quickly." She stroked a pointed fingernail down her neck. Her eyes teased seduction while also veiled with a subtle evil. "I'm told there is a species who can withstand my excessive needs, but I don't know what that is. So, I am always searching for a new species to test him, or her, out. So to speak."

Kir raised a brow.

"Werewolves don't do it for me. I ruled your sort out mortal decades ago. It's why I've retreated deep into Daemonia. There are thousands of breeds and species buried within its decrepit bowels."

"Why not stop? It seems a dangerous quest, if not distasteful."

"Distasteful, perhaps to one who does not require the

vita as I do." The demon ran a finger over her bottom lip, her head tilted in thought. "I've had many children, you know. Like any female, I have emotions and dreams and desires." She turned away from him and whispered, "All I desire is to hold a child in my arms."

"Then why don't you? You've had many? Have you abandoned them all?"

Sirque lifted her chin and the veil shimmered upon her face in the dull evening light. "If I kept the child—any of my children—I would drain them, or vice versa. Afferous demons feed off one another. Each caress, every hug, every motherly touch, would bring death that much quicker."

"Then don't get pregnant."

"But I want a child!" The demon's hands fisted at her sides and her horns seemed to grow wider, something he thought was a trick of the light.

He didn't know what to say to that. He could understand the need for family, the desire that could be so strong it would press a person to do desperate things. The worst image he could not chase out of his soul was that of Bea sitting before the tub, hands covered in ichor. He'd lost a little of his hopes and dreams that day.

Yet if Bea was half demon like her mother, would she then drain her own child of its life? Surely the faery half of Bea would quell the demon's nature to feed upon its young. The thought of the mother feeding off its infant sickened him.

Sirque paced back toward the window. "Every time I get pregnant, I think that maybe this time the father's genes will vanquish mine. I will be able to hold my child. And then the babe is placed in my arms and I can feel the vita tickle across my skin and all I want to do is feed. I didn't want to abandon Beatrice. I never want to abandon any of them. I simply have no choice. To walk away allows them to live. I give them life."

"Life yes, yet life as an orphan. Is that not far crueler than never giving the child life in the first place?"

"Is it too much to ask to be a mother? To know unconditional love? It is a universal desire, wolf. You see only evil in me. I know that. But I do have a heart. And it does bleed."

And in that moment he forgot that the woman standing before him was some hated species. He even forgot about the horrid horns that marked her so plainly *other*. Sirque was a woman with the same desire as many women: to hold her child in her arms. How sad that she was cursed with such a wicked need.

"You'll find the one who can give you a child to withstand your dark needs someday," he muttered.

She laughed softly. "My daughter must love you. You are kind when you've no reason to be so. Kindness is something I rarely witness. Thank you, Kirnan Sauveterre. Do you love my daughter?"

"With all my heart. That's why I left the pack."

"At a steep price."

He shrugged his shoulders. "I'll heal."

"Prideful wolf. But well-earned pride, I am sure. Where is Beatrice?"

Kir sighed. He quickly explained the pact made between pack Valoir and Malrick, and how the Unseelie king had dishonored the agreement.

"Your pack kidnapped my daughter and sent her back to Faery? That is abominable. Do you know how to travel about Faery? How to enter?"

"No, but our pack was tasked with guarding a portal deep in the city. I was going to give that a try."

"And if you should have success passing through the portal, what then? Have you ever been in Faery?"

"No, but we were given the opportunity to hunt there. It can't be that dangerous."

"It was under Malrick's protection you were allowed into Faery. Without it, you will find the terrain and its inhabitants a challenge."

"If I go well armed—"

"You will invite enemies who are even more well armed. Your mission is impossible."

"Nothing is impossible. It can't be. I have to find Bea!"

Sirque flinched at his bold declaration, then quickly resumed her regal stance. "You claim to love my daughter, yet you would sacrifice your life before you could get close enough to rescue her."

Thanks for the rousing support, he wanted to mutter.

In truth, he had no clue what to expect upon entering Faery. How awful or challenging could it be? Pack Valoir had enjoyed a few months' hunting there. The wolves who had hunted the lands had returned elated and unharmed, boasting of their kills and the utter freedom to run the lands.

Of course, none had attempted to journey to the Unseelie king's home and steal back his daughter to the mortal realm.

The demon rubbed her arms with her palms. Another strangely human motion. His wife's mother? Had Sirque and Bea known each other all their lives, Kir could have easily warmed to the new mother-in-law and welcomed her into his family. Even now he sensed she was much more similar to Bea than she would believe. A lost soul fighting desperately for her truths. And in that moment he sighed, thankful that he had arranged for Sophie's escape. He had done the right thing.

"Would you be my guide to Malrick's demesne?"

Sirque turned away from him again.

"You've been there, yes?"

She nodded. The horns glinted with the dull afternoon sunlight beaming through the windows.

"If you've navigated Faery once, you could do it again."

Sirque shuddered. Kir suspected there must have been bad blood between her and Malrick. He shouldn't ask so much. But the demon may be his only hope.

"I love Bea," he offered. "She is my world. I don't know how to breathe when she is away from me."

She lifted her chin. "You seem to be doing a fair job of it. You haven't passed out."

"Please?" he pleaded.

The demon turned and approached him until her natural sulfur perfume threatened to dizzy Kir's senses. "You swear to me she loves you? How can you be so sure? Perhaps she is pleased to be back in her father's home."

"I told you he ignored her, made her feel less than worthy for her mixed blood."

"That is very much like Malrick. I hate him for treating my daughter with such cruelty. Very well. I will be your guide. For good or for ill. It is the least I can do for the one I wished to hold."

Chapter 26

The siren was as slippery as…a mermaid. Bea struggled against the creature's powerful hold, which tightened about her neck. Scales armored the undersides of her opponent's fingers and they were sharply edged, which cut into her skin. When her eyelids fluttered and her lungs ached, Bea had one clear thought—struggle would be fruitless.

Her hand slipped away from pushing against the scaled beast, and her fingers played across the crystal blade Malrick had gifted her. She managed to grip it, wet as it was, and jab it upward. The siren's grip loosened. She coughed, gasping for air. Her chest gills flapped near Bea's face. The vicious creature slid into the waters.

Her sisters screamed and dived with their injured sister, leaving the azure surface bubbling into smooth, silver ripples.

Bea flopped onto a nearby boulder, panting, dripping with water and siren slime. The stuff was thick and green and—yuck! Her throat burned. It felt as if the siren's fingers were still there, squeezing the life from her. Clasping the crystal blade so tightly her knuckles whitened, she eyed the water. Not a ripple.

She crept farther up the boulder, pushing her wet and exhausted limbs up with her toes. "Who would have thought sirens were so strong?"

Exhausted, she closed her eyes but inwardly cautioned herself not to fall asleep so near the water. She needed to find a safe place.

But the only place she had ever felt safe was in Kir's arms.

The portal pack Valoir had been guarding was located in an underground aqueduct near the Louvre on the right bank. Kir and Sirque walked the limestone aisle that hugged the open water. Overhead, the concrete-bricked walls curved up into the ceiling. These aqueducts had been in existence for centuries. Mortal kings had used them to ferry prisoners and liaisons to and from the palace.

Last year, Kir had walked these same aqueducts with his sister's now-husband, Stryke Saint-Pierre, in a quest to locate demons intent on unleashing havoc in the mortal realm by summoning a foul demon king from Daemonia.

Lately, his life seemed to revolve around his involvement with demons. Perhaps it was a means to force him to stare into the one thing he feared most—an unfounded fear.

Walking ahead of him a few paces, Sirque wore a glamour so humans—they had passed a few vagrants along the way—would only see a tall woman with dark hair in a black leather catsuit, and no horns.

He wore leather pants, a long-sleeved black shirt and the vest Bea had imbued with her faery dust. Though it was light and supple, it felt as if it were armor. Sheathed at his back was the samurai blade from the wall. When he'd considered a pistol, Sirque had shaken her head. He mustn't invite danger. And mortal pistols would never fire correctly in Faery, generally resulting in an injury to the one holding the gun.

"I'm not sure exactly where it's located," he noted as they walked the cobbled pathway. "I wasn't assigned a shift to guard the portal because I drew the short stick."

"The short stick?" she asked over her shoulder.

Thinking about the term made Kir smile. Then Sirque caught him in an all-out grin.

"Whatever it means," she said, "it must be good."

"It's Bea. I was the one elected to marry Malrick's daughter, sight unseen, to seal the bargain. It's called drawing the short stick."

"Not something you should have been thrilled about," she noted. "So why the smile?"

"Because I've grown to love my short stick."

"My admiration for you grows more and more, wolf. It pleases me one of my daughters found someone who loves her."

"Have you met any of your other children?"

"Never. Though, in passing from realm to realm, I have spied on a few. Just to see what they've become. Most have not made me proud. Here." The demoness stopped and put up both palms as if to feel the air before her. "It's right before us. But it's been recently closed from the Faery side, which should make it impenetrable from this side."

"Do you know a way through?"

She nodded. "Let me try some malefic magic. Step back, but remain on guard. If you see me step through, follow closely."

With her back to him, the demoness spread out her arms

and turned her palms up, her fingers testing the air. Then those sharpened black fingernails danced, moved gracefully, as they seemed to be filing through some unseen system of spells or incantations. A low, steady hum surprised Kir with its strangely metallic tone, as if her voice were altered by an electronic device. The tones grew wide, then settled to nothing. She swayed and seemed to clutch at nothing, bringing it to her chest and then pushing it away.

A gorgeous note of the angels lured him closer—and the demoness disappeared. Through the portal?

No time to question. Rushing toward the space where Sirque had once stood, Kir leaped, and the portal's invisible skein crept over his face, hands and torso as he glided through it and landed on a lush patch of knee-high grass.

He rolled to a stop, landing on his back, his sword arm flailing right and the blade cutting with a *swoosh* across the grass. Sweet summer smells of loamy grass and verdant earth perfumed the air. Looking up, the sky, vast and wide, was different from the Paris sky. Not gray, or laced with trees dropping their leaves. This blue was unreal, bright and thick, as if a painting. And he could taste it, fresh and crisp at the back of his tongue.

He scanned the landscape. Vast green grass stretched as far as he could see. Yet the trees were…trees. And rocks and flowers scattered here and there were the same as the rocks and flowers in the mortal realm. No bizarre colors like a purple sky and yellow grass.

"This is Faery?"

"You don't seem impressed." Sirque appeared above him, offering a hand to pull him upright.

"It's gorgeous. But it doesn't look very menacing to me. Should be a nice jaunt through the meadow, eh?"

Sudden, intense pain at his back tore through Kir's shoulder muscles. He gritted his jaw and swung about to face the culprit. Before him stood a creature as wide as it was tall. Blocky, and with fists like tractor tires. It cracked a yellowed grin.

"Me like to suck marrow from werewolf's bones," it said.

Sirque spoke from behind Kir. "Welcome to Faery."

The first swing from the troll's fist skimmed Kir's shoulder and put him back twenty yards, his heels skidding through the tall grass. He knew he would only stand a chance against the blocky opponent in his *were* form.

The troll's bellow reeked of a stench greater than any Hell pit Kir could imagine. It charged, feet pounding the ground so that Kir felt every step thud in his veins.

Kir shifted, pulling off his clothing as he did. His bones lengthened and spine stretched. Fur grew over his skin and his maw formed into a deadly, toothy snarl. He achieved his werewolf shape within seconds. His werewolf lunged and clamped its jaw about the thick Achilles portion of the beast's ankle. Whipped about as the troll yowled and beat the air with its fists, the werewolf bit deeply into skin and muscle. The blood was acrid and the wolf almost let go, but if it did, such surrender would mean its sure death.

The wolf sensed another presence when a fierce slash of white fire curled about the troll's belly and squeezed as if a lasso. The flames were so hot the werewolf released its prey, stumbling backward from the brightness. Flame cut the creature it had been fighting in two.

The werewolf shook off the eerie shudder of near-death and sat, collapsing against a tree trunk, where he instinctively shifted. Kir always came out of his werewolf with a start. He shifted on the mossy ground, alert for danger, his nose scenting death and a metallic remnant of what could only be the white flame he'd witnessed.

* * *

The blue sky was too much for Kir's eyes. He saw no sun, though the brilliant azure burned his retinas. He blinked repeatedly and found himself stumbling across nothing more than the ribbon-thick grass. The air was too fresh, too pure, almost muffling.

He'd shoved down his pants first before shifting, so they were fine now—not a single ripped seam—as were the boots he'd swiftly kicked off. But he'd gotten to his shirt too late and the seams down the arms had split as well as tearing up the back. Complete loss. The vest, though, was intact and it glinted.

"Fine armor," Sirque commented as she now walked beside him. "Enchanted."

"Yes, Bea touched it."

A rise in the land brought him to the top of a hill dimpled with tiny pink flowers. Looking down the steep incline, he managed to catch his breath. Below stretched a forest. A darkly brilliant forest that sparkled in luscious invite, yet the needlework of black branches boded ill. He could imagine those needles cutting his skin, aggravating the wounds he'd gotten from the troll. And he'd only just healed from the banishment.

"This is the place," she announced softly. "The Unseelie court resides down there within the darkness."

Kir sensed her reluctance. Not willing to return to a place that harbored perhaps both good and bad memories. Should he send her off now? She had shown him the way. He could certainly handle himself from here on. Unless, of course, another troll lurked nearby. He wasn't sure what to call the white flame the demoness had utilized, but he deemed it a handy weapon. As well, he appreciated the companionship, even though the demon wasn't much for talking. And...she was family. He didn't want to send her off until he had reunited with Bea, and they were allowed an official meeting.

"Onward," he said.

Descending the grassy hill, he used the momentum to rush toward the forest. The grasses were flat and he avoided the mushroom crops. If he stepped on one, it would release a poisonous mist into the air, or so Sirque explained.

"Faery is much like time travel to the uninitiated," she said.

"How so?"

"This realm embraces all ages your humans have endured over the centuries. Past, present, even future. Do not be surprised by anything you see. And know that time is not as you believe."

Weird but sound advice.

As he neared the forest, dark shadows flew from the grotesque border of menacing trees. Bats? The creatures screeched and dived for him. Huge creatures the size of a man.

The first to arrive before him opened its maw to expose fangs and long hissing spittles of glow-in-the-dark drool. Wings slashed for Kir's face. A razor-edged wing cut across his cheek.

"This is not a welcoming committee!" he cried in frustration.

"Did you expect one?"

He swung his weapon. The blade flashed in the darkness and cut through the thing with an ease that made him glance back to ensure he had actually struck something. Two halves of the creature landed on the black stones that tiled the ground. A sparkle of dust glittered about the fallen body, and it dissipated.

Sirque brandished white flame from her fingertips.

Each laser-direct shot sliced through one of the flying bats and cut it in two, the halves landing on the ground with a splat.

Kir nodded approvingly. If he had some firepower like that, things would be easier. But he hadn't time to marvel. There were four remaining, and they flew at him as a pack, snarling and sweeping their stiletto-tipped wings as weapons.

As he swung, he was distinctly aware of his own waning strength. Faery had challenged him at every turn. He struck one, then another, with a backswing, leaving but two.

"What the bloody hell are these things?" he yelled as he geared up a two-handed swing for another oncoming. "Faeries?"

A winged beast soared toward him with open maw screeching. No language skills, then. Easier to kill. He decapitated the thing. The air sparkled with glittering faery dust. Perhaps all inhabitants of Faery bled ichor.

He did not. And the scent of his blood was weak, a warning that he had taken another injury and must be cautious. He'd never make it to Bea if he could not restore and heal his wounds.

And yet, above all the smells surrounding him, the scent of honey surrounded, a strange death knell.

Sirque strode over and lifted his head by his hair. "Still with me, wolf?"

He nodded. She dropped his head and he bowed it to the ground.

"I hope you didn't expect this was going to be easy."

He had when he'd first arrived in this bright and beautiful land. Foolish wolf.

Once when he'd been a child, Kir's mother had told him a faery tale that had made him cower under his bedcovers long after she'd kissed him good-night. It hadn't been the dark Faery king or the lovesick human woman who had scared him from his wits. It had been the evil forest Madeline had described with great detail that had given him the shivers.

The trees had eyes; their branches were creeping, moving arms. And the moss could drown a man while the vines choked the breath from him. Trees that could shift and move but never within a man's eyesight, always after the man had walked far enough to lose sight of the branch that reached for his hair. Ground that shifted so subtly beneath a man's foot the moss-heavy carpet would eventually lead the man on, not his path, but one the malicious world of Faery had destined he journey.

Tiny creatures lived beneath toadstools and peered out from the darkness with violet or white glowing eyes. Snickers and giggles that sounded in the man's head like wind or leaves brushing against one another were really voices whispering treacherous deeds.

Kir strode the thick mossy carpet with careful footsteps. Sword held in his right hand, with his left he traced the air before him, as if he expected something to form from thin air and gnash at him. And why the hell not?

Sirque followed closely. He'd taken the lead out of an innate desire to protect any woman. She did not argue the point, although he suspected, after witnessing her surprising arsenal, she could handle herself without assistance from him.

Everywhere, the forest seemed to lower its boughs and branches and wrap about him, perhaps zipping up the path whence he'd come. But he did not look backward, because ahead the forest opened to a vast and wondrous auditorium of darkness and light and rich emeralds, azures and crimsons that flickered to gray and black as quickly as he noticed their vibrancy.

Walking forward he was tickled by long vines trailing from the ceiling many dozens of stories overhead. Kir brushed his fingers over one of the vines and realized it was actually a tree root. The air above was filled with them, like hair spilling from a maiden's head. Were the maiden a hag. And the ceiling was not branches or trees but, rather, earth.

He'd arrived at the Unseelie court; he knew it to his bones. People milled about in the vast courtyard, not yet realizing they had company. Not people, faeries. Of all sorts, shapes, sizes and design. Many as large as he, and dozens more as small as a dragonfly. A buzz of faeries. A dark enclave of glamour. This was the place of his nightmares.

Sirque stood beside him, silent and not looking around as he was. The veil now hung over her face. Sulfur softly emanated with her breaths. Of course, she had been here before. He could sense her intake of breath and the subtle shiver of submission as she took another step to place herself completely behind him.

Kir scanned the courtyard to determine what had disturbed the demoness. He decided the tall dark-haired faery with the silver-and-black wings who approached with an entourage of half-sized creatures skittering about and behind his legs must be the Unseelie king.

To be greeted directly by royalty?

Deciding he must play this properly if he were to elicit any help from Bea's father, he dropped to one knee and bowed his head, acknowledging the Faery king.

The man clapped once, scattering those in the mossy courtyard until it was quickly vacated. Kir stood and offered his hand. "I am Kirnan Sauveterre. And you must be Malrick, Beatrice's father."

The man stared at his offering of a goodwill handshake and reciprocated quickly. It was a firm yet reluctant grip. The man's eyes were silver, and Kir immediately mixed silver and red to come up with pink. Where was his wife?

"This is an unmeasured surprise," Malrick said. "I'm sure you have come for your wife. But first things first."

With a flip of his hand, the Unseelie king commanded a crew of faeries armed with halberds from the shadows. They stepped up behind their master.

"Take the demoness in hand," Malrick said with a bored sigh.

"Why?" Kir demanded. He stepped to the side to stop one of the guards from grabbing Sirque.

"She knew when she left Faery so long ago that if she ever returned, she must forfeit her life."

Kir swung a look to Sirque. Lifting her head regally, the demoness nodded acknowledgment. She had known when he'd asked her to guide him into Faery she could not return? Why had she not said something to him? He would have never asked her to risk her life.

Hell. She was doing this for her daughter.

"Step aside, werewolf," Malrick said. "This is not your concern."

"She is my mother-in-law. Of course she is my concern."

A halberd slashed the air before him, stopping him from getting to Sirque. The guards quickly surrounded her, and, with a glance to him, she shook her head, begging he not interfere.

"Take her away," Malrick said.

"I won't let them harm you!" Kir called. "You will see your daughter. I promise you that."

"Such bold promises, wolf." Malrick stepped around him, walking in a circle to take him in.

The king was dressed in something Kir had seen in

medieval paintings in the Louvre. He guessed the silver threading in the fabric was real, or some kind of faery metal. He wore a thin band of black vines about his head, and at his fingers wrapped more black vines. To study his narrow face and dark hair, and the bright bold eyes, Kir could place him as Bea's father. Unfortunately.

"I've come for Bea."

"She's gone."

"Gone?"

"She wandered off. Never has liked to spend time with dear old dad."

The man was insolent. He couldn't imagine spending an hour with him, let alone surviving a lifetime, as Bea had.

"I love your daughter."

Malrick looked down his nose and aside as he said, "Love is fickle."

"Perhaps yours is, but the love Bea and I share is true and strong."

The man assessed him in a quick stride from head to foot. Malrick nodded. "I'll give you that. You did come to Faery, after all. That bonding mark on your hand."

Kir lifted his hand and displayed it for the king to look upon. "It glows brightly when Bea and I hold hands."

"True love, then. Very good. Hmm… Well, I suppose I can at least point you in the right direction."

The Unseelie king gestured to a short servant, who scuttled away with a squeak and a giggle. Then he proceeded to give directions that sounded easy enough to follow—until he got to the part where Kir should fly over the finger of underforest.

"I'm not much of a flier," Kir said.

"Right. A ground-lurking werewolf. Well, that's not a problem. I may not have been the best father to Beatrice—"

"You were no father to her."

"Ahem. Yes. But I've so many children. It is difficult to pay them all the attention each requires."

"You took enough time to ensure Bea felt badly about being a half-breed. You turned her siblings against her."

"Are we to argue semantics, or do you wish my help finding Beatrice?"

Jaw tight, Kir nodded. "I want your help."

"Then I gift you with this fetch."

The servant lured forward a small creature tethered to a gold chain. It had pink wings and a long, snakelike tail. Very snakelike, in fact. As if a snake with wings.

"Do not release it from the chain or it will fly off," Malrick warned. "Keep it to hand and it will lead you directly to my wayward daughter. It is a consolation I offer you, since you freely stepped forward to take my daughter's hand in marriage."

"An act I will never regret," Kir said proudly.

"Bea has found love, then."

"She has." He took the chain from the servant. The fetch dodged toward him, putting its long violet nose in his face.

"She needs to scent you. Learn you."

"Has she a name?"

"No. Merely a servant."

Malrick easily dismissed all living things. And Kir felt he must leave now or lash out at the insolent Faery king. No time for posturing. He had a wife to find.

"Your pack," Malrick said. "They are fickle to send back my gift."

Bea had indeed been a gift to his soul.

"The pack acted appropriately in the face of your betrayal. But they are no longer my family."

"I can smell the wolfsbane in your wounds," Malrick said. "I could heal that for you."

Kir bristled and flinched when Malrick reached toward him. An offer of kindness?

"No," he said. "I wear the scars with pride. A sign that no man or pack can tell me how to live my life. I live for Bea now. And I will find her." He managed to execute a half bow. "I'll be back for Sirque."

"Don't bother."

"I won't leave her behind. She is Bea's mother."

"Who doesn't care a whit for her."

"She cares too deeply. And that is her curse, as you must know. I made her a promise that she would see her daughter. If you harm her, you will have declared war against me."

"Such a bold wolf."

"That wasn't a threat, Malrick. It was a promise."

Chapter 27

Tired, hot and dirty, Bea huddled at the base of a huge tree. The moss-frosted roots formed a nest around her that was far from comforting. Her feet bled dark ichor. Now she understood why her ichor had darkened since going to the mortal realm: her demon half was rising. Her hair was a tangle that no amount of conditioner could ever manage. She had cuts and bruises from fighting with the siren. Apparently, her mother had pissed off those mermaids.

The sprites that fluttered overhead repeatedly dive-bombed her, chattering manically in tiny tones she understood as curses. She didn't bother to bat them away because that seemed to egg them on more.

This world was no longer her home. She didn't like it. She had no one who gave a care for her here. Yet did anyone in the mortal realm care?

"Oh, mossy misery."

He hadn't come for her.

"Kir," she whispered, sending the name into the atmosphere as a prayer. He'd promised to always be there for her.

Stroking the pale lines of the bonding mark on the back of her hand, she whispered, "I love you, no matter what."

Perhaps his pack had convinced him that sending her back was for the best. He'd agreed and hadn't been able to face her before they'd taken her away. Or even if he had not agreed, he would have done what was right for his pack. It was his family. He'd lived with them for decades. And who was she but a woman he had known a short time? Sure, they had bonded. But could that bond survive the bond of family the pack provided Kir?

She'd been unable to carry his child. Surely she was not meant to be in his life. Perhaps she should seek the exiled Wicked and claim her true home.

"No. I love him. No matter what."

Tracing the intricate bonding design, she wondered if Kir was perhaps doing the same thing at this moment. Every part of her being wished that he was. She needed him to miss her as much as she missed him. Their love had been real. She would not believe anything else.

The fetch soared with such intent Kir felt sure it would break the delicate gold chain. It was on Bea's scent. So he raced after the critter, dodging low-hanging tree limbs and jumping over mossy mounds, roots and rocks. They'd been moving steadily for hours. And despite his catalog of injuries, he wasn't tired. Nothing could stop him from finding Bea.

They raced past a lake where mermaid tails slapped the surface and carrion birds circled overhead. Focusing on his path, Kir called to the fetch, "Faster!"

If he could shift to wolf shape, he could make this journey twice as fast, but there was no way to then hold the chain. So he pushed himself. His only thoughts were on Bea. Her bright pink eyes and coal-dark hair. That gorgeous body she had no reluctance showing him frequently. The sadness in her eyes on the evening he had found her after the miscarriage. And the glee that could fill her very being when she was content and her wings unfurled.

She was his heart, his lover, his sadness and his joy. His tiny pole dancer. His short stick. His naked ninja faery. He loved her more than anything in his realm. And he would not rest until he found her.

Suddenly the fetch cawed and the chain snapped. The useless portion he held dropped along his leg. Kir raced faster, but the fetch flew high into the sky, no longer forward but upward. The fetch dived into a grotto shaded by trees. He heard a female yelp.

Could it be? He raced forward, landing on a clearing carpeted with moss.

From around the wide tree trunk sprang a disheveled dark-haired faery, crystal blade held high above her head. She shouted a weak, rasping warrior's cry. Not much energy left in her bedraggled body, but still she was determined to protect herself.

At the sight of him, Bea dropped her arm and the blade. "Kir?"

Joy washing through his system, he fell to his knees before her.

Bea took a wobbling step forward. "Y-you came for me?"

He held out his arms. Shaking as if frozen, she finally snapped out of the shock and ran into his arms, her body crushing hard against his and toppling them to the ground in a grateful hug. She wrapped her arms up around his head, her face buried at his neck. She smelled like the forest and, suspiciously…fishy.

His wife was back in his arms, skin against skin, heartbeats pounding against heartbeats. Nothing felt better.

She sobbed uncontrollably, and Kir couldn't prevent his tears. It felt good to release his fears and anxiety, so he let them go with a shout of joy. He hugged her and rolled to the side, then to his back again because he didn't want to crush her. Yet if he could crush her into his soul, he would do it. He didn't ever want to lose her again. And he would keep his arms about her until she begged for release.

"Did you think I wouldn't come for you?" he asked.

"I prayed that you would, but I couldn't know if your pack convinced you to forget about me."

"I left the pack. They didn't want me to go after you. I'd choose you over the pack any day. Oh, Bea, I've found you. You feel so good."

She reached down and clasped his hand. The bonding mark glowed and warmed their clutch.

And she kissed him. He'd gone too long without her kiss. He sat up, bringing her with him, her legs wrapping about his back and her fingers clutching in his hair. She tasted earthy and sweet. He'd missed her taste. The feel of her skin against his. The sound of her sighs against his mouth. The eddy of his heartbeats as they settled into calm.

Kir remembered what Sirque had told him about her need to feed off the vita of others. He wouldn't take the time to explain it all to Bea right now, but he knew the best thing he could do for her was to simply hold her.

"Take all you need," he whispered. "I am yours."

And Bea did. She made contact with his skin, not knowing it was a visceral need as she kissed him deeply. Her palms conformed to his neck, bleeding from him the energy that would restore her. And when he thought to feel drained, weaker than any man should from his excursion through Faery, Kir only felt light and renewed in his wife's embrace.

"Take me home," she said.

"I will." He pulled her up to stand and held her against his chest. Not about to let her get too far away. "First we have to return to your father's home."

"What? No. Kir, I just got you back. I don't want to return to that man's castle. It's not my home. Home is with you, and only you. He kept me in a dungeon for three days!"

He bracketed her face and kissed her forehead, calming her worries to sniffling sobs.

Between sniffles, she whispered, "Don't you want to get out of this crazy place?"

"I do. And we will. But your mother is back at Malrick's castle."

"My—my mother?" He brushed the tangled hair from her lashes. Ichor glistened on her skin and her clothing was torn. She looked as if she'd been through hell, but she was standing and had been smiling. "How did my mother get here? In Faery? How do you know her?"

Kir filled Bea in on what had transpired after she'd been returned to Malrick. He finished by telling her about finding Sirque waiting on his stoop when he finally returned home. "Word had reached her in Daemonia that her daughter was looking for her."

Bea gaped. It was a lot to accept. And all Kir wanted to do was take her home and erase the past few days from both their memories.

"Walk with me," he said, turning the direction he had traveled. He could scent the path he had taken now and guessed they could be back at Malrick's demesne before nightfall. "I'll explain it on the way. Trust me?"

She clasped his hand. "Always. But tell me why it's so important we go back for my mother?"

"Because Malrick has ordered her execution."

Bea listened. Kir told her everything while they raced toward her father's home. The last place she wanted to return was Malrick's demesne. But as she learned more about Sirque through Kir, she realized she was curious to meet the woman who had abandoned her. Sirque had only left her because, if she had kept her, she might have killed her.

Her mother's demonic nature was that she took vita from others through skin contact. Bea's hunger for ichor and blood wasn't necessary for survival? Then there must be some way she could kick that habit to the curb for good. Though, even now she was thinking a sip of Kir's blood might tide her over, renew her depleted energy.

Still, holding Kir's hand kept her strong. Perhaps there was something to the skin contact. But really? It was that she held her husband's hand again. He had come for her! She hadn't doubted he would. Maybe there had been a moment when she thought all was lost, that moment when she'd been picking siren slime from her hair, but…no, she'd known he'd find her one way or another.

"We're going to grab Sirque and run, right?" she asked.

Her father's home was not far off. Just over the slash of trees fenced before them. The bold white sun neared the violet horizon. They had but an hour, according to mortal time. Faery time? It could change with the snap of two fingers.

"That's my plan," he said. "But you don't think Malrick will allow that, do you?"

"Nope. The guy will cut her head off before my very eyes to show his authority."

"It better not come to that."

"Thank you."

"For rescuing you?"

"That. And for being the one who wanted to go back for Sirque. You could have left her. Could have forgotten to tell me that detail."

"Never. She was the one who led me to Faery and helped me find your father's home, at her expense. I owe Sirque, Bea."

They strolled through the tall grass at a quick pace, and it felt as though, through Kir's touch, Bea was fortified and as if she could race endlessly after.

"So, from what you've told me," she said, "I gather she's a pretty nice chick for a demon."

"You could put it that way. Neither of us will ever get on the demon bandwagon, but...yes, I think she's one we can rally behind. She only did what was best for you, Bea. She hadn't expected Malrick to treat you so cruelly."

"And she knew that if she led you into Faery that she would have to face the execution order Malrick set against her when last she was here. That takes guts."

"Or maybe love."

She glanced up to her werewolf husband. His eyes crinkled in that gorgeous smile she'd feared to never see again. "Yeah, love."

The bond mark glowed and Bea stroked the back of her husband's hand. "The two of us. Always."

"I promise you that, Bea."

"What about your family? You left the pack?"

"Colin, my father...well, I told you."

"He didn't abandon you as you'd thought."

"And I've had a change of heart about Sophie. Mostly. She did some bad things with vampires, but I'm willing to give her a chance once she gets clean. Jacques made sure she was able to escape the Reckoner. And I made sure Colin was there to grab her."

"You are a fine man. I'll be your family now."

"You already are."

The Unseelie courtyard loomed before them, and Bea's skin prickled as her lover tugged her onward. She did not want to go inside. But so long as Kir did not let go of her hand, she could once again stand before her father. She'd show him she had survived on her own. There was nothing he could do to her that would bring her down. Nothing.

As they strode across the black quartz courtyard, Malrick's lackeys scurried about them. Twisting, thorned vines followed their footsteps, never getting close enough to wrap an ankle but giving Bea good reason not to falter and to keep pace with her husband's determined strides.

The air here was different. Cooler; remarkably so. And not so sweet as out in the Wilds. It oozed of Malrick's control.

They stopped before the archway that opened into Malrick's domain. Kir gripped Bea's hand tightly. "Ready for this?"

"No. But I trust you. And I won't leave Faery without Sirque. I owe you both that much."

They crossed the black-and-pink quartz foyer and Kir stopped in the middle, looking up and about. It would be an affront to move beyond the foyer if they had not been received. Yet Bea could hear something… Or rather, she felt it. A deep and lingering sadness.

She'd always been able to sense her siblings' emotions because they had a common bond of a same parent. They were in one another's ichor. So who was sad now?

Her skin prickled and she rubbed her arms. Kir gave her a wondering look.

"Something isn't right," she said. "We need to look around."

"You know the place. I'll follow you." He held his sword up. "Will I need this?"

"Probably." She tugged the crystal blade from her waistband. "It's coming from this direction."

She shuddered, because she knew the spiraling staircase to her right led into the bowels of Malrick's castle. Down there was a place no sidhe wanted to purposely enter or be taken voluntarily.

"Hurry. Executions are usually held at sunset, but Malrick never did take a deadline seriously. We might already be too late."

Rushing down the stone stairs, Bea felt Kir's hot breath at her back as he followed closely. He wasn't about to let her get too far from him. Blessings for that.

The steps coiled endlessly and formed into the long earthen tunnel that she had followed out from her imprisonment. Eventually the walls gave way and the tunnel opened into the dungeon.

Avoiding one particularly bold spider dashing across the next step, Bea cried out. Kir caught her arm. His strong, steady hold reassured. And then she heard the inhuman cry echo up from below. It entered her pores and tugged at her muscles, pinching them painfully.

"Hurry," she said, and rushed forward, taking the stairs two at a time. "He's torturing her."

The demoness's wrists, hips and horns were nailed to the stone wall. Thick black blood oozed from the nails, which flashed silver. Bea gasped at the sight. The first vision of her mother, and under such cruel circumstances.

She couldn't speak, couldn't force out a yell for her father to cease his torture. She tasted bile in her throat and could but cling to her husband's arm. Kir pulled from her grasp, pushed his way past Malrick, who stumbled in the werewolf's wake, and shoved away the elf who wielded the razor-lined lash against Sirque. When the elf threatened Kir with the lash, the wolf growled, showing him his fangs.

The elf looked to Malrick, who stirred up brilliant blue faery flame in his hands.

Oblivious to the pending danger, Kir pulled the nails from Sirque's horns. The demoness's head dropped onto one of his shoulders. Next he slammed his body against hers to hold her while he pulled free the nails from her hips.

Faery fire hit Kir on the back. He growled and threw a silver nail toward Malrick, who countered the attack with a subtle gesture of his hand. The wolf fought at the flames that crept over his bare shoulders while he fought to hold up Sirque, for to let her go now would see her supported only by the nails in her wrists. The flames licked up his leather vest and then…disappeared. Bea's faery dust had worked its magic.

Bea watched her father build another ball of blue flame in his hands. As he drew back his arm to lob the flame, she caught his arm. The flame dropped to the dungeon floor. Malrick thrust her away from him, then he paused, seeming to realize who he had pushed away.

Sirque cried out as the final nail was pulled from her wrist. Kir hefted her over his shoulder and turned to stand defiantly before the Unseelie king.

"You are quite the werewolf, Kirnan Sauveterre," Malrick said. "You defy my flame to rescue a miserable demon?"

"She is family. And you broke yet another promise." Kir spit on the floor between him and Malrick.

Bea wanted to shout with glee to see her husband stand

up to the mighty Faery king, yet she would not be so bold without expecting major retaliation.

Malrick sighed and spread out his arms in resignation. "You have earned my respect, wolf."

"Then you will grant me one favor, my lord?"

"I know what you request. You want the demoness. Why?"

"She is Bea's mother."

"She does not give a care for Beatrice."

"Not true," Sirque managed.

"She's done nothing to earn this treatment."

"We had an accord," Malrick stated. "She never returns to Faery. I would not concern myself with her ever again."

"She was only looking for me," Bea pleaded. "You are a monster!"

"I am no more a monster than she is," Malrick insisted. "And to show you how amiable I can be, I will give the valiant werewolf a choice. He may leave Faery through the portal in my home with either my daughter or my ex–demon lover."

Malrick tilted his silver eyes on Kir. "Choose."

Chapter 28

"I've never liked being forced to a decision," Kir said, stalling for time. He didn't know how to get around this situation. Certainly Malrick must suspect he would choose Bea.

But he could not abandon Sirque. He'd made a promise to her.

The demoness struggled, so he let her slip down to stand beside him. He supported her across the back as she valiantly stood on her own. She had to be in excruciating pain, but he had no sense of how long it took a demon to heal.

"This demon's death will bring you no satisfaction," he said.

Malrick shrugged. "Of course it will. I will know my dishonored word has been avenged."

The man sought a balm to soothe a compact of words? As had Etienne in support of pack Valoir. How lives were ruined with mere words.

Sirque's body panted, her shoulder falling against Kir's chest. She couldn't realize she rested against him. Defeated, she was weak. He needed to see her back to the mortal realm or, perhaps, Daemonia, where she could heal by feeding off the vita from others. But remembering her need for skin contact, he slid his hand across her back, seeking the slash in her leather clothing, where his palm pressed against her cool yet bloodied flesh.

As for Bea, she stood behind her father. Kir wished she were standing in his arms. He only wanted to take her home and make love to her, to give her the skin-on-skin contact that she also required for healing, for her very survival.

"There is no third option," Malrick said. "You must choose."

"If I choose one or the other," Kir offered, "then I request the one not chosen is set free in the Wilds."

"Why?"

"To struggle to either her death or her freedom should she find a portal."

Sirque's snicker against his arm was felt more than heard. She approved of his request. He knew she could survive after witnessing her strength on his journey here.

"Would that not please you more to see one of them fight for life?"

Malrick looked at Bea. Did he not want his daughter to suffer that fate once again? Could he possibly care about her? Kir couldn't imagine a father being so cruel—no, not even when he'd believed his father had abandoned him—but the sidhe were a breed that he would never completely understand. Even the demoness had a heart, for he'd discovered that while talking with her.

Malrick gestured with annoyance. "Very well. You may take one to the mortal realm with you, wolf. The other shall be unloosed in the depths of the Wilds. No weapons. No provisions. No mercy."

Malrick snapped his fingers and Bea's crystal blade soared into his grip. A nod of his head set his henchmen to task. They tugged Sirque from Kir's grasp, but he sensed the demoness moved willingly toward her fate. Black blood oozed down her arms and spattered the henchmen's knees as she dropped to land on all fours beside her daughter. Her head bowed, and her horns clacked on the stone floor.

They held Bea beside Sirque, who managed to lift her head and look upon her daughter. Bea, too, looked over her mother's face. Black tears stained Sirque's cheeks and painted her mouth. The resemblance was in their dark hair, the shape of their faces and the glint in their eyes. Even tortured, Sirque's eyes brightened at the sight of Bea standing so close.

"I am sorry," the demoness whispered.

"I forgive you," Bea said. She swallowed and reached out to grasp Sirque's hand. The bond mark glowed as did the markings on Bea's feet. And Kir thought the demoness's veins darkened beneath her skin. "Kir told me everything. How you can't touch me..."

"I can feel your life," Sirque said on a gasp. She tugged her hand out of Bea's grasp. "My daughter."

Malrick shook his head. "Dramatics." He clapped his hands together sharply, snaring Kir's attention away from the women. "Choose!"

Kir met Sirque's eyes. With the slightest nod, she acknowledged his difficult decision. He wanted to thank her for bringing him back to Bea. For having the unselfish heart to bring him to Faery. This was going to hurt. All of them.

He nodded once. The demoness closed her eyes.

"I choose my wife," Kir said.

Malrick whisked his arm before him and the room flickered with the blue faery flame. A mad humming sounded in Kir's ears. He wanted to press his palms over them to shut it out, but suddenly he felt a hand in his. Clasping, clinging. The world toppled. His boots stepped left and right into a secure stance. He clutched Bea to his chest.

And then they stood still, holding each other in the cold, reflecting shadows of an underground passageway. A river flowed slowly by. The Seine. He recognized this as the portal where Sirque had led him into Faery.

"Home," he whispered.

Bea lifted onto her tiptoes and kissed him. "Home. Now..." She clasped his hand and kissed the back of it. Bright pink eyes met his with hope. "What is your plan for rescuing my mother?"

Kir insisted on taking Bea home before revealing his plans. She was on board with that. After lingering in her husband's arms as they stood inside the foyer of their home, she finally forced herself away from the warmth of his body and tugged him upstairs.

"Showers!" she announced. "I've never been so desperate to be away from you than I am now. I must smell like a siren and look worse. I don't even want to look in the mirror."

Kir cupped her face as they topped the stairs. "You are gorgeous. A little smudged here and there." He rubbed his fingers over her forehead and jaw.

Clothing was shed on the way to the bathroom, and Bea was first in under the hot stream. She unfurled her wings and let the water spill over them. And when he joined her and slicked his fingers over her wings, the heady electricity of passion shot through her system. All the faery dust that covered his skin was washed away in a spill of sparkling liquid that swirled about their feet and down the drain.

For a moment in Faery she'd thought he'd abandoned her. What a fool she had been to consider that. As she turned to him now and hugged her breasts against his chest, the man stroked the top arcs of her wings until she bent her fingers into his skin and dug in her nails.

"Oh, Kir, I don't ever want to be away from you again."

He nuzzled kisses along her jaw and at her neck while one of his hands slipped around to slick over her mons and into her folds. "I'll do what I can to be here for you whenever you need me."

He hadn't made a promise, and that was better for Bea. Because promises could be broken, and who knew what the future held for them? She'd always have an arrogant, controlling father who did as he pleased. She felt sure she'd not seen the last of him. As for her mother, they needed to rescue her, or at least try. And she knew her brave werewolf husband would give it his all.

"Love you," she whispered.

The strokes at her wings, combined with the consistent pressure at her clit, enveloped her in a dizzying orgasm that commanded she do nothing but receive. To fall into Kir's strong arms and bask in the love he gave her.

He lifted her and held her body against the hard landscape of his abs and hips, which allowed her to splay her arms back and touch the edges of her wings. She pulled them out and wrapped each wing about them as if a cloak, and Kir bent to lick the gossamer fabric.

"You beguile me, Beatrice. I am happy to be a wolf without a pack so long as I know that you will always be waiting to catch me in your wings."

She'd forgotten about his banishment. He'd purposely allowed it to happen so he could be free to go into Faery to find her. An immense sacrifice that she might never completely comprehend. For she did not understand family, and the tight bonds that could enmesh an entire pack. Yet the scars she felt on his back proved their bond was stronger.

"I want to be worthy," she whispered, feeling the shivery sweetness of orgasm slowly melt through her bones. She leaned forward and nestled her head against his chest. "Thank you, Kir."

"We'll figure things out together, yes? The future is what we make it. It'll be good."

"I know it will be."

He leaned over and turned off the water. They toweled each other off. Bea wrapped the towel around his hips and shimmied it back and forth. Bowing, her wings still out and shimmering off the water droplets, she licked the head of his rigid cock.

He groaned and again his fingers found the solid arcs of her wings. He held on as she took him in her mouth and licked him as if he were a dessert made for a hot summer day. She loved this man and she wanted to please him and own him.

Her fingers trailed down his powerful thighs and she bent her wings forward to caress about his legs and hips, drawing them up to hug his back. Enveloped within her enchantment, her werewolf husband let out a howl that she recognized as joy. His hips bucked and he spilled into her mouth. She took all of him, reveling in their bond.

Reaching down, he clasped her hand, and the bond mark glowed brightly. And Bea knew that it wasn't she who had done the enchanting but, rather, her werewolf husband who had enchanted her.

Kir didn't have a plan for getting Sirque back, but he'd be damned if he wouldn't come up with one. Clad only in jeans, he paced the living room. Bea wandered in from the kitchen. It felt great to have his naked faery back.

She handed him a goblet of wine and sipped her tea. "Turn around. Let me take a look at your back."

He did as he was told and didn't wince when she touched the one spot where he felt sure claws had cut into his rib bones. The final strike from Jacques.

"Almost completely healed. It's been four mortal days. You should have healed faster."

"Blame it on the wolfsbane," he said, turning to pull her onto his lap as he sat on the big easy chair. "And a few weird creatures in Faery I don't even have names for." She set the goblet on the coffee table for him, then snuggled up to his bare chest.

"Banishment is cruel and unusual punishment. Couldn't they have let you walk away with a 'don't let the door hit you on the way out, buddy'?"

"That's not how it's done. When you belong to a pack, you abide by their ways, good, bad, old and new. They are instituted for a purpose."

"To humiliate you?"

"To show other wolves that I was banished."

"But it wasn't because you did anything wrong. Oh, I wish you hadn't had to suffer just for me."

"Just for you? Always for you, Bea. Always."

He hugged her to him, slipping his hand between her legs. She slid her arms down his and opened her legs to give him free rein over her. Such luxury to be back in this realm, melting in her husband's arms, with not a care in the world. At least, not a care she wanted to consider at this moment. Soon, she would do that.

Gripping the hand Kir was not using, she pulled it to her mouth and kissed him, then tongued the join between his thumb and forefinger. He liked that, and to show it, his other hand pressed a little deeper, slightly harder, focusing on her core, leading her to a blissful, trippy abandon that made her feel as if her wings were out and soaring through the air.

The bond mark glowed about their clasped hands. And it seemed to encompass Bea's whole body as, with one perfect stroke of her husband's finger, her hips bucked and her body released her into their shared love. She cried out and reached back to clasp his hair, pushing her fingers into it and then down to his neck, where she clung as her body spasmed and rode the wave of pleasure.

Chapter 29

Kir did have a plan after all. And the Jones brothers agreed to help this time around because it didn't involve going into Daemonia. Faery was a new and intriguing conquest for them.

Pushing the living room furniture to the walls to expose the tapestry carpet, Kir prepared the room as Certainly Jones had instructed. Bea stood at the end of the couch, eager to help her hubby, but he lifted the whole thing at the center and managed it himself.

"Show-off." She teased a coil of hair about her forefinger. "So you really think this will work? Magic kind of freaks me out. And those brothers are even freakier."

"You swooned over them when they were here before."

"Swoon? Me? No." She cast her look aside. "Maybe a little. But no. They're so dark."

"And your mother is not?"

She settled onto the couch, cross-legged, catching her chin in her palm.

"I'm sorry." He leaned over her and kissed the crown of her head. "It's what she is. She really does care about you. And we will get her out of Faery. No matter what."

"You're too kind to me, lover. You've sacrificed so much for me."

"And you have not? Bea, you left your home for me. You carried my child."

"And we both know how well that went."

"It will happen again."

"But what if I do have a child and, like my mother, I can't touch the baby? Oh, Kir, I'm not so sure about starting a family now."

He sensed the fear in her tone and felt a trace of it shiver down the back of his neck, as well. There was no promise that their future would go smoothly. And he'd never forgive himself if they did have a child and Bea was unable to hold it.

Kneeling before Bea, he clasped her hands and kissed the palms. Pressing his face into her palms, he closed his eyes and prayed that this night would go well. He'd worry about the rest of their life as it came to them. One day at a time.

"Whatever the future holds," he said, "I'll be there holding you and we'll face it together."

Her mouth spread into a smile and she bowed to hug him, her hair spilling over his face and neck.

The doorbell rang, and, after kissing his wife, Kir then winked. "You ready?"

"Bring it."

The Jones brothers were dark, focused and—okay—still a little sexy, Bea decided as she watched them prepare the living room for the grand spell they had detailed to her and Kir. A salt circle was standard and, apparently, so was whiskey. Both men imbibed while setting up the spell area. A lot. As did Kir.

Should she be getting drunk? It might lessen her anxiety. But someone had to remain calm and sober should the spell actually work and Sirque was rescued.

They weren't really drunk. And TJ did offer Bea a quaff from his bottle, but she politely refused.

"Now." CJ, the tattooed twin, stood before the salt circle, whiskey bottle dangling near his thigh. Both men were shoeless and oozed a dark sensuality. "TJ and I have determined that neither of us, unfortunately, can make the journey into Faery."

"Much as I'd kill to venture into that realm," TJ added, "we'd have to perform such a complex set of wards to even begin to make the journey that it would take too long."

"I'll go," Kir offered. He stepped up beside Bea and put an arm across her back. "Just tell me what I need to do."

TJ, who had taken to lighting black, white and red candles around the perimeter of the salt circle, shook his head. "Has to be a blood relative."

Bea realized that CJ was looking directly at her, and she felt the connection of his jade gaze like a bullet piercing her heart. But, of course, it made sense. And she was willing to go back to Faery to find her mother, but…

She looked up into her husband's eyes. "What if I don't make it back?"

"She can't go," Kir stated.

"She has to," CJ said. "And don't worry. We'll send your doppelgänger, Bea. You'll remain firmly ensconced in this realm at all times. Trust me." He winked. "It's a magic trick."

She did not feel the levity; nor was she inspired with confidence. Kir rubbed his palm up and down her arm. But she stepped out of his grasp and moved toward the circle. "I'll do it." She took her husband's hand and gave it a squeeze. "I can do this."

"I know you can. But I'm not sure it's safe. Can I go with her?" he asked CJ.

TJ stood beside CJ now, shoving the lighter into a front pants pocket. Both gave Kir that don't-question-just-do look.

"No," Kir said. "I won't let her go alone. I'm sorry for dragging you guys all the way over here—"

Bea tugged on Kir's arm. "We can't let her remain there. She was so weak. Malrick tortured her. She'll never find a way out on her own. You promised her, Kir."

"Right. I promised her. That means I should be the one to go after her and risk the danger involved."

"Blood only," CJ reiterated. "If she doesn't go in, we won't be able to hold the connection on this side."

Bea stepped before Kir and grasped both his hands, pleading with him in a silent gaze. Letting him know she wouldn't stop until she knew Sirque was out of danger.

"The witches say I'll be safe," she entreated softly. "And it won't even be me who goes to Faery." Which, she didn't really understand. Her doppelgänger? This could get interesting. "Let me do this, Kir. For as much as you needed to walk away from your pack for me, understand now I have the same desire to walk toward and rescue my mother."

He nodded. His kiss was long and lingering, and though the twins stood watching, Bea surrendered to the soft warmth of her husband's mouth and the sure heat of his embrace.

"You won't drop her hand during the whole procedure," CJ said to Kir. "I noticed you two are bonded. That'll provide the lock that holds Bea to this realm."

"We need to do this now," TJ interrupted. "The moon

is at its zenith, and it could take her days, weeks, to find the demon."

"Weeks?" Kir asked.

TJ shrugged. "Faery time is different from mortal time. What may seem like moments on our side could be a lot longer over there."

"We've talked enough. It's time for action." Bea gripped Kir's hand and the bond mark glowed. "Just don't let me go and I'll be fine."

She sucked in a breath. Saying the words and believing them were two different things. But she did have faith that her husband would never let her go.

Kir nodded, conceding silently. "What do you need us to do?"

"Bea, step in the circle," CJ instructed. "We've already explained the doppelgänger will arrive in Faery and you'll search for your mother. You'll feel Kir's hand in yours, but you won't see him. No matter what you do, Bea, don't drop his hand. You, too," he said to Kir.

"Never." He squeezed Bea's hand as she stepped over the line of salt.

TJ added, "We'll be able to home in on Sirque through Bea's blood, so we should be able to place you quite close to her."

"Ichor," Bea said. "I don't have blood in my veins, but ichor."

"Right. And perhaps a bit of demon blood, eh?" CJ suggested.

Bea nodded. She could never be disgusted by her demon half again after meeting the brave, proud Sirque and witnessing the tremendous sacrifice she had made to help Kir find her. That was one amazing demon chick.

"Then let's get this party started," TJ announced, and, with a swallow of whiskey, he then spewed it out toward the lighter he'd reignited. A spray of flame lit the room, and the brothers began to chant and walk the circle in dancing steps.

Bea smiled at Kir, then swallowed and closed her eyes. She didn't want to look at him anymore. She'd seen him smiling back at her. That is how she wanted to remember him if she never saw him again.

The moment Bea's doppelgänger entered Faery, Kir felt it. Her grip loosened in his, and he had to clasp her hand with both of his so as not to lose his hold on her. The bond mark glowed as if a beacon. She was close to him, yet so far away.

CJ had warned him not to step across the salt line or to break it with his boots. But now, only two minutes into the spell, he strained to hold on to Bea, so much so that he leaned backward to counterweight his body so it didn't slip forward. Her pull was tremendous, but he suspected it was more Faery trying to pull her in completely rather than her petite strength.

The Jones brothers had ceased chanting and now hummed in a resonant tone that reminded him of holy voices echoing out from a monastery. The twosome embodied strange, wicked magic.

The candles flickered at his feet, the flames dancing back and forth as if wind brisked through the room; all windows and the patio door were closed.

He shouldn't have allowed Bea to do this. He couldn't bear to lose her again. And he doubted Malrick would be so amiable as to allow his daughter to return for a second time without facing dire consequences.

His palm was slick with sweat. Kir dropped one hand to wipe it along his pants leg, then slapped it back onto Bea's wrist while he wiped the other hand.

"Hold her hand!" CJ warned.

He quickly resumed the clasp and the bond marks glowed brighter than he'd ever seen. It was as if their skin opened to let out the inner light from their very souls. He wasn't sure what he would do were Bea not in his life. He didn't need children. He only wanted his wife, safe in his arms.

"Ah, hell."

Kir jerked a look to CJ. "What? What's wrong?"

TJ leaned forward, across the circle, inspecting Bea's face. Kir couldn't see it because she leaned away from him, straining forward as if she wanted to run free from him. Her body was here in this realm, but her consciousness was in Faery.

"What is it?" he yelled, bracing himself to maintain the stronger pull from his wife.

"There's ichor dripping from her eyes," TJ said calmly.

"She's bleeding." Kir shook his head. "We've got to stop this now!"

"It's not much," TJ verified. "But I've never seen this when we've done the spell before."

Heaving the air in and out of his lungs, Kir struggled with Bea, who suddenly seemed to come back and struggle with him. The candle flames grew, stretching higher than the men's knees. Sulfur filled the air.

And then, Kir's body tumbled backward. He hadn't let go of her hand. He couldn't have…

"Bea!" he cried as his shoulder hit the floor and he rolled to the side.

Yet he rolled over on top of his wife's body, and knowing she was there beneath him created a rush of relief through his body. He collapsed on top of her, hugging her, burying his face in her hair with no intention of letting her go.

"It worked," he heard one of the twins say.

"She's badly injured," the other said. "Won't survive."

Kir held tightly to Bea, breathing in her sweetness, her Faery sparkle and trusting heart. Even as he processed what the witches were saying, it was difficult to move away from his wife. She could have been lost to him.

"I'll never lose you," he said against her cheek, then kissed her closed eyelid, which was slippery with her ichor tears. "I love you."

"Me, too," she whispered softly from within the tangle of her hair. "Go help my mother. Please?"

With another squeezing hug, he finally pulled himself away from Bea and turned on bent legs to lean over the salt circle alongside the brothers. The demoness lay in a pool of black blood. One horn had been severed at the temple. Scratches marked her face and neck, and at her chest a wide wound pulsed up thick black blood.

"Can you heal her?" he asked the brothers.

"Not a demon," TJ said. "We work dark magic, not malefic magic. I'm not sure a warlock would be capable of such."

"Is she going to survive?"

Kir turned to Bea, who sat up now and had asked the question in a little-girl voice. A little girl who had only just found her mother and needed that promise of a familial connection.

"Truth?" TJ said from over Kir's shoulder. "She's in a bad way. I have no idea."

Bea scrambled over to Kir's side and he took her hand when she leaned over Sirque's body. She whimpered and touched her mother's face.

Sirque stirred. The witches stepped aside, leaving them to this terrible moment. A moment Kir sensed would not end well.

"Bea," Sirque whispered. Blood drooled from her mouth. "You…saved me?"

"Oh, Mother." She lay upon Sirque's damaged body and nuzzled up to her. "I wish we had been made differently so we could have shared this hug long ago. I love you."

A smile curled Sirque's mouth and she nodded, accepting her daughter's love. "Love," she whispered. "So exquisite."

"You need to heal, Mother. How can we help you?"

"Daemonia," she said on a sigh.

"It's probably her best chance for healing," CJ said from where he stood outside the circle. "We do know how to expel demons out of this realm. Rather easily, in fact."

"Then you should do it," Bea said. She kissed her mother's cheek and squeezed her hand. "Come back when you are well."

Sirque closed her eyes and the witch twins took over, restoring the salt circle and then chanting in the Latin that neither Bea nor Kir understood.

Kir slid his hand along Bea's and bent over to kiss her cheek. "She will come back someday."

"I know. It was good I got to see her now, though." She tensed as suddenly the brothers' magic lit the room with a blue glow and the demon in the center of the circle was gone. "Until we meet again, Mother."

Chapter 30

Some months later...

Snow coated the yard, yet the sun was high and Bea hadn't bothered to put on a coat. She wandered into the backyard shed on tiptoes, licking her fingers of chocolate. Kir brought her *pain au chocolat* every morning for breakfast, left it bedside with a glass of orange juice, then slipped out to work in his shop until she rose.

Leather had been stretched over an intricate wooden frame. The frame had been fashioned by a furniture craftsman Kir had met a month earlier. And the leather, now covered with gorgeous handiwork, gleamed with Bea's faery dust.

Kir sat on the floor before the object. Glancing over his shoulder, he turned and set a hammer down beside him on the cardboard that served as a rug beneath his work space. "You're not naked."

"It is twenty degrees outside." She teased at the short hem of the sheer pink nightie with the dragonflies embroidered around the skirt. "You don't like it?"

"Come here, Short Stick."

She straddled his hips and settled onto his lap.

"Oof," he said.

"Oh, come on. I haven't gained that much weight. Have I?" She grabbed a thigh and wished it was a little thinner. And she wouldn't reach around to gauge how much she'd gained on her ass. That way lay Crazytown.

"You are gorgeous." He spread his palm over her blossoming belly. "Abundant with life." He stroked his fingers over her skin and then down to tease between her thighs.

"And for some reason horny as heck lately. Must be the demon in me jonesing for your touch. Are you busy with the project or do you want to take this sparkly bit for a ride?"

"Let's rock the little guy up and down."

Bea smoothed a palm over her stomach. "What makes you think it's a boy?"

"I just know."

"Yeah? Well, you know it could be a werewolf."

Bea stood so Kir could unzip his jeans and shuffle them down. "Yep."

"Or it could be faery. Could be werewolf faery. Or even werewolf demon."

"I know that."

"What if it's demon faery werewolf?"

He shrugged. "I don't care what it is. Only that our baby is healthy and happy. Will that work for you?"

"It will. So long as I can hold him in my arms, all will be well. I love you, Kir."

"I love you, Bea."

And their lovemaking gently rocked the cradle behind them and stirred a glittering cloud of faery dust about them.

Three months later Bea gave birth in the spring on the day the first anemone bloomed. The faery midwife handed her the squirming infant, swaddled in soft wrapping, and left the happy couple alone in the bedroom of their home.

Kir kissed Bea on the forehead, and, happy tears spilling from his eyes, he bowed to kiss his son on the pert little nose that was a match to his mother's nose. "He's perfect."

"Everything is perfect," Bea said on a tired sigh.

She closed her eyes and concentrated on the warmth of her son's head against her chest. Skin against skin. So tender. So luxurious. Did she sense the need to draw him tighter to her and feed upon his vita?

No. And she never would.

She hadn't seen her mother since the Jones brothers had sent her back to Daemonia, though Sirque had sent a liaison with word that she was doing well and would come to visit when she could.

When Kir tried to take the baby from her, Bea gladly relented and fell into a blissful peace as she watched father and son standing in the sunlight beaming through the window.

Finally, family was hers.

* * * * *

I hope you enjoyed Kir and Bea's story! Most of the paranormal romances I write for Nocturne are set in my Beautiful Creatures world. They don't have to be read in any specific order, but if you like a secondary character, they may have their own story for you to check out. Here are the stories you can find at your favorite online retailer for some characters in this book:

TJ's story is THIS GLAMOROUS EVIL
CJ's story is THIS WICKED MAGIC
Blyss's story is MOONLIGHT & DIAMONDS
Edamite's story is CAPTIVATING THE WITCH

CAPTIVATING THE WITCH

Chapter 1

The evening hours in the Council's archives were indeterminable from the daylight because the vast archives were located two stories below Parisian ground and formed a labyrinth of rooms, cubbies and hallways over many acres. It was like something out of a fantasy movie with the secret passageways and mysterious decor that might suddenly open to a dark chasm so cold your breath would fog, or a dimly lit library whose ceiling soared many stories high, or instead a small Regency-styled tearoom smelling of lilacs.

And sometimes after the witching hour things started moving.

Nestled in a room filled to the industrial iron-beam rafters with dusty old tomes and spiderwebs, Tamatha Bellerose noticed the thoroughly modern fluorescent lighting flickered. Someone was either accessing a security camera or one of the biometric-scan doors. Probably her boss, Certainly Jones, was on his way to remind her—as he did at least once a week—she didn't have to work so late.

Tamatha didn't mind. Since being hired to work in the Archives three months ago, she had been in a witch's information heaven. While she had been hired for general filing and straightening, it was approved that she would spend time studying as she had mentioned that was her reason for seeking the job. Not a problem for her boss. And when Certainly had suggested she choose one of the messier storage rooms—the one housing all demonic artifacts, texts and accoutrements—she'd been thrilled.

Diabology fascinated her. Her grandmother Lysia (whom she had not the pleasure to know) had been a diabolotrist. The tales told by Tamatha's mother, Petrina Bellerose, had been enough to stir Tamatha's curiosity. She wanted to learn everything she could about demons because they were such varied and interesting creatures. And they weren't all bad, as most people assumed. Their species and assorted breeds were as numerous and diverse as the humans who walked the earth.

She'd decided to start with the demons who inhabited the mortal realm, and after she'd learned all that was available, she'd move on to those occupying Daemonia, the Place of All Demons, and then Faery, and then perhaps even Beneath. Many years of work ahead of her to master diabology. She hoped Certainly wouldn't mind if this cleanup project carried on awhile.

There wasn't much else to do in the Archives beyond dusting and looking up things when her boss requested the assistance. The Archives housed the largest collection of paranormal ephemera in the known universe. All spells and grimoires, a copy of the *Book of All Spells*, potions, objects of magical nature and even creatures of mysterious origins. Some were preserved through taxidermy or in creepy glass receptacles. Some were even stored *live*.

Beyond the label of assistant archivist, Tamatha considered herself a keeper of books and historical material that told stories about the paranormal species and shaped their origins and evolution. And that was pretty cool.

Sighing, she leaned over the centuries-old grimoire of *Basic Demonic Bindings* and took a moment to consider how lucky she was to have scored this job. It paid the bills and she got to learn. A witch couldn't ask for much more than that.

Not that she needed the money. She was quite well-off, thanks to nearly a century of wise investments. And she never got so deeply into a relationship with a man that they considered marriage, and thus, joining incomes. That way lay poverty, Tamatha believed. Her last lover, a cat shape-shifter, had been quick to suggest marriage, a combining of their lives. The familiar had been too charming, too suave. And she had fallen for his seductive spell like a cat to nip. Only, she had suddenly remembered one day, while in the midst of a sensual reverie, how much she didn't like cats. And then the family curse had seen to preventing any rash decisions she may have made regarding making the relationship permanent.

The Bellerose curse ensured the females in her family for the past three generations had bad luck with love and lovers. Relationships never lasted. Most lovers went mad. Literally. The occasional unlucky lover ended up dead.

The familiar had been run over by a car a month after suggesting he and Tamatha start a family together.

Over the decades, a few other lovers had died, but maudlin grief wasn't her style. She'd written such expected deaths off as the Bellerose curse and had moved forward. It was something she knew how to do. It was all Tamatha had ever known, for she had watched many of her mother's lovers die, as well.

"But I am hopeful," she whispered.

She was determined to never give up on love. Someday it might stick. And she strove to follow the family motto: Love Often. Yet what was generally whispered after that declaration of love was "because they never last long." Not so much a family joke as the truth.

Why she was musing over the fate of the Bellerose women's lovers was beyond her. Though her mind did tend to wander after hours bent over a book. Not that there was anything at all wrong with that. Tamatha's favorite thing in the world was to lose herself in a book. And to try out new spells.

"I want to test this binding spell," she said and tapped the handwritten text before her. "I think I've got it down. Just say the right words—*scatura*, *demonicus*, *vold*—and voilà!" Bound demon.

From there, she could ask the demon questions and study it while not having to worry it might harm her. Because the best way to learn was from the source. She preferred live studies as opposed to dusty tomes. But she had no demon friends, and none of her witch friends had close demonic contacts, either. Which was a good thing. She didn't run with witches who summoned demons to do their bidding. That was cruel.

She wondered how difficult it would be to locate a demon willing to let her bind it. She had lived in Paris only a little over a year, after moving here from Belgrade, where—well, yes, that shapeshifter affair. Her "friends" list was slowly growing, listing mostly witches, because that was who she generally trusted and understood. But there were a couple vampires and the werewolf/vampire half-breed Rhys Hawkes whom she considered her friends.

Her boss, Certainly Jones—or CJ, as he asked her to call him—was a dark witch who practiced the dark arts.

Didn't make him evil or wrong. The dark was necessary to balance the light, which was what Tamatha practiced.

Though adding diabology to her oeuvre would darken her talents. She didn't mind shadowing her aura. She aimed to be well-rounded in all magical arts, and knowledge of all aspects of witchcraft would help her to understand and relate to others much better. And as long as she avoided malefic magic, she was good with the balancing act the light and dark would work on her soul.

"Tamatha?"

She spun around from the grimoire she'd been perusing to spy CJ's dark sweep of long hair. He stuck his head between the opened door and wall. The tattoo on his neck was a ward against vampires. CJ sported dozens of tattoos and most were spells or wards.

Tamatha found a tattooed man incredibly sexy. Something about creating art on his skin to share with the world. But she would keep it professional with CJ. His wife would appreciate that.

"I'll leave soon, boss. It is after hours, and I wanted to do some studying. I found something interesting."

"It's after midnight."

"Really?" Wow, time had flown this evening. She eyed the teapot on the table, which was empty—five cups ago. "Right. I suppose I should be heading out." Not that she ever slept more than a few hours a night. "I'll be back in the morning, bright and early."

"Tomorrow is Saturday," CJ said as she gathered her purse and stepped into her high-heeled shoes, which she always slipped off when she tucked up her legs in the plush gray velvet easy chair. "I don't want to see you in here until Monday. Got that?"

She saluted him. He winked and left her to straighten the work area and turn out the lights. While her OCD magic generally took care of things in her immediate range, snapping unarranged items into order as she walked by, it worked only in close range. Mostly, humans didn't notice, and those who did, she quickly did a hands-on straighten to make it look as though she'd physically touched the object.

Swiping her hand over a sprinkling of dust on the top of a stack of books, she had to restrain herself from grabbing the feather duster. And then she couldn't resist a quick touch-up. Tapping her littlest fingers together, which activated her air magic, she blew gently over a row of books. The dust swirled and lifted and dispersed into nothing.

With a satisfied nod, she said, "Always better than manual labor. So! Midnight. And a full moon tonight. This night promises a new beginning."

Or so it had said in her horoscope that she'd read on the back of a stranger's newspaper while taking the Métro to work this morning.

"Ha! Horoscopes," she said with a laugh as she strolled down the dimly lit hallway to the elevator, her heels clicking brightly on the bare concrete floor. "I'll take real astrology any day. And that says the full moon brings family and challenge to my life."

Her only living family—her mother, Petrina—lived in Greece with her current lover. Petrina and Tamatha talked once a month. They had a great relationship. Unfortunately—or fortunately, depending on the degree of attachment—Petrina's lover was dying. Again, the curse. Her mother wasn't upset over it. Though she had mentioned something about perhaps giving him some belladonna to help him along so he didn't have to suffer.

As for the challenge the horoscope had promised… "I like a good adventure." But she wouldn't admit that adventure was hard to come by with her nose stuck in a book all day. Her life was exciting. Mostly.

Maybe.

"Hardly."

So she put a lot of focus and energy into her studies. She had mastered earth, air, water and even fire magic. The sigils tattooed on her fingers representing each of the four elements allowed for easy access to a specific elemental spell. She also practiced ornithomancy (divination by birds), alomancy (divination by salt) and pyromancy (fire divination). And her venture into diabology would eventually add demonomancy to that list. As far as witches went, Tamatha was quite powerful. But never powerful enough when the world offered so many opportunities to learn and expand her knowledge.

She stepped into the elevator and tugged at her gray pencil skirt with fingers beringed in lapis lazuli (for truth), amethyst (for grounding and balance) and bloodstone (for healing). The elevator moved laboriously up two floors. She'd left her reading glasses on, and she now tucked them into her purse. They were fabulous cat's-eye frames bespangled with rhinestones at the corners of each eye. She was into the rockabilly look and was pleased it was actually making a style comeback with the humans. Easier to fit in when she resembled others.

On the other hand, she never wanted to conform. That was for uninteresting people who didn't know themselves.

Once out of the elevator, she nodded goodbye to the hirsute night guard, who she suspected was a werewolf, but he never seemed to want to converse, barely looking up from his handheld television as she passed and never offering a vocal "*au revoir*" or even a confirming nod.

Ah well, she couldn't befriend them all. And he was a shapeshifter, so yeah, nix that.

Located on the Right Bank in the 11th arrondissement, the Council headquarters opened into a dreary alleyway that was far from parking or any Métro station. Out of the way and unassuming. Tamatha could do without the ten-minute walk to the closest subway. She lived across the river in the 6th, near the Luxembourg Gardens. It was a fine walk on a sunny day, when she remembered to bring along walking flats. Not tonight, though, with the promise of rain thickening the air.

Muttering the words to the demon binding spell, she delighted in how easily she remembered things like Latin spells or even long ingredient lists for poultices and charms. If only her luck with men could be so simple and long lasting.

The curious thing about the family curse was that no one was really sure how it had originated, nor had anyone tried to vanquish it. Sure, the Bellerose women were independent and much preferred lovers to a more permanent husband. But Tamatha had already had her share of lost lovers since she'd started dating in her late teens in the 1930s. She was ready for some permanence. For a good old-fashioned love affair that might result in something more promising than death to the male party.

Warm summer raindrops spattered her cheek and she picked up into a sort-of run. The fastest she could manage in four-inch heels and with a tight skirt was a penguin waddle.

Touching her middle fingers together to ask for a rain-parting spell, she dodged left into a cobblestoned alleyway she knew was sheltered with close-spaced roof ledges—and she ran right into a man. He had been walking swiftly as well, and when they collided he let out an "ouff" and gripped her by the shoulders.

The first thing Tamatha noticed in the moon-shielded

darkness was the glint of something shiny and black at his temples, beneath the hairline, and the barest scent of sulfur. Demon? A brief red glow ignited in his eyes.

She reacted. *"Scatura, demonicus, vold!"*

"Wait—"

It was too late for his protest. The man dropped her, his arms slapping to his sides and his body going rigid. He wore half gloves on his hands, and his exposed fingers crooked into ridged claws. His feet stiffened within his boots and he teetered, falling backward, his shoulders and head hitting the brick wall of the building but a foot behind him.

His eyes glowed red and he growled at her through tight jaws. "Witch!"

Chapter 2

Edamite Thrash had been minding his own business, racing against the rain to get home, when he collided with a deliciously scented female with skin like ivory, hair the color of silvered snow and wide green eyes. It was as if entering another realm when he'd touched her and she had surrounded him with citrus, sensuality and softness, and then—

Damn it. He couldn't move his limbs. And his veins felt as if ice flowed through them. The chill was moving down his thighs and toward his calves. Every muscle strung tightly. The witch had bound him.

"Get this…off me," he hissed, thankful he could still speak. Though he clenched his jaw tighter. And his body leaned against the wall. How soon before his boots would slide on the wet pavement and he toppled? "Damn you! Witch!"

"Oh my goddess, it really worked!" she said with more enthusiasm than he thought appropriate.

The witch peered into his eyes as if looking for something she'd lost. Even in the darkness her giddy thrill showed in the gemstone gleam of her gaze. Stepping back, she looked him up and down. From the top of his slicked-back black hair, down his black suit and trousers, to his leather boots. Ed had never felt more humiliated. So inadequate. If he could lift a hand he would make her regret it. In his trouser pocket he felt his mobile phone vibrate. No one would call him at his private number unless it was important.

"I've always wanted to bind a demon," she offered with a gleeful clasp of hands before her. Many crystal rings flashed in the moonlight and he noted the small tattoos on the midjoints of each of her fingers. Sigils of some sort. Nasty witch business, no doubt. "And I did it!"

"Against my will," he snarled. "Take this binding… off me, or…" To make the sounds leave his mouth was a monumental task. "I will kill you, witch!"

Her happiness flattened to curious concern as she tilted her head and tapped her lower lip. A plump pink lip that looked all too tempting even in his bound, defenseless state.

What was he thinking? Witches were disgusting.

"You actually think that threatening to kill me will convince me to release you?" she prompted.

Probably not. But he'd been speaking reactively not rationally.

"Fine. Please, witch—" Oh, how he hated to condescend to her sort.

"My name is Tamatha." She offered her hand to shake, and when he could but look at it, a pitiful statue tilted against the wall, she dropped her hand. "Sorry. My bad. I learned the demon binding spell this evening. Must be the full moon. It's magical, isn't it?"

Ed inhaled a deep breath to calm his anger. He had to do something if he was going to talk his way out of this one. "How about I promise not to harm a hair on your witchy head if you remove the binding? I mean, what are you going to do with a stiff demon anyway?"

Her lips curled to an expectant smirk, and her eyes brightened as they strolled down the front of his torso to *just there.*

And Ed realized what he'd said. Really? Her mind went *there*? Well, he could entertain a few lascivious thoughts about those lips— No! This situation was embarrassing and ridiculous. And never would he entertain anything with a witch. Been there, done that. Learned his lesson well.

"Please, Tamatha?" Right, appeal to her personally. Befriend the enemy.

"Before I release the binding, tell me your name," she entreated, "and what breed of demon you are. I'm studying diabology. I'm very interested in your species."

Yikes. The woman was some kind of fangirl. That creeped him out. Just his luck with women, though. They either wanted to marvel over his oddities or run screaming from them.

"If I give you my name, you've control over me," he said tightly. His jaw muscles felt like stretched iron. "Not going to happen."

"Oh, but I— Oh, yes, I see what you mean. Witches can control demons with their full names. Could you maybe tell me what kind of demon you are? I'll release you then. Cross my heart."

The gesture of crossing her heart disturbed Ed. He would have flinched if he wasn't bound. He'd once been told about the witch's crossed heart but couldn't recall what it meant. A wicked gesture with malefic intent?

He didn't want to give her anything, but her knowing his breed wasn't going to hurt him any more than this wicked chill icing his veins. "Corax demon," he said. And then, to keep it light and perhaps her mood light as well, he offered, "Such fortune that I run into a witch who is practicing her spells this ugly moonlit night."

"Oh, it's not ugly out. You think it is? Rain is cleansing and it washes away the icky city smells."

"What I think is that we are done conversing. The cold." It took all his effort to curl his fingers upward into an ineffectual claw. "It's icing in my veins."

"Oh! Really? That must be a side effect of the spell. Yes, I think I recall the binding, if left on too long, will paralyze. There was also the side effect of chilblains, headaches and possible extended, er—" Her eyes dropped to his crotch again.

Ed gritted his jaws. Really? His cock *was* hard, now he noticed. Even more humiliation. Gorgeous as she was, this chick was one wacky witch. Who smelled like something he wanted to bury his nose in and suck down whole—damn it!

"*Vold, demonicis, scaratus*," she recited.

With but a sweep of her hand before his chest, the chill exited Ed's veins downward, seeming to sluice out the soles of his boots. His shoulders relaxed, as did his legs. He started to go down. The witch reached to help him, and in her sudden panic, she grabbed him by the head. Her palms slapped warmly against his temples. The horn nubs that jutted up but millimeters through his hair heated and glowed beneath her touch.

He never let anyone touch his horns. Mercy, but that felt too good. The contact provided enough energy transfer to allow him to straighten his legs and catch himself before sprawling on the ground.

Coming upright before her, he matched her height, which was a surprise, but then he decided she must have been wearing high heels. Excellent. That would make it difficult for her to run when he strangled her.

Ed gripped her by the neck, squeezing as hard as his anger would allow him to squeeze, and—

The demon kissed her.

When Tamatha had expected him to hit her, to bruise her with his terrible clutch about her neck in retaliation for the binding she'd put on him, he instead…kissed her.

And he was still kissing her.

Her pink leather shoe heels backed up against the brick wall and she wobbled, but he caught her about the waist with a sure and guiding hand, not breaking the incredible, shockingly hot kiss.

This kiss was the furthest thing from retaliation. So she surrendered to the weird moment and even forgot about the rain spell, reveling in the spill of warm summer rain down her neck and cheeks.

This man kissed her as if he knew her. Had tasted her lips before. His mouth was firm and demanding, intent. Nothing about him being a demon repelled her. Everything about him made her want to get closer, dive deeper and seek his insides. To study him for more reason than that he was demon. If she could run her hands over his skin, she would. She must.

She dropped her shoulder bag and pushed her hands over his shoulders and teased the short, dark hair at the back of his neck, gripping it to hold him at her mouth. And then she glided up the back of his scalp and forward. Her forefingers glanced over the adamant growths at his temples she suspected were horns. Interesting. And he answered her greedy coax by dashing his tongue against hers and daring her to meet him as he deepened the kiss. Which she did.

The sulfur she'd originally scented was no longer noticeable. The crisp, cool tang of his aftershave filled her senses with ice and cedar. She would never forget this man's scent.

What *was* his name? Sure, she could control him with his name, but she wouldn't. Maybe. The binding had been an unintended reaction. But what joy that it had worked! Of course, then he had called her a witch with such vitriol she had tasted his hatred for her as if it were acid on her tongue.

If he would stop kissing her she could step back and be wary.

On the other hand, right now, lack of wariness suited her fine.

He muttered an appreciative moan against her mouth, and then as suddenly as he'd kissed her, he pulled away and wiped his lips. "Wha—?" He winced and shook his head. "What the hell? Why did I…? I did not just kiss a witch."

"Uh, yes, you did. And it was awesome."

"Not awesome. No! Witches are…vile." Again he wiped his lips, and Tamatha cringed. He admonished her with a wagging finger before her face. "You made me do that."

"No, I—"

He snapped his fingers, abruptly cutting her off as if she were a child being scolded by a rude teacher. "If you want to keep breathing, stay away from me, witch."

And he stalked off, glancing over his shoulder at her once. He slapped his hand against a thigh, tugging a phone out of his pocket, and stomped away.

Tamatha offered a wave. Silly. And stupid. He'd been offended by kissing her? She hadn't made him do a thing. He'd wanted to kiss her.

Vile?

"Not so pleased about kissing you, either," she muttered.

But she couldn't quite bring herself to wipe off his kiss. Instead, she tapped her mouth and decided to stick with the good memory of his demanding and sensual lips against hers.

"I kissed a demon," she said in wonder. And for as much as he had been repulsed, she could not summon a tendril of disgust. A smile curled her rain-sprinkled lips. "And I liked it."

He clicked to answer the ringing cell phone as he stalked away from the repulsive witch. She had tasted—well, not vile, but rather sweet. Though he'd not admit that out loud.

"Thrash! You gotta help. They're getting closer. I can't get out of here!"

It was his friend Laurent LaVolliere, a fellow demon whom he considered family, for their grand-relations had once formed the Libre denizen centuries earlier here in the very heart of Paris. Laurent sounded out of breath and frightened. The man was a strife demon; it took a lot to frighten him.

"Tell me where you are, Laurent."

"The Montparnasse!"

"Where in…the cemetery?"

"Their skin… Ed, it's falling from their faces. And… stuff is oozing from their mouths. There's so many of them. I can feel their dark magic. So…powerful. I can't move!"

The terror in his friend's voice sent a shiver down his spine. "I'll be right there. Hold on."

Ed shoved the phone into his pocket. Yet something compelled him to glance over his shoulder. The witch was nowhere to be seen. Talk about tormenting demons under the full moon.

But he couldn't bother with a silly witch and that ridiculously hot kiss. Laurent was in trouble.

He spread back his arms and tilted back his head. The sensation of feathered barbs piercing his flesh always hurt like a mother. The price he had to pay for shifting. His molecules rearranged and did their own thing and his form separated into dozens of soot-winged ravens. As one entity the conspiracy of ravens swooped upward and soared in the direction of the cemetery. Beyond a vast city garden, the graveyard marked a dark blot amid the roofed and pavement-tangled city.

When he came to human form with a shiver of his body to gather in his energy and shake off a feather or two, he stood in a dark graveyard packed with tombstones, mausoleums, crumbling stone crosses and moss-frosted angels. Fully clothed, a phenomenon beyond his explanation, he wore no trace of his previous form. He could smell the anomaly immediately and felt its presence as a tightening in his horn nubs. And the witch ward on his forearm burned as it had not previously in the alley.

When his eyes landed on the band of growling creatures—who were wrapped in shredded linens, some of their hair gone and skin indeed falling away from some of their bones—he heard his friend's scream. And witnessed his destruction.

Laurent let out one agonizing shout at sight of Ed: "*Les Douze!*" Then his body was torn away at shoulders, hips and head. His remains did not immediately ash as with most demon deaths.

One of the hideous creatures sighted Ed. He reactively sent a stream of energy mined from his vita, his very life force, toward it, which manifested as black smoke, enforced with demonic magic. The force should knock it from its feet and slam it into the nearby tombstone, breaking its body and killing it. The current of black energy coiled about the creature. Instead of succumbing to defeat, the zombielike thing merely swayed as if an annoying breeze had washed over its decrepit structure.

The rest of the creatures spied Ed. The one next to the thing that had taken his energy zap as if a mosquito sting dropped Laurent's disembodied arm and growled at him. One opened its mouth and the lower jaw unhinged.

"Didn't think zombies existed," he hissed.

Zombies were not tops on his list. He never watched the popular television show because they were so unbelievable. The dead did not come back to life. Right?

The group of things—whatever they were—groaned and stalked toward him.

Ed knew when he was overwhelmed, and he was going to count his lacking ability to put the one off its feet to lingering remnants of the sexy witch's binding spell.

"Find your rest, Laurent!" he shouted, then shifted to a conspiracy and flew out of there and back to his home, where he landed on the rooftop, fell to his knees and caught his palms on the concrete surface.

It was raining harder, and he prayed no lightning snapped the sky. Lightning worked like an electrical jolt to his bones, no matter how distant the occurrence.

Shifting into and out of his humanlike demon form took a lot out of him. He rarely utilized the skill because he could generally get where he needed to go by car or on foot. He'd be exhausted for hours now. But he was safe at home. Safe from…

"What the hell killed my friend?"

Chapter 3

Les Douze was French for The Twelve. And something about that moniker rang a bell in Ed's memory. Perhaps he and Laurent had discussed it once? But why, and what did it mean?

After searching for hours through the database his office maintained—hacked from Hawkes Associates—Ed learned The Twelve had been a coven of witches from the eighteenth century who had been accused of witchcraft by the locals and burned to death in the Place de Grève, which was now the Place de l'Hôtel de Ville, or city hall. A remarkable and grisly event that the human Parisians had talked about for decades and the real witches would never forget.

That verified what Ed suspected. He rubbed the small, solid black circle sigil on his forearm that had burned when he'd first landed in the cemetery. Indeed, those creatures had been witches. But what sort? Witches were generally *alive*. Not even generally, but rather, exclusively.

Those things after Laurent had been remarkably zombielike. With skin falling from their limbs, their only audible sounds had been grunts and groans. Strange, metallic gray stuff had oozed from their mouths. But really? Had *dead* witches killed Laurent?

"But *Les Douze* were burned," he muttered, closing his laptop and leaning back in his office chair. "They were reduced to ashes. Things don't come back from the dead. Not usually."

He'd heard the rumor about a tribe of revenant vampires who had been resurrected from the dead. And sure, he guessed dark magic could bring anything back to life. A dark witch or warlock could conjure such a monstrosity. But it would be a real zombie. Zombies were shambling bone sacks. Their brains had to be degraded or completely gone. A revenant could not feasibly survive for long.

As far as he knew.

Ed wasn't up on zombies and dead things. He didn't want to be, either. But he had watched his friend get torn, literally, limb from limb. He couldn't ignore that horrific incident. And no doubt, Laurent had tried to communicate something about *Les Douze*.

The office was quiet and vast. Black marble stretched the floor and up all the walls. It was peaceful here six floors above the big bustling city. Sometimes too peaceful. But then again, something always happened to shake him to the core and exercise his diplomacy and survival skills. Like impossible zombie witches killing his friend.

Thinking about witches made Ed shudder. Demons and witches had a strange and volatile relationship. Most witches could not control a demon unless they had originally summoned that demon. Likewise, demons hadn't much control over witches. But the most powerful witches could control demons and use them for nefarious means.

Every demon child was told scary tales at bedtime, and Ed's mother had loved to frighten him with tales of wicked witches.

There's nothing you can do to outrun them. He recalled the creepy, dramatic voice of his mother, Sophie, as she'd lean over the bed and speak to the sheet he'd pulled over his head in fright. *If you ever see a witch, Edamite, run!*

Of course, then his mother would laugh and leave him shivering in bed, wishing his father were actually married to his mother and living with them so he could run to him for a sympathetic hug. It hadn't been that his mother was vindictive. Ed guessed she simply never realized how those tales had freaked out her son.

Unfortunately, such childhood frights had not completely warned him off witches. He'd dated two. Two too many.

The first had been flighty and fascinated by his demonic nature, yet had only lasted so long as he could endure her silly human propensity to gossip, shop and text, text and text some more. The second had tried to enslave him and had come so close that he'd felt her power strip him of his innate magical defenses. It had been three days of relentless torture he would never forget.

But he was a grown man now. He was a high-ranked demon in the city of Paris, thanks to his not showing fear in the face of challenge and his tendency to take charge and get things done. He was respected and revered by his kind. And witches should walk a wide circle around him.

Not kiss him.

You were the one who kissed her.

Funny thing, that. She must have used magic to get him to lock lips with her. Why she would do that was beyond him. Must have been a distraction so he wouldn't strangle her in retaliation for the binding. Weird way to go about shifting the balance of power. And how had she, a witch, controlled him when she had not summoned him?

"She must have great power," he muttered.

But did it matter? He should not give another moment's consideration to a pretty witch with wide green eyes and soft lips, whose derriere had wiggled teasingly in her tight skirt. He'd learned his lesson. Witches could never be trusted.

There were more important things on the table now.

Some very powerful magic had been present in that cemetery. It had torn Laurent apart. As well, he'd felt the air crackle with the unseen magic. A force greater than the creatures he'd witnessed, perhaps? He wielded demonic magic, but if the tales of demon/witch relations were accurate, it was never effective against witches for long. And he suspected his ability to use magic against witches had irrevocably weakened, thanks to his ill-fated romance with Witch Number Two.

Yet, if it were witches, he was going to need some powerful magic to figure this out. At the very least, provide him with answers, perhaps some suggestions as to how to approach the creatures he had seen.

Had Laurent's death been a bizarre but singular event? Did he have to kill them? How to kill them? Only another witch's magic might serve the killing blow.

Could he lower himself to work with a witch? There must be someone else who could tell him about witch magic. The werewolves and vampires Ed called allies likely wouldn't know much. He considered contacting John Malcolm, the exorcist he kept on his payroll. The man was more versed in demons and ghosts. Though he had begun dabbling in witch finding. It was a medieval, yet very necessary, practice that few specialized in nowadays.

Ah hell. He'd give it a go and contact a witch. For Laurent's sake. The man had been a good friend; he deserved the investigation, if not downright vengeance. And Ed would rather jump into a situation with a knowledgeable enemy than wait for a less informed ally to wander along and half ass the situation.

He pulled out his phone and dialed Inego, one of his field assistants. "I need you to find the most powerful witch in Paris," he said. "Bring John Malcolm along."

"The nutty one with the crazy eyes? Isn't he an exorcist?" Inego asked.

"Yes, but he's added witch finding to his oeuvre. He should be able to track one for you."

Tamatha had encountered a corax demon. She wrote the term in her purple-glitter-covered notebook and underlined it. The breed was related, somehow, to the *Corvus corax* species of ravens. Perhaps the demon could shift to raven form? Many demons possessed shifting abilities. She'd have to look it up when she got to work on Monday.

What she did know was that the breed could be very grumpy following a kiss. And not at all friendly. She wasn't going to write about the kiss in her notes, though.

She set the notebook aside and it automatically straightened on the bench to align with the painted brown wood. She pulled out from her purse a pair of black rhinestone-bespangled sunglasses. The high sun warmed the Luxembourg Gardens today. The air smelled green and alive. A nearby pear tree scented the air sweetly. Yet she wished she were inside, two stories belowground, sorting through dusty pages in the archives.

But she would follow her boss's suggestion that she not return to work until Monday. Perhaps a relaxing weekend was needed. So to put herself in the vacation mood, she had given herself a mani/pedi this morning. The gray, sparkly polish glinted in the sunlight and went well with the silver rings she wore and her hair. She'd got her silver hair from her mother, whose shade had been slightly darker and tinted blue. Petrina had told her Grandma Lysia's had been blue-black.

The park wasn't as crowded as she'd expect on a sunny day. It was early yet and most were probably at home eating breakfast, save for a few mothers and their children scattered around the pond tracking sailboats.

Tamatha worshipped nature and was pleased she'd found a place to live so close to this lush garden escape. The few people who did wander about also soaked in the sunshine. When had the Parisian men started wearing such tight, brightly colored pants? Not at all garish, the style showed off some nice thighs and well-shaped derrieres. Had she really been away from the dating scene for so long? She preferred a stylish, gentlemanly look, groomed hair and maybe some stubble and a mustache.

"And tattoos," she said with a smile.

She had many. Some were spell tattoos; others were personal, such as the Bellerose family crest she wore on her right biceps. It featured a bell-shaped pink rose surrounded by black and gray shaded arabesques, and the family motto Love Often was inked in Latin—*Amor Modum Saepe.*

She recalled the corax demon had tattoos on his neck. A vampire ward similar to the one she wore in white ink (more discreet). And the backs of his hands had been virtually blackened with ink, though maybe that had been the black leather half gloves creating the effect; she'd looked so quickly. That was the only body art she had noticed because he'd worn a suit and buttoned-up gray dress shirt, which had given him a *GQ*-with-an-edge look. And his black hair and brows had drawn her focus to his pale gray eyes.

Eyes that had briefly glowed red. She wondered now

if the glow was something that happened without his volition. Was it controlled by emotion? Anger? Reaction to surroundings? Instinct? Was he aware when they turned red? All of the above?

So many questions and so many books to read to learn the answers. The prospect of research thrilled her.

She smoothed a hand over the volume on European demon breeds she'd taken from the Archives, thinking reading was pleasurable, but an afternoon sitting across a café table from a sexy demon, asking him anything and everything she wanted to know, would prove more desirable. Gazing into his eyes. Drawing in that interesting icy cedar scent…

Tamatha straightened abruptly and slammed the book shut. "You do not have a thing for him," she admonished. "He called you vile."

The guy must harbor the age-old hang-up most demons had toward witches. She thought it silly. But some habits died hard. And she knew more than many witches who still avoided vampires because the longtooths possessed the ability to steal a witch's power through bloodsexmagic—biting, and draining them of magic while they had sex. Ugh. Nothing sexy about that scenario whatsoever.

She had never dated a vampire and generally preferred human men. They were easy enough to figure out. Though she never got too serious. The family curse and all. While she'd never been directly responsible for a death, there had been that time she'd mixed magics and a windstorm had uprooted a tree and sent a branch straight through her lover's heart. He'd hit her once, and she'd feared him every time he'd walked through her door. Had he got what he deserved? It wasn't for her to judge, but certainly she hadn't cried over his death.

What she wanted was a challenge, someone to seduce and stimulate not only her mind, but her body, as well.

"I don't even know his name," she whispered, then sighed again. Chasing the mysteriously sexy demon out of her head was proving impossible. Ah well, a little daydreaming never hurt anyone.

Nearby the octagon pond, Tamatha heard a splash. She saw two feet upend over the edge of the pond and a sailboat bobbled frantically. A child had fallen?

Heartbeats thundering, she reactively touched her middle fingers together to activate her water magic and whispered a controlling spell. A *whoosh* like a tidal wave curved toward the pond shore, spitting the kid back onto the pebbled ground. A mother shrieked and rushed for her soaked child.

And Tamatha exhaled with relief. "Whew."

Chapter 4

Ed looked up from his laptop to see Inego and Glitch forcing a squirming, struggling—bound—woman into his office. A plastic grocery sack hung over her head, though the long silver-white hair that he recognized so well spilled out beyond her shoulders.

"What the—?" He marched up and pulled the bag from her head.

"You?" she gasped. Lifting her bound hands, the fingers of which having been completely wrapped up with thin white cording, she asked, "What in all the moons?"

"What is the meaning of this?" he asked Inego (of the twosome, the one who he suspected had more brains). "I asked you to bring me the most powerful witch in Paris."

"She's it, boss. We saw her save a boy in the park. Didn't even have to twitch her nose to do it, either."

"Did John verify it?"

"Yep. He picked her out before that happened. Said his

witchy radar was going off the scale and told us to check her out."

Ed stepped back from the witch and noticed she looked as surprised as he. Though that could have something to do with the ropes and the rough treatment she must have received when brought here. If John Malcolm had verified her power, then it was possible. He'd had no idea she was so powerful.

On the other hand, she had bound him with nothing more than a few words.

Well, well. This could get interesting. If not…uncomfortable.

"What are you up to?" she asked. "I thought you hated witches. Called us vile."

Indeed he had. Not the best way to start a working relationship, but he could manage. "I needed to speak to you," he said. Could he really do this? *Did* he need a witch? Especially one so distracting as this one?

"So you—you kidnapped me?"

"This is not a kidnapping."

Though when she shook her bound hands between them and gave him an incredulous gape, he couldn't deny it did look nefarious, if not downright cruel.

"Now you know what it feels like," he said reactively. "To be bound."

Her jaw dropped, stupefied. He couldn't help a vainglorious smile. So he wasn't keen on condescending to her sympathies. The witch had bound him. And it had hurt like hell.

To his men he said, "I didn't tell you to tie her up. I just asked you to bring her to me."

"She's a witch, boss. We had to tie her up or she'd put a spell on us. Malcolm told us the marks on her fingers cast spells if she can use her hands."

Ed considered that one and conceded with a nod. "True. Good call, men."

"Oh, I am so out of here." The witch backed away, bound hands beating the air with her words. "Most powerful? Maybe. Most pissed off? You better believe it."

Glitch rushed to grab her by the arm and she struggled, kicking her high-heeled shoe and landing the pointed toe on his thigh. Yikes. That had to hurt. Glitch yowled and hobbled off, clutching his wound. Inego grabbed her other arm.

"Enough!" The minions glanced to Ed.

The witch pleaded with her thrust-up hands. "I can still throw magic with my hands bound. But I'll be much more compelled to listen if you treat me with respect."

Indeed. But could he trust her? She'd once already used witchcraft to soften his anger and make him kiss her. Her mouth was a pretty pale pink today. And those eyes. Had he ever gazed into such vivid green eyes? There were things in them. Mystery. Adventures. Worlds.

Hell. No. He wasn't gazing.

"I'll count to three," the witch threatened. "Then I'm bringing out the big magic."

"Boss?" Glitch asked on a worried wobble.

"What kind of minions are you?" Ed said to them. "You're frightened of one little witch? You managed to get her here without taking harm."

"I'm going to have a bruise," Glitch whined and clutched his thigh.

"Where did I find you two?" Ed muttered, pacing before the threesome.

Right. He'd rescued the dastardly duo from exile to Daemonia after both had been caught with their proverbial fingers in the cookie jar. Working a V-hub and selling vampire blood to their fellow demons. They were two stupid lunks who had needed direction and a purpose. Which he was trying to give them.

And the best way to lead was by example.

Ed thrust out some minor magic in a black curl of smoke that melted the ropes bound about the witch's hands. "My men should not have been so cruel. I apologize."

"Yeah? Too little, too late, buster. This is nuts!" She turned and marched out of his office, the tight skirt she wore luring his gaze to the sensual wiggle beneath the pale green fabric. Yeah, so gazing was good. Real good.

Inego and Glitch cast him wondering stares, which blew his gaze off course.

"Idiots," Ed hissed. He strode after the pissed-off witch. What was her name? "Tamatha!"

Instead of turning right to go down the hallway to the elevator, she'd unknowingly taken a left and now stood like a captive doe before the wall where his secretary normally sat. At least the secretary was spared this scene, though. She was out having a baby demon that could very likely be born with scales, thanks to her affair with a dragon shifter.

"I'm so sorry." Ed walked up to her and tried to put his hands on her shoulders to calm her, but she slapped at his wrists and hands. "Tamatha, please, I want to talk to you."

"They put a freakin' plastic bag over my head!"

He managed to pin one of her shoulders against the wall and worked to wrangle her opposite wrist, to calm her, to make her listen to him. And to be prepared should she try to fling more magic his way.

"I could have suffocated!"

Indeed, he had best give more detailed instructions next time he sent his men after such a pretty, delicate creature who— "Ouch!"

Pressing his forehead to the wall beside her head, he rode out the pain of a direct hit from her pointy-toed shoe to his shin. Damn, those things were sharp! He was probably bleeding. He didn't want to risk looking because he still had her in a loose but compliant hold.

"Sorry," she said softly. "I didn't mean to hurt you. I'm not cruel. But you bring up my defensive instincts."

When her hand stroked over his cheek and temple, a wave of strange desire shivered through his system.

"Tamatha," he gasped. A lush tide of delicious warmth overtook his muscles and his body melted against hers. He could not…resist. "Oh, goodness and light."

Bracketing her face with his hands, he kissed her like he'd never kissed a woman before. Sweetly. Reverently. With such a longing that it must have shown all over his skin in the shivers he felt riding the tattooed surface. Her breath spilled over his lips and entered his pores. Her aura of lemon perfume surrounded him with a sticky sweet allure.

He was falling, succumbing, slipping into a strange kind of submission…

Realizing he was once again kissing the witch, Ed abruptly broke the connection. "Ah hell." He looked at his hands, still gently bracketing her face. And there, on her face, the glint in her eye as the curve of a smile tickled onto her perfect lips. "What did you do to me?"

"Me? You're the one who keeps kissing me. I didn't do a thing but get kidnapped and roughed up by your henchmen. And then you pressed me up against the wall and had your way with me." She cast her glance aside. "Not that there was anything wrong with your way. Which is why I haven't wielded magic against you. Yet."

"I believe I should be thankful for that. Why is it every time I see you I want to…to…?"

"Hurt me?"

"I don't hurt women. I just want to—" he made a motion to shove but curved his fingers away from touching her "—push you away. Witches are vile."

"So you've said. Repeatedly. Great way to kill the mood, buddy." She shoved his chest, but he didn't step away from her.

"Yes, but if you are so repulsive, then why do I end up kissing you every time we meet?"

She tilted her head and tapped a finger on her lips. Those luscious, sweet, soft lips demanded more thorough attention. And so he would see to it they had it.

Ed again kissed her, this time pushing his hands through her hair and caressing the softness that spilled over her shoulders in waves of unnatural silver. Goddess hair, he thought. Not of this realm. He pressed his body along hers. To feel her, to take her all in…

"Ahem," she muttered against his mouth, and he sensed her need to push him away, when all he wanted to do was get closer than close. Inside her. Intimately. Her gaze veered over his shoulder and to the door of his office.

Ed glanced around behind him. Glitch stood in the doorway, observing with a smirk and dancing gaze. The idiot didn't need to say a thing.

What luck that the most powerful witch in Paris was also one who attracted him like no other and promised to give him dreams that would keep any sane man begging for more. She was a witch, but she wasn't one of those nasty witches his mother had warned him about. She couldn't be.

But then, that was the same thing he'd thought about Witch Number Two before she'd tried to enslave him.

Ed gripped Tamatha by the wrist and pulled her toward the office, but she planted her feet and tugged.

"We need to talk," he said hastily.

"I'm not going in there with those creeps leering at me. A plastic bag," she reiterated. "Seriously!"

Releasing his hold on the stubborn witch, Ed gestured toward the idiots. "Leave. Go do…that thing I needed you to do."

"What thing, boss—?"

Inego shoved his partner out of the doorway. "You know, that *thing*. Sure, boss. We're out of here."

"There is no thing," Glitch argued as they strolled down the hallway.

Exasperated by his employees' incompetence, Ed pushed his hands over his hair, and then remembering his guest, he took a moment to vacillate on what he was about to do. Make nice. With a witch. Because he needed one.

First, he had to determine if he could trust her.

He gestured to Tamatha that she enter his office. "Please?"

With an impertinent lift of her chin, she strode through the doors, quickening her pace as she passed him and walking to the center of the black marble floor that stretched far too long to his desk. This office was too large and ostentatious, but he'd got the rental for a steal because a mass murder had taken place in it a few years ago. He had sensed the malefic vibrations in the air—and still did on occasion—and he'd had it smudged more than a few times, but that never seemed to clear the negative energies.

"I don't know your name," she said. "You know mine. Tamatha Bellerose."

"Bellerose," he repeated, but didn't recognize the surname. "Pretty, like its owner. My name is Edamite. You can call me Ed."

"Edamite? I've never heard that form of the name before. I would say 'glad to meet you, Ed,' but I'm not terribly thrilled about this situation." She cast her gaze about the room, briefly noting the few items displayed on the wall. "Generally my dates are a bit less…kidnappy."

She shivered and embraced herself. The blouse she wore was a sheer, filmy black thing that showed a glimpse of the black lace bra beneath. And on her arms, beneath the sheer black, he made out a tattoo, but couldn't remark its design. Smaller symbols had been inked on the midsection of each of her fingers. Spell tats, no doubt. And there at her neck was a white ink symbol he recognized. A vampire ward. Smart witch.

He rubbed his forearm where beneath the shirt was the witch ward. It usually tingled when a witch was near. And it did now. But why hadn't it when he'd run into her the other night?

"Cold?" He passed her by and walked to his desk, intent on maintaining his calm and not rushing over to steal her into his embrace and devour her again. What was up with that? He was not lusting over a witch. That way lay trouble.

"Something awful happened in this room," she said, her gaze still taking the area in. "Have you smudged the place?"

"Half a dozen times. Never seems to chase away whatever morbid stuff remains. I've given up on trying."

"I could do it for you and it would work. Whoever has smudged it previously wasn't bleeding into the very pores of the stone beneath our feet. Earth magic is required. Murders," she said suddenly and with knowing. "I don't want to stay in this room much longer."

"Okay, fine, Tamatha, but give me two minutes, please?"

"If that's how long it will take for you to explain why you had me kidnapped, then…go."

"It wasn't a—" Ed surrendered the argument with an exhalation. "My men are assholes. I apologize for their ineptitude. To get to the point…" He spread out his hands before him. "I need a witch."

He didn't know if he could trust her yet. What was he saying? Why hadn't he a plan? Damn, she was so gorgeous. He'd say anything to have another kiss.

Really?

"Well, well." She lifted her chin and assumed a haughty pose, which was made all the more attractive by the tight skirt and slender gams and that curly goddess hair that Ed could still feel crushed between his fingers.

"Well, well, what?" he asked.

"I'm studying diabology and demonomancy. It so happens I need a demon."

"You mean to study? To put under a microscope and observe?"

"Oh, not like that. Maybe a little. Textbooks and dusty old grimoires are excellent resources for learning, but I'm more of a hands-on kind of girl. I would love to have a demon to talk to and ask questions. Learn things."

He smoothed a palm over his hair. She was annoying and she was appealing. And he wasn't sure which side was going to win out, but she was the only witch he had right now. And apparently a powerful one. He wanted to play her carefully, lest he became one of those demons from his mother's faery tales. They had never survived to the end of the story.

"I don't do the bug-under-the-microscope thing," he offered.

"You want a powerful witch? You gotta bargain, buddy."

So that was the way of it? The magic he'd felt filling the atmosphere in the Montparnasse cemetery had been incredible. Immense. He needed dark magic to fight it, but more likely, light magic to win against it. And Tamatha looked like a witch of the Light.

"*Are* you a witch of the Light?"

She nodded. "Mostly."

Well, she was honest. And her hair spilled like liquid silver over her shoulders. It was gorgeous— Ah! He had to focus.

"You said you are studying demonomancy? That's controlling demons. How do I know you won't try to control me? Er...*again*."

"I'd never do such a thing. I've never summoned a demon, either. It's wrong to exert your control over others."

He lifted a brow at that one.

She shrugged. "Well, you know, I have to practice my spells. The binding was a reaction."

"So you said. But it was an exertion of control."

"Guilty. I do have a thing for keeping things orderly, which I've been told is also a means of control." She glanced around the room. "I'd show you my OCD magic, but this place is spotless. Too cold."

Yes, yes, so he didn't do the decorating thing beyond the few magical items on the wall he displayed from the stash he'd acquired over the years.

"I don't think I can trust you, witch."

"You pronounce 'witch' as if it's an oath or curse word."

Now it was his turn to offer a shrug. "Your kind and mine have never been friends."

"I promise you I won't try to control you again, Ed."

"Witch's honor?"

She drew a cross over her heart, which gave him a shiver.

"You know what it means when I cross my heart?" she asked.

He shook his head. "Something bad, I'm sure."

"When we witches cross our heart, it is the truest and most sealing bond to our word."

That didn't sound so awful. Rather noble, even. Hmm...

"It would mean a lot to me," she said, "if you would agree to answer some questions and let me, well..."

"Study me?"

"Not under a microscope."

Mercy, he didn't want this alliance. All his rational instincts screamed—*stay away from the witch!* Yet the louder voice moaned in anticipation for one more kiss. Could he control her with seduction? Because he had to keep her under thumb to keep his risk low.

But, oh, the things on her he'd like to feel gliding beneath his thumbs.

"Fine," he said. "So you agree to be the witch I need, if I agree to be the demon you need?"

She nodded. Her high-voltage smile beamed to match those world-filled eyes.

"You don't even know why I need a witch," he countered.

"I assume it's to cast a spell. Do you need me to clean this office?"

"Uh..." He strolled the floor, walking slower as he passed beside her. She smelled like lemons hanging fresh in the tree, sweet yet spiked with a bite of sour that a man desired to lick purely for the tangy thrill of it.

How to ask for the magic he needed without sending her running? What witch would agree to work against her kind? He hadn't enough information on *Les Douze* to know if she would be open to his needs. What *were* his needs, beyond to destroy some dead witches? If they really were witches.

He had to work up to that slowly. Convince her that she wanted to stop those witches, and not because a demon had asked her to. How to do that?

She tilted her head. A lift of her brow not only took him in, but also teased. And a crook of her finger and a lick of her lips delivered the coup de grâce. Yeah, seduction. The woman was a master at it. And she hadn't to do anything more than quirk one of those luscious brows. He could kiss her again. Right now. Pull her to him by curling his hand around the back of her neck and bruising her mouth with his until she gasped for freedom.

The most powerful witch in Paris? He'd expected someone more…dark. And haggish, actually. Older, too. Although, he shouldn't judge by appearance. Paranormals who lived centuries had a tendency to age so slowly one could never know if the sexy young vixen eyeing him was in her third or fourth decade, or perhaps her third or fourth century.

But he'd never get anywhere if all he did was make out with the woman. The way he could get her to help him was to keep it businesslike. Professional. And he had to check out her skills, make sure she was up to par.

"Right, the murders," he muttered, grabbing the opportunity. "Can you cleanse this office?"

"That's the reason you kidnapped me? To ask me to clean your office?"

He nodded. No sense arguing the kidnapping. It had gone down that way, and he wasn't proud of it. "Like I said, my men can be indelicate."

"Seems a rather dramatic effort for something so anticlimactic."

He could give her a climax if that was what she wanted— Ah! No. He had to stay on point. *Business, Ed, business.*

"I do like to clean rooms," she said. "But I'm not sure. It seems a little suspicious."

Because it was. Kidnapping a witch just to wave around a smudging stick and chant a spell?

"Why such a powerful witch to do a cleansing?" she

asked. “I mean, the room is tainted, but any witch could do this.”

“You yourself noted the previous efforts have been worthless. You must understand my need for someone with a bit more skill?”

She bristled proudly, tugging at the ends of her lush hair. On the side of her littlest finger was another tattoo. Words. Probably a spell. Ed didn’t try to read them. One never knew what horrors reciting an unknown spell could unleash upon his head.

“Ask me something,” he volleyed.

“What do you mean?”

“Something you want to know about demons. It’s a trade for your trust.”

“Oh.” She wiggled her shoulders. The excitement that she exuded was like a natural pheromone, so effortless and addictive. He breathed her in as if he were the lucky observer of an exotic flower who only put off her scent a few minutes a day before closing up. “Okay. Let’s see… I know you’re a corax demon. Can you shift to a raven form?”

“I shift to a conspiracy of ravens.”

“Oooo.” When she made that sound, she pursed her lips deliciously. Ed squeezed his hands together behind his back. “Can I see your horns?”

“No!”

“But those nubs at your temples. That’s where they come out?”

He nodded. They grew to full length when he was angry. Or sometimes when he was aroused. He couldn’t control the anger horns, but the other time, when he was having sex, was an option he employed if he wanted to heighten the experience. Because to have his horns touched? Oh, baby. Yet, sadly, he’d attempted it only once before. She’d run screaming. He'd learned his lesson about what to reveal about himself when having sex with a human woman.

She pointed to his gloved hands. "Why do you wear those? More horns?"

Actually, thorns. The thorns on his knuckles grew when he got angry, and they were deadly sharp, leaving a poison in his victim's cuts that could kill. The half gloves were a safety precaution because he didn't like to kill people. Not unless they deserved it.

"Forget it," she said suddenly. "I have to leave this room. I'm not properly warded and this malefic aura is creeping me out."

"Fine. Can you return later to cleanse it?"

"I can," she said, walking backward toward the door. "If you promise we'll talk afterward."

"Research and a cleansing? It's a date."

"It is?"

"Uh, er…a business date. I mean, you know. Why else would I have you brought here?"

"Did you request me specifically or did those idiots grab any witch off the street?"

They had grabbed a witch John Malcolm had deemed most powerful. Lucky for him it had been the one witch he wouldn't mind spending some time with.

"Does it matter? I've stated my need. You've agreed to meet that need, as I in turn will meet yours by answering your questions. We are in accord."

"Sure." She nodded and gestured toward the door behind her. "Can I leave now?"

"Of course. You're not my prisoner."

"Will I run into your henchmen on the way out?"

"No. I promise. And again, I apologize."

"I'm not one to hold a grudge. I forgive you for your

odd means to hiring a witch to clean this office. Thank you, Ed. I'll return later. Ten?"

"Sounds fine. I'll be here. Alone."

She raised a curious brow.

"No henchman," he reassured her.

With a nod and wink, she left him standing there, watching her retreat. That sexy swing of hips and the brush of her long hair across her elbows was like poetry. A raunchy poem with a lascivious plot.

When she had turned the corner toward the elevator, Ed let out a low whistle. "Now to win her trust," he muttered. "And destroy some dead witches."

Chapter 5

Tamatha fixed her hair in the mirror and touched up with a little pencil to her right brow. Her hair was naturally white with silver tones, but she liked to soften her darker brows with gray pencil. A smooth of powder across her forehead and a touch of pale pink rouge to her cheeks. She never wore lipstick. Just a little lip balm. Because what man wanted to kiss a woman with greasy red lips?

And she'd already got two—no, three—kisses from Ed. A man who fascinated her as much as he disturbed her. Because he had sent minions to kidnap her! But then he'd kissed her. And then he'd acted nervous and kind of shy, so she could hardly blame him for the rough stuff. She could certainly blame the minions. But not Ed. Right?

She, the most powerful witch in Paris? Hardly. Certainly there were many witches more powerful. While she had mastered all four elements, she was sadly lacking in the various -mancys and study of specific magics. Perhaps only a warlock or thousand-year-old witch might be so powerful. But if she had copped to the truth, he would have tossed her out in search of the real deal. And by all means, she wanted to work with him.

To learn about demons, of course.

It wouldn't be because she found him handsome and was intrigued by his many tattoos and didn't want to end what his hot kisses had only begun.

Maybe a little.

"I have a date with a demon," she said as she spun into the bedroom to check her closet for an appropriate dress. Something sexy and yet it was a business date, so no lace and nothing too low cut. But always body-hugging.

"A date with a demon who kidnapped me," she corrected herself, her enthusiasm wilting as her fingers slid over the red silk wiggle dress. "What are you doing, Tamatha?"

"I should ask the same." Amberlee, a fellow witch friend, had stopped by an hour ago with some fresh rue and megabytes. Amberlee practiced tech magic. She wandered into the bedroom and plopped onto the end of the queen-size bed. Her bright red bob contrasted with her severely arched black brows, but both matched her red-and-black-striped dress. "You're talking to yourself, *mon amie*. Or are you working a spell? Am I interrupting?"

"No. Did you get the memory installed on my laptop?"

"Yes. Now you have ten times as much space to ignore on that tech device that always has dust on it."

"I'm not much for technology. I prefer paper and pen."

"Then why the upgrade?"

"I do like to store the photos I take with my phone. The laptop serves as an excellent photo album. I'd like to photograph my grimoire someday and keep that safe."

"Let me know when you do that. Tech magic tends to

distort grimoire text. The two magics clash. You won't know it until it's too late and your valued grimoire has been completely erased. You'll need a spell to properly store any information."

"Good to know."

Tamatha pulled out the purple velvet dress and held it before her. The fitted fabric would hug her slender frame and accentuate her cleavage with a sweetheart neckline. The black lace collar had skulls worked into the intricate stitching.

"I adore that one," Amberlee said. "Sensual with a touch of goth. So you've seduction in mind?"

"You think it's too sexy?"

"I'd do you wearing that dress."

"Yes, well, you'd do me, him and it, so I won't take that one personally. Who, or what, is your date tonight?"

"A werewolf from pack Conquerier. Sweet guy. Intense sexual appetite. He likes to howl."

"Nummy."

"Yeah, I like to howl right along with him. Especially when he hits the sweet spot with his fingers. What about your date?"

"It's not really a date. I'm going to cleanse an office for a guy. A demon, actually." She caught her friend's nod of approval.

"Demons do it devilishly," Amberlee said. "Or wait. Is this to do with your venture into diabology? Please tell me you don't intend to simply study this guy."

"Yes, study is exactly what I had in mind." She pulled the dress off the hanger. "I have already performed a binding spell on him, and he didn't hold that against me. Not too much. Maybe a little? I certainly won't hold the kidnapping against him."

"The—what? Slow down, Tamatha. I seem to be missing something here. Some demon kidnapped you? And now you're going on a date with him?"

"Suffice, we had an interesting meeting. And tonight..." She slipped into some high black Louboutin heels with purple tulle bows on the toes. "After the business of cleansing murdered spirits is completed, I want to talk to him. Learn about him. This date is strictly for the purpose of furthering my demonic research."

Amberlee put up a palm as she shook her head miserably. "You're killing me, Smalls. You and your work ethic. Please say when such research is concluded then the dress will come off. Maybe show the demon a few of your tattoos?"

"Don't be silly. I never have sex with a man on the first date. That's just gauche."

"What about Love Often?"

"I do. But you don't expect me to love him after one rather curious meeting, do you?"

"I suppose not."

"Besides, I don't know anything about him beyond that he's a corax demon—that means he can shift to ravens—and he's an excellent kisser. And he did have me brought to him, so I can only assume he's got no hang-ups about the demon-witch thing. Although he does seem to say the word *witch* with more vitriol than anyone should. Hmm..."

Amberlee rolled her eyes. "You and your adventurous heart. Be careful, Tamatha. And don't forget your white light before you go."

"Good call. I wasn't wearing it when his henchmen kidnapped me this afternoon. Best to go prepared."

"Henchmen?" Amberlee thrust up her palm. "I won't ask. I know it's wild, adventurous and your kind of weirdness. I'm headed home to pack. The wolf is bringing me to the Rhône Valley for the weekend. He owns a castle. If

I'm lucky I'll get to have sex with him fully shifted. Fur and fangs, baby!"

Tamatha did not disguise a shiver as her friend pranced out, en route for some kinky werewolf sex. Getting naked with a man shifted into animal shape was so not her scene. She'd never thought about sex with the familiar in his cat form. But she did like her men interesting.

"And, apparently, with horns," she said to her reflection.

Unzipping the dress, she stepped into it and pulled it up. Purple velvet seduction? So maybe a little flirting could be allowed. After the business.

The air held the dry, sweet scent of sage and lavender long after Tamatha had finished the cleansing. She'd focused her energy toward the marble floor and walls where the vibrations of whatever vile act had occurred in this room lingered. Lives had been stolen. More than one. In hideous manner. She didn't want to know the details. It wasn't important. The spell captured those remnants, and with the use of her air magic, she sent them through the window and into the ether to dissipate.

Barefoot, she stood up from her kneeling position on the floor in the middle of the salt circle she'd poured earlier. Eyes still closed, she swept her hands over her head and down her body to clear away any negative energy that may have latched on to her. And then, drawing her hands up her body from toes to crown of head, she replaced that sensitive open aura with a white light.

When she opened her eyes, the demon stood three feet away from the line of salt, hands shoved in his black trouser pockets. This evening he wore a gray-striped business shirt without a tie, and the open collar revealed tattoos or sigils that climbed his neck. Sleeves were rolled to his elbows, revealing yet more black ink in various designs.

Gave him a bit of a gangster vibe. Add to that the dark hair parted neatly at his right temple, slicked back with a bit of pomade, and his gray eyes that held a hopeful curiosity, and he took her breath away.

Oh, what another kiss might lure her to do. Like unbuttoning that shirt and running her palms over his chest, which was nicely muscled, because the shirt stretched over some well-honed pectorals.

Of course, that meant he was strong, and she still didn't know him at all. Would he harm her? She had a tendency to overlook danger. She preferred to see the best in most; the worst only after they'd proved their lacking worth. She *had* slapped the binding spell on him, so he could still hold some residual anger.

Tamatha shivered, but the sudden rise of insecurity reminded her she'd been in the office alone with him for over an hour and he hadn't harmed her. And she did wear the white light.

"It's good," she said.

"Cleansed?" he asked incredulously, his body leaning forward in expectation.

"Of course. Can't you feel it?"

Straightening, he spread out his palms, half-covered by the gloves, and looked about the candlelit office. Tamatha had requested only the six white candles provide the lighting while she smudged. Unnatural light would have decreased the spell's efficacy. "I don't feel anything."

"Exactly." She stepped out of the circle and slid her feet into the pumps.

In the circle remained the extinguished candle, a calcite wand, which aided in clearing negative energy, and her amethyst-hilted athame. She'd collect them before she left. They needed time to rest, and if any residual dark energy remained, the salt would leach it out.

"You'll have to vacuum the salt later. Give it at least eight hours to allow any remaining dark energies to dissipate."

"Me and salt…" He mocked a shudder.

"Ah, yes, demons and salt."

"Not so pretty."

Well, she wasn't a maid, but she couldn't stand for things to be out of order. But she also didn't intend to stick around all night. He'd have to deal with cleanup duty on his own. "So is that wine for drinking?"

Ed grabbed the bottle from a marble-topped vanity by the wall and from the cupboard underneath pulled out two goblets. "It is. Thought I'd bring out my best Beaujolais if you managed to work your magic."

"Thanks, but I'll take information for the cleansing." She accepted the goblet he handed her. She quickly sipped and averted her eyes from the dark tattoo that crept up under his ear. "No remaining evil in this room now. Unless, of course…"

"Unless I create the evil myself?" he volleyed at her. His eyes had a means of dancing with hers in a challenging yet sensual manner. A defiant smolder. Such a look stirred in her core and tightened her nipples.

She shrugged and resisted falling into that appealing challenge by taking another sip of wine.

"You know, not all demons are evil. We get a bad reputation from media and silly movies."

"Oh, I know that. Your species is vast and varied. Though, the majority can tend to be nefarious and malefic. I sense you straddle the line between good and evil."

He didn't respond, and she followed him to the black leather tufted couch. She sat first, in the middle, and he moved over and sat three feet away from her. Humph. Yes, well, it wasn't a date. Maybe?

"The same goes for we witches," she said in an attempt to defend whatever it was about her he wasn't willing to sit close to. "We're not all vile. Very few of us are."

"I've grown up listening to faery tales of your sort. You must allow me my ingrained childhood fears."

"Really? A big strong demon like you feels faint around a little ole witch like me?"

"No one said anything about fainting. I just like to stay on alert when in the presence of…your sort."

"Yikes. What does it take to win you over? I've cleansed your office. I've kissed back as good as you've given."

He put up an inquisitive finger. "About those kisses."

"What about them?" Pressing a palm into the black leather, she leaned a little closer. "Want to try it again?"

"I, uh…" He actually cringed from her, which gave her pause. She sat up straight and tugged at her skirt hem. Really? Those faery tales he'd been told as a child must have been some doozies. Probably featured the classic hag. Oh, how inaccurate they could be. Most of the time.

"You said you wanted to ask me things," he offered as if tossing the suggestion out to deflect her sudden sway toward romance. "Ask away."

"Awesome," she said with little of the enthusiasm she should have.

The man had the weirdest ability to attract her while repelling at the same time. She shouldn't take it personally. But when one was kissed so well and thoroughly, it was hard to not want more.

Perhaps since they were in his office he assumed a work attitude. Though it was late, she had no idea if a secretary lingered in an office down the hall or even if his henchmen were on the premises. Business it was, then.

Kicking off her shoes, she pulled up her legs and leaned an elbow on the back of the couch so she faced him. On the floor, her shoes righted and snapped into an orderly side-by-side position.

"What the hell?" the demon asked.

"My OCD magic. I like order."

"And control, as you've mentioned. But really?"

"I can't control it. I used to control it, but eventually the urge to straighten got so strong it took on a life of its own. It works in about a five-foot range."

"So things snap into order as you walk by?"

She nodded.

"Weird."

"Really?" Toggling the fragrant wine goblet in her hand, she asked, "Says the corax demon who can shift to raven form."

"More than one raven—an entire conspiracy. And that's not weird. It's genetic."

"It's still weird. Does it hurt? How is it controlled?"

"It stings like a mother for two seconds and then I don't feel anything but the freedom of flight. Multiple times over. When I'm in that form, all the ravens fly in sync and are controlled as one by me. But if I need one part of me to do something, I can break off and fly solo. It's complicated. Of course, shifting takes a lot out of me. I don't do it often. Driving usually gets me wherever I need to go."

"Is that feather on your neck related to ravens?"

He stroked the tattoo, which appeared as soft as a feather and seemed to undulate under his finger as if touched by a breeze. "It is. It's not a tattoo but a demonic sigil. Unlike a tattoo, the sigils simply appear on my skin. It's not ink but darker pigmented skin cells. This feather is the top of the complete sigil that stretches the length of my spine. All corax demons sport something similar."

"That's fascinating." She leaned forward but cautioned herself from reaching to touch him. Much as she wanted to nuzzle her nose against his neck and breathe him in, she would not go there. Not when she could sense his need to lean back as she neared him. "Were you born here in the mortal realm or did you come from Daemonia?"

"Mortal realm, born and bred. I have a certain distrust and dislike for those from Daemonia."

"Why?"

"My opinions are not important to your research, are they? Let's stick to facts and avoid the personal." He tilted back the rest of his wine and got up to refill, and then he returned to the couch with the bottle and topped off hers. He remained a good distance from her. Which annoyed her. "Next question."

Nothing personal? He was protective of himself. Perhaps she'd read too much into his incredible kisses. Way to anticipate a fabulous date night. Not.

Oh, who was she kidding? She wanted details more than she wanted kisses.

Yeah? Tell yourself another lie, Tamatha.

Shaking off the nuisance inner voice, she allowed her eyes to glide about the office to the marble walls and across the windows. The desk and wine cupboard were topped with the same black marble streaked through with silver mica. Above the vanity sat three objects on separate shelves, which had been lit by halogen beams before she'd requested only candlelight.

"Is that an alicorn?" she asked of the object on the center shelf. "If so, I'm stunned."

"I buy and sell objects of magical nature. And yes, the three items are a genie in a bottle, an alicorn and a bit of angel dust on the third shelf."

Wow. A genie in a bottle? He'd better not let that loose or he'd be responsible for a world of hurt. The angel dust intrigued. It was terribly expensive to buy at the Witch

Bazaar, and she'd never the interest in testing its efficacy. Angel magic was the most powerful of all magics in the mortal realm. But if handled improperly? The witch may wish herself dead as opposed to experiencing the brutal backlash.

But the alicorn continued to draw her interest. Unfortunately, fascination was quickly overwhelmed by a sadness that tugged at her very core.

"There's so much positive energy leaking from the alicorn now that I've cleansed the room." Her heart shivered. "I could almost cry. Did a unicorn get slain?"

"I'm sure it was taken from a dead unicorn," Ed offered.

She gasped at his utter lack of concern, or perhaps he simply hadn't such knowledge. "Unicorns don't die, Ed. They are immortal. Oh, that's awful." She sipped the wine, not wanting to consider the alicorn anymore.

"Back to the questions about me," Ed said. She suspected it was an attempt to divert her from the alicorn. Good call. Maybe he was more attuned to her feelings than she suspected.

Very well. What else did she want to know, beyond that he could buy an item that had likely been stolen from a living being and had caused it much pain? *Don't think about it!* Her eyes strayed to his desk, which harbored only a closed laptop. She had no idea what he did. Buying and selling magical objects? He employed henchmen, as well.

"What do you do, exactly?"

"That's a faintly personal question."

"I mean here. In this office. What's your job? Is it to do with the collection on your wall? Is it related to you being a demon or is it a means to a living?"

He scruffed his fingers over the back of his head. "Let's say I head an organization dedicated to keeping the peace."

"That sounds entirely too heroic for—"

"For what? A demon?" He sighed and propped an ankle over his knee, rapping his fingers on the couch arm. "What *are* you wearing that keeps me at a distance from you? Is it a protection spell?"

"Huh? Oh. But I thought you..."

She thought he'd wanted to keep it all business. But instead he wanted to get closer? The man's duality was aggravating. Of course, he hadn't kissed her since she'd arrived. Unfortunately. And did his aggravation over not being able to get close to her have to do with his wanting to kiss her?

And why couldn't he— Hmm... She hadn't thought of that. "I always pull on a white light when I do a job. It protects me from any rogue elements or vengeful souls that I may not have control over."

"And demons?"

"From most breeds, actually," she said. "You can feel it?"

He tilted his head back on the couch, closed his eyes, then smiled. When he sat upright, he turned to her and touched her hand but retracted quickly as if bitten.

"Sorry," she offered.

"You must not have had the white light on earlier today when we kissed."

"I didn't. Your thugs surprised me and I wasn't calm enough to call it up."

"Could I ask you to take it off now?"

The look he gave her melted her insides and made her question if he'd asked her to take off her white light or, instead, her clothing. Yes, please?

She swallowed softly. "Depends."

"On my reason? I don't expect you to trust me, Tamatha. Or to feel safe. But I have kissed you, and... I'd like to do it again. But we can't do that unless I can sit closer to you and feel comfortable. It physically hurts me to be this close to you now. It's like tiny electric sparks are emanating from your body."

"Wow. I had no idea my white light was so powerful." Then again. "Oh, but, you know. Most powerful witch in Paris, here. Of course it's going to feel like that."

Whew! Fast save. She had to be careful. He had provided her a reason to keep him in her life; best not shatter that reason.

"If I take it off, will you tell me about those tattoos on your fingers? If that's not too personal a question."

"Yes, and it's a little personal, but some of the sigils on my skin are related to my genealogy."

Satisfied, she exhaled and then swept a hand over her from head to toe and pronounced, "*Exsolvo*." The white light slipped away.

"I felt that. Like prickles skittering over my skin." He rubbed his forearms, then inhaled a deep breath. "Wow. Now I can smell your perfume. Lemons. I like that. It's different."

"I preserve my own lemons. My house always smells like a lemon orchard. It's a scent my grandmother wore, though I only know that because my mom told me. Grandma Lysia died long before I was born. So, those tats on your fingers?"

"Demonic runes. They are tribal. The history of them goes back centuries, maybe even millennia. They designate me corax and my location and alliances. As well, they provide protection within the demon community and rank me to others."

"That's a lot of information from a few crossed lines. Are you in a denizen?"

"Always been a lone demon. I prefer it that way. I, uh, don't play well with others."

"You're playing nicely enough with me." His smile was a little shy and she liked that he was willing to relax now. "Tell me about those dark marks on your neck."

He slid closer and pulled aside his collar to expose the design. Tamatha leaned forward only a little. Didn't want to spook him. "These are demonic sigils that form on my body as I age," he said. "It's indicative of many demonic breeds but not all of them. Major life events imprint on my skin. And some are spells and wards."

"Really? That's so cool. I didn't know demons could do that. So a life event? Like what?"

"Anything. Dangerous encounters. Life-changing events. The move to Paris from Italy a decade ago. Defeating Himself's plans to send a dangerous demon into this realm. Growing into my horns. And I've already explained coming into my shifting abilities with the feather."

She eyed the hematite nubs at his temples and then tapped his gloved knuckles. Ed pulled away.

"Does that hurt when I touch them? I touched the ones on your temples earlier this afternoon when you had me pressed against the wall."

"I know you did. That touch was…" He blew out a breath laden with what she guessed was repressed lust. "Just take it easy, will you? Should you get cut, the thorns on my knuckles are capable of imbuing poison into your bloodstream, resulting in death. As for the horns on my temples…they are…sensitive."

"Oh." She'd take that sensitive as meaning *sensually* sensitive. Interesting. But she wanted to learn more about the thorns. They were a new bodily enhancement to her. "Poison? So you never take the gloves off?"

He clasped his hands together. "Only when I'm alone."

"Bummer. Must make for some weird—" She almost said "sex." Tamatha swallowed the last of her wine awkwardly. "So that mark on your lower neck looks like a scythe, actually."

"It imprinted after I got my horns. Puberty stuff, like the feather. This here." He traced his inner wrist, which featured a series of black wavy lines, almost as if a drunken bar code. "Was a fight with a werewolf. I won. And this one is a witch ward." He tugged up his sleeve to reveal a small, solid black circle on the side of his forearm.

Tamatha smoothed her fingers over the ward. He didn't flinch. Nor did she. "For or against witches?"

"It was supposed to be a sort of warning alarm should a witch come too close. Apparently, this one is bogus since I'm not feeling so much as a tingle from your touch. I'll have words with Sayne next time I see the guy."

"You had an ink witch tattoo you with a ward against witches? Doesn't that sound a trifle ironic? I mean, did you really expect it to work? It came from a witch."

He shrugged and a tiny smile softened his dark features. Compelled by his levity, Tamatha touched the corner of his mouth briefly. "I'm glad it doesn't repel me," she said.

"It has alerted me to other witches previously. I'm sure it's because you are so strong. Of course, that makes little sense. Unless you've a ward to repel my witch ward?"

"It may be my white light." Which she'd taken off. Hmm... That was weird, but not so startling she need worry about it. They were sitting here now. And he no longer seemed repelled by her presence.

And he leaned forward to kiss her, but stopped, their faces but a breath from one another. "I told myself I was going to keep it strictly business this evening."

"Me, too."

He considered it, frowned, but then nodded. "Right. So..." He tilted his head and nudged her nose with his. He smelled like leather and icy cedar. "I've always thought that nothing happens accidentally."

"Oh, it doesn't. There are no coincidences in this realm. I'm very sure our running into one another in the alley was destined. Though for what reason, we've yet to learn."

"Destiny is a big concept. Serendipity sounds cooler." He pressed his forehead to hers. A hint of wine on his breath compelled her closer and to close her eyes. "Demons and witches have a brutal history," he said.

Tamatha nodded. Witches had often been demon conduits through the centuries, along with their faithful familiars. But she didn't want to discuss their reasons for hating one another right now. Not when she could feel the pulse of his heart in the air and the cool hardness of his horn nub against her skin.

"This isn't history, Ed. It's right now. We're writing our own pages."

"I can get behind that. There is something I want to ask you," he said, breaking their connection by a few breathless inches, "but after I do, you'll not like me so much as you do at this moment. So I'm going to keep that one in my pocket for now."

"I can deal. Later will always be there waiting. I've asked enough questions for one night. I want to set work aside."

"No more business." He exhaled. "This you-and-I thing is really odd for me—"

Enough small talk. If he continued on that tangent he'd talk himself out of so much fun. "Kiss me, Ed."

She tilted up his chin with her forefinger and took the lead by kissing him. He responded nicely by not uttering another protesting word. Relaxing back against the couch, his hands spreading down her sides, he lured her on top of him. His hands glided down the purple velvet to her hips and she knelt between his legs because the skirt was too narrow for her to straddle him.

Lemon and cedar mingled as the two of them breathed in one another, tasting wine and anticipation, touching warmth, hair and the pulse beats of desire.

She spread her palm over his neck and felt a soft flutter. A demon sigil that marked him as corax. Cool. She hadn't read anything about sigils in her research so far, but knew she'd passed her hands over a book or two that detailed demonic sigils. When she returned to the Archives she'd head straight for those books.

"Do all demons have markings like this? Or wait, you said it was only certain breeds?"

He tilted a frown up at her, but it quickly softened to a light wonder. "Witch, do you want to research me or kiss me?"

"Honestly? Both." She teased a fingertip at the corner of her mouth. "But first I'd like you to stop calling me witch as if it were a bad thing."

"Sorry, Tamatha of the pretty green eyes." He clasped her hand and pulled it up to look at the side of her smallest finger. "Since we're asking about skin markings, what's this tattoo mean? Beatus?"

"Be-aye-tus." She pronounced the word properly. "It's Latin for 'blessed be.'"

"Special. A witch offering a blessing to a demon? Wonders never cease."

"I suppose I should be more cautious around you, but I can tell a lot about a person from his kiss."

"Is that so?"

"You're trustworthy."

She didn't miss his wince and then told herself she was being too trusting. She knew nothing about this man. But that was why she was there. To learn. And to learn one must set aside caution and dive in for the experience.

"So you must kiss a lot of people to have developed such a skill?" he proposed.

"I never kiss and tell." She traced a finger down the feather on his neck and delighted when it fluttered under her touch. "I'd like to see them all."

He waggled a finger at her. "That would involve removing clothing. And I suspect you're not that easy."

"Oh, I'm not." She tugged down her skirt and started to sit, but then immediately turned to lean into him. Because she couldn't not look into his eyes. "But kissing you is something I'd like to do more of."

"You perplex me." Grabbing the wine bottle and their empty goblets, he motioned she move aside so he could stand. "You say you want to ask me questions, do research," he said and set the bottle and glasses on the vanity, "but your body says something entirely different."

"What about you? The man who claims to be wary of witches and yet you were the one to ask me to take off my white light so you could get closer."

"Touché. You don't have a lot of fear, do you?"

"You keep assuming I should fear you. Is there something you're not telling me?"

There was. She could tell in his pause. Must be that thing he said he'd wanted to ask her, but that would make her not like him. Should she ask him about it? Asking might bring whatever they'd started to a screeching halt. Must be the history he had with witches. Well, she'd have to change his mind and teach him that some witches were trustworthy.

Tamatha stood and placed a hand on her hip as she paced before the couch. "Let's make a deal. We both want something from each other, yes? And whatever it is you want from me, I am going to assume it's not a simple office cleansing."

He nodded and swiped a palm over his mouth, and behind that swipe she saw his smoldering smirk. It was sexy, yet secretive, and the unspoken lust in his eyes made her heart thunder and parts of her simmer and grow wet. Oh, so wet.

"Whatever you want from me is a doozy," she decided.

"On the scale of trivial to doozy, I'd say you are correct."

"Must be dark and dangerous if you're so nervous about it."

"I'm not nervous. *Nervous* is not a word in my vocabulary. I am confident."

"If a trifle cautious."

"Caution is smart."

"Like I said, I can read a person, and you are nervous. You can't stand close to me. You keep touching your face, fidgeting. And you won't look me in the eye."

"And you are too perceptive. But I'll let it go because you're so pretty."

She twirled a finger within her hair. "You think?"

He clasped his hands together before his mouth and considered it a moment. Were it not for the black markings, he would appear a businessman standing in his high-tech office. An organization that sought peace? Dare she believe such a ruse?

"I need a witch," he finally said. "At least, I think I do. It's to do with my mission to keep the peace."

So it was a mission? That was…big. And magnanimous. Yet what reason could he have to be so secretive about it?

"I feel as though I need powerful magic to help rectify the situation." And at that moment his phone rang. He put up a finger that he needed to take the call. "Yes," he said to the caller. "Another? I'll be right there." He tucked the phone in his inner suit coat pocket. "I'm afraid I've an urgent appointment."

"Oh." She bent to gather her wand and athame from inside the salt circle. "Right. It's late anyway."

"After midnight."

"Yep, and I have work in the morning."

"Where do you work?"

"In the Council Archi—er…hmm." Should she actually reveal that to him? She hadn't been told to keep it a secret. It wasn't as though she worked with secret stuff. And most paranormal species were aware of the overseeing Council.

"The Council Archives?" he guessed. "Sounds like a bunch of stuffy old books."

"It is, but books are awesome. I could live in the stacks, reading everything about all things. I never want to leave. My boss usually has to remind me to go home."

"There is something about librarians that arouses most men's imaginations."

"Is that so?" She stood from collecting her things, then swiped the toe of her shoe through the salt circle, effectively rendering it but a broken circle of salt and no longer a protective barrier. "I've never considered myself a librarian. Bookish, I guess. But I know how to party it up. I'm down with all that."

Ed chuckled. He took her hand, and when she thought he would lead her to the door, instead he kissed the back of it. Clutching a candle and the knife to her chest, she sighed at the chivalrous move. But when he licked her skin, she flushed to her core. Goddess, what would that feel like on other places on her body? Like her breasts?

"Tasting me?" she tried lightly.

"We demons can tell a lot from taste," he said. "That's a freebie for your research."

"It's only a freebie if you explain yourself. What can you tell about me from tasting my skin?"

"Let's talk on the way out, shall we? That call was urgent." He led her down the hallway, and as they waited for the elevator, he again clasped her hand. "I can taste the wine in your blood and a salty remnant of the *pommes frites* you downed five or six hours earlier. Possibly on your way home from our less-than-stellar encounter here earlier."

"There's a Greek restaurant down the street from my apartment. I love their fries and chicken gyros. Tell me more."

"Your blood pressure is slightly elevated." He winked and smirked. "I'll attribute that to being here with me, your hand in mine."

She shrugged, acquiescing to that one.

"You are indeed very powerful because I could feel those electric vibrations tingle at my tongue, as if the white light, but I can differentiate and know it is your magic. You've been on this earth for about a century…" He tilted his head. "I can feel the ancient ways in you, but not so old that I sense you were around preautomobile."

The doors opened and they stepped into the elevator.

"You're very good," Tamatha said. "I was born in the 1920s."

"I assume you've taken a source?"

"A decade ago."

When a witch wished to maintain her immortality, she had to consume the live, beating heart of a vampire once a century. Witches called them sources; vamps called them ash. Nasty work, but immortality was well worth the mess and vulgar taste.

"And you emanate light," he finally said. "And joy and curiosity. But I didn't have to lick you to learn that. Such lightness is written all over—" he spread his hands before her to take in her shape "—this gorgeous piece of work." He exhaled. "I've that thing to get to."

And she sensed he was giving her an escape from what could turn into an evening of debauchery. That neither of them would protest. Yet she wasn't quite ready to dive in so quickly with this intriguing yet deeply mysterious man.

"Tomorrow night?" she asked as the elevator doors slid open. "Another research date?"

"I'm…hmm. Can I get back to you on that one?"

"Oh? Sure." She'd expected a quick response that he'd love to see her again. Didn't he want to drop the big question on her? So her shoulders dropped as she headed for the door. "I live in the 6th," she said.

"I know. By the Luxembourg."

She cast a look over her shoulder.

"I can smell the pear blossoms and roses from their gardens in your hair. It's a unique blend indicative of the garden on the Left Bank. If I want to find you, I will. We demons retain scents far better than any werewolf can. You're in me now, Tamatha."

And he turned to stroll toward a door set near the elevator bay. Without a goodbye or an *au revoir*. As last night when he'd left her in the alleyway after that devastating kiss.

Tamatha stepped outside under the moonlight and stroked the back of her hand where he'd licked her. With a shiver, she decided to draw her white light back up.

Chapter 6

The last of a few black feathers dissipated as Ed's body re-formed into human shape. He tilted his head to the left and right to stretch the kink in his neck, then shook his shoulders to shake out his clothes and return to normality. Or as normal as it got shifting from a conspiracy of ravens to demonic flesh and blood.

There were other terms for a group of ravens, such as an *unkindness*. He'd stick with *conspiracy*. As it was, he got enough bad press.

The phone call had come from Inego, whom he'd directed to post guards at the Montparnasse. There were no dead witches in the cemetery this time that he could see. Nor a dismembered demon corpse. But between two mausoleum fronts with rusted iron doors he did find a telling pile of ash. Obsidian flakes clued him in that one of his own had died there. Recently, for the red embers and lingering sulfur that tainted the air.

Yet the sickly smell of rot clinging to the air was not demonic. And the ward on his forearm tingled.

"Witches," he muttered. "Again. How is it possible? Unless they are alive and just really ugly?"

No, he'd seen exposed bone on more than a few of them the night he'd witnessed Laurent's murder. Whatever the creatures were, they could not be alive. And they seemed to have a death wish for demons.

Perhaps the situation was more urgent than he'd initially thought.

Kneeling before the ash, he held his palm flat over the pile without touching it. Rising warmth teased at his skin, as if the essence yet remained. He couldn't get a read that would clue him in to what breed of demon it had been or if it had been male or female.

Scanning the surroundings, he wondered if the demon had been wandering about the cemetery—for what reason?—or if he or she had somehow been lured here. Because it was the same cemetery. It seemed too coincidental to be mere happenstance. Could dead witches do such a thing? Or was someone else luring hapless demons to a sure and terrible death?

The thought was disturbing. And he would find answers.

From a witch like Tamatha Bellerose? He wasn't sold on her being the most powerful in Paris, but he wasn't yet prepared to admit to that doubt. She seemed open-minded. She'd even suggested she was not into summoning and then commanding demons to her will. With hope, she would at least hear him out regarding this situation.

He should have been direct with her earlier. But after watching her smudge the office, the whole time he'd slid his eyes over her gorgeous figure and had thought thoughts he wouldn't want anyone to know about. Lust had altered his initial goal. He'd been thankful for the phone call only because he was pretty sure he might have pushed her down on the couch and made out with her right there in the office.

And what was wrong with that?

"Everything," he muttered. "She's a witch."

He stood, then strode quickly toward the south entrance and slipped through the unlocked gate. He spied Inego parked down the street in a black Audi and slid into the passenger side.

"I posted guards at the front gate like you asked, boss."

Ed rubbed his lower lip, in thought. Would any future victims really enter through the front gate? If the victim was demon, he or she could enter by a number of means, through shifted shape or by simply leaping over the fence at any point in the periphery. More guards may be necessary.

Beyond setting a demon out for bait, he had no idea why these killings were occurring. "Do you have any idea who the demon was?"

Inego shrugged. "He was in the process of being made dead when I decided to get the hell out of there. But he did have this." The lackey handed a bowie knife to him. "It was lying on a stone sarcophagus. I grabbed it 'cause you know how I like weapons."

The blade was crude iron, not polished steel. Demons worked well with iron, especially cold iron. The inlaid pearl handle was etched with a demonic sigil, but it was so worn it was difficult to determine the original design. In the hands of its owner the sigil may even glow and provide strength or serve some fierce magic.

"This sigil…the curve of it and that crossed line… It looks familiar, but I'm not sure. I'll have to clean it up and see if I can match it to a sigil on file. Looks like it's back to the office."

"Will do." Inego shifted into gear and turned the vehicle toward the Right Bank.

Ed had shifted the other night and again tonight. Too much, too fast. Already draining numbness toyed with his brain, thanks to the most recent shift. He probably wouldn't get farther than the couch in his office before falling into a dead sleep.

He closed his eyes and tried to banish the dreadful scent of death and rot from his senses. Dead demons generally did not smell when they dusted, but this one had reeked of sulfur. It could have been ripped limb from limb. There was no way to know by studying the remaining ash. As with vampires who ashed when staked, so did demons. But also similar to vampires, the younger demons could die and remain in bodily form or even only ash partially. So Ed knew the victim had to be at least a few decades old. Which helped him little in identifying the demon.

He absently tapped the blade on his thigh. The sigils could help in identification. He'd do that at the office. If he could get the memory of that awful smell from his nose. *Think of something sweeter.* Roses and pear trees that dotted the Luxembourg grounds. And lemons…

"Why do I keep kissing her?" he whispered.

"That pretty little witch?" Inego asked.

"Huh? Oh." He'd drifted into a reverie, lured by his exhaustion. He didn't want to have this conversation with the idiot who would put a plastic bag over someone's head thinking that was safe.

"We did get the right witch for you, yes? If you'll pardon me, boss, you two seemed familiar with one another."

"Yes, she's the right one." In ways even he couldn't comprehend. Yawning, Ed settled, flexing his spine into the comfortable leather seat. "I've kissed her both times I've seen her. And I don't know why. Witches disgust me. I had no intention—"

"You're bewitched," Inego offered. "The witch *made* you kiss her."

Bewitched? At the time, he'd jokingly suggested that she had made him kiss her. Because if he had been in his right mind, he would have never so boldly done such a thing. Maybe?

Bewitched. That made…a lot of sense. And what reason had she to tell him the truth? She'd wanted to soften him, keep him from harming her. Of course she had used witchcraft on him.

The car stopped behind his building and Ed stepped out, telling Inego to remain on call and keep his guards posted at the cemetery. Next time, he said, call him at the sign of anything suspicious. He needed to catch the demon before it was torn asunder.

"Bewitched," Ed muttered as Inego drove off. "She isn't playing fair."

Balancing a shoulder bag full of books on demons and curses and sigils, along with her purse, a plastic sack that held the high heels she'd traded for flats for the walk home, and the small plastic cup of pineapple gelato she had picked up when walking down the rue de La Huchette in the 5th, Tamatha licked the tiny plastic spoon clean and almost groaned out loud at the goodness of the tangy Italian ice.

On the days when she walked home after work, she always treated herself to gelato from Amorino. But as the first drops of rain hit the creamy treat, she cursed and rushed across the pebbled grounds of the Luxembourg. Her apartment backed up to the royal garden.

Pausing outside the lush hornbeam shrub that bordered

the park because the angle of the rain didn't reach her there, she finished the last of the gelato, then made a toss for the nearby garbage bag the city posted near trees and street poles—when a demon caught the empty cup and made the slam dunk for her.

"You."

"Me," Ed said as he approached. An irrepressible smile curled his mouth into something she could only wish he would press against her lips. "You didn't expect me? Didn't we have a date?"

"I thought you needed to think about it?"

"I thought. And here I am."

"Well, then here." She handed him her heavy bag, and when the rain began to pummel them both, they dashed down the alleyway that hugged her building. Once inside the cobblestone courtyard and sheltered by the roof over the landing, lightning crackled the sky.

"Inside. Quick," Ed said, and Tamatha followed orders without even thinking that he'd sounded demanding. "We've got to stop meeting in the rain," he offered as he followed her up the three twisting flights of time-worn stairs.

"I like the rain."

"It annoys me. And sometimes it hurts."

She pushed her key in the lock, turned it and shoved the door inward. "It hurts? I think I read something about that. No, that was faeries. Rain in the mortal realm can burn their skin."

"It works the same on some of us demons. Especially so when there's lightning. It crackles in my veins like electricity and messes with my ability to shift."

"Oh, I'm sorry. But I'm going to make a note of that."

"I'm learning to expect nothing less from you."

"You can drop my bag there by the door."

She strolled past the tiny kitchenette and into the living room. Her bedroom was on the opposite side of the room beyond the curvy pink velvet sofa. With a dash she deposited her shoes before her bed, then returned to the living room to find Ed looking around. The pale pink sheers were pulled back to reveal lightning splintering the sky.

"It's not the Shangri-La, but it's my home. So, another date?"

"Sure, but first I'd like to get straight to the point."

"The point?"

He walked right up to her and grabbed her by the shoulders. Not so gently. And he wasn't giving off "I'm going to kiss you now" vibes. "You've bewitched me."

"I—" Tamatha's apprehensions dropped. Aww. What a sweetie. Mr. Darcy redone in demonic flesh and blood. Although…he hadn't said it in quite the manner Darcy would. Not a hint of romance in his tone or mention of his body and soul. Which meant… "Are you serious?"

"That's the only explanation for my compelling need to kiss you every time I see you."

Was he for real? The guy couldn't accept that maybe he *wanted* to kiss her? Way to make her feel special. Not.

Tamatha pulled from his grip and pushed her rain-jeweled hair over a shoulder. "I don't work love spells or anything romantically related. That's trouble waiting to happen. No spells cast as a means to provoke you to kiss me, I promise. Though, *bewitchment* is a term that encompasses a certain romantic desire or feeling toward another. Seriously, you think I'm *making* you kiss me? And you can't imagine any other reason, on this entire planet, why you'd want to kiss me? Maybe you just…want to?"

"Well, sure, but…" He sighed and swiped a hand through his hair. The move made her yearn to know the feel of his fingers gliding through her hair. "I thought…

Uh…hmm…" He tapped his lip. "Because when we do kiss, it's so easy. And I've never been this way around a witch before. Because I have trouble with— And things never seem to last. Most especially if she—"

"She what? Ed?" She touched his cheek and then dared to stroke across his horn nub.

He gripped her hand quickly. "You shouldn't do that."

"What? Touch your horns?"

He tilted a serious stare at her.

"Does touching your horns make you…horny?" She tried not to laugh, or even giggle, but the idea of it was clearly ironic. "I'll keep my hands to myself. I didn't know."

"Yes, well, now you do. Lesson number one in Basic Demon Knowledge. Don't touch the horns unless you're invited to."

She nodded respectfully. "Kind of like faeries and their wings. You touch their wings and it's supposed to be sexual, like touching their breasts or their…" Her eyes dropped to his crotch, where a noticeable thickness caught her attention. "Wine! I'm sure you'd like some wine."

She hustled into the kitchen and was glad for the half bottle in the fridge. Needed to restock. And ugh, this was a white. Not the most romantic of wines. But then, apparently the demon was feeling put off by romance. Unless, of course, she considered what had appeared to be a hard-on.

So was he hot for her or not? She couldn't shake the awful feeling that he believed his kisses had been commanded by a force outside him instead of a reactionary pull to make contact with her.

To her, using magic to mess in the affairs of love and romance was almost as big a no-no as commanding demons against their will. Love spells could be quite effective. Until they were not. Be careful what you wish for and all that.

"Stick to business," she reminded herself. "But he did mention something about a date."

And she was keen on love. Often. But to be clear, the family motto encompassed all kinds of love. Familial, friendly, social, romantic, love for animals, love for food. Heck, love for bugs, grass or old cars. One must simply love life.

Out in the living room, Ed had opened one of the tall windows, and the noises from the restaurant below mingled with the clatter of rain on the windows and streets.

"Close it halfway," she said. She straightened the black velvet pillows on the pink sofa and cast about a glance to make sure no stray underthings were lying about. It was a chick's apartment; that stuff happened all the time. "Or the pigeons will come inside. I hate to bespell those poor things. They never seem to fly right afterward. Though I do use the occasional stray to practice ornithomancy."

"Divination by birds," he said and adjusted the window to make sure the opening wasn't quite so pigeon-wide. "That should make for interesting times, me being a corax."

She hadn't considered that, but cool. "Would you allow me to divine your conspiracy?"

"That sounds strangely sexual," he said with a wink.

And Tamatha actually blushed. So he did know how to flirt.

"White," he said as she handed him the goblet. "I do love a dry sip."

"Is that a demon thing?" she asked, slipping into research mode. From the table she grabbed a notebook that she always left lying around for moments of inspiration. And she put on her glasses, as well.

"No, I just love a good white. So we're right to business." Ed sat next to her. "I guess our dates always start that way, eh? That's cool— Wow."

"What?"

"Those glasses are incredibly sexy on you. All the rhinestones and the way they draw focus to your bright green eyes."

"Hmm, must be the librarian thing you mentioned."

"You're not put off that one of my fantasies is exactly what you are?"

"Why should I be?" She leaned in close enough that his cedar scent overwhelmed the wine. It stirred her desires and softened her muscles so she felt like falling into his arms. "I like to play with danger."

"Right, the dangerous-demon thing. I'll give you that. I'm not safe, by any means."

"And how does not being safe play into your work, which is to bring peace? I don't understand that. What kind of peace and between whom? Other demons?"

"I said that was personal. You want basic demon facts, and that's what I'll give you. You know about our sigils." He pulled back his coat collar to show the black ink work, which wasn't ink work at all but an innate coloring in his skin. "You know about our sensitive taste."

"Right. And you can travel by shifting to a conspiracy of ravens. Can I see you do that?"

"Not now that I've learned you might like to use my ravens for divination. Besides, I'm all tapped out for a while. Just getting my strength back after doing it twice in a week."

"It drains you that much?"

"Shifting to dozens of birds and then re-forming back to a complex human body? That requires a lot of energy."

"Then why did you do it recently?"

"Next question."

She didn't like that he felt he couldn't be totally honest with her, but Tamatha would use caution. He was here and that was what mattered. "You know, I could help you with recharging your energy after a shift."

"How so?"

"I'm sure I've a spell of some sort that'll hasten your healing. Because that's what it is. Healing from the shift."

"Something to keep in mind. But pardon me if I maintain a healthy distance from your witchcraft."

"Right. You and your caution."

On with the research. And yet she wasn't as compelled to learn about the textbook stuff so much as delving deeper inside the man. A man who had just flirted with her, even if it may have been accidental on his part.

"Tell me something daring. Intimate. Do demons have sex the same way most other species do?"

He chuckled, shook his head. "Yes, we do. Though we come in all shapes and sizes, with different means, muses and fetishes. And some of us fellows are ribbed." He winked and sipped his wine.

"Ribbed?" She again averted her gaze to his crotch. "Like…you mean?"

He nodded, his grin irrepressible. "For your pleasure, my lady."

Mouth open in awe, she didn't know what to say to that one, so she let it sink in. Interesting. And…oh, baby. Now he expected her to continue with the interview without wanting to make out?

"That was too much too soon, wasn't it?" His gaze over the rim of the goblet reached in and caressed her thumping heart. Oh, how he had mastered the smolder.

"No, that was perfect. Great. I'm writing that one down."

He tugged the notebook from her grasp. “I don’t want to be a footnote on your pages, Tamatha. Let’s stick to conversation and leave the dictation for some guy with an ego. Is that okay?”

“Fine.” She crossed her legs and settled back with the wine goblet in hand. A ribbed penis? *Oh, mercy, think about something else.* Like her pattering heartbeats. No. Her moistening hands. Double no! “So you know how old I am. What about you?”

“Thirty. Just turned.”

“But you are immortal?”

“Unless someone stabs me with a salt blade or injects my veins with a salty brew. That stuff is killer. And it’s everywhere. You can buy it at the local *supermarché*. It appalls me. I had to call in the building housekeeper to clean up the salt you left on the floor.”

“I thought you said you had a secretary.”

“Out on maternity leave.”

“Aww, babies are so sweet.” She caught his lift of brow and figured she’d better explain. “To look at. Not to have. Dear me, I don’t know that I’m very maternal. I like to play with them a bit, then hand them back to the mother when they start to cry.”

“So you won’t be continuing the Bellerose family through your progeny?”

She shrugged. Babies were so far off her radar right now. Had always been that way. And she suspected the conversation would never get where she wanted it to go if she delved into talking diapers and snotty noses.

“Can you eat salt in food?”

“Minimal amounts won’t kill me, but I have a chef who cooks meals for me once a month and leaves them in the freezer. Salt free.”

She loved to cook, but sometimes cooking for one was

a pain. Part of her desire to find a man who lasted longer than the family curse was so she could actually settle into the domestic-goddess mode and see if she liked it. Creating delicious meals for someone she loved? Sounded divine. Having children? She'd reexamine her priorities if and when she ever found a lover worthy of giving her children.

"Have you ever killed anyone?" she asked Ed.

"That's a personal question."

"Sort of. Sort of not. If it applies to a demon's necessary means to survive—"

"It does not. I am not a vampire who sucks the life from mortals, nor do I thrive on skin contact as would an afferous demon."

Tamatha reached for her notebook, then relented. "I'll remember that one. Maybe. Probably not. I'll survive. So, no killing."

"Killing is sometimes not necessarily murder."

"Oh. Yes, you're right. Murder is premeditated. A man might be faced with the kill to protect himself..."

Yet the fact he had to designate the difference— No, she wouldn't go there. Couldn't. Not with him sitting right there, but inches from her, overwhelming her senses with his ice and cedar scent and his—his very being. Yes, just being nearby, the man captivated her. And he made her desire. And want. Simple as that.

"Do demons possess a form of bewitchment?"

He quirked an odd look on her. "Not that I know of. You feeling bewitched, little witch?"

She nodded and then caught herself. "Course not." She took another sip of wine. "Oh, goddess, yes. I'm not much for avoiding the truth. There's something so compelling about you."

"It's your voracious need to learn what I am, to peel back my skin and study my innards."

"Oh, I don't do innards. Can't even manage most spells that require viscera or organs. Gross. It's your outsides and what's in here that interest me most." She tapped his temple below the horn nub. "Can I see your horns? They must extend out, yes?"

"They do, and I will not bring them out."

"A sex thing?"

"No, more like I'm not willing to display myself like that for you to preen over. Besides, they react more with my anger than anything."

"Oh, well, then I'm all for keeping you happy. But you did say something about having your horns touched making you horny."

"Tamatha, I can handle the questions. Even flirtation. But whether or not you realize it, your fascination is ribald."

"Really? What if it's genuine curiosity?"

He clasped her hand and squeezed it. "I'm trying not to push you down and kiss you right now. Is your intent to spoil my focus?"

Yes, yes and yes! "Wouldn't want to unsettle you."

"Now you're teasing."

"I won't deny that. What would you say to my research involving trying some spells on you?"

"No more binding. That hurt like hell. Much worse than lightning stinging in my veins."

"I promise I won't use such a dangerous spell again. Nor would I try to cast you out or eviscerate you."

"I appreciate your thoughtfulness. So I must subject myself to lab experiments now?"

"Would you?" she eagerly asked. "I might like to try a spell or two to connect with the sigils on your skin. See if I can divine—"

"You are entirely too excited about stuff you should not be."

Her lips formed a moue.

And he noticed her waning enthusiasm. "But I like that about you. You are uncommon. And I suppose being the most powerful witch in the city, I should expect as much from you. Always eager to learn and try new things?"

"Absolutely."

"I can't agree to be your lab rat. I admit, I'm protective of myself. Don't want anyone messing around…inside me, with magic or otherwise. But I will consider things not requiring evisceration if you give me some time to…"

"Trust me?"

He nodded. "Exactly. And now it's my turn to do a little research." He tugged her hand, bringing her closer to him, and nudged his nose against her neck. "Lemons. Delicious."

A pleasurable shiver traced her skin as his explorations moved him slowly along her neck and up toward her ear, where he kissed the lobe, then nibbled it softly. She clasped his hand tighter, wishing he were not wearing the half glove but knowing it was for her protection. His warm fingers twined within hers, and that was enough.

"Have you any witch marks?" he said after a kiss to the underside of her jaw.

"Why? Are you suddenly on a hunt?"

"No, just curious. You got to ask your questions, so I thought it fair to ask a few myself. Let me take a closer look at this tattoo on your arm." He slid down her dress sleeve, exposing her shoulder and bra strap, and traced the tattoo with a finger. "Looks like a rose, but bell-shaped."

"You got it on your first guess." His touch rubbed against her skin. All parts of her softened, luxuriating in the sensation. Tamatha wanted to fall forward, crushing her breasts against his chest, but she cautioned her eager need for the sensual connection. "That's the Bellerose family crest."

"Is it a magical tattoo?"

"No, just pretty."

"What do the words mean? Is it a spell?"

"*Amor Modum Saepe.* It's Latin for 'love often.' It's the family motto." But she wouldn't tell him the unspoken part. No man deserved such cruel knowledge of his future.

"So have you loved often?"

"I've loved my fair share for a woman who has been on this earth for nearly a century. What about you?"

He shrugged and leaned back against the sofa. She sensed she was losing him to his intense need to keep his personal stuff private.

So she quickly said, "And so you know, I've not any witch marks. At least, not that I've seen. Though when I was little I wanted to have a beauty mark at the corner of my mouth like a glamorous movie star. I used to put a dab of chocolate there after lunch."

He leaned closer again, his eyes dancing over her mouth. "Too bad you don't still do that. I'd love to lick it off."

He kissed her and Tamatha sighed into him. The man had switched from business to pleasure and she wasn't going to point that out to him.

The kiss wasn't like most. It wasn't greedy. It didn't try to command. Instead, it was more tentative and perhaps a little cautious. Even when he traced her teeth with his tongue and pressed a hand across her back to draw her closer, she felt he wasn't quite relaxing into her. The man had a healthy fear of witches. So perhaps kissing her was more daring than satisfying.

Still, his mouth on hers felt marvelous. And she could allow him the slow exploration because that would only grow the trust between them. Her fingers glided along his neck and she felt the feather sigil flutter. As if a bird beneath her touch, ready to take flight. The energy was incredible, the power. And yet it never took off. And she remembered his mention of being drained from the shifting.

Suddenly his mouth left hers, and Ed stood.

"Put your shoes on." He tugged her up from the couch and waited for her to slip into her shoes, then pulled her down the hallway. "It's stopped raining. Let's go to the park."

"Why? We were doing fine…"

"Because if we're out in public then I won't be able to ravage you."

She tugged him to a stop at the front door.

Ed bowed to study her face. "You're thinking about getting ravaged, aren't you?"

She nodded and her smile burst.

He slid his hands up her arms and pinned her wrists above her head. He kissed her there against the wall and she felt his erection nudge her hip. And then he pulled her down the stairs and into the safety of the public courtyard.

He wanted her. And she wanted him. But he was ever cautious.

She couldn't think of a single reason why someone would fear her so much. "I thought we were going out?"

"We were—are. I need to ask you something but I'm not sure how."

"It must be really bad if you can't bring yourself to ask me. Don't you think I'm a big enough girl to handle it?"

"I think you're a powerful witch who might have the answers I require. And I also think you need to trust me more before that happens. And I need to trust you."

Tamatha sighed. "Fine. But I'm not a very patient

woman. I'll keep bugging you about this. And you've no one to blame but yourself. You did bring it up."

"That I did. I'll just have to distract you." The phone in his pocket rang and he kissed her instead of answering it. Points for ignoring the technology.

But after five rings, a pause and a renewed set of rings, she pulled from the kiss. "Answer it."

"It's one of my…" He checked the phone and smirked.

"Minions?" she provided. "You know how weird that is, to lay claim to having minions?"

"I prefer to call them field assistants."

"I distinctly heard you call them minions when I was at your office."

"Fine. I am Edamite Thrash, the evil overlord of the demon sect in Paris. Are you happy?" He turned from her to talk to the caller.

"Edamite Thrash?" she whispered. That was the first time she'd learned his whole name. Well, it didn't include his middle name, so she still couldn't control him with a spell. Not that she wanted to. Or needed to.

The name was indeed of the evil-overlord persuasion. Yikes.

"I've some details regarding an urgent matter I need to attend to," he said, tucking his phone away.

"Once again rescued by the phone call," she said.

"That's not fair."

"I count three times you've been whisked away from kissing me by that blasted thing."

"I'm sorry. Evil-overlord stuff."

She blew out a breath. That title was not as funny as he apparently had hoped it would sound.

"To make it up to you I promise if you'll meet me tomorrow night I'll turn off my phone."

"Can we talk then? Will you reveal the evil overlord's ultimate plan to take over the world?"

He smirked. "I should have never said that."

"I know you're kidding."

"Do you?" He kissed her on the cheek and then opened the front door of the building. "Tomorrow, then. Thanks for the wine and kisses."

"Don't ever thank me for a kiss," she said. "Just spending the night missing me will suffice."

"I can do that." He winked and closed the door behind him.

And Tamatha blew out a breath. "I don't know what is up with him. He's cold and then hot for me, and then right back to business. Maybe I *should* look into a love spell? At least then I could have him all to myself for more than an hour here and there."

Edamite Thrash?

She sucked in her lower lip. She'd have to look up that name at work tomorrow. Just for research's sake. Not because she suspected he was the evil overlord he jokingly claimed to be.

On the other hand, she didn't know him at all.

Chapter 7

After cleaning the knife Inego had found at the cemetery and applying a bit of demonic magic to the blade to lift the engraving, the sigil was then easily matched in a database Ed kept on the local demon denizens. It was Laurent's Libre denizen, and the second victim had been a friend of Laurent's whom Ed knew, but not well. That was why the sigil had seemed familiar to him.

Pacing beside his desk as he racked his brain on what to do next, he suddenly noticed…something. Like a darkness humming above his head, yet it wasn't something he could see, only feel. It was odd, and it lingered.

He stretched his arm up and tapped at the air. He didn't feel anything tangible, but instinctively it felt intrusive.

"Dark magic? I thought she'd cleansed this office?"

He cast a glance toward the genie bottle displayed on his wall. That thing was always lit from within, and at times it would roil with an angry redness that wanted out.

He'd never let the genie out, no matter the three wishes he should earn. Because after a man had been granted those wishes? The genie was granted freedom.

The city of Paris would never be prepared for the wrath of a genie who had been contained within a tiny bottle for millennia.

Blowing out a breath and shaking his head, he dismissed the odd feeling as angry genie vibes. Or it could be nerves after everything that had happened lately. A demon had a right to be on edge after the things he'd seen in the cemetery.

"Zombie freakin' witches. Whoda thought?"

He couldn't erase the memory of watching Laurent being torn asunder. Had the same happened to the demon who had owned the bowie knife?

The Libre denizen traced back centuries, which was how Ed knew Laurent. Their respective grandfathers had founded the denizen together, choosing the name Libre, which meant *free*, to signify their escape from the domination of their witchy owners who had originally summoned them to this realm. So the sigil on the knife had also been Ed's grandfather's sigil. And while Laurent currently oversaw the Libre denizen—or had when he'd been alive—Ed had never any desire to join them. He stood on his own. No one told him what to do.

Were the witches in the cemetery going after the demons in one particular denizen? He had no idea if these were the first two deaths or if others had occurred. He'd send Inego out to locate the acting leader of Libre, to ensure all other members were accounted for. It was the only lead he had.

It was time to get over his mistrust for witches and tell Tamatha what he knew. With the access she had to the Archives, perhaps she could fill in some of the missing spaces for him. Such as more information about *Les Douze*. What were they about? And were they actually dead or just really old and decrepit?

"No, have to be dead."

He typed Les Douze into the browser search and it brought up a paragraph he'd read earlier detailing the mass burning of a dozen witches in the Place de Grève in the eighteenth century. The article didn't detail their crimes, save only that a group of men and women had accused the witches of heinous occult activity.

Of course, hundreds of years ago, a woman merely had to look at a man wrong or even refuse his vulgar advances and he'd accuse her of witchcraft. True witches had managed to avoid capture and ultimately a hideous death. Though, not all. Ed knew well a good fear of a specific breed could cling to a man's psyche even after he met one who he felt should not be threatening.

Tamatha could be threatening. She was very powerful, and he had the memory of the binding to prove it. But he didn't fear her. Not physically. Emotionally? Hell, he didn't want to answer that one right now. But he did know she could sense his reluctance to simply relax and trust her.

He was stronger than that. He'd once faced Himself and defeated a nasty crew of wraith demons. He wasn't going to let one little witch make him shiver.

He tapped the computer screen. One of the accuser's names was listed. LaVolliere. He had the same surname as Laurent. A relative? But Laurent was demon. Demons weren't big on surnames or carrying them through the generations. Ed had always assumed it was a name Laurent had taken to make him fit in with humans.

And besides the surname, mortal men had accused *Les Douze*. Maybe. That was according to reports, which had been detailed by a human. Of course, a human would only assume the accusers had also been human. Demons were once expected to appear as creatures, hideous and deformed with tails and hooves.

Had demons in corporeal form accused the witches? It would serve adequate reason for those *things* in the cemetery to want revenge against their accusers. But why now after so many centuries? And how had they managed to rise from the grave to achieve such revenge?

He was missing something. He needed to clear his mind and think about other things. Only then would his distraction allow focus to the fore.

He picked up the phone and dialed Tamatha. With luck, she would forgive his hasty retreat last night and meet him for dinner. And he'd show her how relaxed and trusting he could be in her company. He could get lost in her eyes. The best distraction he could imagine.

"That place salts even the desserts," Ed offered as he strolled arm in arm with Tamatha down a narrow street in the 1st arrondissement. He'd asked for her recommendation for a restaurant but she hadn't any in mind. He wasn't hungry and neither did she seem to be in a rush to eat. And walking closely as twilight settled the sky in violets and pinks was some kind of all right.

"The new park layout is pretty," she commented and veered down the narrow, cobblestoned aisle leading toward the Bourse de Commerce, the old Commerce Exchange, which now housed the Paris Chamber of Commerce. "Let's check it out."

They filed around the domed structure, past the Medici column and into the recently remodeled gardens of Les Halles, beneath which stretched a massive shopping complex that offered everything, including lattes, music, movies and high-end diamond watches.

They strolled across a lawn and Tamatha inhaled the scent of flowers and commented on the green texture of the air. Ed had never considered air to have a texture but he had to admit it did. Clear and crisp and, indeed, green. The water feature dribbled over smooth cement forms and he felt the whole experience surreal. He was holding hands with a pretty woman and talking about the scent of flowers. As if normal humans on a date. As if there was nothing whatsoever odd about him—or her, for that matter—and everything was peachy.

Maybe it was all romance and roses? This feeling of comfort with a witch was new to him. The difficult part was to not rush away from it. To just enjoy. He liked holding hands with the girl. A pretty woman who had chosen to spend time with him. And he felt a sense of pride that she deemed to walk alongside him and no one else. She could be his girl.

No, she can't.

And that, he realized, wasn't even a witch thing. It was just that he didn't know how to do the romance thing, and even if he tried, it could never end happily.

Enough sappy stuff. He veered toward the cobblestoned street that paralleled the Saint Eustache Church and noticed the farmers market. Some stands appeared to be packing up for the night, but a few were still accepting patrons and serving food. The spicy rich saffron, rosemary and sausage carried on the air and wove it into a fiery, yet enticing texture.

"Paella," Ed said and tugged Tamatha along.

He paid for a huge plate, grabbed two plastic forks, and then they found a spot on a concrete step before the park and shared the meal. A trio of dancers had set up a boom box and were busking for tips with some stunning moves.

"This is delicious," Tamatha said, her knee touching his as she sat close. "I've never tried it before."

"Really? I love this mishmash of rice and sausage and veggies. If I had any cooking skills at all, I'd make it once a week. And this is not salted. I know the guy. He's got a heart condition, so he watches salt as if he were a demon."

"Awesome. I happen to have some mad skills with the pots and pans."

"Is that so?" He waggled a brow as he forked in another steamy bite.

"I like to try new things. I'll have to look up a recipe for this online."

"I volunteer to be your taste tester."

"Deal." She tilted her head onto his shoulder. "You know, I'd love to have a guy to cook for all the time."

Ed mocked a choke on his next bite. "Did you just say, in a roundabout way, you are looking to get married?"

"Did I? Oh, no. I mean, someday. But no. I didn't mean that about us." She spooned in a bite of rice.

Ed would love to have a woman cook for him. But marriage? Absolutely not. Well. Yes, someday. Maybe? Ah, who was he trying to fool?

"I don't think I'll ever marry," he said, casting his gaze beyond the dancers and across the park where a half-dozen young men tossed a Frisbee back and forth. "Never had much luck with women."

"Really? There's always men."

"I prefer women," he said, tilting his head to bump it softly against hers. "But thanks for offering me hope." Then he laughed and folded the empty plate in half. "I have never discussed anything remotely domestic with a woman before. It's usually..."

"Wham, bam, thank you, *mademoiselle*?"

"Uh..." Close, but he wasn't going to reveal that to any

woman he was interested in. Especially not a woman capable of retaliating with magic.

"It's okay. Like I said, I'm not in the market for marriage."

"Just following that family motto, eh?"

"It does include more than romantic love. It could mean loving paella. Which I do. And going for walks with a handsome demon. Which I also love."

"All right, then, let's continue the walk and talk. Where to?"

"How about we check out the church behind us? I've heard it's beautiful inside. Can you go inside?"

"Of course I can. What? You think I'll sizzle to ash if I encounter the holy? You don't need to research demons to know that holy symbols are just that, Tamatha. A symbol. Belief is what holds all the power."

"True. But baptized vamps can't touch the holy."

"So there are some exceptions." He stood and offered his hand. "Come on. Let's go see if this demon starts to sizzle."

Ed stood before the stone statue of some pope flanked by two angels in the narthex of the Renaissance-style Saint Eustache Church, the largest church in the city. He did not feel as though his skin would begin to sizzle and flake off until he had been reduced to a heap of black ash at Tamatha's feet.

On the other hand, he did feel…odd.

Never before had he been in a church or cathedral. He did not subscribe to religion. It seemed to be the root of war, greed, patriarchy and hatred among the human population. He preferred a spiritual approach to life, blessing the nature and earth he lived upon and giving thanks for his existence. All were equal and came from the same star stuff, after all. Yes, he was a fan of Carl Sagan.

So while he hadn't known what to expect when crossing the threshold into this holy structure, he had prepared to not be surprised at whatever may come. And right now he felt a weird compression against his skin. As if something were trying to intrude, move inside him.

He shook his hands, hoping to fend off the feeling.

"It's gorgeous, isn't it?" Tamatha spun and cast him a beaming smile. Tonight she wore a peach dress with a lacy neckline that danced about her full breasts. Her hair was coiled in victory rolls on each side of her head and trailed down the middle of her back. She studied the massive stained glass window, which was surprisingly heart-shaped. "I do love stained glass."

Well, there. An opportunity to escape this infernal establishment and hopefully save face by not turning into a raging madman as he tried to shake off whatever it was pushing into him. If he thought about it, it was similar to the intrusion he'd felt in his office last night.

"You've seen one church window, you've seen them all." He clasped her hand and tugged her toward the entrance doors.

"But we've hardly looked around. You're starting to sizzle, aren't you?" she asked as he pulled her outside into the night.

"No, sweetness, I am not sizzling." He tugged at his tie and assessed his composure. The intrusive feeling was gone. Whew! Maybe he would have started to sizzle? "I have stained glass windows at my place."

"You do?"

"You'll have to come over sometime if you admire stained glass. They are quite remarkable."

"That sounds like you're suggesting another date."

When he nodded, she bounced on her toes. He liked her enthusiasm, yet he could never be sure if her excitement was that she got to spend more time with him or that she was gaining opportunity to research and study. Should it matter? It meant he got to spend time with her, and that was all right.

"Tomorrow night," he offered. "I'll order in."

She kissed him, there in the shadow of the church's sacred walls. Passersby strolled on the cobbled path between the church and park, not paying them any attention, or perhaps they were and Ed didn't notice their reactions. Because he couldn't focus on anything but Tamatha when they kissed. She may not have used witchcraft to get him to like her, but he truly did feel bewitched.

And there was nothing whatsoever wrong with that.

Chapter 8

After pulling on a white light, Tamatha strolled the stacks in the demon room. Set into the far wall was a small iron door that led to the live and pickled specimens. A person had to bend over to pass through. And about the door flurried a constant blizzard of snow. She could feel the chill from here. She'd been in there a few times, but today she merely wanted to look up the corax demon.

An entire wall of books focused solely on defining the various demon breeds loomed before her. A few crooked volumes straightened as she approached, and dust flew off the pages to sift through the air. Suppressing a sneeze, she reached for a volume labeled *C* that sat with its alphabetical compatriots. It was thicker than most, but not as thick as the *S* and, surprisingly, *Z* volumes.

Back at the study table, where she'd left a steaming cup of peppermint tea and a plate of chocolate biscuits, she settled in and paged through until she found the corax entry. Rather short, but it did provide a few details.

Tens of thousands of years old, the breed was originally entirely raven in form until they began mating with other species that had mastered human shape. Their evolution was swift and they quickly became a trusted entity among their kind for their ancient heritage yet progressive manner. The demon's sigil is the line of raven feathers down their spinal column and their sense of taste is especially valuable for reading others.

"They gain knowledge by consuming the hearts of those who hold such knowledge? Ugh." She set the book on the table and pulled her legs up to clasp her arms about her ankles. "Ed eats hearts? That's..."

She couldn't pronounce the vocation awful, because she had done it. Once. But if he murdered innocents merely to gain knowledge? Or did he consider it killing? Either way, it was awful. And it didn't seem as if it were a part of his nature, that he needed to commit such an act to survive. Knowledge was an enhancement to one's wisdom.

"Maybe I shouldn't have looked you up," she muttered. "Ed, the demon who looks like a gangster and has minions like an evil overlord, and yet...he can't be. He's very mannered and...his kisses."

She sighed and clasped the clear quartz crystal suspended around her neck. For clarity and truth.

"Who are you, Edamite Thrash?"

He trusted Tamatha. He did. Maybe. Hell, with another demon death he didn't have time to waffle. But could he spring it on her? Tell her why he'd sought her in the first place? She had expressed exasperation over his avoidance of the subject. Certainly she wanted to know what he had to ask of her.

But accepting that information could be difficult. Could a witch work against her own? *Were* they her own? Those decrepit monsters in the cemetery couldn't be from the Light. Of course, he didn't know for sure.

One thing he did know: witches ran in tight circles, or rather, covens. All for one and one for all the cackling hags. Dread to those who went against one of them. Witch Number Two from his past had garnered much of her power from her two sisters and they in turn had met with their coven weekly. It made him shudder now to remember how easily she had seduced him into trusting her. Her dominatrix tease had fired his desires. He'd been crushed by his own lascivious curiosities.

His phone rang and Tamatha's profile displayed a female silhouette against a pastel square. He'd have to snap a pic next time he saw her. Trust her? Probably never. But he did need her and he did know how to play nice.

"Sweetness," he answered.

"Aww, I like when you call me that. Cheers me up."

"You need cheering up?"

"A little. I've a terrible backache from crouching over the floor all day on all fours. I hit a smelly spot in the demon room here at the Archives and discovered a stack of molding books. Had to scrub the floor but I think I salvaged most of the books."

"Would a back massage do the trick?"

She cooed and Ed could feel her anticipation shiver up his neck in a pleasurable way. Yes, he wanted her here. Now. In his arms. At his mouth. Wrapped about his body and filling his senses with lemons.

"Come over," he said. "I'll make dinner."

"I thought you didn't cook?"

"If you promise not to notice the containers in the garbage, I'll pretend to plate the meals with such a flair you would never bother asking if a chef made it."

"Deal. I don't know where you live."

He gave her the address to his place, not far from where his office was in the 10th, and the warning that she mustn't be surprised at the building. It had been in the family for ages, and it had once belonged to a religious organization.

Smirking, he hung up and glanced out his office window to the stained glass windows a few blocks away that curved along the wall in his penthouse apartment. From one of the windows, the archangel Michael pointed his sword directly at Ed. He always got a kick out of that one.

He tried to keep his nose clean and avoid angels. Wisdom any demon would do well to follow.

The man's place was fancy, yet the gorgeous gray-and-turquoise palette added a subtle tone. The main floor was open, and the kitchen was set off the living area and two steps up. Everything was tiled in gray marble. And the place was not square or rectangular—but circular. Not a straight wall in the place—at least, not on the main floor. He told her the bedroom and bathroom were up the open stairway that was railed with ultramodern steel cables.

One half of the circle was walled along the kitchen; the other half, in the living area, emitted the setting sunlight in shards of myriad color from the stained glass windows that curved about that side. Once a former headquarters for a Catholic diocese in the nineteenth century, Ed had explained. Tamatha got a kick out of learning it had been in a demon family for half a century. The saints depicted in some of the windows must surely cringe whenever the current resident passed by.

She wondered if he'd had to have the place unblessed. She had read how to do it once, but hadn't ever thought it an important skill. So many strange yet wondrous facets to the man's life.

She could fall in love with a guy like Edamite Thrash if she didn't think he was hiding something huge. Or that he killed. But if love weren't in the cards, she wanted to have fun with him. And sex. Ribbed for her pleasure? Oh, mercy, she needed to further her studies on that.

Two warm hands suddenly massaged her shoulders from behind, and he leaned in to kiss her on the cheek. "You like coq au vin?"

"Love it. Smells delicious. You were right about this place being startling."

"It takes some getting used to, but I enjoy the colors streaming in more than focusing on the pictures depicted in the glass. Religion can be so theatrical, yes?"

"I bet some long-dead church elders would roll over in their graves to learn who lived here now."

"I think I felt that group roll when I moved in. Had the place cleansed."

"Whoever did it performed a much better job than in your office."

Though she did sense a tendril of…something. It was almost like a sheen over her head, something shaded with darkness. Perhaps it was just Ed's presence. The demonic inhabiting this former religious haven? That had to mess with the room's aura.

His hands worked down her spine to just below her bra strap and she cooed in pleasure. "Oh, yes, right there."

"Why does the Council have you doing the dirty work of crawling about on your hands and knees as a maid?"

"I didn't mind the cleanup work. And if I hadn't done it, the mess would have sat for decades longer, surely. The Archives are ancient and I'm sure some books haven't been touched for centuries. Goddess, that smells so good. I'm a lot hungrier than I realized."

He ended the all-too-short massage with another kiss to her cheek, then wandered into the kitchen. "Wine?"

"Yes, please."

She sat on a stainless steel stool before the glass-topped kitchen counter, where he had placed two settings and poured her a goblet of red. He placed a plate of food before her, along with silverware, which reacted to her by straightening alongside the plate.

"Really?" he said.

"What can I say?" She lifted a fork and dived in without further explanation. If he were around her for any length of time, he'd get used to her OCD magic.

The kitchen was a stainless steel and glass marvel. Tamatha felt as if she were sitting in a nouveau chef's laboratory, tasting his wares. The meal had been premade and featured small servings à la high-tech cuisine, but man, how good was the side of caviar soaked in kir?

It was weird to watch Ed eat with his half gloves on. She bet he took them off when he dined alone. Had he ever harmed anyone with his thorns? She stopped herself from asking, thinking to keep dinner light instead of veering toward research. Besides, the side glances he cast her and those tiny smiles during their conversation about the history of the building were enough to satisfy her. The shiny nubs at his temples didn't bother her at all, though she did want to rub them again.

To test his lust.

And when she moaned over the grapefruit mousse, Ed gave her a raised eyebrow. Realizing she'd been imagining a lusty embrace instead of the food, Tamatha blushed and used the napkin to hide her foray. "So good," she murmured. "My compliments to the chef, whoever that may be."

She finished the fruity mousse and set her plate in the dishwasher. She cleared Ed's dishes as well, finding she liked stepping into the domestic role. Taking care of a man. At least, as much as he would allow it. She did know he was protective of himself and his surroundings. A closed man.

When he was not making out with her.

Her demon boyfriend? Yes, she could consider having him as a boyfriend. But if she went that far into the relationship, then there was always the family curse to consider. So she wouldn't label him yet. For his own safety.

She paced in the living room before the stained glass windows. He'd eaten without even tasting his food, she guessed. He was preoccupied. And she could guess with what. The same thing he'd had on his mind since that day he'd ordered his henchmen to bring her into the office.

But what she was more curious about was his morals.

It was time to get some answers from him. And maybe he'd pop the question he so wanted to ask her. For good or for ill, she wanted to hear it.

Pushing her hair over a shoulder, she smoothed down the blue velvet skirt that flared out at her knees. Her heels—black with blue lace around the edges—clicked on the stone floor over to where Ed paced, and she stopped before him and took his hand.

They both spoke at the same time.

"Do you kill?" she asked.

While he asked, "I need you to cast a spell. Kill? Tamatha? I thought we'd discussed this already."

"I know but—it wasn't really a discussion." She shrugged. "I looked up the corax demon. There was something about eating hearts..."

"Ah, that little detail."

"Little? I think it's a rather big detail myself."

"I suppose, but no. I do not kill. It is not necessary for my survival. My breed can gain knowledge by consuming the hearts of others, but people die every day in a big city like Paris. I just have to be there when it occurs. It's not a difficult task. I don't touch them. I tap into their heart. If I need it. Which isn't often. Rare, even. I'm not making this sound very good, am I?"

She didn't know what to say to that. It sounded weird. Then again, who was she to waggle her finger in blame over eating a heart? She'd done it to maintain her immortality. Of course, she had done it only once.

"What kind of knowledge is so important you would commit such a grave act?"

"Information on local denizens. Or other species that may have invaded the city. It's all a part of the keeping-the-peace thing."

"That you don't want to elaborate on."

"It's what I am, Tamatha. We eat knowledge. I was born that way. Can't change it. Though trust me, I wanted to when I was a teenager. Teenage angst, you know. Even we demons have it."

"I can relate to having problems when I was younger. Though I can't remember a time I've ever had angst about being a witch. Maybe knowing about how cruelly some treat my kind. I mean, witch burnings? What kind of history is that to grow up with?"

"I can't imagine. Your breed has endured much through history."

"Thank you. I just needed to know…"

"I'm not a murderer?"

She shrugged. "It would have been a deal breaker."

"I see. So we're at the deal stage?" He crossed his arms

and strode to a window. Red and azure light beams spilled across his face and the sigils on his hands. He was beautiful. And dark. And an enigma she never wanted to completely learn, because to do so would spoil his mystery.

"No," she said, "I just— Well, you know. I couldn't have continued to see you if that had been the case."

He nodded, not turning to regard her. "Are we doing something here? The two of us? Beyond the obvious need for knowledge we seem to want to get and give to one another?"

"Uh, don't you think we are? It's not necessary to kiss a woman to answer her questions. I just thought..."

This time the look he cast her felt genuine and real. His smile wasn't cold. And a bit of the smolder filled his eyes now. "I do like kissing you. You'll have to forgive me my skittishness. I thought I was over that with you."

"Your thing about bad luck with witches."

"Yes." He held up his hand, the half gloves revealing only the heavily tattooed and sigiled fingers. "Unlike many species who can walk among the humans undetected, my differences are visible. Women get a look at my thorns, or wonder about the weird black growths at my temples, and let's just say it spoils the romantic mood."

"But witches should understand."

"Yes, well, your kind tend to be either oddly fascinated..." He grinned at her and Tamatha felt a thread of guilt heat her face. "Or... I'd rather not explain right now. I had a bad experience with a witch. But that's my past." Again he assessed her with that knowing accusation. "I think I should probably not question this thing we have too much. Maybe just enjoy it while I can."

"Good plan. Love often," she provided.

"Yes, that family motto of yours."

"Good words to live by. Love is good for everyone."

"You are quite the optimist."

"And you tend toward pessimism."

His shoulders dropped with a heavy sigh. "I suppose I am. But I won't offer excuses. Take me or leave me."

"I'll take you." She winked and danced her fingers along his arm and up to thread them through his hair. "Tell me, Ed. What was the reason you needed a witch to cast a spell for you? Are you calling up a fellow demon? If it's bad, I still want to know. I need to know. You can trust me."

"I do know that. I want to tell you exactly what I've been involved in lately. I need your help. But..." He glanced around, limning his gaze along the walls and even the ceiling. "I've felt the intrusion lately. Like a sort of supernatural spy cam. I think someone is tracking me or somehow...listening."

"Really?" She joined him in his search of the invisible snoop. If she focused she could match her earthbound vibrations to that of the marble inside his home and sense any anomalies. She had noticed something earlier that seemed a bit off but had thought it from him.

"Might be a witch," he added. "I can't tell."

"I can put up a shield for us to talk under so no one can hear."

"You can?"

"No problem. Uh..." She tapped her lips as she sorted through the possibilities. This was fun stuff. She rarely got to utilize the shield of silence. "The bathroom is upstairs? You secure the front door and meet me up there."

Grabbing her shoulder bag, she skipped up the black metal stairs and into the bathroom, where she pulled the shower curtain aside to reveal the freestanding black claw-foot bathtub. A narrow stained glass window featured a white lily, but the sun was on the other side of the building, so it was muted. The lily was the heraldic fleur-de-lis and symbolized chastity and virtue. "Yes, perfect for keeping secrets."

Inside her bag she kept an emergency kit of supplies. Enough salt to pour a thin circle around the tub. A small red-and-black candle she set on the vanity. Some crushed valerian sprinkled over the salt for silence. And a spritz of lemon oil around the door frame to block intrusive entities finished the job.

By the time Ed stood in the bathroom doorway, she had completed preparations.

Kicking off her heels, Tamatha climbed into the tub and, peering through the parted gray fabric shower curtains, gestured to her reluctant demon lover to join her.

"Seriously?" He approached, arms crossed over his chest, and sniffed the lemony air. "This is going to work?"

"It'll give us the privacy we need. I promise. Careful. Step over the salt. And kick off your boots. You shouldn't be wearing boots in the house anyway."

"Yes, ma'am." He studied the salt circle for a few long seconds, then drew in a deep breath and did as requested, climbing into the tub and crouching on the opposite edge, facing her. The curtain darkened their little tent, but a candle placed between their feet glowed up beneath their faces.

Tamatha reached out and adjusted the broken salt line to close it up, containing them within the circle. Ed reacted instantly. His head jerking backward, he grasped for the tub edges and grimaced, jaws tight.

She placed a palm over his heart to adjust the volatility of the circle. Whispered a few Latin words, "*refragatio subsisto*." His heartbeats thundered and then slowed.

Ed relaxed and exhaled. "Whew! This is a powerful circle."

"I never do anything half-assed," she said and leaned forward to kiss him. "Most powerful witch in Paris, remember?"

"That is probably the first time I've ever voluntarily stepped into a salt circle. You do bewitch me, Tamatha."

"Never purposely. Now." She clasped his hands between them. "Tell me—what has been troubling you so much you resorted to kidnapping a witch?"

"Will you ever let me forget that one?"

"Probably not. But you've been wanting to ask me since then, right?"

"Yes, but I had to know I could trust you first."

"Hence the romance and wine?"

"Honestly? Whatever happens romantically between us is separate from this, which I consider business."

"Good to know. So you do consider this a romance?"

"It's certainly not a tragedy." He kissed her.

She was miffed he couldn't claim the word but decided to mark it off as caution instead of lack of interest. "So tell."

He clasped his hands before him and pressed his fists against his mouth. She sensed his anxiety, but wasn't about to give him a pass on this one. She needed to know what it was he was so passionate about that destiny had brought the two of them together in a means neither could have resisted.

"I need you to perform a spell for me. Maybe a spell. I'm not sure. But a searching spell might be a good start."

"I already said I could do that."

"Right, but it might be vast or maybe small. I feel as though I'm asking a lot. It's to do with…other witches."

She gaped at him. She'd expected demons. What could he want that required a spell against her own? She didn't perform magic against the Light. It was unthinkable.

She leaned forward, feeling the heat from the candle flame warm her hands. "I know witches aren't in trouble with vamps again. Has it to do with demons?"

"Demons and witches. A particular denizen of demons and perhaps one particular coven. Maybe. I don't know. I'm trying to piece things together and I need your help to do that."

He took her hands and held them above the candle flame. The amber light warmed their grasp. "Demonic magic won't work because we've very little sway against witches."

"As do witches against demons. We generally can't command a demon to do our bidding unless we've conjured that demon to this realm in the first place."

"Right, but you can take us out and...bind us."

"True." She hadn't considered that at the time. Why had she been able to bespell him in the binding? Were there exceptions? Another note for her research list.

"I need a witch to perform a spell that will— Let me explain first."

Within the glowing confines of the bespelled bathtub, Ed told her everything.

"I witnessed a coven of witches murder a demon a few days ago, not ten minutes after I ran into you in the alley. And the other night after you cleansed my office, that phone call I got sent me to arrive after another demon had been slaughtered. I had initially thought it was a random killing, but now with two in the same cemetery and possibly by the same witches, I'm thinking this could escalate, and I don't want that to happen."

"Keeping the peace?" she asked.

"Exactly. I've been able to piece together some basic facts. But I still don't know exactly what is going on. The demon killed was a friend of mine. Laurent LaVolliere. And the second demon was from Laurent's denizen."

"And you think a coven is killing off a denizen of demons?"

"I don't know. Are the witches going after any demon they can find? Or maybe they are focusing on a specific bloodline that originated in the eighteenth century. Or it could be that specific denizen."

"What makes you think it's related to a bloodline from the eighteenth century?"

"Tamatha." He clasped her hand to the side of the candle. "You know how witches use familiars to call up demons and then can control that demon to do their bidding?"

She nodded. "I've never done it myself. Seems cruel."

"Exactly. The demon never asked for such slavery. But generally after the intended task is completed, the demon is released or escapes. But a coven in the eighteenth century used to enslave their demons and use them until they literally burst into dust or collapsed from exhaustion."

He splayed his hands out and continued. "What I have learned from some online research is that, in the eighteenth century, a coven was brought to the pyres and burned right here in Paris where the Place de Grève used to be."

"In the courtyard before city hall."

"Yes. In the article I read, two accusers were listed by name. And of course, no one assumed anything at the time but that they were human. I suspect they may have been the very demons the witches had enslaved. Yet they had been able to occupy human bodies to make the accusations.

"It was clever on the demons' part. Revenge against their oppressors. And it did serve to set them free, for their persecutors were burned."

"Clever indeed. And I can hardly feel sympathy for a coven who would do such a thing." She stroked his hand reassuringly. "How do you feel this is related to the demon deaths you've witnessed?"

"I believe the coven that was burned is the very same who are now murdering descendants of that denizen who accused them," he said.

"But if they were burned at the stake…how is that possible? They'd have to be…revenants."

"You said it, not me. But that term perfectly fits what I've witnessed. They've risen from ash, Tamatha. I don't know if they were conjured by another witch or were able to manage the transformation back to life themselves, but I know the coven's name because it was the last thing Laurent said before he died. They are *Les Douze*."

"The Twelve?" Suddenly Tamatha's heart thudded against her rib cage. She clutched her chest. "I've heard of them before. But from whom and why? I can't recall what I know about them."

"Whatever they are, I think they're back. As zombies."

Chapter 9

He'd confessed his idiotic thinking. And she hadn't laughed at him. Did she trust him after all?

"And you learned this by witnessing one of your friends being killed by these zombie witches?"

Ed nodded and rubbed Tamatha's clasped hands softly. "Laurent and I were close because our mothers were when we were younger. Our distant relatives were in the same denizen that Laurent led, or used to lead. That denizen was formed in the eighteenth century after they escaped enslavement by The Twelve."

"But you're not in the denizen?"

"I'm not affiliated with a denizen. Evil overlord, remember? I'm a stand-alone kind of guy."

And after discussing his ability to gain knowledge by eating hearts, he kicked himself for not considering such in the graveyard. If he had tapped into Laurent's heart, he might have some answers. Of course, it wasn't a practice he utilized often, so it hadn't been fore in mind. Hell, just getting out of there had been. But he wouldn't reveal that moment of lacking bravery to Tamatha.

"Come on. I've laid something incredible on you, and I'm feeling drained by this salt circle." He leaned forward, pressing his nose to hers and kissing her lips. "Can we get out of the cone of silence now?"

"Yes, I'm sorry. I forgot about that. Let me clear the salt for you." She did so with a shuffle of her hand over the salt line, and once he was out, he turned to help her from the tub. She snuffed the candles and set them back on the vanity. As she cleaned up her supplies, Ed noticed she wasn't even touching the things as they straightened and aligned on the vanity. That OCD magic could come in handy on cleaning day.

When finished, she leaned against the vanity and crossed her arms. Candlelight kissed her glossy lips with an enticing glint. "I need to think about this, Ed."

"Of course you do. What I ask of you is immense. I'm not even sure what it is I'm asking you for. *Is* a spell required? What *are* those witches? They look dead to me. They must have been summoned by someone."

"Who else could be involved?"

"I have no clue. I need to do more research, but I don't have a very extensive database or the means—"

"The Archives. Now that I know what is going on, I'm sure I can find information in there." She hastened down the stairs, and when he thought she would rush away, she sat on the stool before the kitchen counter. "I think we should finish the wine."

He poured her a goblet of wine and none for himself.

"You don't seem very worried that a gang of dead witches might come for you."

"I don't worry so much about myself as I do other demons getting killed and the possibility of chaos should this coven become sloppy and reveal themselves to humans."

She tapped a beringed finger against the goblet rim. "You and that 'keeping the peace' thing?"

"Exactly. Let's say I make it a point to ensure Paris stays relatively demon quiet. In the long run it's good for us all."

"You really are a good guy," she said on an incredulous whisper. "I think an evil overlord can be beneficent if the henchmen he leads are doing good. But what bothers me is I don't know how those witches could have risen from ash."

"Witchcraft? Do you think someone else—another witch—could have summoned them?"

"Makes more sense than dead witches rising on their own. Oh." She pressed a hand to his chest. "We shouldn't talk about this out here. I haven't warded this area."

He swept her into his arms. "What was shared in the cone of silence stays in the cone of silence. Promise?"

She nodded. "But—" Another shiver and this time she pushed out of his arms. "Agreed."

"You want to leave?"

She looked at him and shook her head. "I'd much rather finish our date. And this wine."

"We could watch some television, chatter about random things. Kiss?"

That got a smile from her. But he was pushing it. He'd dumped a huge revelation on her. He could hardly expect her to want to make out. It was really hard for him, though, not to think about kissing her. All the time.

"I want to ward this place," she said with determination.

"I have wards."

"Against witches?"

"Surprisingly? Not. Else you would be in pain right now."

"I felt the intrusion you spoke of when I first entered. There's something not right about this place."

"It's probably the same thing I felt. Heavy, like it's trying to invade my skin."

"Yes." She shuffled through her shoulder bag. "I'll need more supplies. I'll have to do it next time I visit. If it's a witch who has been getting into your place and spying on you and we want to have a conversation without worry of it being broadcast, a ward is necessary. Would you let me try?"

He clasped her hand and leaned across the counter. "But if you ward against witches, then I won't be able to bring you home and ravish you."

A flutter of her lashes teased. "Ravishing sounds wonderful. I'll put a niche in for me. The warder usually does that anyway. Did you know that? Whomever you have ward your home generally leaves an entry for themselves. I hope you trust the person who warded it previously."

"I did not know that, but I do trust the fellow. And I trust you." He walked around the counter and took her hand as she got off the stool. "I'm suddenly compelled to do this."

He kissed her below the jaw, there at the base of her earlobe where he loved it most. Always her hair spilled over his face, tickling, and the scent of lemons was sweetly fresh.

"Mmm," she cooed and slipped her hands up his chest. "Let the ravishing begin."

Ed spun her and her shoulders met the wall. He kissed her mouth, tasting wine and her sigh. Her dress buttoned from breasts to hem, and he unbuttoned the first and then the next. "Do you mind?" he asked.

"No, this is just the thing we need to take our minds from more dire things. It's not wrong, is it?"

"What?" He kissed the top of her breast as he unbuttoned yet another button. Mmm, soft, luscious, flesh-smelling, tangy sweet.

"Us ignoring that other thing."

"The world will be fine for a few minutes. We need to do research, yes?"

"Right. Oh…yes. That's nice. You going to go…all the way down?"

"I am." His fingers danced over her stomach and continued to unbutton. Tamatha tilted her head against the wall and closed her eyes. "Pink lace," he commented on her matching bra and panties. Two more buttons, and he spread her dress open to look over her long, lithe figure. A tattoo at her hip featured an owl, wings spread, soaring toward him. "What does an owl symbolize?"

"Athena," she offered, "the Greek goddess of learning."

"Most definitely you." He glided his hands over her stomach, feeling the muscles beneath tighten and release in his wake. "You are gorgeous, witch."

She smirked. "You didn't say that with quite as much accusation as you once did."

"You are undeserving of my scorn." He licked from one breast to the other and cupped them in his hands, cursing the fact he must wear the half gloves. But it was for her protection. "You smell so good. I want to taste you."

"No objections to that. But when you taste things, are you always getting a read like you showed me in the elevator?"

"Not unless I want to." He dashed his tongue from between her breasts and up her neck. "Anything you don't want me to know about you?"

"No. And I much prefer this method of your gaining knowledge to the 'eating the heart' method."

"Agreed."

"Let's get you a little more comfortable." She unbuttoned his shirt and he helped her to pull it off. When she tapped his gloves he shook his head.

"My thorns contain poison. One little slice..."

"Yes, I won't forget that. I can deal." Her hand spread across his chest and her eyes danced with marvel. "So much dark hair. And so soft."

He chuckled. "If I got anything from my werewolf father, it was thick hair. Good thing, too. I don't worry about going bald."

"Mmm, and it goes down further." Her fingers walked down his muscled abdomen and teased at the dark hairs below his navel. "Your father is a werewolf? I didn't know that."

"Was that something I was supposed to provide during your questioning?"

"Maybe, but I've realized you protect yourself, first and foremost. So, half wolf, half raven?"

"I've never thought of it that way. Raven-shifting is simply an innate skill of mine. If I have to label myself, it's simply 'demon' because I have no werewolf qualities beyond the abundant hair."

She tickled her fingers up through his chest hair and tapped his mouth. "Let's go up to the bedroom, demon. I want to get you naked."

"More research?"

"I'll never tell."

"That means yes."

"Maybe."

Oh, it was a yes. And he didn't mind at all.

Ed grabbed her hand and led her up the stairs. He flicked on the lights, which were set around the ceiling cornice and beamed subtle halogens every ten feet around the room's circumference. Not too bright, but enough light so he could admire every sensual curve that designed her body.

Tamatha strode across the room, dropping the blue dress in her wake. Pink lace panties barely covered her sweet, peach bottom. She turned a teasing wink over her shoulder and crooked her finger for him to come to her.

Ed unzipped his trousers and Tamatha slid them down his legs. As he stepped out of them to stand in nothing but dark blue, form-fitted boxer briefs, she walked around behind him, her fingertips drawing over the sigils on his shoulder and gliding down his back where the black lines formed an art gallery of life events.

"You have so many marks back here. These feathers trace your entire spine. The same as the one on your neck. Oh! They connect."

"Yes, it's one long trail. The feathers are indicative of the corax breed," he said of the long black sigil that started at the side of his neck and trailed down his spine to the top of his buttocks.

The feathers were thorned along the shafts and seemed to have a depth, as if she could push her fingers into the blackness. Tamatha stroked the feathers and marveled over their subtle movement upon the steely muscle that wrapped his body. It was a two-dimensional drawing that took on three-dimensional life under her touch. Amazing. This was going in her notebook.

"Born with it," he added.

"Really? A baby with tattoos?"

He shrugged. "A sigil. Unlike tattoos, sigils alter and grow as I age. I imagine it was but a fine line down my spine when I was a baby."

He let out a pleasurable moan as she danced her fingers along the pale gray marking at the back of his hip. It was circular but again thorned and tribal in style. Most of his sigils were, and she associated it with the deadly thorns on his knuckles he wouldn't allow her to study.

"First official fuck," he said with a gasp. "That one."

"Really? You've a sigil to mark the first time you had sex? Do you have one that tallies every time you get it on?"

"Cheeky of you, but no. You think I would have a back full of hash marks?"

"Would you?" She rested her chin on his shoulder and hugged him from behind. "Don't tell me. It's not important. Besides, I've lived four times as long as you."

"Should I be asking about your tally marks?"

"I take my lovers with a discretionary eye. I have had my share over the decades. Let's leave it at that."

"Love Often, eh?"

"Exactly."

Returning to stand before him, she glided her fingers through his chest hair, marveling over the soft thickness. His abs were hard and ridged, a count of three rises and falls as she moved lower. She stopped at his boxers but then couldn't stop herself from pressing a hand over his very obvious erection.

"Oh!" She met his curiously wondering gaze. "You really are..."

He nodded. "For your pleasure, my lady."

"I need to take a look at this."

He gripped her wrist, halting her from tugging down the boxers. "Tell me first—are you curious or is this for your research?"

She shoved him backward to land on the bed. "Both."

Tamatha's demon lover winked and clasped his hands behind his head as she shimmied down his boxers and tossed them aside. His erection was impressive, regally straight, and—

"This is so cool. It really is ribbed." She ran her thumb

over the definite ridges that circled from below the bold, thick head of it. She counted four and they were spaced about a finger's width apart. "This is going to be fun."

"I have never had a woman take such delight in my penis before."

"Really? I'm sorry for you."

"I mean—well, you know, it has never scared anyone off."

"I should say not. I want to play. You okay with that?"

"You play all you like, sweetness. Did you want me to join in while you're playing?"

"No. Lie back and—" she gripped his hard rod "—take it all in. I know I'm going to enjoy this."

"I'm going to have to change my thinking regarding your research," he said as she tickled her tongue around his penis corona. "Oooo, yes. Research. Goood."

Trying a few strokes up and down his length, she noticed he didn't have the usual salty tang that most did. He was clean and perhaps even a little cool, as if he'd come in from a brisk outdoor walk and the chill air lingered on his skin. Yet with every stroke she could feel heat replacing the coolness. Ed groaned and muttered something about her having her way with him being perfectly fine. She lashed her tongue over each of the ribs on his length. They were so firm and like a sex toy waiting for her to experiment.

Shimmying off her panties, she straddled his hips and directed the head of him against her folds. Wet and hot, she needed connection. His molten heat steamed her skin. Mmm, she pressed hard, using his erection to satisfy her achy need for contact. Rocking her hips, she rubbed the ribs against her clit, dragging his penis up and down, increasing the friction and luring her pleasure to the edge.

"You know exactly what you like," he said. "Ah, that's so good."

"Good? This is sofuckingsweet."

Now was not the time for chatter. Because the focused sensation of his hot cock gliding over her swollen clitoris was rapidly conjuring a heady storm in her core. With her free hand she clasped her breast and squeezed the nipple, rocking her hips faster and faster. Ed's encouraging moans spurred her to press his length harder to her.

And with a thrilling shout, an orgasm swept through her system, shivering and quaking and spilling through her pores. Tamatha gasped and stopped humping him as she quivered into the delicious surrender.

Ed sat up and swept aside her hair, then kissed her breasts. "You are incredible, witch."

The sweetest accusation ever.

"So good," she said on a gasp and kissed him quickly. Hungrily she devoured his taste.

"I can taste your fire," he said. "The hot, fiery magic within you. It's powerful."

He lifted her by the hips and she wrapped her legs about his back as he lowered her onto his stiff, wanting erection. The man groaned deeply as she enveloped him. He pulsed and swelled within her. Swearing, he hissed, then lifted her by the thighs to rock her up and down upon his shaft.

Still fluttering in the orgasm, she squeezed her insides about him, coaxing him to join her in the bliss. And with a few more glides up and down, her lover bucked beneath her and shouted. He clasped an arm across her back and clutched her to him as he came along with her.

Bodies trembling, breaths gasping, together they fell back onto the soft gray bedsheets, panting as they rode the exquisite wave.

Tamatha kissed him. He bracketed her head, dashing his tongue in deeply and mimicking the actions his penis had made inside her. He was still inside her, both at loins and mouth. Sweet possession.

She glided her hands through his hair and traced the glossy horn nubs. Breaking the kiss, she slid upward and licked one of the hard nubs, which felt like warm hematite against her tongue.

"Holy—whoa." Ed gripped her about the waist. "That's..."

"You like that?"

He nodded as she licked him again. "Never had a woman do that to me before. Actually, I never allowed it. Why, I have no idea. I'm going to come again if you keep it up."

That was an invitation she wouldn't pass up. She tested the other horn, and it was warm and solid, smooth, and didn't taste like anything. Ed's gasps and increased breathing enticed her to lick harder and to swirl her tongue about the circle of it. And *like that* his chest bucked, his hands slapped the bed, and within her, she felt his cock harden again as he came.

Her lover groaned from his very being and pulled her down to collapse on top of him. Tamatha nuzzled her cheek against his shoulder and clasped a hand within his fingers half-covered by the leather glove.

"That was incredible," he muttered. "How'd you know to do that?"

"Just being curious." She hugged her breasts up to his panting heat and nuzzled her cheek against his chest. "You're a nice big cozy snuggle."

"No one has every used *nice*, *cozy* or *snuggle* to describe me."

"It's the truth. Can you handle that, Evil Overlord?"

"My evil cred may take a hit, but yes. Bring it."

Chapter 10

Tamatha woke to a beam of red light dashing across her face and smiled to realize she lay in Ed's bed after spending the night snuggled next to his gorgeously muscled, sex-warmed body. But he wasn't in the bed now. Turning her head, she found he stood near the wall, looking up, as if following a spider along the ceiling. But she couldn't see anything.

"What is it?" she asked sleepily.

"You can't feel it? Something is trying to intrude." He shook his hands over his head as if to chase away the invisible entity. "What is it?"

She sat up and closed her eyes, tapping her littlest fingers together to invoke her connection to air magic. Instantly, a malevolent feeling fell upon her bare shoulders and teased at the back of her neck.

"Oh, shit, that's malefic magic." She threw aside the sheets and hopped out of bed. Grabbing her bra and panties and hastily putting them on, she then rushed down to the living room.

"What is it?" Ed followed her. He wore only boxers and his hair was tousled. He looked so eatable. And she would get to that. But first.

Emptying her bag on the couch, she sorted through the magical accoutrements and grabbed the amethyst-hilted athame. "I forgot all about warding this place last night. You distracted me." She winked at him.

He nodded acknowledgment. "I aim to please."

"You did please. More than a few times. But we forgot the important stuff."

"You said you had to go home for supplies."

"I do, but shoot. Maybe I can work with what I have. I have to do this now because something malefic is trying to get in."

"Maybe I've something you can use?"

"Unless you have a store of salt somewhere, I don't think you can."

"Fresh out of that condiment. What do you need me to do?"

"Stand back and let it happen." She dipped the athame into a vial of blessed rainwater, then walked to the center of the living room and stood before the stained glass windows that beamed in colorful morning sunlight.

"I have never seen a more beautiful witch," Ed commented.

Smiling to herself, Tamatha redirected her focus. Reveling in a compliment from her lover could threaten to lower the efficacy of any spell she attempted. Drawing in the air before her, she marked out the sigil against malefic magic and recited the incantation. Tapping her little fingers together, she activated her air magic and focused her inner eye to encompass the entire building Ed lived in, including the surrounding streets.

A pulse of power echoed out from her being and pushed through the air. Behind her, Ed swore in quiet fascination. And when the energy returned and entered through her soles, she closed off the ward and sealed it with a final dash of the athame across the invisible sigil she had drawn before her.

Turning to the fascinated demon, she nodded. "It's done."

"I felt that. But I don't see anything."

"Exactly. The best wards are invisible yet strong. That should hold. But not for long. I didn't have any sage to make it stick. And blood might even be required to really put up a good block against the intrusion. Malefic magic is way out of my realm. It's beyond diabology, which I'm only beginning to study. But I put it off for a while. You think whatever has been trying to get into your place might be involved with the cemetery killings?"

"Possible. In my line of work, I'm always dealing with nefarious people."

"Evil-overlord stuff?"

"Yes, but this feels like it is to do with the current situation."

"I need to do some research on *Les Douze* today. Do you mind if I shower here? I want to head straight to the Archives from your place."

"Not at all. You want me to join you in the shower?"

"Oh, yeah. Do you have a vacuum?"

"A, er…vacuum?"

She smirked at his apparent lacking knowledge. "You know that electronic thing that you push through the house to suck up dirt?"

"Ah. I have a maid who does that once a week."

Tamatha shook her head. "Bachelors. How about a broom?"

He winced. "Perhaps? Why the compulsion to clean?"

"I want to sweep up the salt around your tub so you can get into it with me."

"I think I remember where the broom is kept."

The depths of the Archives' room that harbored grimoires and all documents and tomes related to the species of witch was Tamatha's favorite room. It was the largest room with high, arched ceilings painted in the fresco style of da Vinci, though there were no religious scenes, but rather depictions of Samhain, Beltane and the great Hecate. This room contained twice as much information as any other. Witches were the most abundant of the paranormal species.

It was a workday, but Tamatha had nothing more pressing to tend to. Dusting and tidying she achieved by slowly pacing down an aisle of books. Her OCD magic took care of straightening, dust dispersed in her wake.

She paused at the end of the aisle where the fluorescent lights didn't reach. This far quadrant of the room repelled modern electricity. It was where the books on malefic magic were kept. Old-fashioned candle sconces provided lighting, and two beeswax candles took to light with a snap of her fingers.

A familiar shiver crossed her shoulders. Malefic magic had been trying to infiltrate Ed's home. That made her suspect whoever was behind whatever was going on was a witch who practiced malefic magic. But witches didn't practice such magic. If so, they were branded a warlock and shunned from both the Light and Dark.

The only warlock Tamatha was familiar with was Ian Grim. She didn't know him personally. Never had a reason to work with a practitioner of such foul magic. There were dozens of other warlocks, surely, but she'd need to do more research if all paths led that direction.

Stepping forward, she felt the shadows creep over her like black ink spilling over her skin. The hairs on her arms tingled. Hisses lured her to the left of the bookshelf. Scents of decayed thyme and earth infused the air. A low growl sounded more from within her head than before her. It was the magic toying with her.

She followed intuition, hoping it would guide her.

Something skittered off on a multitude of feet, not across the floor, but within the pages of the dark, bound volumes lining the shelves. Even though she fluttered her fingers along the spines, these books did not align as did all other things when reacting to her OCD magic.

"Most definitely malefic," she whispered. Quickly she pulled up her white light. "Should have done that earlier. You're slipping, Tam. Too much demon on the brain lately."

But, oh, what a demon. And she'd had him on more than her brain. Her lips, her breasts, her stomach. Mmm… between her legs. Her thoughts drifted to the king-size bed and Ed leaning over her, tending her every sensual hot spot…

One slim book slid out a quarter of an inch, dusting the air with a mist of emerald smoke.

"Really? And I was just getting to the good part of the daydream."

With a sigh, she snatched the volume, which moaned until she'd returned to the fore of the room and set it on the table right on top of the sigil carved into the wood that would render all magics useless. It was a contained spell and focused only on text, so it could not vanquish a spell tossed at her from a visitor or fellow archivist. Not that Tamatha worried. The Archives were secure.

She planted herself in a wicker chair that creaked, kicking off her high heels. Study of the heavy volume found the gold leaf had worn away from the title, but the words were impressed deeply into the scuffed brown leather. And the fore-edges of the pages were not deckled, but rather, when she pressed them tightly together and then fanned them slightly, revealed a scene that depicted horned and tailed beings. She loved surprises like that. Yet the book wasn't a malefic grimoire, but rather a genealogy.

"Weird. Why was it shelved with those dark books?" It felt safe now that she preened over it in the light. "Why am I surprised? Isn't as if there aren't hundreds of misshelved volumes."

She had been meant to pull out this volume, and that was the important thing.

It wasn't difficult to track down a page detailing the witches of *Les Douze*. They had been burned in 1753 in the Place de Grève. The area was now the square before the city hall, and a merry-go-round held court where once violent hangings, burnings and all sorts of criminal executions had taken place through the centuries. A couple decades later, use of the guillotine had literally stained the streets red during the Revolution.

The page in the grimoire shivered under Tamatha's touch and a minute twinge of sorrow entered her veins.

She quickly withdrew her finger from the book. "Whew! Powerful stuff."

Many a grimoire or book in the Archives were filled to the endpapers with whatever magics it detailed and often harbored memories and emotions that could bleed into a reader's very being. It was the reason most chose not to work in the Archives. Anything could happen. Including escape from the pages. CJ had captured an elemental the first week Tamatha had worked there. It had been left next to a book of cherubs, and the magics had combined. A drunken bacchanal had ensued. Of course, with no alcohol on the premises, the cherubs had stolen tea, and well, as CJ told it, tea could get a cherub drunk faster than vodka to a teetotaler.

Lifting the book to check the magic sigil was indeed directly beneath the volume, she set it down with a bit more confidence. She trailed her finger down the list of twelve, whispering each name as if a prayer as she did so.

"Macarius Fleche, Alyce Doran, Lucian Maldove." The list included all twelve coven members and ended with "Martine Chevalier and…"

She paused before speaking the final name written in tiny cursive. A name all too familiar to her. Tamatha's heartbeats sped. It couldn't be. Her mother had never mentioned…

"Lysia Bellerose?"

Her heart dropped in her chest. She gasped to catch her shallow breaths. That was impossible. Of course, nothing was impossible. And there were no coincidences. It was right there in black ink on the stained page.

Her grandmother had been one of the witches of *Les Douze*.

Chapter 11

After Tamatha had left for the Archives, Ed dressed, slipped on his gloves and selected a deep purple tie to go with the steel-gray business shirt. He pulled on the black Zegna suit coat and stepped into his leather shoes. He would go in to the office because he wanted to put contacts on the alert should he need them.

And figure how dangerous it could be to piss off a warlock. Though it seemed as though, if it really was a warlock, he was already in fine fettle. Ed didn't mind facing a new and powerful opponent, but he did like to know what he was dealing with. With hope, Tamatha's research could fill him in.

He took the elevator down and checked the part in his hair in the mirrored wall. His finger dashed over a horn nub but it didn't feel like it did when Tamatha did that. When she touched him there it was like sex coursing through his veins and congregating at the base of his cock to an instant hard-on.

For all appearances, he and Tamatha were hitting it off. Doing the boyfriend-and-girlfriend thing. But he didn't want to get his hopes up. Because…he wasn't boyfriend material. Women never stayed in his life for long. And when he finished with what he needed Tamatha for, she'd leave him. He felt sure of that.

He wasn't meant to have love.

Besides, he was merely research to the witch. She wanted to study him and, yes, even have sex with him to see what it was like to have sex with a demon. She might like to believe differently, but he knew better.

He sighed as the elevator doors glided open. Striding out the lobby and through the main doors, he headed down the street toward his office building. Once across the street he felt something pull over his skin and he stepped through it, as if emerging from a thickness.

He stopped and looked back over the street. "Her ward," he decided. "A powerful witch indeed. I'm lucky to have found her. She'll help defeat *Les Douze*."

And that should be all that mattered.

Of course, he knew better. Somewhere deep inside, the idea of love rattled his better senses and scared the crap out of him.

Hands shaking, Tamatha carefully sipped the mint tea. The one name on the list of twelve witches kept flashing at her like a warning light. Truly, was her grandmother involved in the terrible murders Ed had detailed?

It didn't make sense. Her mother had never spoken a disparaging word about Lysia Bellerose. Petrina had not talked about her often, but when she had, it had been to tell Tamatha of her grandmother's wisdom and spell-crafting expertise. Lysia had been kind, lovely and wise. Her magical knowledge had been vast. She'd had diabology under her belt and had sought to study angelology before her abrupt and cruel demise. She'd never caused a death, nor would she participate in magic that could result in such evil. Born in the early sixteenth century, she had lived two and a half centuries and had given birth to five daughters, three of whom had survived the birth. Yes, Lysia had been burned at the stake—the sad fate of many a witch who had tried to help humans by teaching them simple remedies that embraced herbology and healing skills.

"Burned at the stake alongside eleven others," Tamatha whispered.

To imagine such a horror chilled her veins. Had all twelve pyres been lit at once? Or had one been lit and then the next, so that the witches at the end had to endure the screams and agony of their coven mates before the flames got to them? The thought of it made Tamatha moan.

Tea spattered her lap, and she set the teacup on the saucer with a click. Blowing and whispering a spell instantly dried the dark skirt fabric, which didn't show a stain.

She turned the page in the book to read more. Within the fragile pages of a history ledger that detailed the bloodlines of witches of the Light, she located her grandmother, Lysia Bellerose. None of the females in the Bellerose family—should they marry—had taken their husband's name. It just wasn't done. If they fell in love and felt the need to make a home with the man, they did so. Without the official document. All their offspring carried the Bellerose name.

It was how witches often did things. The matriarchs were the strongest and wisest in most families. Male witches were often considered lesser, which wasn't necessarily true when comparing skills, but it was an old and revered train of thought.

Tamatha's father had been a witch, but he and Petrina

had drifted apart after fifty years with one another. *People are not meant to have such long monogamous relationships*, her mother had once said. *But if it comes to you, try it, embrace it and welcome it for as long as you feel comfortable. But never stay beyond the expiration date*, her mother had also warned.

Love often.

"And deeply," Tamatha whispered. "For it never lasts."

The idea of marrying a man for the romantic ideal of happily-ever-after didn't fit when the twosome were immortal. Ever after took on an entirely new meaning when compared to the fifty or more years some humans enjoyed in marriage.

Yet Tamatha teased the idea of monogamy. Dating was tedious. Lovers were essential, though. And she'd never been bothered that they left her life more frequently than they stayed. Only three of her former serious lovers had died when they'd been dating. Henry had been a mortal who'd fallen off his bicycle, hit his head on a sharp rock and bled out. Joseph had been a fellow witch who had insisted that using arsenic in a spell was correct—he'd choked on his foaming saliva. The familiar had died after they'd broken it off. All the others she'd dated had come and gone with the same desire for freedom as she had. Save Byron, who had gone mad and had literally been carted away from her in a straitjacket.

And Ed, well…

Well.

She wanted him to last. To not go mad. To not die. And to be in her life longer than most. Because he fascinated her and appealed to her desire for the new and unknown.

But most of all, she wanted to help him. She'd agreed to help him with whatever he needed to figure out the situation of demons being murdered by witches. But could she?

magic could put a never-ending tangle of poisonous snakes on a man's feet and render him insane.

But that was the past.

And now…

Had Lysia managed to come back on her own, along with her eleven coven mates? Didn't seem possible. Which only left someone else summoning the dead witches.

"What malefic magic has brought back twelve witches from the dead?"

Tamatha set the book on the table and closed her eyes, placing her fingers lightly over the pages. She inhaled and exhaled deeply but could divine no hidden clues beyond the printed text.

Dare she involve herself in this? It couldn't end well if it resulted in her grandmother's destruction. And a witch never worked magic against her own. It was unheard of. The Light and Dark would ostracize any witch who worked against them, which was how some became warlock.

But if Lysia truly were back and killing demons, Tamatha couldn't stand by and allow that to happen. Why hadn't her mother told her the details of her grandmother's death?

She had to give her a call, get to the truth.

Tugging out her cell phone from her purse, she texted her mother. Petrina never answered calls. She preferred her daughter text her and she would return a call when she olitry. Could they not see the humans who had accused them were simply men and women? Demons had tails and fiery red eyes. Yet the witch finder had noted that he did not doubt *Les Douze* were in alliance with demons and the very Devil himself.

"*Himself,*" Tamatha corrected herself when she read the lowercased word. One always capitalized the name of the Dark Lord. And a wise witch would never say the name three times, for that would serve as an invite to Himself, who had a tendency to appear to a person in the guise of their greatest temptation.

She mused that should he appear on her doorstep, she might lunge into his arms and kiss him, for surely the Devil would appear to her as Edamite Thrash.

She shook her head of the terrible notion. Best not to spend time considering *you know who.* Back to the text.

"Grandma must have known something," she said. "Of course, if they were really demons, she would know. She was a diabolotrist. If anyone could recognize a demon on the spot, it had to be Grandmother. But why had demons accused *Les Douze*?"

Had Ed figured it out? They had to compare notes.

She pulled up the ledger against her chest and settled into the chair, clasping the book as if it would fly away. "How terrible to have been burned at the stake. Alive."

Prickles shivered her skin. Most witches shied from

had a moment. She typed: Questions about Grandmother's death. Urgent.

If that didn't result in a return call within a few hours, she'd worry that her mother was hiding something.

Until then, she had work to do. But she couldn't concentrate on her demonic studies. Maybe there was something in one of these books about witches raised from the dead? Should she look up zombies?

Setting the teacup on the side table next to the teapot, she then pushed a tall wooden ladder along the dusty metal pipe to move it down toward the spell books. The books closest to her on the head-level shelves shifted to attention. This room was partially organized by topic, such as spell books, grimoires, herbals, incantations and hexes, et cetera. But within those categories there was no organization.

Looking over the vast shelves overstuffed with books, she shook her head. It was going to be a long yet interesting day.

Ed crossed a street lit with neon gleams from nearby restaurants and bars. It was midnight and he didn't want to sit in the office or at home. Tamatha had called to say she was spending a late night at the Archives and not to look forward to seeing her. He never thought he'd miss seeing a woman daily, but he did. He tried to remember her scent. It was lemons, but he couldn't summon the memory in his nose.

Really? He couldn't remember the scent of a common fruit? He was acting stupid. Pussy whipped? Yes, he was.

Best he focus on business. He'd send Inego and Glitch to check on the cemetery guard. He hadn't heard word from either, so he assumed no new zombie-witch action there.

A horn honked and he flipped off the driver as he crossed the street.

"Nice," a familiar voice called from behind the wheel.

Ed turned a look over his shoulder and chuckled. "Kir! You see?" He splayed out his hands as he approached the car. "I knew it was someone worthy of my scorn."

He joked. But he always sensed if either of the two of them held scorn toward the other, it was his brother for him. His werewolf half brother. They shared the same father, Colin Sauveterre. Kir had a thing about demons. He hated them. Although, he was getting better. He seemed to tolerate Ed.

And as hungry as he was for family, Ed tolerated the wolf's tolerance.

Kir found a parking spot and the lanky wolf climbed out and gestured toward a tapas bar. Good call.

The place was touristy, but Ed and Kir found stools at the end of the bar where one of the neon wall signs had blinked out, and it was as far from the '80s-themed karaoke stage as they could possibly get.

Kir drank whiskey while Ed preferred absinthe. It had an acrid bite that appealed to his ultrasensitive palate. He could read old things and stale mossy forests in some of the better absinthes. This one was too processed, nothing but a chemical note.

"Thought that stuff was illegal," Kir said of Ed's foggy green drink.

"Only in the States. But it's no longer like they used to make it in the nineteenth century, I'm sure. Rarely do I get a buzz off this stuff."

"Maybe because you're not human?"

"Possibly." He clinked his glass against Kir's and the two tilted back healthy swallows. "So what brings my werewolf brother to the red-light district? I thought you

Kir swung a look at him.

"It's a weird story. I'm dealing with it. You know I like to keep a finger on all demonic activity in Paris. Unfortunately, I need Tamatha's witchcraft skills to help me figure things out."

"Tamatha Bellerose?"

"You know her?"

"I know of her. Weird silver hair and kind of a retro look? She is a gorgeous number. And smart, according to her friend Verity Van Velde."

"I had no idea my brother hung out with witches." Ed mocked a shiver. "You do get around."

"If I can't go near another werewolf, then I'm open to any and all friendships offered. As you should be open to having a relationship with the witch. You have had bad luck with women."

"One witch in particular. So what makes me think this one could be different?"

"You won't know until you try."

"Your happy vibes are annoying, wolf. I can see why your wife kicked you out this evening."

"I'm heading home soon. With ice cream in hand, she'll be happy to see me. The baby will be sleeping. Do you know that faeries prefer going skyclad?"

Ed raised a brow.

"Isn't often I come home to a fully clothed faery."

"Nice. I thought witches did the skyclad thing, too?"

"See? You've so much to look forward to when dating a witch."

"I wouldn't call a binding something to look forward to."

"Well, if you're not into her, then dump her."

"I can't do that."

"Course not." Kir finished his whiskey. "Because you

like her," he teased as he stood. "I gotta go. You need any help with whatever this zombie-witch situation is?"

"Not yet. But I'll call if I need you. Thanks, Kir. It was good to talk."

"Yeah, we're cool." He nodded and headed out.

That "we're cool" meant a lot to Ed. Their camaraderie, while still weak, would grow. Maybe someday they could do brotherly things like—who knew—golf or fishing? He could get into a little outdoor adventuring, though he suspected Kir's form of fishing may be in wolf shape. Ha!

So maybe he shouldn't be so worried about a relationship with a witch. He shouldn't look at it that way. It was a relationship with Tamatha. Didn't matter what she was—witch, demon or otherwise—he liked the woman and how she made him feel.

Yeah, things could be good for him.

So long as he avoided attracting the attention of twelve zombie witches.

Chapter 12

Something nudged Tamatha's elbow. She startled and looked up from the open book her cheek had been smashed against.

"Morning, sleepyhead."

"Huh?" Peeling strands of hair from her face, she straightened and winced at the muscles that pulled in her neck. She'd fallen asleep last night while reading about the local covens. "Is it morning?"

"That it is. Is my husband such a cruel boss that he makes you work all night?"

A tall, red-haired witch, who wore the corseted black Victorian dress as if she'd invented the goth style, winked at Tamatha.

"No, I was doing some research. I want to advance my knowledge on diabology."

And now, apparently, witches. Had her mother returned her text? She glanced about but didn't spy her phone in the scatter of books neatly arranged before her.

"Wow. That's a lot to study. But interesting?"

"It is."

"You find much on demons in a witch's grimoire?" Vika tapped the book cover.

"My interest wandered. What is that delightful smell?"

"CJ is brewing tea in the office. Oh, but, sweetie, you've a Post-it note stuck to your forehead."

Tamatha slapped a palm over her forehead and claimed the pink slip of sticky paper. A spell for night terrors had been noted on it. Why that had caught her attention she had no clue.

She sighed and pushed the compendium on witch families away from her. No luck with tracking her family back further than what she already knew. And she'd thought to look into Ed's family, but Thrash wasn't listed in any of the genealogical lists. It had to be a false name or moniker.

The scent of lemon and thyme drew closer, but Tamatha again sighed. She really liked Ed. As a friend. As a lover. But what he'd asked her to do was not something with which she felt comfortable. To kill her grandmother? Again? She didn't want to offend him or lose the chance to learn more about his breed. And if witches were killing demons, then someone had to do something about it.

Right?

"What's up with that?" Vika asked as she pointed to Tamatha's face.

"What do you mean? Have I more office supplies stuck somewhere?"

"No, that melancholy sigh. Ah..." The witch sat across the ancient table from Tamatha and spread her hands over the assorted grimoires, lists and compendiums. Her black fingernail polish glinted under the flickering fluorescent lights. "You're heartsick."

"What? No."

"Then it's a new love?"

"Why does it have to be love?"

"Because I can read it in your irises."

Tamatha touched the corner of her eye, wondering if that could be true. Iridology was the practice of reading fortunes in irises. And Vika was a talented witch, but she'd always thought her main focus water magic. Of course, most witches had many other practices besides their principal magics.

"Tea!" CJ entered carrying a wooden tray replete with pot and cups. The dark witch's long black hair was teased back into a leather binder behind his neck, and he was barefoot. The lack of footwear wasn't odd; Tamatha had come to learn the man was more comfortable without shoes on.

"I see you shook her awake, Oh Dark Queen of Mine," he said to his wife, and then to Tamatha he said, "We wondered about you earlier."

"Earlier?" She cast Vika a wondering gape. "How long did you two stare at me before you decided to wake me?"

"I figured you needed the rest. We've only been in the office an hour. You see it in her?" she asked her husband, who handed her a cup of tea with an extremely tattooed hand.

CJ offered a cup to Tamatha and then peered into her eyes. His dark ponytail fell forward over his black shirt. The twosome were goth defined, and never had Tamatha met a more perfectly paired couple. "Oh, yes, a new love, eh?"

"Seriously?" Tamatha sipped the tea. She shouldn't be surprised that two witches who were madly in love could see something like that in her. But she wasn't in love with Ed. Far from it. They were friends. Who liked to kiss. And fool around. And the sex the other night had been off the charts. "He's just a guy I know."

"Ooo, tell me more." Vika winked from over a sip of tea.

"It's not important. Not related to my work here. I shouldn't bother either of you."

"Bother me all you like," Vika said. "I love some salacious gossip."

Wrapping her fingers about the comforting warmth of the teacup, Tamatha offered, "It's not salacious." Because she'd keep the naughty parts to herself. "Ed is a demon I ran into one night, and he's agreed to answer some questions to further my knowledge about the species."

Vika raised a brow, accompanied by her thin but knowing smile. The expression said so much Tamatha blushed. CJ, thank the goddess, had made his way to the door, and she hoped he'd leave because the last person she wanted to discuss her love life with was her boss. Only when he did quietly wander out did she lean forward across the table.

"His name is Edamite Thrash, and he's so handsome," she said. "He's got all these demonic sigils on his skin that look like tattoos. And he's got this *manner* about him. So virile. Very sexy."

Vika squealed.

And CJ dashed back into the room, toppling his cup and spilling tea onto the concrete floor in the process. "Edamite Thrash? Oh, no, not him. You can't date him."

"Wha—why?" she cautiously asked the dark witch.

"Do you know who he is? *What* he is?"

"Yes. He's demon. And he has an office not far from here—that's how I ran into him," she said to Vika. "I was walking to the Métro one night after work. And he's kind. And smart. He says he heads an organization dedicated to keeping the peace and it's true."

CJ blew out an angry breath. "Tamatha, that man is reprehensible. Thrash heads a demon mafia."

"Mafia?" she spit out unbelievably.

"CJ, what do you mean?" Vika asked. "I haven't heard of a demon mafia in Paris."

"It's discreet, but Edamite heads it and rules over Paris. If any demons want to get in or out of this realm, he'll know about it. And he'll stop whomever he doesn't want here. No matter what it takes. He used to deal drugs to his own sister."

Sister? He hadn't mentioned a sister to Tamatha, only the father who was a werewolf. A drug dealer? Reprehensible?

"He's a nasty piece of work. Tamatha, you need to be careful around that demon," CJ insisted. "Better yet, I don't want you seeing him again."

She stood up from the chair and closed the book before her. "I don't think you get to tell me who I can and can't date. You may be my boss but you're not my father."

Vika cast a stern glance toward her husband. "Tamatha is smart and she's a big girl. She knows what she's doing." But the look she then cast Tamatha was filled with question and concern.

Actually, now that she'd heard about the mafia thing—and a drug dealer?—Tamatha wasn't at all sure what she was doing, but she wasn't going to let anyone know that. "I do know what I'm doing. And I always wear a white light around him."

"Seems to me if you trust a man you shouldn't have to go to such measures." CJ crossed his arms tightly. "I'm concerned for you, Tamatha. Just, please, be careful?"

"I always am. Thanks for the tea. I put in an all-nighter, so I should be leaving."

As she passed CJ she saw him sweep his arm out in

her peripheral vision. Tamatha spun quickly and put up a blocking spell with her palm. His magic bounced off the invisible shield and moved the air in tangible waves.

"What in seven mercies?" she asked, affronted. "Were you going to cast a spell on me?"

"I wanted to put a protection spell on you."

Vika stood and clasped her husband's hand. "Leave her, lover. It's not wise to mess in another woman's love life. Only bad things can come of it for both you and her."

Thoroughly admonished, CJ crossed his arms, yet he maintained his stern gaze.

"Have a good day, Tamatha," Vika said. "Call me if you want to talk!"

Tamatha waved at the twosome and quickly exited. Really? He'd thought to put a spell on her without even asking? Well, the man was a dark witch. She supposed he was accustomed to doing as he wished.

"Mafia?" she muttered. "What does that mean?"

Could the man truly be the evil overlord he'd confessed to?

Instead of heading to the Métro, Tamatha veered toward Ed's office building. Along the way she stopped at a café. The shop had begun selling to-go drinks à la American style, and she ordered a foamy cup of decaf chai with extra cinnamon. Her vita could use the warming spice.

With her bag of books slung over one shoulder and cup in the other hand, she paused before the glossy black marble wall of Ed's building and leaned against it. The cool stone surface against her shoulders felt good on her muscles, which had kinked from sleeping with her head on a table.

The sun was not out, but she didn't feel imminent rain. Of course, Paris was a bitch when it came to the weather, and one minute it could be high sun, the next pouring kittens. She really should invest in an umbrella and carry that in her bag. Because she couldn't always whip out the air magic to form a protective shield against the rain when around humans.

Man, these books were heavy. She set down the bag and sipped the chai, one arm crossed before her as she watched people across the street filing in and out of a *boulangerie*. A fresh baguette sounded like carb heaven. She hadn't eaten more than a few tea biscuits today.

But fore in her busy brain was CJ's voice saying that word: *mafia*. And then: *drug dealer*. She turned and stared up the side of the building. Six stories up, Ed's office occupied the top floor. She wondered if he appreciated the newly cleansed office, and then that wonder startled her.

Had the bad vibrations been created by him? Had *he* taken lives in that office? He'd said he did not kill, but he'd said it in such a manner that left it open for interpretation. There was a difference between murder and killing. And he was the demon in charge of all other demons in Paris? She knew nothing about his work. While his appearance appealed to her, dark and tattooed, she reasoned that others may look at him and easily pin such style as nefarious. A drug dealer? Possible. Even worse? Maybe.

She hated to think such things about him, but CJ had upset her. And she'd never reason to doubt CJ. He was an honest man, a good witch and a kind boss.

So who or what was Edamite Thrash? He *had* kidnapped her. Could his sudden turnaround and seductions be related to an ulterior motive?

Her phone rang and she tugged it from her skirt pocket. Ed was calling her? She glanced up again as she answered.

"I can see you standing down there," he said. "Saw you walk across the street from the café."

Shoot. She hadn't wanted to be so obvious. But then, she was out of sorts this morning. And the next thing she said proved it. "I heard something about you today."

"Gossip? Was it good, bad or—?"

"Ugly."

"I see. Are you going to give me a chance to defend myself against mere words?"

"Do you kill people?"

"What?"

"It's a fair question, Ed."

"I thought we had—" He exhaled heavily. "Do you think because I'm demon I'm a killer? I thought much more highly of you, Tamatha—"

"Don't make this about me. Certainly Jones told me you head a demon mafia and that you're a drug dealer."

"The dark witch is accusing me? And has he told you how many vampires he's killed lately?"

"Ed, I just..." She squeezed the to-go cup too hard and chai spilled out the top. "Oh!" Milky brown liquid spattered her shoes. "I can't do this right now. I have to go."

"Come up, Tamatha, please. Apparently, things have gone extremely south since I held you in my arms yesterday morning. We need to talk."

Arm held out with the dripping cup in hand, she tilted back her head. She couldn't see him in the window for the glare from the clouded sun. But she could feel his anticipation and anxiety. They did need to talk.

"Please?" she heard through the phone that she no longer held to her ear.

He did deserve to defend himself. And she did want to see him again. Because remembering how great it felt to lie in his arms went a long way in smothering any misgivings she had about him.

"Very well. I'll be right up."

But as she bent to pick up her book bag, she had a thought. Standing close to the building, so he couldn't see her, Tamatha pulled a white light over her body.

"Now I'm ready. For good or for ill," she muttered.

Ed paced the floor before Tamatha, who had refused to sit after he'd offered. She clutched the shoulder-bag handle before her, the book-laden bag hanging heavily before her knees. Her hair was tousled and she had apologized for her appearance because she'd slept in the Archives overnight. She looked a disheveled schoolgirl in her short tight skirt, high heels and white blouse that did not hide the perky nipples beneath.

And that turned him on.

Yet, the vibes flowing from her were anything but attractive or welcoming. In fact, he could feel the repellent electricity skitter across his skin from her white light.

"The day before yesterday we sat in a bathtub sharing confidences. Later, you traced my body with your tongue. And we had amazing sex," he said, stopping before her with hands splayed. "What's happened since then?"

She squeezed her eyes as tightly as her tiny fists.

"Tamatha—"

"Just answer the question I asked when I was standing outside," she insisted.

"I..." So she wasn't going to drop that one. An honest answer wasn't going to win him any brownie points. And the definition he had of drug dealer was much different than hers could be.

"Tamatha, there are some things about me you are better off not knowing. I do what I must. The organization I head is focused on keeping the peace. This mortal realm is not always an easy place to exist for my sort. Nor can peace and anonymity be achieved with mere talk or passivity. Sometimes more persuasive methods must be employed."

"So you have killed? And if you say 'only those deserving' I am so out of here."

He didn't know how to win against this woman. Not that he had to win. *Did* he have to win? He shouldn't look at things that way. He didn't want to spoil what felt so right to him.

So he nodded. "I trust details will not serve your curiosity. It is merely my confession that you seek. But it won't change how I feel about you, Tamatha."

"How you feel—Ed, you brought me into your life because you needed a witch. You didn't seek me because you were interested in me or found me attractive or even—"

"And yet every time I am near you I am compelled closer. I forget the important thing, such as tracking zombie witches, and can only wonder how I allowed myself to become so bewitched."

"Agg!" She dropped the bag and fisted her hands before her, shaking them. He couldn't figure the source of her rage. But it was a beautiful rage. "Every time you say that, that you can only believe your attraction to me is because of some spell I've worked against you, feels like a slap in the face. Don't you know how much it hurts me?"

"Tamatha, I would never hurt you."

"And yet the only reason you can possibly be interested in me is because witchcraft made you do it?"

"No, I—" It did sound horrible when he put it that way. And he didn't believe she'd employed a spell to attract him. "It's a figure of speech."

"That you should know better than to use with me. Oh! Do you have a sister? CJ said—"

"I'll thank you not to rely on the dark witch's information. Rumor is often distorted."

"So you don't have a sister?"

"I do have a half sister, as well as a half brother," he said, but it came out more defensive than he wished. She was forcing it from him, and he didn't like that. But he cautioned his anger. Horns were the last thing they needed in this conversation. "Blyss and Kir are blood siblings. They are werewolves in the same pack. Or they were in pack Valoir. They've both been banished. Blyss doesn't know about me. Kir doesn't think it's such a good idea to tell her about her demon half brother. And I did provide her with some pills, but I'm far from a drug dealer."

Tamatha's mouth dropped open. So much information, and all of it so damning on his part. She'd wanted his truth. A lie would have only hurt her, and he'd meant it when he'd said he would never harm her.

"My half sister didn't want to be a werewolf," he provided in the quiet pause that filled the room. "I have a manner of putting my hands to strange and curious elixirs. I sometimes fancy myself a purveyor of essentials."

Tamatha lifted a brow.

"A stupid title I toss out because it— Ah, never mind. I was able to obtain pills that could repress Blyss's wolf. But she's fallen in love recently and has gotten over that demented need to deny her heritage."

"That's…weird," Tamatha said on a gasp. "Both the need to not be a werewolf and the part about purveying drugs."

"Essentials," he corrected her. Then he mentally kicked himself for the stupid assertion to be right. It was all about control. And he didn't have the control with this witch. And…that suited him fine. He splayed his hands before him. "What else do you need to have verified about me that the dark witch has claimed makes me some mafia king? We might as well get it all out while you're here. Not like

I shouldn't have expected this. Women never stick around me for long. If it's not the horns, it's something else. I knew I couldn't trust a witch."

"What?" Tamatha stepped around the book bag. "That's not fair. You can trust me. But in order for me to trust you, I need to ask the hard questions. To get answers from you so I can then make up my mind about how I feel about you."

He bowed. "Mafia king at your service, witch."

"Don't call me that in that tone. You're mean today, Ed. And what happened to evil overlord? Are you a mafia king or the other?"

He shrugged. "Beauty is in the eye of the beholder. Or in this case, ugliness."

She slammed her arms across her chest, then splayed them out and grabbed the bag. "I need to get away from you and think about this. About everything. About us."

"There can never be an us," he said, following her to the door.

"Is that what you want?"

No. But he wasn't about to bow down to her standards of what was acceptable in a mate and how he should live his life. "Of course it's what I want. Better to nip this romance in the bud while I'm still standing. Not that you haven't attempted to knock me down."

"You're being defensive."

"Coming from the witch wearing a white light."

She bristled, but didn't say anything.

"I'm being truthful," Ed said. "But apparently, you can't accept my truths."

She started to reply but stopped, checking herself. "I'm in no mood. I spent the night paging through books looking for answers to the dilemma you posed to me. I'm trying to help you, Ed! I woke an hour ago with my cheek smashed against a night-terrors spell. That's just wrong. And then you are some mafia kingpin. And you think you can only be interested in me because I bespelled you. I want to go home and—"

"Then leave!"

"Really?" Her bottom lip wobbled. Was that a tear glistening at the corner of her eye? One blink and it would spill over that soft, pale cheek. Damn, she was pulling out the big guns.

And he couldn't resist.

Ed pulled her close and, despite the horrible electricity zapping at his veins, kissed her. Because he didn't know what else to do. Because he was one step away from falling apart and confessing his need for her. Because…

He hadn't meant any of those things he'd said to her. He didn't want this to end. But he didn't want to feel the pain of another woman's rejection. He'd been trying to waylay that, but he was too damned stupid when it came to emotions and relationships.

He did know he needed this intimate contact. And falling into her was a cure for any madness, even lack of sleep, betrayal and the weird mix of witchcraft and demonic magic that seemed to keep drawing them together.

She didn't relax in his embrace, but she didn't stop kissing him. He held her against him, wanting her to know he would always be gentle with her and ever respect her. And he might never get her from his heart now that she had etched a place into it.

But saying those things was too hard. He hadn't the right words for actions best performed in a moment of panic.

When their mouths parted, she said, "I will never bewitch you. Never will I use magic to win you. But if that's the way you feel about me…" She sighed and picked up her things. "Your amazing kisses are not going to change my state of mind. I have to mentally sort through everything I dug up while researching. I'm going to call you later, whether or not you like it."

He nodded, unwilling to refuse that contact and so desperately wanting to be in the kiss again. What was his problem? He'd given her good reason to turn and never want to speak to him again. Hadn't he been harsh enough with her?

But he couldn't be. The witch's rede was something like Do No Harm, and he agreed with that completely.

He held the door open as she passed through. Much as his heart twisted and his fingers ached to run through her hair while he whispered to her how much he wanted her to stay, he resisted that fall to weakness. "I can have Inego give you a ride home?"

The look she cast him told him what she thought of that idea.

"Or not," he said. "The Métro is always good transport. I've things to do. Zombie witches to track. Mafia-kingpin things to, er…sort out."

She didn't reply. He caught a palm over his heart and watched her walk away. He didn't want to lose the best thing that had entered his life in…ever. But he'd never had a good thing before, so he wasn't sure how to keep said good thing.

He touched his lips. She'd accepted his kiss even after he'd fired cruel words at her. Could she possibly care about him as much as he did her?

And that was it, wasn't it? He cared about her.

Chapter 13

Tamatha's notes from last night's research in the Archives were scattered—neatly—on the living room table. Beside them sat chunks of amethyst and quartz for clear thinking. And she'd added a hint of rosemary to her usual lemon perfume this morning for awareness. But after a few hours bent over the notes and not getting anywhere, she'd decided to distract herself from the project. A watched pot never boiled, and a brain forced to come up with a solution did best when it didn't know it was needed.

The vacuum glided over the dark-stained hardwood floors in the apartment. She glanced in the bathroom mirror as she passed by. The green face mask she'd slapped on needed to sit twenty minutes. That was about how long it took to get into all the nooks and crannies with the brush attachment.

Dancing her way down the hallway, she vacuumed up scattered lavender petals as well as rose, saffron and thyme. She hung her herbs and flowers from a double row of hemp twine strung along the hallway ceiling because it was drier there in the inner part of the building, and also, she loved the scents that infused the very walls and floor when walking through the front door.

Cleaning always put her in a good mood for reasons she would never admit to anyone else. Perhaps she'd share that detail with the witch Vika Saint-Charles, CJ's wife. Vika was a clean freak, and she also owned a business that cleaned up dead paranormals from crime scenes.

Tamatha decided she could go forever without viewing anything dead, but that thought switched her brain back to the looming elephant crowding her forebrain. A whole pack of elephants, actually. The demon Edamite Thrash, who could be more evil than she'd ever suspected. And her grandmother and her zombie coven.

She had tried to call her mother again, but she still wasn't answering. Petrina Bellerose would know what to do about this situation.

She hoped.

And after baking a chocolate cake earlier—and then eating a quarter of it—she'd finally banished the heavy dread she felt and had started to look at the situation rationally. Something did have to be done about zombie witches. And with the right information she would utilize her magic to help instead of hinder.

But what to do about Edamite Thrash and the possibility that, despite his dangerous and very mysterious lifestyle, she may be falling for him? Vika had recognized it in her, and so had CJ.

But did Ed feel the same toward her or was it as he suspected? Mere bewitchment. *Could* she enact a love spell without knowing it? Had she attracted him to her by crafty means even she hadn't been aware of? Could a love spell work as her OCD magic did—reactionary?

He had been mean to her in his office earlier in an attempt to get her to leave. And then he'd kissed her! The man had to sort out his feelings for her because he was cold one minute and hot the next.

She wouldn't let him go. She wasn't ready to do that yet. She was only just getting to know him.

"Love often," she whispered. "I could so love the crap out of you, Edamite Thrash."

Even if he were a dangerous drug dealer? Or rather, a "purveyor of essentials." He'd explained that had been about some pills he'd got for his half sister. A werewolf who didn't want to be a werewolf? So strange.

Shaking her head to sweep away the negative thoughts, she spent extra time running the vacuum along the living room ceiling to get at any cobwebs that may be forming. She had nothing against spiders, but sometimes their webs could trap negative energy.

Even over the vacuum she heard the door buzzer, and without clicking off the machine, she grabbed the doorknob and opened it to Ed. His calm expression moved into a curious head tilt. The last person she wanted to talk to right now was him. Yet also, she really wanted to see him. He'd come for her! So maybe he wasn't as ready to give up on the two of them as he'd thought he was.

And then she remembered.

"Oh!" Tamatha slammed the door shut and clicked off the vacuum. She touched her chin and the slimy green face mask slid off on her fingertip. "Oh, bother."

"Come on, Tamatha. Open the door," he teased from the other side.

"You shouldn't see me like this. I completely forgot about it!"

"What's wrong? I happen to like avocados."

Seriously? In the two seconds he'd got a look at her he'd determined as much? Oh, mercy, a woman was not supposed to let her man see her *en déshabillé* with a vacuum in hand. Or with muck on her face.

"The door isn't locked," he said.

No, it wasn't. Her fingers hovered over the lock. One twist was all it required. Too bad she hadn't a spell for vanishing face cream.

"I can simply walk in," the man on the other side of the door suggested.

Why didn't she keep this place warded against demons? Then again, she'd have to take the ward down every time she did want him to cross her threshold. Like now.

Did she really?

Oh, mercy, yes. They needed to talk. And she needed another kiss from him. To know if he was really as interested in her as she wanted him to be.

Tamatha opened the door an inch. "Let me go wash my face first."

"I'm coming in," he announced.

She stepped back from the door as it opened. Resigned to accept that there was no reversing this situation, she shrugged and offered a weak smile. Hey, at least the man was here. That was twenty times more promising than when she'd left him. When he sniffed her face, then dashed a finger over her cheek and licked it, she could have died of embarrassment.

"Avocado and honey," he said. "I like it."

"And I am mortified. Now can I go wash my face?"

He kissed her then, so quickly she hadn't time to think. The heady falling into him swept away her worries, and then when he pulled away a few bits of green were on his mouth, which he licked. "Go for it. But first, I'm sorry. I spoke irrationally in the office earlier."

"You don't want us to end?"

"I...don't. Much as we'd both be better off if we did end this thing we've started. But no, I'm not ready to give up on us yet. Or rather, I'm willing to give it a try. It's not something I've ever done with a woman before. I mean, a relationship built around trust and truth. I want to be with you, Tamatha. To be near you."

"Even with a green face?"

"Don't some witches have green faces?"

"You've been watching too many movies. I don't think green skin is a witch thing. It's more for nixies and the sidhe. I'll wash it off."

He caught her hand before she could flee. "To be totally honest, I came here with an ulterior motive. It's about the situation. I want to bring you somewhere. Show you something. Maybe then you'll understand how much I need your help."

"All right. But first things first." She rushed into the bathroom, leaving the door open behind her. Bending over the sink and splashing water on her face, she lifted her head and called, "Where do you want to bring me? It's ten in the evening."

"I thought you were a night owl?" He leaned a shoulder against the frame in the bathroom doorway.

"I am." She patted her face with a towel. Okay, fine, so she had survived that embarrassing moment and the man was still there. He hadn't fled. Nor had he laughed. And now he was looking at her sans makeup. Another brave feat on her part. She deserved some kind of award for allowing him to see her like that. "Will I need walking shoes?"

"Yes—comfortable shoes and a sweater. It's cool this evening."

She touched up her hair with a few tucks of curls here and there and patted her face with some powder while Ed curiously observed. A dash of blush and some lip balm.

When she turned to him he caught her around the waist. "I liked the green-face look. It was tasty."

Rolling her eyes, she then confessed, "You have now witnessed the process."

"The process?"

"What all women go through to try and look their best for you men. Well, and we do it for ourselves. Mostly for ourselves."

He pressed a hand over his heart. "I solemnly promise to keep the process a secret from all other males. Are you still mad at me?"

"Don't I have a right?"

"Yes. No. I wish you weren't, but I understand. I was downright mean to you."

"You were being defensive until you kissed me. But then you let me go. You run hot and then cold with the snap of fingers. You are a hard man to figure out."

"Yes, well, *mafia* is one of those words that implies evil. I'm not, Tamatha. I am good. Mostly. I do try. Call me an evil overlord with a twist." He winked and that set her heart racing. "*Upstanding* probably isn't a word you'd ever see captioned below my picture. But I'm not as CJ makes me out to be. Can we call a truce for our walk?"

"We can. And don't worry—I like to form my own opinion of people. I do still like you."

"Because you need me."

"For research, of course," she teased.

She kissed him quickly, then scampered into her bedroom. A truce wasn't necessary. She liked being with Ed. And she did trust him. She just had to learn what he was all about and then decide if she could live with the kind of person he was or if that would go against her values. Because one man's opinion—that of Certainly Jones—could be clouded.

"Is your name real?" she called as she snagged a pair of purple suede knee-high boots from the closet. She wore a pink wrap dress, and the boots went nicely with it.

"Real?"

She stuck her head out of the bedroom. "Thrash. It didn't appear on any of the genealogical records when I was researching."

"Right. No. My mother purposely never gave me a surname. Something about protecting me from witches and their spells." He winked at her. "Deeply inbred, that fear of witches."

"I get that. So it's a made-up name?"

"Don't you think it suits me? I mean, it does have a rather evil ring to it."

Putting on her bloodstone ring, she then grabbed a blue cardigan and swung it over her shoulders and headed out to meet Ed at the door. "You like that it has an evil connotation to it?"

"It can be a necessity when I need to be imposing."

"Okay. I don't get that, but as part of the truce I'll let it slide. I won't be able to trace your family line without a surname. Did your mother have one?"

"Nope." He held the front door open. "But I'll give her a call and ask after Grandfather's information if you think that will help."

"Anything might help right now. Where are we going? Does it involve pineapple gelato?"

"Actually, there will be tombstones."

Chapter 14

The Montparnasse cemetery was the second largest in Paris proper, in ranking behind Père Lachaise. Many more cemeteries once existed centuries earlier, but as the city grew—and plague spread—burial sites were moved, covered over and forgotten in favor of urban beautification and outright fear of disease. The catacombs held proof of the rampant rise of dead to the ratio of available burial grounds.

Ed held Tamatha's hand and led her through the gate that he had opened with a wave of his hand. Then he quickly closed it behind them, taking a precautionary moment to scan the street for the police. They dashed down an aisle canopied by the *shush* of ash and lime tree leaves.

He'd expected revulsion or even fear from her when he'd suggested they visit a cemetery in the dark of night. But instead she'd squealed in delight, and even now, she had taken the lead and eagerly trekked down the cobblestone pathway in those sexy purple boots. He could love a woman such as that adventurous, quirky witch.

If he knew how to love. Which he did not.

But she wasn't going to like why he'd brought her here. Why did he feel compelled to add to her already growing list of reasons to hate him? That she had a list didn't surprise him.

So he liked to keep his MO mysterious, which led to others suspecting the worst of him. It was best for the things he needed to accomplish that most did not consider him a goody-goody. One could hardly banish a murderous wraith demon from this realm if he was known to help little old ladies cross the street. So, evil overlord he must remain.

And more good work must be done. Quickly. Because if he didn't take action soon, there would be another demon death. And he couldn't live with that when the city's demons were on his watch. Mafia king? More like Keeper of Demonic Nations. The keeping-the-peace thing included looking out for his own. Most of them, anyway. Those demons who hailed from Daemonia could stay there or go back—*don't let the portal door hit you on the ass, buddy.* Which was why he employed an exorcist specifically trained for expulsions to the Place of All Demons.

He had no idea how to begin explaining this whole mess to Tamatha, so showing her had seemed the best way.

Dropping her leather shoulder bag, which she'd grabbed to bring along after he'd announced their destination, she pulled out an empty mason jar and tweezers. "You don't mind if I get some grave dirt while I'm here, do you? I'm fresh out."

He leaned against a stone sarcophagus and gestured she go right ahead. "So this is like a shopping trip for you?"

"It is!" She skipped ahead and, when she sighted something in the shadows, ducked between two stone monuments so Ed could see only her backside swaying with her movement in a slash of moonlight.

Now, that was a sight. Her ass was nicely curved and a perfect handful. And he wanted to touch it right now. Because after the sex they'd shared, he could only think to do it again. And again. And… Well, then she'd got some bad information about him, and he needed to now resurrect her positive feelings toward him and bury the suspicions so she could trust him enough to share her body with him again.

He filed down the narrow aisle between tombstones and glided his hand over her derriere. Made his horns tingle to imagine her bare skin beneath his stroking fingers. And he moaned in approval.

"Don't tell me," the witch said as she scraped moss from the base of a tombstone. "Graveyards make you horny?"

"Not particularly. But your ass in this clingy dress does it for me." She stood, her back to him, and he glided his hand around and up her stomach to hold her against him. His erection nudged her backside. "Want to make out?" He nuzzled his mouth against the base of her ear and dashed out his tongue to taste lemons.

"I thought you brought me here to show me something?"

And like that, his erection softened. Right. Straight to the bad stuff, then. Well, he wasn't going to regain his good standing in her eyes until he revealed the reasons for her to hate him. And that made so little sense he'd just go with it.

"I did want to show you something."

"We can make out, too," she offered gleefully as she screwed on the jar lid.

He quirked a hopeful brow. A make-out session with a witch gathering grave dirt under the full moon? There were some things a man could never plan for but must always be prepared for.

"Later." She tucked her find into the bag. "After we've talked."

He winced. Yeah, talking. As if that was going to make matters better?

"You probably won't be interested in kissing me after what I have to show you. Which makes this damned difficult for me. But, for good or for ill, it's got to be done. Come on, witch."

He grasped her hand and led her down the twisting aisles, following the scent he could never lose. The scent of a darkly familiar death. Toward the back of the graveyard, close to a stone wall where the crooked tombstones were small yet close and blackened with mold and time, he suddenly stopped because the scent overwhelmed him. Evil and wretched, the musty odor tainted with blood and dust instilled a burning shiver on the sigil at the base of his spine. That one was a sort of "fellow demon recognizing" mark. When he was around others of his kind it tingled. Dead ones? The burn always startled him.

"Oh my goddess, what happened here?" Tamatha stepped right onto the spot where Ed had witnessed the death. "It's fresh, not ancient as the other morbid vibrations I get as I pass through." She looked to him over a shoulder.

"This is where the friend of mine—Laurent—was slain by *Les Douze*."

She pressed her fingers to her mouth and swung away from him, backing slowly from the spot that must harbor the violent imprint of the death. He knew she'd notice it, as she had sensed the lingering remnants in his office.

"I wanted you to feel it," he said. "To know that what I've told you is real."

"There was never a moment I didn't believe you."

That gave him much more relief than it should. She believed in him. The feeling was overwhelmingly of acceptance. And he wasn't sure what to do with that. Especially coming from a witch. His witch ward didn't tingle, not even a twitch.

"I thought if I brought you here you might get a sense of the sort of magic used?"

She shook her head. "Same as what I felt in your home, only tenfold. This is vile. Malefic. It runs over my skin like corpse worms. I don't want to be here anymore."

He caught her as she tried to pass him, hugging her gently but firmly. "Please, Tamatha. It's important to me."

"I haven't told you I would help you."

Now the witch ward on his arm did shiver. "I know that."

"And you've told me nothing about this demon mafia. And besides, there is another circumstance that may keep me from helping you. Please, I need to get away from this horror."

He exhaled and released her. The witch rushed down the cobblestone path. Another circumstance? Why Certainly Jones had put into her head that he was so evil was beyond him.

And then he could understand. Witch Number Two? She must have gone crying to CJ after Ed had managed to break free from her. Had probably told the dark witch all kinds of crazy lies about Ed. Of course, an assumption of guilt, of menace, would be made before a belief of beneficence. Not that he was so good. He had done things. Things he was not proud of. And things he knew had to be done, no matter the evil. But all he'd ever offered Witch Number Two was trust and an attempt at romance.

He had assumed the worst of Tamatha initially. So he deserved her reluctance at best. At worst, her downright refusal to help.

The click of her boot heels had stopped and he could smell lemons wafting over the must and loamy scent of dying tree bark and mold. She waited for him. She'd not run away.

"Please," he said softly.

"But," he heard her whisper plainly. "My grandmother..."

"What?" He strolled up behind her. She wrung her hands together nervously. "Your grandmother?"

Her jewel gaze found his and he swallowed at sight of the tears that glistened there. His heart ached when he suspected she was hurting emotionally.

"It's something I learned going over the list of the twelve witches. I found all their names." She inhaled. "Lysia Bellerose was one of *Les Douze*. Ed, you're asking me to help you destroy my grandmother."

"I had no idea. Ah hell."

How he had managed to choose the one witch in the world who was actually related to one of The Twelve floored him. On the other hand, everything happened for a reason. And that wasn't destiny; that was the way the universe operated.

He took her in his arms and kissed her hair, her eyelids and her mouth. If he could make things better, he'd try, but he felt he had not the capacity or the magic required to do so. Who was he but an evil mafia king? A lowly demon who took great risk in even being in this beautiful witch's presence. If only he could be worthy of her.

"I'm sorry," he said. "I had no idea. I just wanted you to feel it. And now you have. Let me take you home. Sounds like we've a lot to discuss."

"We do. But take me to your home," she said and slid her hand into his. "I want to lie on your sheets and feel you on my skin. Together, we'll figure this out."

His fear of rejection was wiped out with that sweet entreaty. How had he got so lucky to meet this wondrous witch?

Tamatha preceded Ed into his apartment and dropped her things on the floor. She had told him about her grandmother, but right now, she didn't want to talk about it. His cedar scent had got into her senses, and all she wanted to do was lick him. Touch him. Press her skin against his.

He started to ask her something but she stopped him with a kiss. Running her hands down the front of his shirt, she unbuttoned it as she dropped lower. At his pants she unbuttoned and unzipped him and slid her hand inside to grip his thick erection. She rubbed the ribs with her thumb.

"I guess we'll save the talk for later," he said and lifted her in his arms and ran up the stairs with her. Tossing her gently onto the bed, he tugged off his shirt, revealing the dark array of sigils and tattoos. "Sometimes I can't figure you out, witch. You're angry with me and then you can't seem to get enough of me."

"Same with you. We're hot and cold for one another. I want all of you," she said, gesturing with a crook of her finger for him to approach the bed. "All of this darkly interesting stuff." She tapped his chest and traced a finger over a curve. Ink or a natural mark, she didn't care. "But this one looks so faint. It's as if it's disappearing."

He eyed the pale curved lines she touched over his chest. "Not disappearing. Might be a new one. I never know what they're about until they are fully formed."

"Maybe it's to do with *Les Douze*?"

"You never know." He kissed her, pushing her back on the bed and pinning down her wrists. "You're the one who started this. No talk of that now. I've got something for you." He rubbed his erection, which had escaped his pants, against her thigh. "Want it?"

She twisted out of his grip and shimmied down alongside him to lick the head of his thickness. Grasping the sturdy column and squeezing, she tugged him onto the bed to kneel while she sucked and licked and teased him with her tongue. Ed's fingers ran through her hair and pulled it from the pins she'd used to put it up. She wasn't undressed, but that didn't matter. Her nipples were so tight every slip of her dress over them increased the crazy-sexy need to let go.

There was something about taking a man in her mouth that satisfied her need for control. Because he was completely at her mercy and would say and do anything to make her continue. The skim of his gloved hand over her shoulder and down to clasp her breast through her dress warranted a wardrobe adjustment.

Kneeling, she untied her dress at the waist and unwrapped it. Ed pulled the bra straps down, and before she could spin it around to unclasp, he sucked her breast into his hot, wet mouth. His tongue teased her firmly and his fingers crept lower, parting her legs.

She wanted him inside her now. And always. He was like a new drug she couldn't get enough of. She didn't do drugs, but she could do Ed over and over.

Directing his exquisitely ribbed penis inside her, she lowered herself slowly onto his length and grasped him at the back of the neck and with her other hand ran her fingers through his hair. He continued to lick her breasts as she rocked slowly, deeply, indulging in his unique design and thickness. Every movement tugged at her apex, teasing the climax to the fore.

Ed swore and gripped her at the hips. His body tensed, the muscles at the back of his neck tightening. He felt alive in her hands and at her skin. Electric with imminent orgasm.

With a gentle stroke of his finger over her clit, she was coaxed into a rousing orgasm that matched his shudders, and they came together. She wrapped her arms about his shoulders and nuzzled her face into his hair as she panted and gasped in elation.

The thunder of his heartbeats against her chest matched

the fierce pounding of hers. And she clutched him tightly, driving in her fingernails at his shoulders, wanting to push him in deeper, to own him, claim him. To make sure he knew that he was hers.

"This isn't bewitchery," she said on a gasp.

"Yes, I know. It's real."

And with that declaration, the two of them shuddered again, coming softly, fiercely.

Chapter 15

Ed lay on his back, his eyes closed, but Tamatha knew he was awake. Exhausted from great sex, as was she. She trailed her fingertips down his neck, tracing the feather that rippled gently, and then along his shoulder where curls and x's and what looked like maroon flame darkened his skin. Across his dark-haired chest and over his heart she studied the faint markings she'd noticed earlier.

"How will you know what this one means?" she asked, tapping above his nipple where the dark hairs barely disguised the tracing.

"I'm never sure what they mean until they are complete. Sometimes I have to have a demonologist interpret them for me."

"Isn't that someone who studies demons? Like me?" she asked sweetly.

"Yes, but can you interpret demonic sigils?"

"No, but perhaps with more study. Would you oblige me?"

"Study all you like, witch."

She was bothered less and less by his propensity to label her witch. It was no longer the accusatory epithet he'd once spit at her, but rather an endearment.

She slid her fingers over the ridged muscles on his abdomen, and there beneath the dark curls about his penis were faint lines. No sigils on his penis or testicles. The ridges were interesting enough as it was. Man, did she appreciate those ridges.

Kissing the crown of his semierect penis, she then ventured her discovery trail down a thigh. On the thigh closest to her, the dark markings looked similar to the tribal tattoos she had seen on human biker types, though she felt sure this meant something different than "it looks cool" or "it makes me look tough."

"You don't want to know about those," he said. "Ah hell. Tamatha, I've killed when it was necessary to save lives. And when I make a kill, the remnants of that kill are blackened into my skin. I feel the mark burn into me as if I were experiencing a six-hour tattoo session in seconds. Hurts like fuck."

Those were some thick lines, and…a lot of them. She wasn't going to overthink it. And then she couldn't help but think only of it. He had killed. Necessary kills? Was killing *ever* necessary? She didn't think so.

"To save the lives of others?" she quietly wondered.

"Yes." He didn't seem to want to elaborate.

What about killing zombie witches who were killing demons? That was different. Maybe. She had nothing to compare to the instances that had marked Ed's thigh. And she wasn't sure she wanted the full explanation or even details. Her curiosity could only take her so far before she drowned in fascination or fled from revulsion.

And yet if she agreed to help him, she would also be

killing. Twelve witches. But was it considered killing if they were already dead?

Ed sat up and slid off the bed. Standing before her, his hands to his hips, he looked like a tattooed god, a rockabilly hero, a motorcycle gangster, perhaps even an evil overlord. Sexy in his dark and dangerous skin. She couldn't get enough of him.

So she was attracted to a man who would kill? Who was she?

"It's apparent there are things about me that disturb you," he said.

She started to protest, but then couldn't force herself to make up a lie to soften the fact that, indeed, he was right about her being disturbed.

"I thought I was jumping in full circle when I took you to the cemetery. But that was outside of me. The real truth, what I really am? I want to show you," he said. "It's probably the stupidest thing I've ever done, but I feel as though I can trust you."

"Ed, whatever you want to say to me, I'll listen with an open mind and heart. The thing about you killing? Yes, it disturbs me, but give me some time to process it. I believe you only act for the good of others."

"You do?"

She nodded and that sexy smile of his lured her forward to kiss him.

"Call me crazy, but I have to do this. This is me." He stood back and spread out his arms. "Full demon."

"Oh." She sat up, crossing her legs and pushing her hair over her shoulder. "Yes, I'd like to see that."

"Not for your fascination or study," he cautioned, "but because I want to be open with you. To not have secrets."

"I understand."

"Really? Because this is not like me showing up at your door to find you with avocado on your face."

She grasped his hand, offering him a reassuring squeeze. "I do understand. But allow me some fascination. I am studying your species." She let her eyes wander to his erection. "There's so much about you that I like to admire."

He chuckled. "All right, then. But you have to know I'm doing this because I need you to trust me. And… I want you to see the real me, horns and all. Here goes all the marbles." He tugged off the fingerless gloves she had come to accept as a part of him. "Be careful you don't touch my hands when my thorns are out."

She nodded dutifully. And though she was eager and felt like clasping her hands before her in expectant glee, she did her best to contain that giddy curiosity and so shoved her hands under her thighs to watch as her lover transformed before her.

Horns grew from the nubs at his temples, thickening and gleaming as if hematite. They curled slightly over his ears and then abruptly curled back toward his face and upward in about a two-foot stretch. They looked heavy and deadly, like something a matador must fear.

A shrug of his shoulders sifted a darkness over his skin. The diluted, inky coloring spilled down his arms and the sides of his torso and from hips to midthigh. All the sigils and tattoos seemed to darken even more, becoming fathomless, like entries into his very being. The dark pigment hardened and must have been of the same material as his horns. His shoulders shifted slightly, pointing up in smaller versions of horns, as did his hips.

At his knuckles the thorns he had warned her about zinged out like tiny claws. And as Tamatha drew her gaze over his figure, noting the hardened leatherlike skin and horns—even his erection looked thicker and tougher—she picked up the scent of sulfur. And it wasn't offensive, but rather sweet, almost cloying.

Red eyes looked upon her. He was mostly human in form, save for horns and leathery skin, though his center and torso and front and back were yet merely skin sans the dark hairs she loved to run her fingers through. She peeked over the edge of the bed. Regular feet; no hooves. But they were blackened and thorned on the toes, as well.

"This is me." His voice was the same but not. Huskier, deeper and perhaps a little hollow. "Horns and all."

She sat up on her knees and inched closer to the edge of the bed. "Can I touch?"

"I would expect nothing less from you."

He held his hands back and away from his body as she moved forward and— The first thing she wanted to touch was the horns at his temples, but she remembered his warning about how that would make him horny. She'd save that for last, because this form did not offend her or make her want to run from him. He was beautiful.

The hard skin on his shoulders felt cool under her touch, like armor, yet it was pliable and moved like skin. From the border where that armor ended and formed into skin, black veins traced under the surface and tangled with the demonic sigils, giving his unarmored skin a virtual armor appearance.

Down his belly she stroked then grasped his penis. He gasped. And she wondered, "A little bigger?"

"Never measured in this form."

"I think it is. Almost as big as these."

Now she dared reach up and touched the base of one horn. It was slick and glossy, and ribbed as his penis. The black horn curved gracefully before dipping and jutting abruptly forward and up. She glided her fingers about and around and up.

Ed sighed against her cheek. "You know what that does to me?"

"Makes you horny." She kissed him quickly, then stepped onto the floor and gave his backside a once-over. "You've a tail!"

The tail waggled, though it was very un-demon-like. And it had black fur on it.

"I did tell you my father was werewolf," he said. "That's about all I got from him."

"It's so cute!"

"Tamatha."

"Sorry. Not cute. Nothing about your demonic form is remotely adorable." She slid back onto the bed and tapped his muscled stomach. "You are powerful and deadly and look very, very dangerous. So manly."

"Then why do you say that as if it's a tease? Do I not strike fear in your quivering witchy heart?"

"Should you?"

He shook his head. "No. I'm glad you didn't scream at sight of me." He slid a knee onto the bed and, with an exhalation and shake of his body, shed his demonic form, coming back to his human shape in but two breaths. "This is much better, yes?" He kissed her. "Thanks for not freaking."

"Horns and a tail don't scare me." She reached for his hand, but he shook his head. The thorns were yet visible. "Hmm..." She tapped her lower lip. "There must be an antidote to the poison contained in your thorns, yes?"

"Maybe?"

"I'll have to do some research. An antidote might be something to have handy if we are dating."

"Are we dating?"

"Yes, we are, like it or not."

"I adore you, witch." He pulled her closer and nuzzled his face into her hair, kissing the lemony warmth. "You really don't mind the horns?"

"They're sexy, actually. Do you think we could have sex with you in that form? Would it be dangerous to me?"

"Only my thorns," he said. "You just want to take my demon dick for a test drive."

"There is that."

"So that's why you like me, eh? I've got a big package."

"It's sizable no matter what form you're in." She reached for the package in question. "But I like your mind, too. And your quest to keep the peace. That is honorable. And you are handsome as sin. Now, I have a secret to reveal to you."

"Something more devastating than your horribly sweet avocado face?"

"You're never going to let that one go, are you?"

"It's all I've got. You're perfect in every other way."

"Maybe not so powerful as you think." She worried her lip a moment, then blurted, "Ed, I'm not the most powerful witch in Paris."

"Yes. So?"

He acted as though he'd known it all along. Tamatha eyed him curiously. "I mean, I'm probably not even top ten, if you want to get technical. That day you had me brought to your office I wanted to do anything to get to see you again, so I lied and hoped you'd never find out."

"Sweetness, I knew from the moment you stood before me."

"Then why did you let me work for you?"

"Because I felt the same way. Despite my initial reluctance to work with a witch, I didn't want to let you walk away from me."

"What did a witch do to you?"

"Why do you think it's that?"

"Because you're a strong, smart man. A healthy caution for witches is one thing, but you got it bad. So that makes me suspect a bad romance."

Ed exhaled.

"Please tell me? You've shown me your outsides. Let me have a peek inside. Promise I will listen with an open mind."

He kissed her and hugged her but was careful not to touch her with his thorns. "I did date a witch two years ago. I didn't know she was a witch and thought my demonic nature was secret from her. I use the excuse of birth defects for my horn nubs."

"And that works?"

"Human women are much quicker to believe that than the possibility that real demons exist."

"I suppose."

"One once actually made the guess that they were body modifications. Implanted. You know, some humans have things implanted beneath their skin to create art or because they're stupid?"

"That creeps me out. So the witch you dated didn't know you were demon? I find that hard to believe."

"She did. But I didn't know she knew until she'd drugged me and let the magic fly. She tried to enslave me." He sat beside her, exhaling heavily as he ran a hand through his hair. "For three days she worked her magic on me. It was torture, literally. I think her magic finally gave out and I managed to break free. It was hell."

"Oh, Ed. I didn't know. That's terrible. So you, uh…"

"What? You think I killed her?"

"I suppose the torture would have justified it."

"Never. Nothing justifies murder, Tamatha. A killing made to stop evil to prevent more deaths? That's doable.

It can be argued it was a means to save others. But still..." He stroked the dark tribal mark on his thigh. "Impossible to justify. But someone's got to do it, so I guess that means it's me."

She tilted her head onto his shoulder.

"Anyway, after her magic failed, I got out of there. Left her. I haven't heard from her since, though I suspect she might have given Certainly Jones an earful. So you see? Not a big fan of your kind." He turned his back toward her. "One of the feathers is chained still, yes?"

She looked closely, and yes, a feather was wrapped in chain. "Oh, Ed." She held him. "That's because she tried to enslave you? I'm so sorry. This whole situation with the zombie witches killing demons. You've lived such horrors. I can't imagine how hard this must be for you."

"You know something?" he asked softly.

"What?"

"You holding me like this makes up for it all. I don't know how to love another person, but you make me feel like I could learn."

"Everyone is capable of love. And it will come when you least expect it."

"That's the same thing my brother said to me the other night. What about you and your Love Often? It must come to you all the time."

"It does, because I am open to love." She spread her hand over his chest where the faint sigil had begun to form. "Open yourself to the possibility."

"I think I can do that." With a heavy exhalation he tilted up her chin and studied her gaze before speaking. "I understand I'm asking a lot of you to go after *Les Douze* if one of them could be your grandmother."

"There's no doubt, Ed. One of the twelve was Lysia Bellerose."

"Do all the women in your family have the same last name?"

"Yes." She stood and toed the dress on the floor. "And should we marry, we keep the family name. We're not so keen on giving a man so much power as to take his name." She shuddered, and Ed caught the minute movement.

Yes, a powerful witch, he reiterated mentally. Perhaps more powerful than she believed herself. And he honored that strength. Now to use it without tainting their fragile bond. A bond trust may have grown closer when he had revealed himself to her, outside and in. He hadn't planned to tell her about that experience. It had simply felt necessary. Now that he had, he was feeling unguarded, not exactly standing square and confident as he should be.

Open to the possibility of love? It still seemed out of his grasp.

Yet he could only imagine what Tamatha must be feeling now he knew the witch was her grandmother.

"Do you think your grandmother likes wandering around a zombie?" he asked.

She looked up from gathering her abandoned clothes that were neatly folded near the bed (OCD magic at its best). "I never thought of it like that. I haven't seen these zombie witches. How can you be sure they are dead?"

"They were burned in the eighteenth century. I'd call that dead."

"Right. Sorry. It's hard to grasp, you know? I wish my mother would return my call." She pulled on her bra and panties. "There could be implications."

"You think if you cast a spell against your grandmother...?"

"Yeah, I'm not sure. I might have to ask Certainly about this one. That is, *if* I agree to help you on this. I'm not going to commit until I talk to Mom. Is that okay?"

"I am thankful you are considering it. I don't know who else I can ask. There are other witches in Paris, but—I don't want to work with any witch. I want you."

She shimmied her shoulders. "Good answer. I'd be jealous if you asked someone else. And so you know, Ed, I promise you—" she crossed her heart "—I will never enslave you as that witch did."

She'd crossed her heart. That meant so much. He nodded. "Sounds good to me. Back to the plan."

"Do we have a plan? I need to find out who is behind this," she said as she pulled on her wrap dress and searched the bedroom floor for her boots. She picked up his gloves and tossed them to him. "Like I said when I was in the cemetery, I suspected the magic was malefic. Not even dark witches will go there."

"Then who would do such a thing as to raise a coven of long-dead witches?" he asked, pulling on the gloves.

"And why?" she added.

"Well, we know the why," he said, slipping on a shirt. "If they are going after the demons who accused them."

"Yes, but the one who raised them must have that goal, yes?" She began to button up his business shirt, a crisp white number, and he allowed her. "So someone—living—wants revenge against demons in general or just those who accused the witches. That would probably make the someone an offspring of one of the dozen. Or possibly a contemporary, seeing as how long witches can live."

"Do you have a list of those who accused *Les Douze*?" he asked.

"Yes. I found one in the Archives yesterday. What is the name of your relative you mentioned was in the denizen that is being targeted? Because Thrash was not on the list."

"That is a moniker I have used since forever. We demons sometimes take different names for anonymity and—"

"Drama?"

"Nothing wrong with a little evil-overlord drama, is there?"

"Edamite Thrash. That's drama, all right. Is your first name even Edamite?"

"It is. My mother has always been simply Sophie. And since she never married my father, neither she nor I felt compelled to use his surname."

"So there are no family names in the demon species?"

"There are. I'm just not sure what ours is or was." Ed nodded. "I'll give Sophie a call and ask her. Though I'm not sure she'll answer. She and my father are in hiding. She's been off my radar for over a year."

"You two aren't close?"

"We don't hate one another."

Which didn't particularly mean close, either. She sensed it was a sensitive subject for him.

"Probably the witch names are more important in this case," she said. "In order to track them to a possible summoner. Though if we want to nail down possible targets, then we should figure out the demons, as well. I think this could only be a spell cast by a warlock."

"Ian Grim?" Ed immediately posited, as he gestured she leave the top two buttons undone on his shirt. "That's the only warlock I'm aware of, and I know for a fact he's out of town."

"You and Grim are friends?"

"No, but I do know his woman, Dasha. I see her on occasion because I provide her with—er..."

"Essentials you have purveyed?"

"Exactly. But it's to keep her alive when Ian is not

around. Trust me. Dasha mentioned something about Grim venturing through Russia for the summer."

"There are warlocks all over the place. You just have to know where to look."

"And you do?" He bowed his forehead to hers and kissed her nose.

"A lot of answers can be found in books. Sounds like I'll be perusing the pages again this afternoon."

"I wish I could help you, but I suspect the Archives are off-limits to anyone who does not work there. And even more so to one who heads a demon mafia."

"You have to have a badge to get past security," she said and then hugged him. "You're not an evil person. I think Certainly has some bad information. But it doesn't matter."

"It matters to me what you think of me."

"Then you're good, because I adore you. So what are your plans for today? What does an evil overlord do all day?"

He chuckled and picked up his suit coat, and they strolled down to the kitchen, where Tamatha collected her shoulder bag. She intended to go straight to the Archives.

"I've got scouts at the cemetery, keeping an eye out for the witches. And I've a little snafu I'm tidying up over in the Bois de Boulogne. Has to do with humans and Ouija boards and some particularly mischievous incorporeal demons. Sometimes those damned boards really work."

"Oh, I know that. You need any help?"

"No, got it covered. But you'll keep me updated on your list making?"

"I will. And you'll call me after you talk to your mother?"

"Right. So here are the names of the two demons who have died." Ed pulled a notepad from a kitchen drawer and scribbled on it. "I don't know if they are the first two the witches have killed. I could have missed others." He tore off the page and handed it to her. "I'll be thinking of you all day."

"Me, too." Tamatha kissed him, then placed her palm over his chest. "And remember—stay open to the possibilities."

"With you I believe all things are possible."

Chapter 16

Tamatha looked over the list of twelve witches who had been burned alive on August 25, 1753. Lysia Bellerose was the third on the list. It was not alphabetical, nor could it possibly be in order of rank. Or so she assumed. She'd called her mother again and left a message, hoping Petrina could shed some light on her grandmother's life. And death.

But with the list she could trace offspring and perhaps even lovers. Whoever had raised the coven from the dead could be anyone associated with *Les Douze*. Though they must possess powerful magic.

"The most powerful witch in Paris," she whispered as she sat back in the velvet chair, kicked off her heels to let them straighten on the floor below the table and pulled up her legs. "Certainly not me. But who? A warlock? How many warlocks currently live in Paris?"

She had heard of Ian Grim. And Zoe Guillebeaux's

father was a warlock. She couldn't recall his name. That could be an excellent next step. Narrow it down to warlocks and then match that list to the list of relations and friends associated with *Les Douze*.

She glanced to the maplewood cuckoo clock that CJ kept wound and dusted. The woodwork was stained black and two ravens carved above the timepiece cawed over their shoulders. One looked directly at her. Which reminded her of Ed and his ravens. His feather sigils on his skin had moved as if real under her touch. And when he'd been fully demon she could only admire him. She'd thought that first night she'd run into Ed that a full moon would bring family and challenge. And had it ever.

Tapping her lip, she sighed and then remembered… She pulled the list of the two dead demons he'd given her from her purse. More names to help in her research quest.

"It's only been two hours," she muttered. "I'm going to need lots more tea."

But first, she texted Ed that she was researching warlocks. She wondered how he was faring, and then her mind drifted again to last night. How trusting for him to have shifted before her. And fascinating. Truly, she found Ed in demon shape sexy. And not at all frightening. Save for those thorns he always warned her about. The ones on his toes must completely recede when in human form because he'd not been worried about hurting her with those when they had sex.

"An antidote," she said suddenly and got up to head into the demon room. "A foray into something else," she decided, knowing when she focused on something too intensely it never came to her. Distraction was always the best cure for finding anything. As well, having an antidote to Ed's thorns could be something she would like to keep handy.

On the way to the demon room CJ waylaid her. He carried a metal bat and wore a catcher's glove. "Want to help?" he asked.

"What's up?"

"Something got out in the demon room last night. An imp."

"Yes, I want to help. Do I need something like a baseball cap?"

"This will do." He tugged a long steel shaker of salt from his back pocket and slapped it into her hand. "I'll distract and attempt to catch the critter. You salt and exorcise. Can you do that?"

"Depends on where I'm sending it. I've not the skill to expel to Daemonia."

"Nothing so demanding. Just back in the book from which it escaped."

A half hour later, CJ closed the book *Lesser Imps* and called teatime. Tamatha sat on the floor near a scatter of books that had been disheveled when CJ had leaped to catch the naked and giggling teddy bear–sized imp. The books on the floor snapped to attention and found positions on their respective shelves.

Blowing away a strand of hair and setting the saltshaker aside, she let her eyes wander over the book spines and gasped when she saw the title *Demonic Breeds and Their Attributes*. Perfect.

Ten minutes later, she had found the section that detailed the corax demon. The text had been written in the sixteenth century and used *f*'s for the *s*'s and had a lot of *thyne*s and *thee*s. Ancient texts gave her a giggle. A very detailed drawing looked only a little like Ed's demon form. But it did get his ribbed penis and thorns right.

And it included an antidote to counteract the poison from the demon's thorns.

She tugged out her phone and typed in the list of ingredients. There were only three, but one of them would prove difficult to obtain.

"Oh, I can't make that." She slumped back against the bookshelves.

The main ingredient in the antidote? A ground corax demon's thorn.

This time the frenzied call from Inego led Ed to the rue Clotilde behind the Pantheon. Not in a cemetery. And too damn close to public houses and streets. Even set back from the boulevard Saint-Michel, the mausoleum attracted lines of tourists, who filed in and out to peer at the lackluster tombs of famous past Parisians. Ed avoided the crowds and tracked the scent of dead witch down a narrow alley that wended into a courtyard lined on both sides by tall hornbeam.

A calico cat mewled and scampered out of his way. Cats never did seem to like him much. He hissed at the retreating feline and then sniffed the air. The scent of death had suddenly vanished.

Ed spun and tracked the retreating cat. Could it have been…?

"A familiar?"

He rushed after the cat, but it dodged under the hornbeam. Making a leap, Ed landed the side of the shrub, grabbing the end of the cat's tail. Wild hisses and claws went at him as he pulled the critter out from under the scratchy shrubbery. Claws cut into his skin, drawing blood.

"You mangy beast!" He let the thing go and it scrambled under the hedge.

Ed turned and sat against the wall of thick, glossy hornbeam, inspecting the cuts that had gone through his shirt. The white linen was stained black with his blood. Never a drop of red. He'd always been cautious not to fight or do anything that might result in his own bloodshed when near humans.

He sensed the skin healing, but nothing would save this shirt.

"They're damned dead witches!" came a hiss from the other side of the hedge.

"What?" Ed turned but couldn't see through the thick shrubbery. "Who's that?"

"I'm the cat, you asshole. You gotta watch it. Almost broke my tail with your grabby hands. Idiot demon."

"Are you a familiar?"

"Well, *duh*. Ouch. This hedge is scratchy."

"Come to this side and we'll talk."

"Really? 'Cause you know the only reason I've a human voice is because I've shifted from cat form."

"Right, but— Oh." Which meant the guy was naked. Familiars shifted much differently than he did. They never retained their clothing because, well, cats didn't wear clothing. One demonic bonus he should be thankful for. "You stay on that side. I'm Edamite Thrash."

"I know who you are, asshole. I've tracked you through the city before. It's what I do. Prowl and observe. Name is Thomas. And you are after dead witches, right?"

"Right. Do you work for them?"

"Hell no. I don't allow witches to use me for the demon-summoning thing. That's crass. And messy. But I can smell those damned witches a league away. Nasty!"

"Were you following one? Until now I've assumed they were contained in the Montparnasse cemetery."

"Yeah? Well, one got out. But I lost her. One minute she was there, the next…poof."

"She just disappeared?"

"Like Houdini. Why are you after those smelly witches?"

"They're killing demons."

"Nothing wrong with that."

If demons hated witches, familiars hated demons on an equal level.

"If they are able to escape what I had assumed were the bounds of the cemetery, that can't be good for anyone. You know what will happen when humans see a zombie witch?"

"Chaos," the cat said. "I'd offer help, but I don't have a clue, man. You need to talk to Ian Grim."

"He's out of town. You know any other warlocks in the area?"

"Pierre Guillebeaux, but he's off-kilter in the head most of the time. Working on some whacked time-travel non-sense. There's Arius, but that warlock is one nasty case. Walks around in one of those stupid frock coats from an-other time."

A warlock wearing clothing from another time period? Generally that was the case if they had hailed from such a time. Which would make the warlock old enough to have worn frock coats. Perhaps around the eighteenth cen-tury, when the witches had been burned. That could be his witch. "Who is it?"

"What's in it for me?"

Ed couldn't imagine what to offer a cat shifter. "I'm fresh out of catnip. Sorry."

"Asshole." The shrub shuffled and Thomas huffed in resignation. "Name's Arius Pumpelché. But I don't know where to find that one. Rather, I do, but I value my fur. Talk later, asshole."

And with a disturbance in the hornbeam, and an abrupt meow, the cat scampered off.

Ed pulled out his phone and saw the text from Tamatha. She was researching warlocks and an antidote. In reply, he texted the warlock's name.

* * *

"'Arius Pumpelché'?" Tamatha read Ed's text. "Never heard of him. Or her. With a pompous name like that, must be a man."

The scent of cinnamon tea preceded CJ's entrance into the witch room, where Tamatha had returned to her desk neatly covered with her notes. He set down the tray and poured two cups. She looked up to see he was eyeing her fiercely.

"No," she said in reply to his unspoken but duly felt question. "I have not broken it off with Ed."

"Didn't ask."

"I felt your burning question," she said, sipping the perfect brew. If the man hadn't such a talent with tea, she would—well, she would nothing. He was her boss and she did like CJ. And chasing down imps? It did not get cooler than that. "Sit down, will you?"

CJ landed in the chair opposite her. He poured his own tea and sipped, waiting for her to speak. The man had once been possessed by a war demon, as well as other hideous sorts, including grief, pain and chaos. But one would never guess he was so strong as to endure such a trial from his gentle demeanor. Though she knew he could take out a tribe of vampires with a simple tap of his left finger against one of the powerful spell tattoos on his body.

Tamatha pushed her phone aside, on which she'd been taking down notes, and leaned her elbows onto the table. "Did you know there is a coven of dead witches roaming the streets of Paris?"

"Dead witches?" The man's dark brow arched.

"Zombie witches, to be exact. At least that's what Ed calls them. He's been following them and is determined to ensure they don't harm any more demons."

"Any *more*? That would imply— What's going on, Tamatha? And do I need to bring this before the Council?"

"Oh, no, CJ, you can't. This is something Ed is handling." He being the mafia king or evil overlord, which was a moniker she felt sure he used for street cred. "I don't think he'd like it if I brought in the Council. Besides, you know them. They never get involved."

"Yes, they observe." He sipped his tea. "Is this dangerous?"

"The tea or the witches?"

He smirked.

"I suspect so. They are *Les Douze*."

The dark witch placed both hands, palms down, on the table. His look was so serious, again, Tamatha felt his question.

"I have to help him," she replied. "My grandmother was one of The Twelve. It's a weird coincidence that when Ed was looking for a witch to help him, it happened to be me, someone related to one of the dead witches."

"Coincidence? Not with Thrash."

"CJ, you're going to have to put aside your obvious distrust for the man so I can discuss this with you. He's not like most demons."

"And what are most demons like?"

Her shoulders dropped and she blew out a breath. "I don't know. My studies are so new. I know very few. Cinder is the only other demon I know, and he's not even demon anymore. He transformed to vampire years ago, thanks to Parish. But I do believe demons have gotten a bad rap. Not all are evil."

"I know that. But do allow me my prejudices against demons after having had a dozen trapped within me for months after returning from Daemonia."

He'd been on a spell-collecting adventure and shouldn't have been there in the first place. "Yes, well, you did go there of your free will. Not like Daemonia is a recommended travel destination."

"Sometimes a man's gotta do—" he waved a dismissive hand between them "—whatever. I'd never try to justify my stupid acts of indiscretion."

"Did a witch tell you things about Ed? Is that why you've such a bad opinion of him?"

"You mean Paisley Burns?"

She nodded. Ed hadn't given her a name, but she could assume that was the witch who had tortured him.

"She was a victim, Tamatha. Thrash had almost killed her."

"Really?" Tamatha placed her hand on his. "Was that before or after she enslaved and tortured him for three days?"

"Oh?"

"She didn't tell you that part?"

The dark witch shook his head and took a sip of tea. She couldn't blame him for forming an opinion based on the witch's story. Which, apparently, had been a story altered to make her appear the victim when really Ed could have died at her hands.

"Doesn't matter," Tamatha offered. "I trust him. Your opinion, while I value it, isn't necessary."

"I had only Paisley's story on which to base my opinion. You believe she really did try to enslave him? Then I will reserve my judgment on the man." CJ stretched his hand across the table and tapped her phone. "What's that name?"

"Arius Pumpelché. Warlock. You know of him?"

"I do. Do you want to hear my opinion on her, or would you prefer to ignore that, as well?"

Certainly was certainly laying it on thick. But she could handle him. "Her?"

"You've heard of Ian Grim, I'm sure."

She nodded. "That warlock has been around since the

seventeenth century. But he didn't go warlock until he decided to keep his current girlfriend, Dasha, alive after she'd been beheaded by the guillotine during the French Revolution."

"Yes. Keeping dead things alive is a grave crime against both the Light and the Dark. Arius Pumpelché puts Grim to shame on the scale of Bad Things Warlocks Do. She was banished from the mortal realm after an altercation with demons and witches. Necromancy, actually. She'd tried to bring dead witches back to life."

Tamatha straightened. That sounded like the warlock in question.

"Fortunately, she failed and was exiled to Daemonia. I didn't realize she was back in Paris. How did she get out of Daemonia? Is she in the city?"

"I don't know. It's a name Ed sent me. I don't know how he got it, but we both suspect it must be a warlock who summoned *Les Douze*. Who else could summon a dozen witches who were burned at the stake three centuries ago? And if she's attempted it once before?"

"Yes." He rapped his fingers on the table. "But if someone had summoned dead witches, the warlock would need to be in the city, near the place where he or she summoned the witches. And if Arius is in town, the Council needs to be made aware. You're sure I can't help you with this?"

"I'm not even sure what this is yet. I'm still researching. I know that the demons *Les Douze* once enslaved were the ones who accused them, and now it seems those witches are going after those demons' family. Which might explain how Arius fits in. I just got his—er, her—name, so I'm going to do some more research."

"Is Ed's family involved with *Les Douze*?"

"Why do you ask?"

CJ shrugged. "It's no coincidence you and Ed have been

brought together. Your grandmother is one of *Les Douze*. That would lead me to suspect one of Ed's relatives could have been one of the accusing demons."

"Really?"

"It makes weird sense on the greater scale of the universal explanation of things. You two were drawn together for a reason. Maybe the universe is pushing you toward that. I have a bad feeling about this, Tamatha. Sounds like you and Ed might be tied together in a manner that's not necessarily going to result in good news for the two of you. One of you is not going to make it out of this alive."

"That's quite a feeling."

"It's extreme. I'm sorry—I shouldn't guess at things. I am not psychic, nor do I portend futures. But I maintain my belief that Ed is not good for you."

"He's not a mafia king. And you said you were going to reserve judgment."

"Does it matter? I'm only concerned what your involvement with him could bring. Tamatha, I care about you. Both Vika and I do. We don't want you to get hurt."

"I'm a big girl and a powerful witch."

"You are. On the same level as I am."

"Oh, I wouldn't say that."

"I would. You're too humble about your skills. You sent that imp back into the book *like that*."

"It was just an imp."

"Not many witches would have an expulsion spell to hand and be able to react so quickly. If you won't accept my help, you must at the very least keep me apprised of the situation."

"Trust me, I will. And it's not that I don't want your help, CJ. I'm just not sure yet what help I require. And if you did help, that would require you work alongside Ed, so there is that."

"There is that," he agreed. "But if this gets out of hand, innocents could be harmed."

"We both understand that, which is why I've been ignoring my work today and focusing on this."

"Consider this your work," he said. "Organizing dusty old grimoires can wait. I had better put on another pot of tea. You drink whiskey at all?"

She shook her head and laughed. "I'm not much for alcohol, only the occasional glass of wine. Though I wouldn't refuse croissants if the doorman heads out on break later."

"You got it. So can I ask? How did you and Thrash get together in the first place?"

"We bumped into one another in the alley and I bound him with a spell. Then he sent his minions after me because he thought I was the most powerful witch in Paris."

Certainly's brow rose measurably.

"I know. And he knew. But…you know."

He smirked again. "I guess I do. Talk to you later. Uh, the warlock stuff is down there." He pointed to a particularly dark corner of the room. "Do protect yourself with a white light before touching any of the volumes. And if you can turn off the OCD magic, that would be wise."

"Thanks, CJ."

"Promise me you won't try to contact Arius without my coming along?"

She shrugged. "If she's in Paris, I'll let you know."

Finishing her tea first, Tamatha then approached the dark corner and knelt before the lowest shelf. The books smelled musty and of something rotted. Shadows and fear, perhaps.

Shaking out her shoulders, she closed her eyes and drew up a white light, imagining it spread from the crown of her head and down over her body until it tucked under her toes. There was no way to control her OCD magic. She'd hope for the best.

When she opened her eyes a pulsing green glow had manifested around the shelf of books. She tapped the spine of a red leather volume, but it stopped glowing. She moved on to the next. The blue-bound volume didn't inspire her and it also stopped glowing. The third spine of scuffed brown leather sent a chill up her arm when she touched it. The glow burst so that she cringed back to avoid any residual magic.

"This is the one."

She tugged it out and carried it back to the table, opening it to a random page. The page revealed a sketch of a smiling woman with black hair tugged back in a bun and a prominent nose. She looked positively puritan. In elaborate calligraphy, the name scribed beneath the sketch was Arius Pumpelché.

A green glow again emanated from within the pages and a faint scent of smoke teased the air. The image turned up its head and looked at Tamatha. She quickly slammed the volume shut.

"Shit."

A scurry of shivers raced over her skin and she rubbed her upper arms. Muttering a reinforcement spell, she hardened the white light and formed a virtual shell about her body. It was invisible and she could easily move, but she felt the heavy weight of it against her skin.

Better encumbered by protection than not.

Pacing before the table, she summoned her courage and again opened the book. A drop of black ink that she hadn't previously noticed dribbled across the page of tiny scrawls...and began to write.

That wasn't unusual for the magical volumes she had seen in the Archives. But what was unusual was the message: "You've found me. And now I have found you."

Chapter 17

Ed's mother, Sophie, was always elated to hear from him. They talked perhaps three or four times a year. Last year she had disappeared with her lover Colin Sauveterre, who was Ed and Kir's father. There had been a big stink in pack Valoir right around the time Colin had hooked up with Sophie (before Ed had been born). Kir had grown up believing his father had left the pack because of another woman. A demoness. So Kir had always hated demons.

But that wasn't the real story.

Kir had only recently learned that Colin had been forced to leave the pack after Kir and Blyss's mother, Madeline, had an affair with the pack principal. All Colin had wanted was love. And he had found it with Sophie months *after* leaving the pack and his wife.

"So there," Ed had wanted to say to his brother. But he had not because he valued what little relationship he had with Kir.

And he valued the connection he had with his mother. Sophie had become addicted to V—drinking vampire blood straight from their veins to get a high from the human blood rushing within—and had over the years grown distant. Now she reassured Ed she was clean and she and Colin were starting anew. But she needed to stay out of Paris. Sophie was a wanted demon. The enforcement team Kir had formerly headed while in pack Valoir had wanted to deport Sophie to Daemonia for her crimes against vampires, but Kir had helped her to escape that fate before he himself had been banished. Should she return to Paris? Pack Valoir would go after her and exile her immediately.

"Your grandfather?" Sophie said, after he'd explained to her about the twelve zombie witches and the deaths of the demons he suspected were related to their enslaved ancestors. "His name was Rascon."

"And a surname?"

"That was just it, Ed. I'm sorry. But I do recall some of the others in the Libre denizen that accused The Twelve. Let me think a bit and give you a call back, yes?"

"That would be helpful, Mom. If I can track down their relations, I might be able to prevent more deaths."

"You're always so good, Ed. You get a bad rap from your werewolf brother. But I know, in my heart, you do nothing for yourself and everything for others."

He smirked and tapped the back of the phone with a finger. Good ole Mom. He did try. But sometimes it felt as though he were pushing against a wall of hot lava. Impossible to stop.

"How are you, son? You mentioned a witch was helping you with this. Is she someone special to you?"

"Mom," he drawled.

"Oh, so she is." A teasingly accusatory tone, if there

ever was one. He'd not told her about Witch Number Two attempting to enslave him. Some things a man shouldn't tell his mother.

"I should go," he said. "I've got this mess to deal with."

"Of course. You don't like to talk about yourself. So humble. But you watch out for yourself, son. If zombie witches are going after Rascon's relations, then you are a target."

He hadn't considered that until now. But if he was a target, then so was his mom. It seemed *Les Douze* were operating strictly in Paris. With hope, they would stay contained to the cemeteries and their peripheries and away from his mother.

"I will, Mom. Tell Colin I said hello. You two take care of one another. *Au revoir.*"

He hung up as a knock at his door sounded. He eyed the door, unable to see through it, but certainly he detected that luscious lemon scent on the other side. He rushed to open the door and pulled Tamatha in to give her a hug and kiss her deeply.

"Wow, someone's happy to see me."

"You are a bright beacon, witch. You change the air when you're near me, you know that?"

She splayed both hands open near her shoulders. "No magic, I promise."

"You've bewitched me with your beauty, kindness and heart. That's a special magic."

"You are a charmer, Edamite Thrash."

She tapped his chest—he wore no shirt—and kissed him over the heart. "This design is growing darker. Maybe it's related to the demon killings?"

"I won't know until it's fully formed. You hungry? I ordered in. Got vichyssoise warming on the stove."

"I'll get the wine!"

* * *

After the supper dishes had been tucked in the dishwasher, Ed led Tamatha to the couch with a fresh bottle of wine in hand and two goblets. He sat next to her, kissing her first before testing the Zinfandel. "That's bitter."

"I like it," she offered. "It's dark and mysterious. Like you."

"I feel my mysteries have been revealed to you in the course of the days we've gotten to know one another. I have nothing left to hide."

"Nor do I. Oh, but, Ed." She set the goblet on the coffee table. "I was talking to Certainly this afternoon. He suggested that the two of us may have been brought together for a reason. He thinks it could be one of your relatives who was one of the accusing demons."

"We are on the same page. My grandfather may have been one of the accusers. I didn't mention it to you because I wasn't sure. But if you've the list of the witches' accusers?"

"I do, but I assume these were the human aliases the demons used." She tugged out her cell phone and brought up the list she had copied from the textbook. "Check it out."

He took the phone and scrolled through the list. "Rascon." He handed her the phone. "They're not aliases. That was my grandfather's name. I confirmed it with my mom before you arrived. This is weird." He ran his hands over his temples, resting his palms over his horn nubs. "I don't get it. How could we have possibly been drawn together?"

"I think Arius is very powerful. I'm not sure she was capable of placing the two of us in that alley the first night we met, or if she is even aware of our association, but..."

He twisted a look at her. "She?" he insisted.

"Yes, the warlock is a she. And...she knows about me.

She left me a message in one of the books I was looking through for answers."

He turned a gaping question on her.

"It was written in ink as I watched. Something like 'I've found you now.'"

"Hell. Maybe she's the one I've sensed trying to spy on me?"

"It could be. I've been reinforcing my white light to superstrong ever since. Oh, and I've to reinforce your protective wards, as well. I brought supplies today."

"Great. But really? A *female* warlock?"

Tamatha shrugged. "Not so uncommon. But I didn't learn much about her. There was only a short entry about her. Warlock since 1754 because of necromancy. Banished from the mortal realm. No family history. Not even a skills-and-magics list. CJ said she was banished to Daemonia and should still be there. So if she's here in the mortal realm, that means she's escaped exile, which should be impossible for the average witch. But for a warlock, well, I'm sure it's very close to impossible. Even CJ wasn't able to leave Daemonia on his own. His brother, TJ, had to rescue him."

She rubbed her palms up and down her arms. "I'm worried, Ed. I'm not sure my magic will be enough to protect me against a warlock. Or to protect you."

"You don't need to protect me, sweetness." He hugged her against his chest and kissed the crown of her head. "I won't let her hurt you. And you've got your white light."

"Right, but to protect myself from a warlock? I'm not sure. So I've called in backups. Actually, it just occurred to me to do so on the way here."

"Certainly Jones?"

"I'll bring him in if and when we learn it is actually Arius who is behind all this. For now I think I can get the help I need from Verity Van Velde and Libby Saint-Charles. They're equally as skilled as I am. As a threesome we should be able to track Arius, figure out where she is. They should be here soon."

"Here?" Ed stood and looked about nervously. "Why did you invite them to my place?"

"Well, it's where I am, and it's bigger than my *pied-à-terre*, and— Are you upset?"

"No, I just..." He exhaled, his shoulders dropping. "I'm not sure."

"Are you afraid of getting girl cooties in your man cave?"

"I don't think it's so much the girl cooties as—"

"Witch cooties?"

He shrugged and winced, offering his assent to her assumption.

She stood before him and stroked his jaw. "Aw, poor alpha demon is going to have his cave invaded by a bunch of witches and he's not sure he can handle it. You are so precious."

"Tamatha."

"Sorry. I shouldn't tease. But I promise none of them will cause you harm."

"I can look after myself."

"I know you can. But allowing a semicoven of witches into your home has got to be difficult."

"I haven't had much time to process—"

In the kitchen a phone rang. Tamatha rushed to get her purse. "That's mine!"

She said hello to her mother. "It's not late. Only ten. I'm glad you called. There's a situation here in Paris. Yes. Er... I'm going to put you on speaker, Mom. I want Ed to hear this, too." She set the phone on the counter, and Ed sidled up onto a stool next to her.

"Ed?" her mother said. "A new lover, darling?"

"Yes. Ed, this is my mother, Petrina Bellerose. Mom, say hi to Ed."

"*Bonjour*, Ed. Are you taking care of my daughter?"

Tamatha fluttered him a wink and she was pretty sure he blushed.

"Uh, yes?"

"He doesn't sound very sure of himself. How long have you been dating this one, Tam?"

"Not long. We're still discovering one another." She clasped his hand and he pulled it up to kiss. "But he's great. I want him to listen because what I have to tell you involves the both of us in a weird twist of fate."

"Oh, I adore twists of fate. Especially the weird ones. Go on."

Her mother was entirely too cheerful. Tamatha did not want to tell her what she had to, but she could use Petrina's advice. "It's about Grandma Lysia."

"How so, Tam?"

"Do you remember anything about Grandma right before she was burned? Like her friends and allies. Was she associated with any demons?"

"Her lover was a demon. I don't recall his name, but I know it's scribbled somewhere in one of Mom's diaries. Why do you ask?"

"Her lover was a demon? So, could he have been one of the demons who accused her?"

"No, the accusers were humans. I was there. I saw them standing at the fore before the vicious crowd. Utterly common humans."

"Mom, I believe they were demons who had taken corporeal form in human bodies. You know it can be difficult to spot such demons unless you know what you are looking for. And even then."

"Yes, that's true. Hmm… I was quite young at the time. And in such a state. My mother was to be burned as entertainment for those stupid humans."

Tamatha sometimes forgot the horrors her mother had experienced. She couldn't imagine watching Petrina being marched to the fagots. "Could Grandma's lover have turned against her?"

"Oh, Tam, I don't know. Again, I was young and wasn't overly interested in my mother's love affairs. If it were true, such betrayal would have created a terrible curse—Oh."

Tamatha got the same thought as her mother. She slapped a palm over the tattoo on her biceps. The Bellerose women had been cursed in love since the time of Lysia Bellerose. Could it have been because her lover had sent her to the pyre to be burned alive?

"Are you sure he was a demon?" Petrina pressed.

"No, not until I can get her lover's name and check to see if it's on the list. I've traced the records in some books in the Archives and have a list of the accusers. Do you think the Bellerose curse could have resulted because of Grandma and her lover?"

"If he was demon? I'm sure of it. The witches in our family have a sort of organic pull to magics that are most needed. Much like your OCD magic, Tam. It naturally developed because you're such a stickler for order."

Ed tilted his head curiously. It was one of those questioning looks that told her she might have some explaining to do after the conversation with her mother. She squeezed his hand and shrugged.

"It's very likely," Petrina continued, "that the curse could have formed as a result of your grandma's lover accusing her of witchcraft. Oh, how awful. I had no idea. How does your Ed figure into all this?"

"He's a demon," Tamatha said. "And he's been pulled into the murders of demons by—" now he was the one to squeeze her hand "—witches raised from the dead. I haven't seen them. Ed has. He suspects they are *Les Douze*."

Silence hummed loudly on the phone.

"Mom?"

"But Mom is… Your grandmother… She's *dead*, Tamatha."

"Not exactly," Ed offered. "I'm sorry to speak so frankly, Madame Bellerose, but I was able to speak to a demon friend before he died—er, due to witches who attacked him. He said *Les Douze* was responsible."

"So Mom is…undead? Someone raised her from the grave? Tamatha, she was ash. I stood there for a whole day following the burning, watching as they shoveled away the ashes and dumped them in the Seine. I was barely able to save some of her ash in a vial. I don't understand."

"I suspect a warlock is involved. Why she would have reason to raise *Les Douze* is beyond me. But these witches seem to be going after demons who are related to the very demons who accused them. Sounds like revenge."

"Over two centuries later?" Petrina asked. "That makes little sense."

"I know." Tamatha sighed. "I'm sorry, Mom. This is weird. But we can't let it continue. The witches have to be sent back to their place of rest or they will murder again."

"I suppose you are right. If they are revenants…" The woman's shudder was heard over the phone line. "Ed's a demon? How did you two meet?"

"She ran into me one dark night," Ed offered, "and before I could introduce myself, she bound me with a spell."

"Good girl," Petrina said. "Your diabology studies are

coming along nicely. But the two of you have apparently kissed and made up. Is he good for you, Tam?"

"Yes." She leaned over and kissed Ed on the cheek.

"Did you tell him the family motto?"

"Yes—Love Often," she said quickly.

"Right. Hmm..." Petrina said. "Aristo died yesterday."

"Oh, Mom, I'm so sorry."

"It's fine. We knew it was coming for weeks. The cancer was aggressive. I've his funeral arrangements to deal with and then I'm returning to Paris for a few days. I can't let you deal with this alone. This is my mother, after all. She's... What does she look like, Tam?"

"I haven't seen her, Mom. Ed has. She's not in a good way."

"Of course not. If some warlock has commanded her and the others to her bidding, she can't want that. She would welcome her destruction. I'm sure of it. You have to put her to rest, Tamatha."

"I will. I just needed to hear it from you."

"And maybe you can break the family curse?"

"How so?"

"Well, the ideas are swirling in my brain right now. If Grandma could be reunited with her demon lover, and he apologized..."

Ed gaped at Tamatha.

"If you can get us the name of her lover, that would put us on the path to such a reunion. It could work."

"Yes, I'll have to look for it when I return to Paris. I've her things stuffed away in storage. The two of you were drawn together by Mom's magic," she stated.

"You think so?"

"There are no coincidences, darling. If she's in pain, if she wants free of the malefic magic controlling her, she may have very well summoned the two of you. Is Ed's family related to one of her accusers?"

"Yes."

"That makes sense. Oh dear, if it was his relative who was your grandma's lover, then the two of you are reliving that union. Ed may bring your death."

"No, Mom. That's…" Yet Tamatha's heart pounded. Her mother never speculated. She spoke from intuition. And her intuition was never wrong.

"I would never harm your daughter, Madame Bellerose," Ed said. "I swear it."

"Perhaps, but that matters little when family magic is involved. Tamatha, must you work with him on this?"

"Yes. We're woven into this together. I trust Ed. He trusts me."

"Then you'd better tell him the complete family motto. Oh, there's the coroner's car. I invited him over to discuss the arrangements. I'm not sure I can keep a tear from my eye knowing what I now know about Mom. Tamatha, please be careful. And, Ed."

"I have your daughter's back. Nothing will harm her."

Petrina sighed. "I'll try to get to Paris tomorrow evening. The next morning at the latest. Love you, Tam."

"I love you, too, Mom. I'll be okay with Ed. Call me as soon as you get to town."

They said goodbye and Tamatha clicked off the phone. Ed caught his head against his palm and watched as she paced the kitchen floor. "Your mother had no idea your grandmother's lover was demon?"

"She was twelve when Grandma was burned."

"Right. Again, I'm sorry. This has to be difficult."

"It is, but like Mom said, if Grandma is being controlled, she must be desperate for her freedom. I have to give it to her. We need to contact *Les Douze* and hope that leads us to the warlock. I hope the others get here soon."

"The coven about to invade my home." He clasped his hands before his chin and offered a wincing smile to her.

She knew this was hard for him. Perhaps she should have done this at her place, but she felt comfortable here. And she wanted him to be a part of all magics involved. He had revealed himself to her. She would do the same.

"So what's this about the *complete* family motto?" he asked.

Thinking of revealing secrets… Her mother had meant well to bring that up, but could she really tell him? On the other hand, if Petrina suspected Ed could bring her death, wasn't it only fair to explain the dangers to him?

"Love Often," she said. "That's the part the Bellerose women always tell their friends and lovers."

"But there's another part?"

She nodded and kissed him. It was a slow, lingering kiss that didn't need to deepen because the press of their mouths together was enough. A binding that went beyond bewitchery and seemed to combine their very molecules in a giddy bouncing bonding.

"Love often," she offered against his mouth, "because they never last for long."

Ed's right eyebrow arched sharply.

"The curse my mom was talking about is that the Bellerose women's lovers never last long. They either can't handle dating a witch and storm off—those are the lucky ones—or they fall desperately in love and literally go mad with love. They have to be locked up. Or there's the third option."

"I'm not going to like the third option very much, am I?"

"Death," she said. "Usually accidental. Sometimes we bring it on because we just want the man gone. It's that organic magic Mom mentioned, like my OCD magic. It just…occurs. It can be natural, as well. Aristo, Mom's current lover, had cancer. He developed it while dating her. When she said it was aggressive, she meant it. They've only known each other a month and a half. Again, part of the curse."

"You believe cancer can be attributed to a curse?"

"He was healthy when she met him."

He rubbed his chin. "So you hadn't intention of telling me I might develop an expiration date the longer we are together?"

"I was kind of hoping the curse would avoid you. You're cute. I like you," she said in an attempt to lighten the mood. "I'd like to keep you around awhile."

"I'd like to stay awhile. Besides the routine evil-overlord tasks to keep me busy, I do enjoy being with you. A lot. I'd have to be alive to continue to enjoy it."

"Most definitely."

"You don't believe what your mother said about my bringing your death, do you?"

Tamatha sighed. At that moment the door buzzer rang. "My mother's intuition is never wrong," she said as she went to answer.

Verity tossed her deep violet hair over a shoulder and smiled a huge, warm welcome. "Tamatha, it's been too long!" She lunged over the threshold and the witches hugged. Verity was much shorter than Tamatha, so it was a good thing she hadn't put on her heels yet.

"It has been a few years. You are pretty as always. Come inside and tell me all the details of your life. Oh, this is Verity Van Velde, Ed." She skipped over to him and clasped his hand. "And this is Edamite Thrash, corax demon."

"Is that so?" The witch's amethyst eyes performed a once-over of the man. "Pretty."

Tamatha could feel Ed's blush, so she kissed him quickly on the cheek. "Libby will be here soon. And I told her to bring along Vika."

"I thought you said you only needed three witches," he protested.

"Well, I could hardly have invited Libby without her sister. You won't even notice we're here."

Chapter 18

Trying to ignore the presence of four witches sitting in his living room, drinking wine, laughing, giggling and gossiping, was an exercise in never-going-to-happen. Not even notice they were there? Yeah right.

Sitting in the kitchen, nursing a whiskey, Ed picked up that Verity was dating Rook, one of the founders of The Order of the Stake. He knew that man—a vampire hunter—and respected him. So the purple-haired witch checked out. One of the redheads, Vika, was married to Certainly Jones, who was a dark witch who also ranked respectably on Ed's radar. Save for when it came to telling Tamatha bad things about him. Apparently, Jones had not the return respect, but Ed wouldn't hold it against him.

It was the other witch, the curvaceous redhead with a booming voice and a tendency to dance as she talked, who he determined was married to a former soul bringer, who before that was a former angel. Those bastards were all-powerful. And he couldn't ascertain if the dude was merely human now or just resting his abilities. Either way, he'd keep an eye on Libby Saint-Charles, at least, to make sure her husband wasn't nearby.

The conversation had grown quiet, and Ed picked up a few Latin terms tossed about. They were talking about herbs and spells. And Tamatha pulled out the amethyst-hilted athame that she always carried in her book bag. When a clink of metal sounded in the living room, he suddenly felt a curious power fill the entire loft.

He spun on the kitchen stool to see all four witches had pressed the tips of their athames together. A brilliant white light surrounded them in a bubble and then it burst and it blasted him from the stool to land on the floor in a sprawl. His whiskey glass went skittering across the marble floor, leaving a dribble of golden liquid in its wake.

"What the—?"

Tamatha's face appeared above him. "We've supercharged our collective magic. We're ready to go to the Montparnasse cemetery to do a seek-and-find. Together, the four of us should be able to contact The Twelve. You coming along?"

"What about the warlock?"

"If she is involved, we'll try to find out from *Les Douze*, but we want to avoid contact with her until we can be sure. Maybe it would be best if you stayed here." She grabbed his hand and helped him jump to his feet.

Libby sidled over and eyed Ed up and down with a cheeky summation that ended in a smirk of her bright pink lips. "No, let's bring him along," she said. "He'll make good bait."

"Good idea," Vika chimed in. She wore a long black gown and appeared most witchlike to Ed. Add a pointy hat and broomstick? Happy Halloween! "We'll send him in first to lure out *Les Douze*."

Ed stood there with an open mouth and a strange wonder as the foursome debated his value of serving as the worm on the hook. Tamatha was against it while the other three were perfectly willing to shove him to the vanguard to stand before the crew of zombie witches.

And so was he.

"I'm in," he said. He clapped his hands together resolutely. "Let's do this. You ladies going to transport yourselves to the cemetery? Should I shift?"

"We can do you one better."

Tamatha grabbed his hand, and the witches all clasped hands, Vika finally taking his other hand. He didn't have time to ascertain what their next move was but suspected it involved transport—

Landing unsteadily on dew-moistened cobblestones in the middle of a shadow-darkened graveyard, Ed's next thought was that the witches were nowhere nearby. And he was glad he hadn't needed to shift and fly there on his own. He didn't feel at all drained. Now, if Tamatha could teach him that spell, he could get some good use out of it traversing across the city.

He cast a glance about. "Tamatha?" They must have landed elsewhere during transport.

He stood near a mausoleum that featured columns of stacked skulls around the stone entrance. An icy chill skittered over his arms and up his neck. His feather sigils shivered. The dark felt like ink, liquid yet staining. He could see shapes of tombstones and winged stone angels. Nearby traffic sounds were muffled. A raven cawed, sending a familiar vibration through his bones. It was a warning cry.

And then he heard the growl.

Tamatha could feel malefic magic thicken the air. Shadows of tombstones and mausoleums were barely visible in the fog that hung like steam about them. She clasped Libby's hand, and she in turn took Verity's hand. All four witches joined hands as the distinct scent of sulfur mingled with a rotting miasma.

"Ed?" Tamatha called.

"Over here. Where are you? I can't see much— Ah hell. They're here."

Heartbeats thundering, Tamatha fought the urge to rush forward to protect him. Instinct settled her. He was a big boy. He could take care of himself. And she would lose her protection if she dropped the others' hands. Together their magic was a force.

"I can't see them yet," she said aloud to the witches. "Let's focus. Call out their master."

Libby began a low humming tone and her sister Vika matched it with a harmony a few octaves higher. Verity whispered Latin for a channeling spell. It would connect them to *Les Douze* if the creatures were open.

And Tamatha finally caught a glimpse of Ed. He ducked a sweeping hand that clawed for his face. The hand was connected to something. She couldn't make it out, but it didn't look human.

While the witches appeared to be reciting Sunday afternoon chants, Ed fought for his life. *Les Douze*, minus at least two, that he counted, came at him full force.

With a sweep of his hand, he repelled the vanguard with a dusting of black sulfurous smoke that should cause most to gag and tear up or even go blind for a few minutes.

Apparently these dead things were not most.

While a few dropped back and began their zombie shuffle toward a tombstone to the left, the others roared toward him. Ed tried a flick of his fingers to repel them.

Half went tumbling backward, a few spilling over the remaining who stood.

One particularly aggressive creature flung herself at him, grabbing him by the shoulders. Metallic black gunk leaked from her gaping mouth. It looked like melted hematite, but smelled like the worst rotting fish. He gagged and struggled. Claws cut into his skin. The witch ward burned to his bone. Shoving at the thing didn't manage to push it from him, but it did disconnect one of its arms, which then dangled, caught in his assailant's tattered clothing.

"Bait," he muttered. "What was I thinking?"

Anger suffused his veins.

Tamatha chanted the warlock's name, entreating her to show if she indeed mastered *Les Douze*. Her fellow witches' powers bolstered her own and made her voice clear and strong. She felt the air change and sensed the malefic presence, but she couldn't know if it was from the zombie witches attacking her boyfriend or if indeed the warlock was nearby.

And then she felt the burn on her wrist and saw the dark line tracking her veins. She shook her arm, even while still clasping Libby's hand. The red-haired witch saw the black tracing up Tamatha's arm and swore.

"She's here," Vika said, and the witches silenced. "Show yourself, warlock!"

The zombie witches howled and cawed like banshees. Ed yelped. A furious wind ribboned through the cemetery, redirecting some witches who had gone off course of the demon toward him. Yet they hissed as if they'd been stung by the wind, which had to be the warlock.

Verity dropped hands with Vika and Tamatha and slapped at her palms, which flamed blue. Her fire magic had activated against her will. She couldn't control the flames. Vika, a master of water magic, doused Verity's hands with a shower that instantly steamed to nothing, leaving the fire lesser but still amber flames.

The warlock was here, and her power was too strong. Perhaps she even tapped into the combined witches' powers. While the remainder of *Les Douze* retreated behind tombstones and some into the dark maw of an open mausoleum, Tamatha felt her magic drain. She tapped her first fingers together, but instead of earth—which she hoped to use to smother Verity's flames—a sputter of smoke hissed out.

Libby cried out. Red claw marks cut through the witch's neck. And Vika clasped her shoulder as blood oozed through the serrated fabric at her hip. Verity fell to her knees clutching her stomach with smoking hands. She spit out a beetle and cursed.

The icy pain of talons cut across Tamatha's cheek. Losing strength in her legs, she was the final one to drop. Their magic dissipated and the graveyard fell silent.

Ed, who lay sprawled behind a grave, twitched. And then his entire body quaked and she smelled the sulfur. Shifting, the demon slapped a thorned hand onto a nearby tombstone and pulled himself up, ebony horns cutting the midnight air. He growled and clenched his fists. Red eyes searched the darkness.

"The warlock is strong," Vika said as she inspected her sister's wounds. "We'll need stronger magic if we're going to stop that bitch, Tamatha."

"Yes," she said absently, because her focus was on the demon who marched toward her. He did not look happy. "Ed?"

"Witch!"

He gripped her by the wrist. Verity cast a sputtering flame at him, but the demon merely shrugged it off.

"I'm sorry—we tried!" Tamatha said, resisting his strong hold, and she was able to pull free, though in doing so she twisted her wrist painfully and something cut her skin. "Calm down, Ed!"

"They would have ripped me limb from limb," he snarled at her in that hollow demonic tone that was far from sexy now. The horns at his temples cut the air with a tilt of his head. "Not so powerful after all," he assessed of her.

"Leave her alone!" Libby grabbed Tamatha by the shoulders and pulled her away from Ed. "Shift back, asshole. You're doing no one any good in that form and someone could see you."

"Witches!" the demon growled. And with a roar that echoed over the cemetery, he then shifted into a conspiracy of ravens and soared up into the sky.

"That was freakin' cool," Libby commented. "Didn't know the guy could do that."

Tamatha shot her a glare.

"Hey, it was. Is he flying away, then? Nice guy. Not."

"Libby," Verity chastised as she checked Tamatha's injuries. She held a palm over the cut on her wrist and closed her eyes.

"Sorry," Libby said. "Ah, the ravens are circling around and swooping back down. So maybe he's not going to abandon you. But maybe he should. No man has a right to grab a woman like he did you."

"He was frightened," Tamatha defended him. "You would be, too, if a dozen zombie witches came after you."

"Point taken. But I only counted ten. Either they've lost two or a couple were hiding." Libby turned to check on her sister.

The ravens flocked close to the ground, but before talons could touch the cold cemetery pathway, they transformed and coalesced into the dark figure of Edamite

Thrash. He shivered, as if a bird shaking out its wings, then let out a moan as the final remnants of the shift left him.

He'd shifted to demon form without volition, and when that happened, it was because he was angry. Angry that he'd been so ineffectual facing a coven of dead witches. They were zombies. Bags of bones and rotting meat. They should have been easy to defeat. Instead, they'd nearly torn him apart.

And the quartet of live witches who had attempted to stave off the zombie-witch attack had served much less than he'd expected from "combined magic." Which had made him even angrier. Not directly at Tamatha, but again, simply because—what the hell? They. Were. Zombies. They shouldn't be that hard to put down.

And once shifted, with the anger racing through his system, he'd gone after the first person he'd seen—Tamatha.

Ed swiped a hand over his head, reactively checking that his horns had completely receded. He touched his knuckles. No gloves to cover the thorn nubs. He hadn't time to put them on at his home before the witches had whisked him away to Montparnasse. What was that? A trace of red blood on the back of his hand? Wasn't his. And the zombies bled weird metallic stuff.

Had he cut someone?

"No, that's impossible. That would poison—"

He rushed for Tamatha but the witch Vika put up a palm, repulsing him as if with an invisible shield. He stumbled backward against a tombstone, catching an arm across the top to keep from going down.

"No, it's okay," Tamatha said as she pushed away from her friends. "He was out of it. Didn't know what he was doing. Are you okay, Ed? They didn't hurt you?"

That she was more worried about him than herself killed

him. She had talon marks across her cheek. Ed nodded but didn't try to approach her again. He could have hurt her with his thorns.

"Let me take care of you, sweetie." Verity pressed her palms against Tamatha's cheek and closed her eyes.

Meanwhile, Libby eyed Ed with an admonishing glare.

"Your bait worked," he spit at the curvaceous witch.

"Yeah, but the warlock's magic was too strong. We're going to have to go at this another way. If we don't have guns big enough to blow her away, we'll have to combine our powers."

"I thought that's what you just did," Ed protested.

"So did I. Back to the drawing board, as they say. We should all head home and search our grimoires for effective magic. I sensed something beyond malefic."

"It was demonic," Vika said, joining her sister's side and smoothing at the torn dress fabric at her hip. "I recognize the feel of it from when CJ was infested with demons."

"Demonic?" Ed asked. "That doesn't make sense. They are killing demons. You think a *demon* is controlling *Les Douze*?"

Vika shrugged. "I honestly don't know. It was witch magic, for sure. Mixed in with the demonic. Weird. Maybe CJ will have some answers. Verity, you want to take Tamatha home with you tonight?"

"No," Tamatha said, though Verity still worked her healing magic on her cheek. "I'm good. I'll go home with Ed."

All three of her friends glanced to Ed. More admonishing witch vibes. He felt them as a cold shiver in his veins. Duly taken. He should have never gone after Tamatha. She did not deserve his anger.

"Your friends don't trust me," he said. "I don't blame them."

"I'll be fine," she said and gasped as her friend pulled

her hands from her cheek to reveal smooth, healed skin. "Thanks, Verity. I need to rest. This night has taken a lot out of all of us. Not to mention you, Ed." She tucked a hand against her stomach and wandered toward him. "Will you take me home?"

"Yes." He kissed her forehead and stroked the hair from her cheek. Verity's magic had healed her completely; not a sign of damage on her pale skin. As were the others healed. "We'll be in touch," he said, and then he lifted Tamatha into his arms and walked past the witches.

"Dude, we will be keeping an eye on you," Libby called after him.

"I don't doubt that!" he returned.

And then thinking he had had enough of witches for the evening, and that he only wanted to be home as quickly as possible, he considered flying out of the cemetery with Tamatha in his arms. She would be carried aloft by his conspiracy, but even considering another shift gave him a headache. He was too drained. And he shouldn't risk anyone spying a witch flying through the air on the back of ravens' wings.

He landed the sidewalk outside the cemetery and set Tamatha down. Pulling out his phone, he called for a ride. Twenty minutes later, Inego dropped them both off before his building. He scooped his tired witch into his arms and carried her inside.

He laid Tamatha on the couch and only then did he notice her wrist when her hand fell away from her stomach. "You're cut here. The purple witch didn't heal it?"

"Oh, it's nothing." She grasped her wrist and winced. "Must have gotten it when I…"

She hadn't been involved in hand-to-hand combat with the zombie witches. The only wound she had taken from the warlock had been across the cheek.

Ah hell. No.

Ed slapped a palm over the back of his hand. His thorns were retracted, but the cool, hard thorn nubs were always sharp. He had struggled with her in his demonic form. Had he accidentally cut her?

"Tamatha, is that cut from my thorns?"

She shook her head and closed her eyes, suddenly seeming as if she could drop into the sleep of the dead. The poison from his thorn would infect her and not stop until she was dead.

He shook her by the shoulders. "Tamatha? Tell me!"

"Maybe," she said softly.

"No!"

If his poison were coursing through her system— He hadn't time to consider the horrible reality. He had to act. Fast.

"The antidote. I've got to make it."

"No," she said lazily, and her head dropped to the side. "I'll be…"

He remembered the antidote she had explained to him. Some of it. It involved crushing the demon's thorn and mixing it with salt and…something.

"How much salt?" he asked, shaking her again. She shrugged out of his grasp and he grabbed her by the chin. "Tamatha, listen to me. We don't have much time. The poison will kill you. I need to do this now."

"Will hurt you," she whispered.

"Hurt?" Yes, removing his thorn could have a dire effect. Much worse than a simple hurt. "Fuck that. I'm not going to watch you die."

"But my mother's intuition—"

About him dying? "Is not going to be accurate today. Now help me. How much salt?"

She sighed. Her hand flopped lifelessly over the edge of the couch. "Equal parts."

"Salt. Ground thorn. And…?"

"Whiskey."

"Whiskey?" That sounded random, but he wasn't going to doubt. Not when time was crucial.

He didn't own a single crystal of salt. He had plenty of whiskey. And the thorn. That was going to hurt like a mother, and had irreversible consequences, but that mattered little.

"I knew from the get-go when a demon gets involved with a witch he never survives to the end of the story." Good ole Mom and her faery tales.

Ed dashed into the kitchen and picked up his phone. He called the building concierge and told him he had an urgent need for salt. Any kind. Borrow some from a resident and bring it up. The concierge promised he'd be up in ten minutes.

"Make it five," Ed said and then dashed to the liquor cabinet. He yanked out a bottle of twenty-year-old whiskey and unscrewed the cap. Pulling down a stainless steel mixing bowl from the cupboard, he almost dumped all the whiskey into it, then remembered, "Equal parts."

He'd start with the most precious ingredient. Opening a drawer by the stone, he pulled out a bowie knife.

He called out, "How you doing, Tamatha?"

No reply. Shit. He dashed into the living room and found her lifeless, her hair spilling to the floor like a Sleeping Beauty in wait of the prince's kiss.

Ed rubbed his lips. He was the furthest thing from a prince. Why was this happening? She wasn't supposed to be the one hurt. He was. A shake of her shoulder forced her to mutter drowsily.

"I love you, Tamatha. I'm going to save you." Fuck. He was the one who may very well kill her. "I'm so sorry."

The door buzzer rang. He retrieved the glass jar of salt and shoved a ten-euro bill into the concierge's hand. Door slammed behind him, he knelt and partially shifted so his horns grew out on his skull and his thorns popped up on his knuckles.

Placing the knife blade to the hard base of the thorn behind his forefinger, he dug into flesh and thorn.

Chapter 19

Ed blinked through the pain. Black blood gushed from the wound on the back of his hand. He'd cut through cartilage and what had seemed like bone for the tremendous effort it required to remove a thorn from his knuckle. The thorn landed on the marble floor. He bent forward, clenching his jaw and pressing his fist to his gut. Tears formed in his eyes. He felt sure he'd never experienced anything so painful. And he had taken battle wounds from demons, werewolves, vampires and even zombie witches.

No time to lament the agony. He'd suffer his skin flailed from his body if it would save Tamatha. Even more? He'd give his life for hers.

Grasping the thorn, he dashed into the kitchen, grabbed the mortar and pestle—no idea why or how he owned one, but he was glad he did—and began to grind the ingredient.

Blood spilled from his knuckle, so he switched hands and used his right to crush. No sound from the couch, but he could see the top of Tamatha's head, her goddess hair spilling to the floor. Not moving. He crushed harder, finding it a difficult task, but soon enough, he had reduced the thorn to a black powder.

Grabbing the jar of salt, he cautiously removed the screw-on lid. He could touch salt, but the instant it hit his bloodstream he'd be a goner. He should wrap his hand to cover the wound but he hadn't time. So with his good hand, he carefully sifted into the mortar an equal amount of salt over the crushed thorn.

Whiskey to hand, he tilted back a swallow. It scoured down his throat, but it distracted from the pulsing burn at his knuckles. He poured what he thought was an equal amount into the mortar then mixed it together with a spoon from the drawer. The instant the silver spoon hit the mix it began to steam. He whipped it into the sink.

"Can't use metal, apparently." A burn on the back of his wrist began to sizzle into his skin. "Shit!" He thrust his bloodied hand under the faucet and turned on the water. Must have got a drop of the mixture on his skin when he flicked away the spoon.

Finally, skin cleaned, but his knuckle still bleeding, Ed slammed his palms to the marble counter. A new sigil veined its way about his wrist where he'd been burned by the salt, forming a black, thorned chain. That meant only one thing in the demonic realm: death.

Well, wasn't as if that surprised him.

"I can do this. I have to save her. Then it doesn't matter what happens to me."

But how to administer the antidote?

Clasping the heavy stone mortar to his gut, he dashed over to the couch and knelt. "Tamatha?" She was unresponsive, yet when he laid his fingers against her neck, he felt a strong pulse. "I'll have to wing it for this part."

Turning over her wrist, he saw the cuts made by his thorns, which had not healed. And would not, he guessed, for he had seen the purple-haired witch place a healing touch there. The cuts were thin. If he laid the antidote on them, it wasn't as though they would suck it in. Maybe?

"I don't know what to do next," he muttered. "Shit! What do I do? I need those witches back here."

Maybe there was a way to reach them. Pulling out Tamatha's cell phone from her purse, he was thankful the Contacts listed Libby Saint-Charles. When the witch answered she sounded frantic. "It's Tamatha?"

"She's been poisoned by my thorns," he said. "I've got the antidote mixed up. How do I administer it?"

"Injection."

"I…don't know how to do that. I don't have a syringe." Why was he so damned ineffectual? He could keep the demons in Paris under thumb but he couldn't save one witch? "Libby, she can't die. She means too much to me. She's the only— I love her."

"Chill out, demon boy. Close your eyes and concentrate on me."

"What?"

"Just do what I tell you, or I will hunt you down."

"Yes, I'm listening." Ed closed his eyes and pictured the sassy redheaded witch. An angel lover? Wonders never ceased. Something clattered onto the floor near his knee. He opened his eyes and saw the plastic syringe lying there.

"You get it?" she asked.

"Witch, you do good magic. Okay, I gotta go. I have to do this."

"Listen to me, lover boy. Inject it into her heart. It's the best way to initiate the antidote through her system fast."

"Her heart? But—?"

"Do as I say."

"Yes. Okay. Thanks, Libby."

He tossed the phone aside and picked up the syringe. He tried to grab the mortar with his other hand, but his bloodied fingers slipped over the marble bowl. His hand had gone numb. And a black streak ran up the back of his hand from the severed thorn to his wrist. It felt icy and at the same time burned as if he'd stuck his hand into a bee skep.

Managing the syringe with his right hand, he suctioned up the antidote into the device then leaned over Tamatha. She looked too peaceful, her pale pink lips parted and her skin like milk. Her hair even looked softer, like silk. He kissed her eyebrow and inhaled her lemon skin. Fresh and bright. A witch like no other.

A woman like no other.

He didn't deserve her. But he wanted to be worthy of her.

Positioning the syringe over her heart, he shook his head. What if he didn't do this right? His ineptitude could kill her faster than the poison might. Then her witch friends would come after him and—if that happened he deserved whatever they served him.

"I love you," he said and pierced her chest with the needle. He squeezed in the antidote, then tossed the syringe aside and lay across her stomach, hugging her. "Please don't die. We are good together. My world is brighter when you're in it. Tamatha…"

Her body remained cold and immobile, yet he could hear her heart beating beneath his ear. He grabbed her wrist. The wounds had blackened much like the wound on his knuckles. Something was wrong. Shouldn't she jolt back to life? At the very least, gasp in a healing breath?

A knock at his door startled him. If the concierge had returned he could just leave. "Busy!"

The knock came again, fierce and insistent.

"Go away!"

A mist of red smoke sifted under the doorway and floated into the living room at the end of the couch. It swirled like a tornado contained within a human-sized space, and then a woman formed, sitting on the couch arm near Tamatha's shoes.

"Who are you?" Had to be a shifter. Or a witch. Or—He didn't have time to make friends right now. "Get the hell out of here!"

The woman, with bloodred hair and blue eyes, crossed her arms and closed her eyes. Intent on staying put. She wore a deep green frock coat over a revealing black bustier, tight black leather leggings and laced-up combat boots. A white triangle was etched onto her forehead, and on her chin, vertical white lines flowed down her neck. The symbols looked demonic to Ed.

Who was she? She had broached the wards Tamatha had put on this place, so…

And then he suddenly knew. "Arius Pumpelché. Warlock!"

The woman put up a staying hand when he lunged toward her. "Your rage will kill her, demon."

"And your rage has conjured foul witch zombies. What do you want?"

The warlock pointed to Tamatha, so still, and her lips were turning blue. "You neglected the most important part to making the antidote work."

Ed gasped, his chest heaving. He didn't want to take help from a warlock. But he wasn't a fool. "What is it?"

"The spell."

"Spell?" The bleeding thorn removed from his knuckles had weakened him, and yet his anger threatened to bring on the shift to demon form. His wounded hand tightened and the remaining thorns *shinged* out from his knuckles. The horns at his temples grew halfway. "What is the spell?"

"Touchy, touchy, demon. You watch your anger." The warlock held up her open palm to reveal another sigil painted in white. Ed felt an intense sting in his horns, as painful as it had felt when he'd sliced off his thorn.

"Tell me!"

"For a trade."

"Anything!"

Arius opened her eyes and looked directly at him. "I'll speak the spell and you will bring to me the progeny of those who accused *Les Douze*."

So the warlock could set her zombie witches on them and kill them. "Why are you doing this? Why do you need the revenge? How are you connected to *Les Douze*?"

Arius folded her hands in her lap and looked over Tamatha. "She doesn't have long."

"Just tell me!"

"My husband, Martine, was one of *Les Douze*. Your kind killed him, demon. Now I'll take my revenge."

"Why wait so long?"

"I've been…preoccupied."

Tamatha had said something about Arius being exiled to Daemonia for necromancy. "How did you get out of Daemonia? Witches aren't capable."

"Does it matter? I'm here. And I am an impatient woman. You want her to live?"

Ed spread his fingers before him. The severed thorn was drawing out his vita, stiffening his entire arm. The demonic sigils on his skin were on fire, most especially the one that had been forming over his heart for days.

Over his heart? Could it be? Did the new sigil signify

Tamatha making a mark on his life? He felt the most pain there right now. He couldn't lose her.

He slapped a hand over his heart.

"You take the deal," Arius said, "and you will live to love your witch."

"But I am one of the denizen's progeny."

Arius smiled a slimy curve. "I didn't say how long you would live."

"You don't need my help to bring in the others."

"I will to bring in Sophie. She's gone off radar. Even my demonic magic can't track her."

Ed bowed his head. An arm's reach away his lover lay dying. The warlock wanted his mother? He couldn't sacrifice her life for another…

He glanced to Tamatha. Could he?

"You a mama's boy, Edamite?" The warlock's eyes were cold blue shards. Ed shivered. Or maybe it was his life slipping away. He shook his head. And made his choice.

"Speak the spell," he uttered. "And you have my word I will locate my mother."

"Excellent." Arius began to chant.

And Ed clutched his arms about himself. He hadn't promised he would bring in the denizen, only that he would find his mother. But he had no idea where she was. Thankfully.

Chapter 20

Tamatha gasped in a breath. Her back arched and she shot upright to sitting position on Ed's couch. As she looked over her hands, a residual shimmer of something she recognized as magic escaped her pores and twinkled into nothing as if faery dust. Inhaling, she assessed her physicality. She felt energized, as if ready to go jogging or run a marathon.

Her lover fell to his knees before her and bowed his forehead to her leg. "Thank the heavens Above," he said. "I thought I'd lost you."

And why was that? She couldn't recall… Yes, she could. She'd been cut by his thorns while in the cemetery summoning *Les Douze*. She hadn't wanted to make a fuss about it—to give him any reason to feel responsible—until she had started to fade, and then when she'd begun to panic that something might really be wrong, the poison had quickly taken her breath and knocked her out.

"Oh, Ed." She bowed over him, and he abruptly jerked away, stepping back.

"You can't touch me. Not like this."

It was then she noticed his arm was streaked with black, as hers had been in the cemetery. As well, his hand was coated in black blood.

"The antidote," she whispered, checking her arm and wrist. The black lines she'd seen climbing her arm in the cemetery were gone. "You made it yourself?"

He nodded, clutching his arm. His hand hung there, bloodied and seemingly lifeless.

"Thank you," she said on a grateful hush. "But the antidote required— Oh, Ed, you removed one of your thorns?"

He nodded again. "Don't worry about it. I'm fine. I want to hold you but I don't want to poison you again. It was my fault. I'm not good for you. I could have killed you."

He'd cut off his thorn for her? That was so unselfish, so…loving. "You are in me now."

"You say that like it's a good thing. I don't understand."

"So it worked? Just the antidote? I'm sure there was a spell I was supposed to speak…"

"Nope. Everything's cool. Injected the antidote into your heart. Thanks to Libby, I knew to do that." He winced. "I don't ever want to hurt you, Tamatha, but that killed me to plunge the needle into your heart."

She felt over her chest but everything about her was invigorated and hummed with energy. "I'm good. Please, go wash off so I can hold you. I need to get lost in your arms."

He rushed toward the bathroom, and Tamatha picked up the syringe from the floor. "Thorns, salt and whiskey." She thought of the black veins running up his arm. "What horror has he incurred to save me? Oh, Ed."

Did he really love her? Maybe it had been a reaction, seeing her near death. He was an honorable man. Of course he would sacrifice himself for her. For anyone. It was his nature to care about others and not himself. But what would result from removing his thorn?

Dropping the syringe, she ran upstairs into the bedroom. The shower was running. She spun into the bathroom and sorted through the cabinet above the towel closet, finding some medical gauze and tape. When he stepped out of the shower, wrapping a towel around his waist, she motioned he sit on the toilet seat.

"My healing magic isn't as practiced as Verity's. I need to prepare an altar and speak a spell to heal, but I can do the human thing and bandage you up and send good vibes your way."

He held out his hand and they both inspected the damage. He no longer bled, though he cautioned her against touching the severed base of his thorn for fear that it could still contain poison. After he'd pressed a wad of gauze to his knuckles, only then would he allow her to wrap his hand and tape it.

She traced a finger up his arm. His veins showed in black vines that looked hard and felt cold under her touch. He confessed he hadn't feeling in his hand and could shift his fingers only minutely. Bending his arm at his elbow took effort. And there at his wrist was a dark chain of what looked like thorns. Was it a new sigil or had she missed that one, him wearing the gloves all the time?

"Don't worry about me, sweetness."

Always sacrificing, she thought. He didn't even realize how kind his heart truly was.

"I don't know what to say," she confessed. She knew what she wanted to hear from him. Maybe. She wouldn't force it. She mustn't. He'd shown her how he felt about her. Words should mean little now.

"Come here," he said.

Tamatha wrapped her arms about his neck and melted against him. He shivered and clutched her tightly as he buried his face against her neck and hair. He smelled like soap and cedar and ice, and everything she never wanted to let go of.

"I don't know what I'd do without you," he said. "You've become a part of me. See." He tilted back a shoulder and tapped the sigil over his heart. It was fully formed but not as dark as the rest of his sigils and tattoos, which she took to mean it could darken yet. "That's you. You've imprinted on me."

It did look like the Bellerose family crest. "Wow. It's a rose." She kissed the sigil and it briefly glowed red. "Is that good or bad?"

"Felt great," he said with a smile she really needed after the night they'd had. "Makes me forget the pain in my arm and hand."

"You sacrificed so much for me."

"Sacrifice? Please," he said with a grimace that tried to be joking. "It was very little to save your life." He kissed her and the soft touch lured her deeper into his arms. "Let's not argue. I have you safe in my arms. And I never want to let you go. You tired?"

She nodded. "Immensely."

"Let's fall asleep together. But *after* I put on my gloves."

"I'll get them for you. You crawl into bed. The night has been long and trying. You need the rest more than I do."

She rushed down to the kitchen, where he always kept his gloves on the counter by the door. She grabbed them and then paused. An unfamiliar scent lingered by the door. It wasn't Ed's sulfur or anything remotely familiar. From the zombie witches? No, that had been more a rotting stench.

They'd barely escaped with their lives after the warlock's presence had arrived in the cemetery. She hadn't seen her but had felt her there and had known it was the one she'd read about in the book.

"The warlock?" She tilted her head, drawing in the scent again. Dry, metallic, maybe a hint of sulfur?

Could Arius have been here? But she had put up wards to protect Ed from an intrusion. Wards that, admittedly, she hadn't thought would hold up for long against malefic magic.

Embraced from behind by a man in a towel, she turned and helped him put the glove on over the bandages. "You smell that?" she asked.

"What? Lemons and sex?" He nuzzled into her hair and hugged her against his bare chest. "Come to bed with me, lover. I want to hold you so I know that you are alive."

She ran her fingers down his arm that felt colder than the rest of him, and when she threaded her fingers through his, he didn't clasp them. But he managed to sweep her from her feet and toss her over a shoulder with his other arm. And she forgot about the disturbing scent and hoped he had enough energy for a good-night kiss and snuggle.

Morning shimmered a bright blue beam across Ed's partially opened eyes. He put up a hand to block the light streaming through the stained glass window and noted it was from a section of Jesus's eye. If he hadn't burned to hell living in this place, he certainly could survive a little thing like removing one of his thorns.

Though when he lifted his other arm to try to flex his wounded hand, it felt leaden and he couldn't move the fingers. And the chained thorns had thickened. That was not good. But so long as it didn't travel farther than above his elbow, he could deal. He'd have to deal.

What was foremost on today's must-deal menu was the

warlock's bargain. He'd agreed to bring his mom to the witches in the cemetery. He always kept his bargains. But he hadn't let on that he had no clue where Sophie was. It could take a while to find her. And in that while, surely he and Tamatha could come up with a means to defeat the warlock.

He should probably explain his deal with the near-devil to Tamatha, but then she'd want to make it better. And there was nothing she could do. The bargain was his cross to bear. And apparently, old blue eyes glaring at him from the stained glass was intent on seeing him bear it.

He'd have to call his mother. But he wasn't about to give her up to the warlock. He'd tell her to go deeper, to cease all contact with him. Which meant he needed a distraction for the warlock. Perhaps the others in the denizen?

No, he wouldn't sacrifice one for another. He'd have to hope that Tamatha and her witch brigade could find a way to defeat Arius before it came to that. But really, he wasn't about to rely on anyone but himself to make this right. It was his mess. He'd dig his way out of it.

He got up and decided to dress before Tamatha woke. He didn't want her to see him struggling with his gimp arm. He recalled his mother telling him to take care of his horns and thorns. If one were damaged it may never heal and could seriously weaken him. And to lose a horn or thorn? Death was almost assured.

"Let me stop the warlock before that happens," he muttered as he strolled into the closet and plucked out a black dress shirt.

Tamatha was aware of Ed kissing her and telling her he had work to do at the office. She could stay as long as she liked, but he wanted her to call him later. In response, she squiggled beneath the sheets and wasn't compelled to open her eyes. She was so tired.

But when the sound of the front door closing downstairs clicked in her brain, she couldn't sleep anymore. She was exhausted because she had almost died last night. But worse? Ed could have been torn apart by demons.

"I can't lie around." She slid out of bed and pulled on her clothes. "You want a war, Arius? I'll bring you one. There's got to be a way to stop a warlock. And I'm going to find it."

Before Tamatha could begin to search for more information on Arius, she went directly to the demon room in the archives and pulled out the volume that detailed information about the corax demon. Sliding her finger down the inked text, she passed over the first few pages and tapped the word *thorns*.

"Deadly poison," she muttered as she read the details. "Four on the back of each hand. Thorns grow to full length with anger."

The antidote to the poison was listed, as well. Crushed thorn, salt, whiskey. The words to the spell. And as a footnote in very tiny writing that she had to put on her glasses to read, she learned this: "Thorns regenerate if removed, as do horns. Slow process. Improper healing may cause death."

"Hmm…that's good to know. So if he takes care of the wounds, he won't die from it. Good. I wouldn't have wanted him to sacrifice himself to save me."

But still, it must have hurt tremendously. And it crushed her heart to know he'd gone through such pain for her.

She set the book aside and her phone rang. Her mother announced she'd arrived late last evening and had gone directly to the storage chest in the attic and pulled out her grandmother's things.

"I've been reading Lysia's diary since I got in town. I'm so tired. But, Tamatha, I had to call you before I fall asleep."

"What did you find?"

"Lysia's lover's name was Rascon. She doesn't detail that he was a demon, but there is a notation about the Libre denizen here. Could that possibly be his denizen?"

"Ah, goddess. Rascon is Ed's grandfather's name. And yes, he was a demon."

"So it's as I suspected. You two are living your ancestors' love affair. I'm not sure what to think about that." Petrina yawned over the connection. "I'm coming over after I take a nap."

"I'm at the Archives right now, and I'm on to Ed's when I'm done here. I'll call you later, okay?"

"Be careful, Tam."

She stroked her wrist where the cut from Ed's thorns had healed, yet a dark line remained, as if his ink had imprinted under the layers of epidermis. And then she remembered the crest forming over his heart. From her? It had to be because she'd recognized the design. How wondrous was that?

"I will be careful, Mom. Get some sleep."

Half an hour later, Tamatha returned to the witch room. Certainly had delivered a fresh pot of tea, and she poured her second cup. Ginger cardamom today. It was warm and a little spicy. Perfect to keep her anxiety level reined in.

After much digging, and more than a few failed locator spells, she uncovered the *Book of All Spells* under a pile of warding texts, which made sense because they had completely shielded the book from discovery.

This *Book of All Spells* was a copy of the original, of

which a witch who currently lived in America, Desideriel Merovech, was the keeper. Whenever a new spell was created, cast or devised, it was written in the pages. All spells were recorded there. The book was a living thing, a sort of automated Xerox that took down everything the original recorded.

As Tamatha turned the pages, images moved and text rearranged. Whispers of chants, Latin and simple magics were quiet, but she felt them viscerally move through her veins. Scents of must, oil, earth and even the ocean rose.

She found the section on raising the dead. The pages were stale and fragile. Touching it gave her a shiver.

To her, death was fresh, vital and brief. Following death, the bones were returned to the ground or returned to ash. But even before burial, the soul left the body and became a part of the greater consciousness. But zombies? They were vile, wretched doppelgängers of death. Nothing final or fresh about them.

There were quite a few spells for raising the dead. Dead vampires mostly. But as well, dead humans and a few species of paranormals. When she turned to the page that detailed "lifting thyne witches from thee ashy remains," the words briefly lit up in a blink. As if to say, *Stop here, you've found it, this is the page.*

"This has to be the spell that Arius used."

Careful not to touch the paper, for the ink could leach into her skin and impart the malefic magic, Tamatha silently read the spell, being careful not to whisper a word lest it be transformed into something real. The overall spell was simple, but could be enacted only with blood magic. Meaning, in order to raise the dead, one needed the potential zombie's blood or the blood from a close relative of that zombie. As well, a demonic hex was required, which could be performed by only a demon.

"Hmm…" She sat back in her chair, pondering. "Is the warlock working with a demon? Doesn't make sense if she's destroying demons."

On the other hand, alliances could be twisted. The demon could be the warlock's familiar. Or to really stretch, it was possible Arius could have picked up some demon magic while exiled in Daemonia. That made the most sense.

As well, the warlock needed blood.

Tamatha and her mother were directly blood-related to Lysia Bellerose, but she knew Arius had not access to their blood. So it must be another relative of *Les Douze* she had used to summon the entire dozen. Who? It had to be a relation to Arius. She could have used her own blood then. And if not, she had to have the blood of one of the witches or their relatives.

Tamatha spent the remainder of the afternoon going through the list of *Les Douze*, searching their genealogy and comparing names in their family histories, and when she reached number nine, she let out a hoot.

"He was her husband."

The witch, Martine Chevalier, had married Arius Pumpelché in 1750. Naturally, Tamatha had not picked up on that because female witches tended to not take their husbands' surnames. A few years later Martine was burned at the stake with *Les Douze*. Also noted was that his wife, a fellow witch, went mad with vengeance. She was made warlock but a week after her husband's death and not a year later was bound and exiled to Daemonia as punishment for her crimes.

Tamatha tapped her lower lip. "Arius tried to bring Martine back from the dead. Did she have his blood?"

Daemonia was the Place of All Demons. A horrible

place for demons. Likely a literal hell for a witch. She couldn't imagine what the warlock must have endured.

But she was here in the mortal realm now. Or was she? Tamatha hadn't actually seen her yet. She tapped the line on her wrist. Though no witch could access earth magics from Daemonia. Could Arius?

Could a witch escape from Daemonia? Perhaps a powerful warlock…

"Deep thoughts?"

Startled thoroughly, Tamatha let out a chirp and straightened her spine. Compulsively, she spread her hands over the page in the genealogy book. CJ stood in the doorway, a stack of papers held against his chest.

"Sorry," he offered with a curious lift of his brow. "Have you figured things out?"

"You went to Daemonia," she prompted. "How did you get there and how did you get out?"

"It was a foolish venture. Many vampires were sacrificed to open a portal and gain access. I was trapped there, unable to utilize my magics to get out. If it hadn't been for my brother, TJ, coming in to rescue me, I might still be rotting in that bedamned place."

"Arius Pumpelché was exiled to Daemonia," she said.

"Yes, I told you that."

She turned the book on witch genealogies toward him. CJ studied the opened pages. "She's the one behind raising *Les Douze*," she said. "I know it because I felt her in the cemetery last night."

"You tried to conjure her?"

"We called up *Les Douze* and she came along with them. Not in the flesh, though, so I don't know if she's here in the mortal realm or somehow operating from Daemonia."

"She wouldn't be able to work magic in this realm from Daemonia. Which means she's here. But I can't believe we didn't know about her escape. I should check with Cinder. He keeps the tech stuff in order for the Council. See when it happened or how."

"Yes, please do that. Any information will be helpful."

"We'll have to report this. Which will include your name and Thrash's since you two are working on capturing the warlock."

"I'm cool with that. The Council won't stop us, will it?"

"I'm sure not. You are trying to stop evil, not encourage it."

"Though capture wasn't exactly my plan. I'm hoping to..." Tamatha sighed and pushed the book forward on the table. "I don't know what the plan is. I found the spell for raising dead witches. It requires a demonic hex. Do you think Arius would be capable after spending so long in Daemonia?"

"I'm sure of it. Can you handle this, Tamatha?"

She nodded. "With Ed's help? Yes. Can you handle standing back and allowing me to handle it?"

He considered it a moment, then smiled. "Yes. As I've said, you are very skilled. And if you trust Thrash, then I'm of a mind to see if the demon can redeem himself to me. What's this?" He grabbed her gently by the hand and turned it over to expose the mark left behind from Ed's thorns. He stroked it and flinched, hissing. "That's demonic."

"Really?" She rubbed the skin. It didn't hurt. And she entirely expected it to fade completely. "Ed's thorn cut me last night."

"But that's— Well, you are alive, so that must mean someone had an antidote. Tamatha, this is not what I had in mind regarding him redeeming himself."

"It was an accident. We were battling zombie witches and fighting the warlock's magic. It just...happened." She didn't need to tell him the nefarious details; that Ed had come after her in a rage. "Ed was the one who mixed up the antidote and was able to save me. He cut off his own thorn to do it, CJ. Wasn't that heroic?"

The dark witch didn't show any sign he was pleased. Instead he leaned closer and met her gaze. "How did he get the spell? Did you teach it to him?"

"Well, no. He said he injected me with the antidote and that worked."

"Inject—no. All antidotes require a spoken spell. You know that, Tamatha."

Yes, she did. And what she'd just read about the antidote had remarked a spoken spell. "He did mention Libby helped. Maybe she gave it to him."

"Libby Saint-Charles is involved?"

Tamatha nodded. She wasn't about to tell him his wife, Vika, had been involved, as well. He wouldn't like that. Maybe. She couldn't get a read on CJ. Was he angry or being protective?

Again, he tapped her wrist over the healed wound. "The demon is in you now. Forever."

She'd said much the same to Ed last night. Didn't sound so awful to her. In fact, it felt awesome, as if they'd taken a step further with one another.

"Do you know what happens when a demon bonds with a witch, Tamatha?"

"I, well— We didn't bond, CJ. That's a sexual thing, isn't it?"

"It's this." He tapped her wrist again. "His blood exchange with yours."

"It wasn't exactly blood. It was his crushed thorn, along with salt and whiskey."

"He could have gotten your blood on his thorn when

he cut you. And then in turn he injected you with his very essence."

She hadn't considered that. It sounded so not like a party. "Am I going to turn into a demon?" she asked, feeling a little frightened now.

"Worse," CJ said. "You've given the demon control over you. None of your magic will be able to stop him. If he wants to control you in any manner, he can."

"Ed would never do that."

"If he even thinks it, it will happen. You might learn exactly how much the man cares for you now. I wish there was a spell to reverse this, but he's marked you and you are his now." CJ blew out a breath. "I feel terrible just saying that. I'm so sorry. Perhaps I should request the Council put someone else on this matter with the cemetery zombies."

"No, CJ, I can handle this. You said so yourself. Please, give me a chance," she pleaded. "I trust Ed. Besides, I've made my mark on him, as well."

"How so?"

"The corax demon is marked through life with major events and magics."

"Yes, with sigils on his skin that look much like tattoos."

"My family crest is forming over Ed's heart. It's my mark on him, I know it is."

"You mean that bell-shaped flower you've tattooed on your arm? Interesting."

"What do you think it means?"

"Such a significant symbol that represents your family?" CJ's brow lifted. "My first guess would be that he's in love with you."

Tamatha beamed at that knowledge. Ed hadn't said as much to her, but yes, she liked to think that they had grown that close. Close enough for love? She wanted it from him. But she remained cautious because of the family motto.

"But a more learned guess," CJ added, "would be a death mark. You and that family-curse thing. Don't most of the men you women love eventually die? I'd guess the demon is not long for this world."

"I'm going to go with your first guess."

"You do that. It's no skin off me if the demon dies. Then I won't have to worry about you being controlled by him."

"That's very rude of you. And surprisingly unsympathetic."

"Tamatha, be smart. I know you want the romance and roses, but really? Have you *ever* had a relationship with a man that did not end with his death or him leaving you while he was carted off in a straitjacket?"

She sighed and shook her head.

And then she remembered what her mom had suggested. "But I might have a chance to break the curse. If we can reunite my zombie grandmother with the demon lover who sent her to the stake, then maybe the curse will be lifted."

CJ whistled and shook his head. "Mercy, you need to fill me in on everything."

Chapter 21

Ed greeted Tamatha with a half hug. He wanted to crush her into his embrace but his left arm wasn't cooperating. And still he felt weak and drained. Not up to par. As if he'd shifted to a conspiracy a dozen times in one day.

Would the Bellerose death curse get him, too? He didn't want to think about it.

She noticed his lackluster hug and grabbed his hand. He hissed, but then remembered he was wearing gloves and she wouldn't be harmed.

"Still hurt?" she asked.

"Not so much hurt as…numb. I can't seem to move my arm. Don't worry about it." He kissed her. "I'll recover."

But he wasn't so sure. He'd never heard about a corax demon coming back after removal of his thorns and horns. He was up on all demon activity in the city, but…well, just…but. He didn't know. He didn't want to know, either.

"I wonder if I could whip up a recovery spell?" she said

as she glided into the living room, dropping her purse on the counter as she went by it.

"I'm fine, sweetness."

She turned and displayed the inside of her wrist where he had originally cut her. "CJ tells me we're bonded now," she said. "Maybe I've got some of your demon mojo I can tap into."

He took her hand and studied her wrist. A dark gray line showed where the cut had healed. His heart actually constricted as he looked at it. He'd harmed her. Almost killed her. And she was acting as if it were nothing more than a scratch.

"Bonded?" he asked. "Is that like when my werewolf brother bonded with his faery wife? It's for life?"

"Oh, I don't think so. I believe it's more on the lines that we're inside one another now. We might sense each other, maybe even tap into one another's magic."

"I don't want you trying to make this better. You could make it worse."

"You don't trust me?" She slipped her grasp into his and kissed his fingers. Green eyes peered up at him and those thick lashes dusted the air.

He was bewitched, and happy for it.

"I love you," he said and then swallowed because he hadn't expected to say that. But really? "I mean it, witch. I love you."

She hugged him and he tucked his head down and nuzzled into her hair. "I feel the same way," she said. "It feels fast. But right. You know? But also it feels like destiny."

"You mean like with *Les Douze* and the Libre denizen? I don't know about that."

"We were brought together for a reason, Ed. I believe that with all my heart."

"So we were brought together, meant to fall in love,

to ultimately slaughter your grandmother and see me die from the family curse?"

"Don't put it like that. I think we can break the curse!"

That bedamned curse. Something about him dying because he loved her. So he either died from a lost thorn or because of romance. Could he get a peek behind door number three? "The one where I'm supposed to die?"

"Yes, that one."

She was entirely too chipper about the whole thing, but as she led him to the couch, he dutifully followed. What else could he do? If her family curse didn't kill him, the missing thorn surely would.

He sat and she turned to place her hands on his knees. "My grandmother's lover was a demon named Rascon."

"Rascon? But I told you. He's my grandfather."

"I know! Isn't that oddly cool? Ed!" He loved her enthusiasm, but he was having trouble rising to her level. Because that implied nothing more than a sure death.

"How do you know that?" he asked.

"My mother returned to Paris last night and went through Lysia's things. She found some diary entries about her lover Rascon."

Blowing out a breath, he settled back against the couch. Now things were getting freaky. Maybe there was something to this destiny thing.

Tamatha curled up beside him. "What do you think of that for destiny?"

"It's freakin' weird, if you ask me. What makes you think the warlock didn't bring the two of us together as part of her plot to destroy the Libre denizen?"

"Well, I don't have proof she didn't. But I'm erring on the destiny side. It suits me better. Besides, how could she have known about your grandfather and my grandmother? Wait. Maybe she could have."

He should tell her about the warlock's visit and their bargain. *No.*

"I learned that Arius's husband, Martine, was one of *Les Douze*. He would have told Arius about Lysia's affair with Rascon. Which could explain how she's put the two of us together. But there's no worry. Now all we have to do is get Rascon here to apologize to Lysia and I think we can break the spell."

He gave her such an incredulous look that she actually flinched.

"He is still alive, yes?" she asked.

"He is. I've heard about him now and again, but have never actually met him. Not sure where he is, but my mom would know." And the last person he wanted to contact now was Sophie. "So you want my grandfather to apologize to his zombie lover for sending her to burn at the stake? I'm not sure that's going to go over too well."

"We have to try." She clasped his hand, and while she wasn't wielding the fluttery lashes for seduction, Ed's heart still performed a double beat. "Don't you want to avoid death?"

"At all costs. But there's a lot worse things in this strange realm that can kill me than loving you."

"No, there's not. The Bellerose curse is extremely accurate. If you don't die, at the very least, you'll go mad. I do love you, Ed. I want you to be alive and sane so I can continue to love you."

"Sanity and a heartbeat sound good to me. But you're overlooking the key point here. Even if Rascon did apologize and he and your grandmother kissed and made up, and the curse was broken, there's still the problem that zombie witches are destroying demons. They are controlled by Arius. No long-lost love reunion is going to change that."

"I know. But Arius's husband was one of *Les Douze*.

She's doing this for that reason. All for love. Don't you see? That's her weakness. Love."

"I sense love is the weakness in the hearts of most. I wonder why she waited two and a half centuries?"

"Because she was exiled to Daemonia and she's only recently escaped. CJ is checking the details of that. CJ also said Arius would need the blood of one of *Les Douze* to raise them from the dead. She must have some of her husband's blood. If she were to run out, I suspect the zombie spell would be broken."

Ed swore and stood, pacing toward the stained glass windows that curved about the living area. He recalled Arius's visit. The cherry-red hair. The demonic marks. Had she worn some kind of vial about her neck?

"This is nuts," he said. "This all seems to hinge on lovers and their broken hearts. Why do people do that? What is so special about love?"

Tamatha huffed out a breath, but shrugged. "Love can make a person do strange things."

He turned to her. "How many times have you been in love?"

"I, uh…" She stood and approached him. "Does it matter?"

"Not in the greater scheme of things, but I am curious. You tell me your lovers die or go mad. Did you love them all?"

"Oh, no. I can like a lover and enjoy sex with him, but that doesn't mean I love him. Though I can say I've loved from my heart twice in my lifetime. What about you?"

He shrugged and turned to face the window.

"You have loved?"

"Is it important that I have? Maybe I haven't found the right woman until… Saying 'I love you' means something to me." He glanced over his shoulder. "That's the first time I've said it to anyone."

Tamatha's jaw dropped open. "Your mother? Father? Half brother?"

He shook his head and looked away. So he wasn't one of those gushing emotional kind of guys who liked to hug the world and count daisies. His heart was hard and black. He was demon, for hell's sake. He'd never thought love was something he'd know or deserve.

But when he was with Tamatha he did know. And love? He stroked the back of his hand where the glove covered the bandage. He'd cut off his thorn for her. That meant something. Maybe he'd like to have love for more than the short time her family curse would offer him. If he didn't die from his lost thorn first.

The warmth of Tamatha's hands embracing him from behind settled into him like a sigh. Had he fallen in love only to stand before death's door? He couldn't move his fingers on his left hand to even touch her. What the hell was going on with him?

"I might not have much longer," he said. Because he had to. He wanted to be truthful with her. "I think it's because of the thorn. Removal brings death."

"What makes you believe that?"

"Things my mother told me when I was younger. Tamatha, I'm not right lately. And while the black streak has moved lower on my arm, I can't—"

"It's not the thorn," she said. "Your thorns and horns can regenerate. I read it in a book about demons. Unless the healing goes wrong. But you're keeping it clean, yes? If you feel like you're in pain or suffering, it's because of the curse. Oh, Ed." She moved around in front of him and hugged him tightly. "Call your mother and find your grandfather. We need to break this curse now."

"I can't."

"Why not?"

"I can't talk to Sophie now." Might he risk Arius tracking Sophie with a mere phone call? It was possible if she had tracked him in his own home.

"But that's the only thing that will break the curse, that will save our love."

He turned to her and saw such hurt in her expression. Hell, he had thought he would die to give her life. What was one more sacrifice to win her love?

But his mother? He'd known Tamatha a short time. Maybe it was lust? Which didn't explain the imprint over his heart.

Hell, he could not sacrifice his own flesh and blood for a fleeting romance. It felt wrong. And it felt like destiny.

And he didn't want to believe in destiny.

"I'm sorry," he said. "You should leave now."

Chapter 22

Tamatha wasn't sure if Ed would contact his mother. He'd flat-out refused and then told her to leave. She couldn't imagine that he was angry with her and only hoped it was residual effects from losing his thorn that was making him not nice. Because he had only just told her he loved her. He wasn't going to change his mind so quickly, was he?

Even if he had jumped the gun with his proclamation of love for her, she could deal. It was part of the curse. Men started to lose their minds the longer they were involved with her.

They needed Rascon to break the curse.

So Tamatha came around to thinking if she could heal Ed, then he could think clearly. And what she couldn't do without supplies was now possible with an altar and concentration.

Switching her focus to the spell before her, she closed her eyes and lured her inner senses toward her wrist where

Ed's vita connected her to him. She sat upon a velvet cushion before a small altar on the bedroom floor. Red and white candles were lit for healing. Myrrh burned in a pewter tray. And she was skyclad. She wanted to be as open as possible to anything she might tap into.

Whispering a prayer to all the men who had died or gone mad because they had deemed to love the Bellerose women through the ages, she then ended by saying Ed's full name three times. Her soul reached out to him and she drew on the invisible tendrils that wavered through the air and soared through the city.

And when the tendrils seemed to attach and she gulped in a breath, Tamatha smiled. "Feel me," she said. "And heal."

Pacing the marble floor in his office, Ed paused and glanced to the items on the shelves. The genie in the bottle was quiet, the glass dark. The angel dust had been a trade from one of The Wicked, half demon–half faeries who had escaped their exile in Faery. Their irises were pink and Ed had found an elixir administered by drops to change them to innocuous brown. Many of The Wicked had found asylum in the mortal realm, and thanks to his good relations with them, he needn't worry about policing them as well as the full-blooded demons.

And the alicorn. He paused from reaching for it. Tamatha had remarked the good vibes she felt from it and how sad that had made her. Why had he never considered that the creature might have experienced pain to give up such a thing? That it had very likely been stolen from the unicorn since, indeed, the beast was immortal.

He owned many items of magical nature and some were evil. It had never bothered him. Until now.

Tamatha made him see things differently. And that was a good thing.

He should not have been so brisk with her earlier, asking her to leave. But he'd not known what to do. To explain about his mother would have revealed his alliance with the warlock. Not really an alliance. He'd figure a way out of it. And when he did, Tamatha never had to know.

The alicorn sat upon the dusty shelf, seeming to beam out pink vibrations at him. Good, joy, all that was right. And he knew he should be honest with Tamatha. Completely.

"Damn it," he muttered and marched away from the annoying thing. "I'll tell her! I have to. I could be dead from that stupid family curse soon. She has to know I would do anything for her, even if it meant lying to the warlock."

On his way out, Ed paused before the door. An overwhelming warmth spread in his heart. He clasped his left hand over his chest, then unbuttoned his shirt to reveal the Bellerose sigil over his heart glowed. And his body... hummed subtly. As if sensing an intrusion.

"What the hell?"

Then he realized he was using his gimp hand. He flexed the fingers. Without pain. Complete use had been restored to his hand. He removed the glove and drew his thorns out—all four of them. The one he'd cut off had regenerated. Just as Tamatha had said it could happen.

"What kind of magic...?"

It was magic. Had to be. And it was her magic. He knew it as he knew she was inside him, flooding his veins, healing his thorn. It was a weird intrusion, and he didn't like it. He appreciated the healing, but he certainly didn't want the witch to control him like this. It reminded him of that horrible time he'd almost lost his soul to a witch's enslavement.

Reacting to that sudden anger, he thrust out his palm, as if to shove someone away from him.

Tamatha's body was thrust away from the altar by an invisible force. She landed on the end of the bed and tumbled off to sprawl on the floor. "Ouch!"

A silken spill of a sheer red shawl fell over her shoulders, which she clutched about her. Blowing aside the hair from her face, she saw the candles had ignited the altar. With a forceful breath of air magic, she extinguished the flames. Black ash sifted into the air and seemed to take flight…as if ravens.

"Did *he* do that?"

No. She considered the line on her wrist. They *were* bonded. If she could send him healing vibes, perhaps he could do the same. But he wasn't a healer, so instead what had he sent? It had felt violent.

"CJ was right." Ed *could* control her. And he'd been so rough with her. Had he felt her intrusion and shoved her away? If he loved her, why wouldn't he embrace her?

"I'm not going to make an assumption. I did just control him with the healing."

She'd try something else. Like a simple kiss. Something he should welcome…

This time Tamatha's body slid across the floor and crashed up against the window. The glass cracked but didn't break. Maybe she had tapped into the wrong demon?

When a flock of dark birds battered against the cracked window, she turned and stood, putting up her hands in defense. A little air magic would send them off—

"Ravens?" Was it Ed?

Unwilling to use repulsive magic against her lover, she rushed to the unbroken window and opened the sash. The conspiracy flooded in and flocked about her, their wings hitting her hair and forcing her to pull up the shawl as a shield in defense. When she stumbled and landed on the bed, the ravens shifted.

Ed formed over her, his hands pinning her wrists to the bed, trapping her. "What the hell, witch?"

Her demon lover loomed before her, his gray irises edged in red. He was angry? But she had only tried to heal him. How dare he react so cruelly?

"Get off me!"

Ed stood back, shifting his shoulders to stand tall and defiantly over her.

Tamatha almost cast a repulsion spell, but relented at the last moment. "I was testing the connection. And apparently, you can control me, as CJ said."

"Is that so? CJ told you this? You didn't mention it to me."

"Yes, I…" Didn't she?

"You were the one *inside* me, witch."

She cringed at the tone he used to call her witch.

"What were you trying to do? You have no right! This goes way beyond the whole boyfriend-girlfriend thing. I will not have you fucking around inside my head."

"I wasn't in your head," she argued as loudly as he did. Tugging the sheer red wrap about her did not alleviate her vulnerability. "I wanted to give our bond a try and thought you could use some tender care. I was healing your hand. And I see you've got control of it again." He wiggled his fingers, then curled them into a fist and punched his opposite palm. "You're welcome."

"If you would have let me know you were going to do this, maybe I wouldn't have been taken by surprise. But if you believe you have a right to just jump inside me, no matter the reason—" He swept his hand before her and his black smoky magic soared toward her.

Reacting to the threat, Tamatha repulsed it with air magic, following with a frill of fire on the end.

Ed dodged the fizzling flame. "Is that so?"

"You're forcing me to defend myself!"

"And with such flare. I'll see your flame." He snapped his fingers and a swarm of small black-winged creatures soared toward Tamatha. "And raise you an unkindness."

The miniature flock of ravens dive-bombed Tamatha's hair. She shouted, "*Expulsus!*" And the creatures misted to nothing. "Ed, stop!" She held up a palm to deflect his next move. "This argument is ridiculous. We should both be focused on the more important reason we are together right now."

He gripped her by the shoulders and squeezed not too gently. "You were the one freaked about my being able to possibly control you. And then you go ahead and do the same? Tamatha, I trusted you."

She exhaled. Yes, he had. And she hadn't thought of the implications when she'd prepared the altar to send her healing magic. She'd only wanted to help him. But he was right. She should have asked or, at the very least, let him know what she was doing.

"Sorry." She bowed her head. "I was wrong. You are right."

"No, I don't want to be—"

At that moment the cracked glass in the window cracked even more and fell inward. Ed grabbed her about the waist and charged into the living room to avoid the flying shards.

"What the hell?" he muttered against her hair. "What is going on?"

"You flung me against the window with your reactionary magic. It cracked."

"Shit. I'm sorry. I—I could have hurt you. You could have been cut by glass. I didn't want that. I wanted you out of me." He clutched her against him as if clinging would make her safe. "I love you. But that scares me. That's why I reacted so strongly. What are we doing to one another? I threw magic at you."

"I'll never do it again. I promise. I wanted to heal you."

"Thank you. It worked. I love you for that. I shouldn't have reacted."

"I should have told you what I wanted to do."

"Let's make a vow to never use our bond with one another."

"What if it can help the other?"

He shook his head. "Never. Please, Tamatha—it's wrong."

Much as she didn't agree, because if she could help him and vice versa, she would never neglect that power, she nodded. "Agreed."

With a gesture of her hand and a whispered "*Resolvo*," the glass window re-formed and fitted back into the wood sill. "Was that our first fight?"

"I think so."

"Wait. That time you had me kidnapped—"

He kissed her. Because he didn't want to bring up the bad stuff. He was glad she was safe, not cut by glass, and hell—she'd attempted to heal him and had succeeded. Not a thing about the two of them warranted further argument. Only falling into this kiss mattered now.

His hands glided over the silky fabric draped about her shoulders. "You're not wearing much. What is it with witches and the whole skyclad thing?"

"It opens us to the full potential the universe is willing to offer. I needed it to reach you with my healing vibrations. Does it bother you?"

"Does this bother you?" He lashed his tongue over her nipple.

She arched her back, lifting her breast higher. "Nope. But maybe you should check the other one. See if that one bothers me."

His mouth closed over her ruched nipple and she clung to his shoulders, wanting to pull him into her, but not wanting to lose the delicious sensation at her breast. "Mmm, yes."

He lifted her onto the couch and licked down her stomach and didn't stop until his tongue found her clit. His hands glided down her thighs and hiked her legs up over his shoulders.

If fighting led to makeup sex like this, Tamatha could do with the occasional argument. What the man could do with his tongue. Her body shivered and she ran her hands through his hair, making a point of gliding slowly and circling his horn nubs.

He growled against her and the vibration of his voice teased her closer to climax. Gripping his hair, she pulled gently but insistently. Right there. Yes, he went deep and followed with his fingers.

"This is the only way I want to be inside you," he said and lashed his tongue over her skin. "You like that?"

"You've got a magical touch," she said on a rising note, and then she gasped out an exalted cry as the orgasm rocked her world.

In the morning, Ed sat up on the bed and grabbed his ringing cell phone. After his argument with Tamatha he'd rethought his priorities. He would do anything to protect his mother, but that meant he needed to keep her in the loop. He'd called Sophie last night and explained his need for her to stay out of sight and also for contact with his grandfather. His mother must have given Rascon his number.

"Uh, hey, Grandfather. This is a little weird, but there's a situation going on in town that needs your involvement."

"I'm delighted to help my grandson. Can we meet?"

"Yes, soon. But I'm afraid there's no time for getting to know one another."

"If what you need me for is so important, I understand. I'll take you out on the town after the problem has been solved. So what is going on?"

"Do you recall a witch lover from the eighteenth century?"

"I, uh… Why do you ask?"

"It seems that after the two of you parted ways, a curse was fashioned. That very curse is now affecting my lover and me. And a warlock has gotten involved, as well. The warlock has been killing the progeny of your former Libre denizen."

"That sounds like a mess. But why the interest in my lover?"

"You remember her?"

"Yes. The witch, Lysia Bellerose."

"You two were in love?"

"What do you need, Edamite? Tell me."

"I need you to apologize to Lysia for accusing her and sending her to the stake."

Silence reigned on the other end of the line. Ed assumed Rascon was sorting through memories. They must have loved fiercely. Surely he would want to make amends by explaining his reason for siding with his denizen and accusing her so cruelly.

"I'm afraid I can't help you with that one," Rascon said.

"I don't understand. You must have been forced to accuse *Les Douze* by your denizen."

"No. No force involved. You see, I was the one who led the denizen in accusing those heinous witches."

Chapter 23

The look Ed gave Tamatha made her sit upright on the bed and press a hand over the sigil on his chest. His heartbeats thundered beneath her touch. So much so that her heartbeats sped up. "What is it?"

"Rascon, please," he said to the caller. "Meet me and let's talk about this." He tossed the phone aside. "My grandfather hung up on me."

"Why? You didn't say a thing about Lysia being a zombie. I don't understand."

"We suspected that Rascon was forced to go along with his denizen in accusing the witches?"

She nodded.

"He was the one who led them in the accusation. He doesn't want anything to do with apologizing to Lysia. So I guess that's that with breaking the curse. At least we can still try to take out the warlock. Because you know, we're so powerful and have all the skills to do that."

His sarcasm set her back. Tamatha clutched the pillow

to her chest and watched as he dressed. They had to break the curse. More than stopping *Les Douze*, she wanted the curse broken. So she could have Ed. For longer than most. And if that was being greedy, then sign her up for the trophy. She'd take the greed award and wave it proudly.

"What's the plan for the warlock?" he asked as he buttoned up his black shirt and tucked it in his pants. "Are you witchy foursome working on something?"

"Vika and Libby are digging deep into their family grimoire and Verity is trying to contact Ian Grim. Supposedly the warlock owes her one."

His manner was curt and she sensed he was ready to give up on it all. But he didn't seem like the kind of man who could do that. Otherwise he would be some witch's slave right now.

"What if we could get Arius's husband to somehow tell her to stop?" she asked. "He's one of *Les Douze*. It must be horrible for him to be controlled and to exist in such a condition. Surely he must want it to end."

"Doesn't sound like a party the warlock would like to attend. Or me, if you intend to dangle me as bait again."

"Never. I promise. But you did volunteer to it the first time."

"You don't have to beat me with the stupid stick more than once. I learned my lesson. Though, I'm not complaining. Just don't need to try a stupid thing more than once. What about your Certainly Jones? He's a dark witch. He must have a warlock-fighting trick or two up his sleeve."

"You don't think I can handle this?"

"You alone? No." He stood at the end of the bed, arms crossed over his chest. "Do you?"

"Thanks for the faith."

"We don't need faith, Tamatha. We need a bloody miracle."

"What about the two of us working together?"

"We've tried."

"But now that we're bonded?"

"I thought we'd made a promise not to—"

"To use our bond against one another. But combining forces and working as a team?"

He sat beside her and clasped her hand with his restored hand. Kissing the back of hers, he rubbed the back of it over his cheek, lingering, then said, "We do make a good team."

"Yes, and if Arius has some kind of demonic magic—which we suspect—she's mixed that with her witch magic. So can't we do the same?"

He kissed her. "I love you."

"Really? Because I had thought you might have changed your mind after our altercation last night."

"I was acting naughty. Reacting when I should have merely been grateful. But we kissed and made up, yes?"

"I do like your kisses. Especially the ones right here." She touched her crotch and smiled up sweetly at him.

He bent to kiss her there. "I love you. I love you. I love you. And I'm actually beginning to believe it's real the more I say it."

She stroked his cheek. "Why have you ever thought you were not worthy of love?"

"An evil-overlord thing, I guess."

She snickered, but she knew he was being too hard on himself. And if he'd always believed such, it was a real and tangible emotion that he couldn't simply erase because their relationship had opened up a vein to love. It would take time, and that was cool with her.

"I love that you are willing to love," she said. "Often?"

"Sure. But only you."

"Good answer. So have any more demons been killed since the last?"

"No. But I'm not hanging out in cemeteries keeping watch."

"I thought you'd posted guards?"

"No reports of foul deeds from Inego."

"What if the warlock has no choice but to show?"

"Still pretty sure she's not going to attend any party we decide to throw."

"Ed." She tossed aside the pillow and crawled to the end of the bed. Still naked, she knelt and pulled him to her by the front of his shirt. "If we kidnap her husband, then I think she'll show."

"Kidnapping a zombie witch? Eh. I'm not so sure about that one. Despite their decrepit appearance, those things were strong. I'm not sure I could fight them off if they came at me full force again."

"Have you a better idea?"

"You're serious?"

She nodded.

"Possibly with our combined magics." He shuddered and twisted a look over his shoulder.

"What?" she asked, but no sooner had she spoken than she felt a weird intrusion that shimmered over her shoulders. "Something's in here with us."

"It's the warlock," he said. "Put up wards!"

Tamatha dashed to her altar and scrambled to light the black candle. Her fingers slipped and she dropped her beryl wand. It broke in two. She gasped. She'd owned that wand for decades. It had teemed with the earth's energy and always enhanced her spells.

"Ah, shit."

Ed's utterance did not inspire hope in her. Turning slowly, she saw the warlock standing in the center of her living room before her boyfriend. She wore skintight red leather, thigh-high boots and a rich emerald frock coat. Her face was marked with white sigils that didn't look like any kind of magical sigils with which Tamatha was familiar.

And in one hand she wielded a menacing ball of green flame.

"*Protegendum!*" Tamatha called up a protective shield before Ed and herself in a flash of white light. The warlock's flames bounced off the shield protecting Ed.

"Thanks," he said. "I needed that." To the warlock he asked, "Are you Arius Pumpelché?"

"You know I am, demon. You had one job to do and you failed."

"A job?" Tamatha asked. "Ed, what is she talking about?" The warlock's smirk crept over Tamatha's skin as if corpse worms. "Ed?"

His hands gripped in and out of fists at his sides. He winced, then tilted his head toward her and confessed, "She wanted me to bring my mother to her in exchange for providing the spell that accompanied the antidote that healed you."

"You broke that promise, demon."

"You said you didn't need a spell," Tamatha said. She'd forgotten CJ's concern that a spell had indeed been needed. "You've spoken with the warlock already?"

"I lied because I didn't want you to know I'd made a deal with this bitch. I was desperate. You were near death."

"Spare me your lovers' squabble," Arius said. "You are fated to die as it is, demon. You, Edamite Thrash—" she touched her throat and squeezed the two white lines together and Ed gasped for breath "—are the progeny of Rascon, who accused my husband of witchcraft. I watched him burn at the stake!"

"Yeah?" Tamatha said, stepping up behind Ed. "Well,

wasn't your husband, Martine, one of the witches who kept the Libre denizen captive and controlled them?"

"He was." The warlock straightened, offended at that obvious question. Yet she lowered her head, aiming her gaze on Ed. "They should have been thankful for the entrance to this realm. The demons had no right to accuse the coven so. They gave them life on this realm."

"Life as a slave," Ed defied her through gasping breaths. "Witches have no right!"

Tamatha felt the pain of his suffering in that statement. He knew too well how a demon could suffer at the hands of a witch.

Arius pressed her fingers tighter at her neck. Ed choked.

Tamatha eyed her altar for something, anything she could use against the warlock, but she didn't think herbs and some rose water would help much. Ed was choking but he was strong. And he was still talking, so he was holding in there.

As long as they kept the warlock talking, maybe all she would do was talk. Then she noticed the faint shimmer over Arius's image. And she realized it was just an image.

"She's not here," she said to Ed. "It's a projection."

"Indeed." Arius turned to her. "Stay out of my business, witch, and I'll let your demon lover live."

"You made this my business when you decided to raise my grandmother from the dead. She doesn't want to be a zombie. And I'm going to help her have peace. As well as your husband. How can you do that to him?"

Arius dropped her hand from her neck and Ed sucked in a heaving inhalation.

"Martine knows it's for revenge. I've waited centuries for this. And I won't have two meddling nobodies screwing it up." The warlock thrust out a blast of fire that ricocheted off Ed's shield, as well as Tamatha's, but it ignited on the sheers hanging before the window.

Tamatha pressed her middle fingers together and recited a water spell. Rain spilled from the ceiling, soaking the entire room. It also wiped away Arius's image.

"You took the warlock out with water?" Ed scratched his head. "What next? Flying monkeys?"

"She's not defeated. That was just a message." She ceased the rain spell and pushed her wet hair over a shoulder. "A little air magic should dry things up nicely." With a few recited words and a sweep of her hand about the room, the water evaporated as quickly as it had formed.

Ed pulled her into his arms.

"You okay?" She touched his throat.

"Yes, but she was able to permeate your protection spell. I could feel the demonic magic in it. It was familiar."

"She's obviously studied while in Daemonia. I think if we want to defeat the warlock, we need to turn her revenant spell against her."

"And how do we do that?"

"We get my grandmother and the warlock's husband on our side."

"I've already said Rascon isn't going to help. And I do know the zombies would rather munch on me than listen to anything I've to say."

"Right." She took his hand and turned their palms up. Tracing across the gray line that marked her wrist, she said, "We should be strong together, yes?"

"I'll give anything a try once. Twice if it feels good."

She kissed him. "Then let's go talk to some zombie witches."

"Aw, and here I thought you'd understood what I'd said about doing things that feel good."

"We'll have sex later," she said. "Zombies first."

He followed her down the hallway. "I'm not sure I'm keen on how you prioritize, but okay, then."

They didn't get out of Tamatha's apartment because the front door opened to reveal Petrina holding a faded red leather-bound diary. Petrina's eyes brightened at the sight of her daughter, and she swept in to hug her while Ed stood back, observing. The mother looked as young as the daughter, yet she was decidedly bohemian in fashion. He took that cue from the flowers woven into her hair and the long flowery dress she wore. Beads wrapped both wrists nearly to her elbows, and rings competed with the tattooed sigils marking her fingers.

"Mom! This is Ed."

When Tamatha grasped his left hand, he was again thankful for having got back the feeling in that hand and arm. And when Petrina pulled him in for a hug, he had a moment of wonder when her hand slipped down and over his ass.

"Whoa." He stepped back and bowed, offering a *Namaste* to the touchy-feely mother. "Nice to meet you, Madame Bellerose."

"It's Mademoiselle," she stated with a wink as she breezed by him and into the living room. "Tamatha, I've brought your grandmother's diary— Oh." She paused in the center of the room, looking about. Her nostrils flared. "What was here?"

"The warlock sent a hologram of some sort to give us a warning that we've a battle ahead of us," Tamatha said as she took the diary her mother handed her and began to page through it. "She's a she."

"Really? A female warlock? Makes sense. No man could survive that long in Daemonia with such vengeance in his heart. He'd die after a few years. We women are strong."

"Unfortunate for the poor witches she has raised from the dead," Ed felt it necessary to point out. "How to fight this warlock?"

"Oh, you are adorable." Petrina stroked his cheek and glided her fingers down to touch the feather sigil on his neck. "Nice. I do love a tattooed man. I taught my daughter well, I see. Are you sure you're happy with this one?" she asked Tamatha. "If not, I could take him off your hands."

"Yes, Mother, very sure," Tamatha offered absently. Her attention was deep in the pages of the diary. Much to Ed's peril.

Petrina circled him, eyeing him up and down. He'd never felt more like a piece of meat hanging in the charcuterie until now. And usually an assessing look like that from a woman should make any man feel great. If not propositioned.

"So you are living in Greece?" he managed when Petrina stopped her gaze at his mouth. "I've heard the water is as blue as a sapphire."

"Yes, sure." She dismissed the comment with a flip of her hand. "So. Fighting a warlock. Let's put our heads together, shall we? Ed, you can put your head against mine anytime."

Thoroughly embarrassed by her wink, he did catch Tamatha's teasing smile. If he survived the mother, he imagined he could stand against a gang of zombie witches and one pissed-off warlock.

Chapter 24

Petrina shivered and slid away from Ed on the couch where she had been sitting close enough to have babies with him. Tamatha overlooked her mother's behavior because she was who she was. Sensual, seductive and flirtatious. She'd never worried her mother would steal a boyfriend before, and she didn't now. What did worry her was the shiver.

"Mom?"

Petrina stood and paced to the window, pushing her fingers through her long blue-silver curls that spilled tiny queen's-lace blossoms in her wake. She was never without flowers, even in winter.

"I can sense your demon lover's death." She turned a sad eye on Ed and clasped her arms over her stomach, shivering once again. "Soon."

"You ladies and your weird family curse." Ed gestured dismissively as he got up and gathered the teacups from their afternoon brainstorming session over how to kill a warlock. “I’m good.”

“You don’t look it,” Petrina commented. “You’ve gotten paler since I’ve arrived.”

He made a doubting face. “Just some residual stuff from nearly being torn apart by zombie witches, I’m sure. I’m good. Let’s get this show on the road. You said you needed some supplies from the graveyard? And that you wanted to try and contact one of the witches without the warlock’s interference?”

“Yes, we should get going.” Tamatha tucked her grandmother’s diary in her book bag and ran into her bedroom to slip on some knee-high boots. She called out, “Mom, get the nightshade from the fridge!”

“Will do!” But when Petrina passed him by, allowing her gaze to slither up and down him, Ed felt as if she had walked over his freshly mounded grave.

He believed the Bellerose curse was real. And admittedly, he wasn’t feeling top-notch. But he wasn’t about to step back and allow the women to do all the work. They needed him. And he’d die to help Tamatha and her family.

Because he loved her and she was the best thing he never knew he wanted. Crazy maybe. But certainly worth the ride.

He flexed the fingers on his left hand. All functional. So what was making him feel as if he’d run a marathon and could use some oxygen?

The man waiting for them inside the cemetery gates appeared unremarkable to Ed. So much so that he wandered right past him. But Tamatha recognized him from the etching she’d seen in the demon genealogy book.

“Rascon?”

Ed spun around and walked back, putting an arm

around Tamatha's waist. Petrina drew up her white light and whispered a demon protection spell.

"Grandfather?" Ed asked.

The man looked about seventy and had gray hair and olive skin. Not at all pale like Ed, but Tamatha had never met his mother, so he could have got his paleness from his werewolf father. Rascon wore boat shoes and a canvas hat and vest along with canvas pants and a gray T-shirt. Unremarkable. Almost had a tourist vibe. One would never pin him as demon. Especially not a vindictive demon who had once sent his witch lover to the stake to be burned alive.

"Yes, Grandson, I am Rascon." He didn't step forward, but Tamatha was well aware he'd taken in her and Petrina. The old man was sharp. "I couldn't let things go the way we left them, so I deduced you were on your way here when I saw the three of you leave the witch's apartment."

"How did you know when I—?"

He must have used demonic magic to trace his grandson from the phone call. Or GPS.

"You followed us?" Tamatha asked. "What do you want? If you're not going to help us—" Ed squeezed her hand, and she decided it wasn't her place to do the condemning. She felt her mother move up close beside her and leach her white light onto her. Thankful for that, she knew with her and Ed's new bond, that light would also protect him.

"If you've come to hinder us, you'll have to go through me," Ed said. "I'm just trying to keep the peace in this city. It's something I've always done."

"I know." Rascon shrugged. "Your mother told me you're a fine young man, what with you keeping a watchful eye over the city and keeping our species in line. You're someone to be proud of, Edamite. I'm sorry, but this one thing in my past won't go to rest, much as I'd like it to. I had to do it," he said to Tamatha. "*Les Douze* needed to be taught a lesson. We were not pets to control. We were *and are* thinking, breathing, living souls."

Tamatha nodded. "I agree. But weren't you in love with Lysia?"

"Eh. It was a ruse. So she would trust me and release me. I was the last one *Les Douze* released. We formed the Libre denizen with the intent of ensuring no witches ever controlled another demon again. It was a lofty goal. We hadn't the skill or the manpower to accomplish such a task. But we did take down a dozen of them. I'm sorry. I know you two are Bellerose women. I can feel it in my veins, the latent command that yet lingers and always will." He shivered. "Lysia was so powerful. But understand that I did it for my freedom. You've much worse to deal with now. Someone has conjured *Les Douze*?"

Ed stepped before Tamatha. "It's not your problem. And I'll have to ask you to leave. I'm sure you'll have nothing against us, once again, putting *Les Douze* to rest, so just...leave."

"Who raised the witches?" Rascon asked.

"Arius Pumpelché," Petrina provided. "Know her?"

Rascon hissed. "Crazy witch. Tried to raise her husband from the dead right after he was burned at the stake. It was a fine day when she was exiled to Daemonia. But she's here?"

Tamatha nodded.

"While in Daemonia," Rascon said, "she used the demons to learn their ways and gather their magics. She is reviled by us all. And she will be a force to fight unless you've demonic magic."

"Which I do," Ed offered.

"Not powerful enough," Rascon said. "Even if you should combine your magic with your witchy lover. Arius is warlock times ten with the added demonic knowledge. I remember her too well, and that was when she was not so powerful." Rascon sighed. "Perhaps you should simply let her complete her act of vengeance then let her slip away."

"So you're cool with her killing your daughter Sophie?" Ed offered. "And me?"

The demon met Ed's question with a startled moue. "Not my Sophie?"

"Arius is after *all* the relatives of the Libre denizen. I told Mom to go deeper into hiding, but unless we take care of the warlock, she'll never be safe." Ed tilted his head side to side, stretching his muscles and gearing up his fortitude. "Like I said, we've got this under control."

"One more demon on your team would only increase that control," Rascon suggested. He stepped forward. "If I can help you take out that bitch of a warlock, then you have me. You have my word I will give my all."

Ed glanced to Tamatha, who nodded. He didn't want the old man involved. He looked ineffectual and weak. And he hadn't wanted to help originally. What gave him hope to trust him?

"Let me protect my family," Rascon offered.

"Excellent," Petrina whispered and gestured to Rascon to follow her. "We're going to summon some zombies. Are you in?"

The elder demon followed the witch. "Zombies are new to me, but I'm always willing to give things a try. Twice if they feel good."

Tamatha glanced to Ed and smiled. She didn't have to say anything. So he'd inherited his grandfather's penchant for reckless adventure.

Rascon agreed to talk to Lysia if they could summon *Les Douze.* That might negate the curse and in doing so gain Lysia as an ally and perhaps even allow her to introduce them to Martine Chevalier. The key to defeating Arius.

Before Tamatha could enter the salt circle she and her mother had poured onto the cobblestones before a massive family mausoleum, Ed tugged her aside into the shadows created by a mourning angel.

He kissed her slowly, savoring the feel of her mouth on his. Lemons overwhelmed and he smiled. "I love you."

"I love you, too, Edamite Thrash. That's why I'm doing this. I want to break the curse. And now that your grandfather is on board, it's very possible it could happen."

"I still don't trust him. He came to see me too eagerly. And then to return after I'd asked him to do the one thing he would never dream to do? Something doesn't feel right."

"It's love, Ed. Rascon has a love for his family. His daughter. And you. He wants to protect you. Believe in love, will you?"

"I believe I love you." He kissed her again.

"That's all that matters. So you two will need to stay outside the salt circle."

"I have no problem with that request."

"Right, but..." She tugged him back before he could walk toward the circle. "That means you'll be, uh...you know."

He didn't have to think about what she meant before it popped into his brain. "Really? Again? I'm starting to feel like a worm on a hook."

"Yes, but you're a sexy worm. And you're still wearing the white light my mother put over us, so that will help a little."

He shook his arms. "I don't feel it. But that's how it's supposed to be. Got it. Let me do this, then."

He gripped her hand and slid it up over her wrist.

Tamatha could see the family crest on his chest glow through his shirt while she felt the heat on the healed wound on her wrist. Their bond was strong. And with a sudden puff of black smoke, she felt as though she'd been covered over with something intangible.

"My style of white light," he said with a smirk. "The double protection should be just what you need. Now come on, witch. Let's go play with zombies."

Nine members of *Les Douze* remained. Ed had taken out one during their altercation the other day, and the other two, well, Tamatha didn't know where they were. She'd asked her mother what Lysia looked like. She'd died before cameras had been invented and no one had ever sketched her.

Petrina had smiled and said how often people had remarked that she had looked so much like her mother. Save that Lysia's hair had been much darker.

Okay, so Lysia was her mother's twin. Zombified.

And which one was Martine? She could pick out at least two zombies that looked remotely male. It wasn't easy looking at any of them. Flesh hung off exposed bone. Metallic ooze stained their tattered clothing. Missing hair and teeth, also, some cheeks missing.

But there. That one. It had to be Lysia. She stood tallest and had most of her hair. It was bluish black, darker than Petrina's but definitely of the same shade. Interesting how as the generations had progressed their hair had got lighter. Tamatha cautioned herself not to slip into fascination.

The zombies shambled closer. Ed and Rascon stood behind the salt circle in which she and her mother stood.

Sprinkling ash from a velvet bag into her palm, Tamatha recited a ward against the dead. Holding up a hand and now reciting a spell, she called on the wind to prevent their approach.

"Lysia?" Petrina called out. And then on a gasp, she murmured, "Oh, *ma mère*."

The zombie Tamatha had suspected was her grandmother yanked her head up from its sideways tilt and eyed them both. She opened her mouth and metallic ooze drooled down her chin.

"Oh, Grandmother." Tears wet her eyes. She wanted to embrace the tattered remains of her grandmother and… change her. Bring back her life. But that was impossible. One could never return a person to their original flesh-and-blood mentally-stable state after death.

The warlock was nowhere to be seen. Tamatha must work quickly.

"Rascon," she said, signaling the demon step forward. "Talk to her!"

"Right." The demon's first steps were confident and sure, but after five or six he slowed and his fingers flexed by his sides.

Meanwhile, Ed stepped to the side of the circle beside Tamatha. He reached across the salt line and, with a grimace, grabbed her hand. The mark on her wrist blazed brightly and he nodded, teeth gritted. It hurt him like hell to cross the salt line, but he wasn't going to let her go.

Goddess, but she loved him.

The zombie in the lead studied the approaching demon, then snarled. "You lied to me!" Lysia yelled. Her voice was graveled and hollow but she was understandable. "You made me believe you loved me!"

Rascon removed his canvas hat, pressing it over his chest, and put up his hand placatingly. "It was a necessary evil, Lysia. You enslaved me."

The witch hissed at him.

Rascon turned to them and gave a shrug.

"Give it your best," Ed said.

His grandfather nodded and with a breath of bravery turned back to the zombie. "Please, it's been centuries. Can you forgive me?"

"For doing this to me?"

"I did not bring you back from the dead, Lysia darling. That was—"

"Don't say the warlock's name," Tamatha said quickly. "We don't want to invite her to the party too early."

Rascon nodded. Then he dodged to avoid Lysia when she charged him, but she still caught him about the neck with a clawed hand. The other zombies began to mobilize and get antsy.

"I have to help him," Ed said as he let go of Tamatha's hand and rushed forward to help free his grandfather. A tangle of limbs and shouts ensued.

Tamatha stepped forward, but her mother caught her hand on her shoulder. "Stay safe in the circle, Tam."

But her lover was in danger. He couldn't realize the whole coven was closing in on him. She tried throwing more repellent magic. Flame burned only briefly on the zombies before quickly extinguishing. She was reluctant to use fire. How cruel to wield the killing fire against them once again? And her grandmother. While tugging at Rascon's hair, she flung Ed away into the groping arms of her dead cohorts.

Closing her eyes and spreading the fingers of both hands before her, Tamatha focused on Ed and their connection. "Strength," she commanded and felt the surge of power infuse her system.

"Whoa!" Ed called, and he cocked a grin at Tamatha. "I felt that." Turning, he sent out a wave of demonic magic toward the crowd of zombies. That separated them and sent a few flying.

Yet Lysia was still tearing at Rascon. Ed gestured to throw magic at the twosome. Then he appeared to think twice and instead reached for his grandfather, managing to pull him away from the threat. Fabric tore and Ed landed on the ground at Lysia's feet.

The witch growled and lunged for him. She'd torn his shirt away from his chest. The zombie stopped abruptly before plunging her clawed fingers in through his rib cage. She pressed her palm to the sigil over his chest. "The Bellerose crest?"

Wincing at the obvious painful connection, Ed offered, "It's your granddaughter. She's imprinted on me. We are in love."

Lysia jerked her gaze up to meet Petrina, who nodded and said, "This is Tamatha, Lysia. Your granddaughter. She was born over a century after your death."

"My granddaughter loves a nasty demon?"

"He's good, Grandmother," Tamatha said. "He thought he was sacrificing his life to save me a few days ago. Fortunately, his life was spared. But he's weak still because of the curse that was created when Rascon betrayed you. All men who love Bellerose women go mad or die. I want to love Ed forever, Lysia. Please. Help make that happen."

The witch righted in a spitting spray of metallic ooze. She wiped the stuff from her forearm, which showed more bone than flesh. "This was a foul punishment. Why?"

"A warlock brought you and your coven back to seek revenge against your accusers."

"Just so!" Lysia said, slapping a palm to her chest.

"But, Grandmother, the warlock is killing all the accusers' relations. Ed is Rascon's grandson. The warlock wants him dead, too."

"We're trying to break the spell cast by the warlock," Petrina said. "The one who was married to Martine Chevalier."

Lysia cast her gaze toward one of the males wearing tattered damask breeches. Torn lace hung around his neck, which exposed the thorax. One arm was missing. Had to be Martine.

"Exorcise me back to the grave," Lysia said decidedly. "And all will be well."

"All will be well if you can forgive Rascon."

Lysia jerked her gaze toward the demon, who struggled with two zombies, though they seemed to have lost steam and one merely gnawed on Rascon's wrist while he pushed against the other's forehead to keep it at chewing distance.

"A Bellerose woman never bows before a man," Lysia said. "Most especially a demon."

"I require no subservient gesture!" Rascon said as he shoved off the biting zombie. "Nor forgiveness. Simple understanding that I acted to protect those of my breed is all I ask of you. It is what my grandson Edamite does now. And I believe he loves your granddaughter with a true heart, Lysia. He can be trusted as I never could be."

Lysia dropped to her knees before Ed, who still lay sprawled in cautious submission. She placed her hand over the Bellerose crest and he gritted his teeth. When Tamatha made to move for him, he shook his head at her. "I can feel your grandmother's sorrow," he said. "She is in so much pain." He groaned as the intensity of his experience increased.

"Good." Lysia stood, breaking the bond. "Someone knows what I have endured. You, demon, will carry my pain. If you should think to harm my granddaughter, you will know my pain tenfold."

"That will never happen."

"Demons lie. But I hope you are an exception." Lysia nodded. "I release you from my hatred, Rascon, but I will never forgive you." She crossed her arms and wobbled. Once a zombie… "Now, send me back to the grave, if you will."

Not sure if the Bellerose curse had indeed been broken, Tamatha hadn't a chance to ask about it. Green lightning sparked the air around them, zapping a few of the zombies dead. And suddenly standing before them stood the warlock in full demonic tribal war paint. In one hand she held a staff that glowed red and in the other a misshapen creature's skull. Around her neck hung a red vial on a leather cord.

"Let's party," Arius said.

Chapter 25

"Martine!" the warlock called. One of the zombies moved forward from the pack, seeking the commanding voice. "Get behind me, husband."

The male zombie in the tattered damask breeches shambled over behind the warlock.

Ed joined Tamatha's side in the salt circle and clasped her hand. She in turn clasped her mother's hand. She wasn't sure where Rascon was, but he'd served his purpose. Only time would tell if the family curse had been broken.

Right now, she had a more dire problem with which to deal. The vial hanging from Arius's necklace must be blood. The blood of her dead husband? Had to be. It was key to sending the zombies back to the grave.

Petrina began to chant a reinforcement spell that would increase any magic they used. Ed cast up a black smoke that surrounded them in the salt circle. He'd stepped into the circle?

"How'd you do that?" she whispered, with a glance to the salt.

"Must be our bond. I can feel it prick at me, but since your grandmother took her hand off me, I feel a hell of a lot better than I have for days. Strong."

Maybe the curse *had* been broken?

Lysia spit and called out to her coven with a rangy howl that would have called werewolves had they been in the vicinity.

"Yes," Arius directed with her staff. "Gather, witches! There is one of my targets standing before us now. Search for the other! He was directly responsible for the flames that ate away your flesh and blood."

Two zombies shambled off in search of Rascon.

Arius put back her hand holding the staff and Martine grasped it. Tamatha thought he held the staff more for support since his head seemed dangerously close to falling off.

Fingers coved to bracket her head, Arius began to chant. It wasn't Latin, and her voice seemed to double and then break off into unison of horrific sounds.

"She's speaking in demonic tongues," Ed said. "Shit!" His entire body cringed and their bond allowed Tamatha to feel his pain wash through her system. Electric and sharp, it cut at her from within.

"Break your bond right now," Petrina demanded, "or you'll never have the strength to fight the warlock. Drop his hand!"

She did so, reluctantly shaking off Ed's hand, but when he responded by also pulling away, she knew that even though it hurt in her very soul, she had done the right thing.

"Gather flame," she recited and began to draw up her magic.

Arius laughed odd, wicked laughter that crackled like

ice. But when Lysia suddenly turned and began to stalk toward her, the warlock silenced. “Mind your place, witch!”

And Tamatha took a moment to regroup. Zombies were flesh and earth. So a little earth magic… Focusing on the surrounding graves and the little space of land between them, she called up the earth, which exploded around them in a cloud of darkness.

Ed mixed in his dark smoky magic that seemed to adhere to the earth particles and spark when it hit the zombies. Some cried out; others fought against the substance as if it were flames.

A command from Arius shook the electrified earth from the air and it landed with a thump all around them.

Ed glanced over his shoulder at Tamatha. His eyes glowed red. “I’m feeling a bit unkind right now. Pardon me while I try a different tactic.”

Spreading out his arms and tilting back his head, he shifted. Black ravens took to air and coiled above the warlock and her unholy crew of zombies. Commanding a break-off, a single raven from the unkindness dived toward the warlock and snatched the vial of blood in its beak. The warlock’s staff caught the end of a feather, but did not hamper its escape.

The raven circled, dodging a flash of green flame as the warlock shouted at it in defiance. Tamatha saw the thing drop from the raven’s beak. She held up her hand and caught the vial.

“Destroy it,” Petrina ordered.

Dropping the vial, Tamatha crushed the glass under her boot heel and stomped it furiously. A mist of red smoke sifted around her feet. Salt from the circle crept toward the crushed glass and soaked into the blood.

At that moment the zombies shifted alliance and turned on Arius. The warlock’s staff shot out random sparks of green, but she could not control her dead minions. Demonic curses filled the night air, crashing against the protective shield Tamatha and Petrina stood behind.

It was the male zombie Martine who shuffled up to Arius and shoved his hand into her chest. The warlock gasped for breath. Martine pulled out her heart and tossed it aside to his cohorts. The feast that ensued was enough to make anyone go vegetarian.

Ed landed inside the circle and shifted back to human form, coming complete with his arms about Tamatha. "You okay?"

She nodded. "Yes, almost finished."

Petrina's chanting grew louder. She sent out exorcising vibrations while Tamatha recited the exorcism, commanding the dead to return whence they came. The zombies responded. As the warlock's body wilted onto the cobblestones, her hair was tugged out and chunks of flesh were taken as repayment for her vile magic. The zombies began to wither. The metallic material gushed from their mouths and ears and noses, and soon there was nothing but a spreading puddle of the shiny substance.

"It's too awful."

Ed hugged Tamatha tighter. "Don't watch. Your mother has it under control." And he swept his hand before him, sending a black cloud over the massacre, obliterating their view. "Rascon has gone."

Tamatha nodded and hugged him tighter. "He served his part."

Petrina stopped and dropped to her knees, exhausted from the spell.

And when the black smoke cleared, nothing remained but piles of ash, still smoking as if a funeral pyre. The white-boned skull the warlock had wielded rolled to the edge of the salt circle and cracked in half.

"We'll bury them," Ed said. "This time for good."

"I can put a fastening spell on them to ensure that," Tamatha said.

"You can?" He pulled her to him and kissed her soundly. "Did I mention that I love you?"

"Yes, but you can tell me again and again. I'll never tire of hearing it."

"Come on, you lovebirds." Petrina snapped her fingers and three shovels appeared before them. "Save the lovey-dovey stuff for later. Pineapple gelatos for all after we've laid my mother to rest."

Epilogue

It was three in the morning by the time they returned to Tamatha's home. Petrina collapsed on the sofa and fell instantly asleep, while Tamatha led Ed into the bathroom and they showered together.

They made slow, quiet love under the spill of warm water. She didn't want to think about what had happened in the graveyard. And pressing her fingers over Ed's skin, tracing the dark ink and following that path with her tongue was a distraction she needed.

As the two of them came, their mouths together and their gasps muted by the connection, she hugged him tightly about the neck as he pumped inside her. "I love you," she managed through tears.

"You've made me believe in love," he said. "And if that isn't bewitchery, I don't know what is."

"Look," she said, holding up his hand. "The thorns chained about your wrist are gone."

"So they are. I guess I defeated the death curse after all. Your grandmother did good work."

"As did your grandfather."

"I'll give him a pass on his strange disappearance. Maybe we'll talk someday. Hey. I made it to the end of the story!"

"What does that mean?"

"It means my mother's faery tales weren't always correct. Kiss me, lover. Give me some more of that love often."

In the morning, the threesome headed out for the patisserie where Ed treated them to croissants and coffees. But they couldn't pass Amorino without stopping in to buy pineapple gelato.

Petrina hugged Tamatha and then handed her her gelato so she could turn and hug Ed. "You be good to her," she said to him. "You may have dodged the family curse, but I'm pretty sure Lysia put a new one on you."

"She did. And not to worry. I adore your daughter and will spend every moment trying to earn her respect and adoration."

"You won't have to try too hard. You're a good man. Cute, too."

"All right, Mom, enough flirting." She handed her mother her treat.

"I'll be going, then," Petrina announced. "All is well in Paris. And I've a plane ticket to Andalusia. I do love those bullfighters."

"You need a ride to the airport?" Ed asked.

"No, I've Jacques, who is always willing to give me a lift when I need one." She winked and blew a kiss to Tamatha. "Love you, Tam. Love often. I think this one will last longer than all the rest." She turned and strolled off, her long pink skirts dusting the cobblestones and her blue-silver hair pulled up in a messy bun.

"I like your mom," Ed said and sneaked a bite off the top of Tamatha's gelato cone.

"Hey! You should have got some for yourself."

"No sharing?"

Tamatha studied her treat. Seriously?

"So that's the way of things, eh? You'll share your magic with me and risk my very life to save a dead family member, but you won't let me have the sweet stuff?"

"But…it's pineapple."

He tucked his nose against her neck and licked her skin. "Good thing I prefer lemon. Mmm…you saved my life," he said. "The curse is lifted."

"We don't know that for sure."

"I do. I feel great."

"That's what they all say. And then hours later they're plastered to the side of a Mack truck or struggling within a straitjacket."

"Sweetness, have some faith in our love. I know your family curse is broken. It's as simple as that."

"Very well. Simple as that. What about Grandmother's new curse?"

"I will never harm you, so I've no worry about that one. If pineapple is your favorite, I don't know what else we can do to celebrate."

"I can think of a few more things."

"Such as?"

She waggled her eyebrows and slid on a teasing smile. "Sex."

"That's always a celebration. You mentioned a *few* things?"

"Yes. Call me crazy—or wait. Don't call me crazy. Call me impulsive, but…"

"What?"

"Would you be my boyfriend, Edamite Thrash?"

"I will. If you can handle being the evil overlord's woman."

"Why don't you make that 'his gorgeous sidekick, the most powerful witch in all of Paris.'"

"Works for me." He kissed her and spun her in a hug that toppled her gelato to the ground. But it didn't matter. Tamatha loved Ed. He loved her. And together they would make bewitching magic.

* * * * *

I hope you enjoyed Ed and Tamatha's story. If you are interested in reading about some of the other characters mentioned, you can find their stories at your favorite online retailer.

CJ and Vika's story is
THIS WICKED MAGIC

Blyss and Stryke's story is
MOONLIGHT & DIAMONDS

Kir and Bea's story is
ENCHANTED BY THE WOLF

Libby and Reichardt's story is
THIS SOUL MAGIC

Desideriel and Ivan's story is
THE DEVIL TO PAY

Verity and Rook's story is
BEYOND THE MOON